BLOOD TEARS

By

Raven Dane

United Kingdom • France • Germany • Spain

Blood Tears

By

Raven Dane

Copyright © 2005

All rights reserved. No part of this publication may be reproduced, stored in a retrieval system or transmitted in any form or by any means, electronic, mechanical, audio, visual or otherwise, without prior permission of the copyright owner. Nor can it be circulated in any form of binding or cover other than that in which it is published and without similar conditions including this condition being imposed on the subsequent purchaser.

ISBN 1-904181-71-6

WRITERSWORLD
9 Manor Court
Enstone
Oxfordshire,
OX7 4LU
England
www.writersworld.co.uk

DEDICATION

This book is dedicated to Helen Hollick, Rachel Cropper and Charles—my much loved trinity of believers, who never lost faith in Blood Tears, and without whose unswerving help and support Azrar and co would never have lived beyond my imagination.

Also a big thank you to Muse, U2 and Keane —your music kept me sane while typing away in my lonely office!

To Jordan Scott-
Here you are, Jordan, the book I promised you over lunch in Hampstead, at last!

To Janice,

Welcome to my world of Secrets & Shadows

Enjoy the journey!

[signature]

Do the Dark Kind weep tears of blood,
When they lose their sons to the Light?
A whole ocean of blood tears could not erase,
One salt tear from our eyes.

Fragment of Dholma folk verse discovered and translated by Aubrey Weingard in 1810.

Prologue

The white roses first caught his eye as he glanced around the bedroom; at least a dozen or more glacial buds arranged in a crystal cut glass vase. Perfect yet strangely cold – as if the blooms could only thrive in snow-melt water. Above them hung a portrait of a young woman, a silver silk shawl draped softly over her slender shoulders. The woman's Slavic features were delicate and portrayed with a gentle, slight smile, her face framed by silvery layers of fine, pale blonde hair.

Her eyes were an extraordinary colour – a lustrous gold – strange and ethereal, yet reflecting an inner warmth. She gazed confidently from the portrait, a woman who, with her unique insight into the darkness dwelling in human hearts knew too much of this world...

He saw beyond her fey beauty and the freshly offered tribute of the roses. As if mesmerised, he was drawn to her necklace, a generous waterfall of dark blood-red rubies and a dangerous rage welled within him. To anyone else, the lavish display of fabulous jewels would represent only opulent decoration. To the man, torn between hatred and fascination, they were the potent symbol of the woman's eternal damnation. For shamelessly, she wore a necklace of blood tears.

PART ONE

Thunder on the Horizon

Chapter One

Isolann, Upper Balkans, 1925

In near complete darkness, a black stallion picked its way through tangled undergrowth obscuring the narrow path through the forest. It moved lightly, precise as a ballet dancer, lifting its hooves high away from bone breaking roots that lay tangled like traps on the forest floor. The horse gained its courage from its rider, the Jendar Azrar, who sat in the saddle relaxed and straight-backed: a consummate horseman. Above, the dense canopy of night-shadowed trees blocked out the light from the stars and moon but the broad-chested horse did not hesitate or stumble over any fallen branches or exposed tree roots. The stallion took its signals from its rider, who with his sharp, nocturnal vision and ancient knowledge of the woods was at one with the darkness like no other creature in the forest.

The rider breathed in the many scents hanging in the misty night air rising up from recent rain; the rich earthy smell of leaf mulch on the forest floor, and the telltale pungent traces of deer and wolves. Suddenly, horse and rider jolted alert at the sound of pitiful whimpering: an animal, alone and frightened. Pushing forward through the undergrowth, the Prince traced the source of the faint but urgent sounds of animal distress. He dismounted and searched through the dense, bramble-snarled tangle to find a very young wolf cub, a wretched scrap of cold and hungry grey fur. It was very small, perhaps the runt of the litter.

The Jendar searched but found no sign of the rest of the pack. They would not have fled at his approach;

something else must have made them abandon the cub. Only one source could panic a wolf pack in these woods, his domain. Humans.

He gave a low growl of rising anger, hoping the invasion was not from any of his own people, the Pact nomads. Had his long isolation made them less mindful of his presence? The thought of the age-old agreement between the Isolanni and their Prince being violated after all these years agitated him. No, it must be rash and desperate peasants from neighbouring Svolenia, in the grip of yet more hardship. They would be fair game. To reach this far they would have ignored the warnings of their people's ancient legends, and avoided contact with his people. These were foolish and ultimately ill-fated choices– they had ignored warnings, which might have saved their lives.

Gently, he scooped up the tiny wriggling cub and secured it within the folds of his clothing where it would not come into contact with the harmful aura of his icy power. He remounted, anxious to intercept these trespassing humans before they harmed any more of his forest creatures. The only game to be hunted in these woods was man.

Jendar Azrar no longer stifled his growing hunger, but let it rise within him in a tide of urgent craving. He glanced up at the setting moon, a few hours of darkness remained, the burning scourge of dawn still held at bay by his closest ally, the night.

He rode on with a new urgency, searching with his sharp senses. His nostrils flared - the unmistakable scent of humans! The pungent odour of fear-tinged, male sweat and beneath that, the coppery promise of hot fresh blood. The Prince smiled, disdainful, contemptuous. This was too easy! A clumsy trail of broken branches and deep footprints indicated the passage of four men. The bravado needed to cross Isolann and enter his forest meant they were probably young, fit and strong – ideal prey for a Dark Lord's needs. He gave a low growl, anticipating the pleasure of a good hunt, the challenge of tracking down a courageous human full of fight and defiance.

Sandor shook with fear. He hated the dark tangled forest; he trembled at the muted sounds of unseen creatures and the cold breath of the night wind. Despite his considerable height and broad-shouldered strength, the unknown terrified him. He tried to edge closer to the camp fire, his clothes rank and sodden from the earlier heavy rain, but one of the other men angrily kicked him away with a cruel and mocking laugh.

"You're blocking out all our light and warmth, you great clumsy oaf."

What hurt him the most? The constant barrage of blows and kicks, or the cruel names? Sandor needed only warmth and food to survive but he desperately craved kindness- just the occasional gentle word or a proffered smile. Every moment of rare compassion towards him was etched in his memory: the farmer's wife who once gave him a bowl of oats with warm cream and honey and the old man who allowed him to shelter in his barn for the winter. He always worked hard, didn't argue or fight back. But his life never got any easier.

Facing another winter of loneliness and starvation, Sandor had reluctantly agreed to accompany these foul men into the Land of Secrets and Shadows. Only bad things lived there, he knew that, for he had listened well to the tales told around crackling kitchen hearths and campfires. His new companions though, believed it all to be superstitious nonsense. They had heard the other stories, the ones that told of a fortune in gems waiting to be discovered in an abandoned castle that lay deep within the forests that carpeted the foothills of the Arpalathians.

Forests that teemed with game: bears; deer; wild boar and wolves, a life-long fortune to be made in hides and flesh. And of course, a castle that hid a wealth of precious gems.

Sandor wanted only to be fed and sheltered but the men had promised him hard cash too. Money could buy him food and warmth, but now with the night pressing closer in, he just wanted to be back in Svolenia - anywhere, however harsh, however cruel. Anywhere that was away from this terrible place.

Old Presco, grumbling to himself, gave Sandor a sharp kick in the ankle. "Get up and fetch more tinder, and make it dry this time, you lumbering idiot."

The old man glanced up at Sandor, squinting at the big man with his mean little eyes, feeling confident the oaf would not retaliate; he did not have the wits to answer back let alone hit out in anger. He tossed a leather flagon over to Sandor. "And fill this water bottle while you're at it."

Sandor nodded meekly and though shaking with fear, slowly moved away from the meagre warmth and tenuous protection of the fire to seek dry kindling. It would be a difficult task, the surrounding forest dripped with steady rainfall, intense enough to get through the tightly-packed canopy and soak the pine-scented floor. As he moved away into the darkness, he tripped over a tree root, falling heavily and gashing his cheek. He clambered back to his feet, the mocking laughter and jeering taunts of his companions brashly invading the forest's unnatural, eerie silence. He wanted to keep walking, away from their scorn and constant acts of cruelty, but where could he go?

Ahead in a small clearing, came the sound of men's harsh voices, blatantly masking their fear. Without a sound, Azrar dismounted and secured his horse by tying the reins to a tree. He slid the sleeping cub into a saddlebag and stood, hidden, watching them, unseen and silent. One of the three younger humans trudged off into the trees, perhaps to hunt or gather firewood. He must have taken too long for his companions' liking, for the other two became angry, and swearing loudly went in search of him. They left behind an old man frantically cutting up the carcass of a hind, muttering his fear that the wolves would come to steal his kill. Or him!

Azrar stifled a menacing growl of anger at the desecration of his woods and moved swiftly. The kill was quick and efficient; the old man's neck snapped, cleanly broken, with the twist of one hand. All the Prince's senses were honed to acute awareness, anticipation surged through him. He was all hunger, all burning ferocity. The superficial outward imitation of human form was now torn away by the intensity of his true nature.

With ease, he tracked the remaining humans, his senses gathering information about them as he followed their trail. One was heavy set and slow moving, possibly slow-witted too, from the evidence of his clumsy progress. Another was tainted, his blood rank, steeped with the creeping onset of disease. The third was agile, fast and strong, well worthy of being Azrar's prey that night.

Unwittingly helping their silent pursuer, the men split up. First, the heavy-set man. The Jendar found him filling leather water bottles from a fast-flowing stream. Swift, silent, Azrar pounced, holding his hand across the man's mouth preventing him from breathing long enough to lose consciousness but still live. He gagged him, tied him to a tree then went in search of the others. He caught another intruder, the diseased human without effort, instantly dispatching him by snapping the man's neck. This was tedious, Azrar growled, he needed some worthwhile prey.

Stillness held the forest in a tight grip as if every night beast paused and held its breath. The tension hung in the air and the remaining Svolenian hunter realised there was something seriously wrong. He grasped his rifle tighter, reassured by the familiar, comforting weight of wood and metal and the lingering smell of cordite. Risking alerting bears or wolves, he called for the others but there was no answering reply, only the sinister silence, unbroken even by the scurry of night creatures. He still did not regret scoffing at the old villagers' warnings of the danger that dwelled in this forest. They were just stupid and ignorant superstition riddled peasants. The only danger in this wood was from wolves that were no match for his modern gun.

The graveyard silence continued, a trickle of cold sweat began to pool at the base of his spine. Where the Hell were the others? They could not have run away in disarray, he would have heard their shouts of alarm or the clumsy crash of breaking branches. He called out again, angrily, fighting back the dangerous, weakening effects of rising fear. If his worthless cousin, the old man or the simpleton had left him alone in these woods or fallen asleep, they would pay dearly for it.

He shouted again, "Come out you, bastards! If this is your idea of a joke, Presco, sod the wolves, I'll kill you myself!" Only silence answered him, no chaotic flutter of fleeing startled birds, not even a breeze rustled through the branches. The forest held its breath, a malign spectator, ghoulishly anticipating a drama, one with him at its centre. A show that could only end in bloodshed and death. But it would not be his. "Watch all you like, I am the hunter, I have the gun!" he yelled to the impassive trees. Alarm made him more belligerent, raising his rifle to his shoulder, he fired upwards at the hidden sky above the woodland. As the thunder from the loud retort echoed and died away, the uncanny silence returned. "I'll give you morons one last chance, let me know where you are or I'll start firing into the trees."

His taunts were met with absolute silence. With a sudden clarity he knew was not alone anymore. It was not his fellow hunters... He strode forward, making a deliberately noisy progress back towards the camp, aware that unless suffering winter starvation any wolves that might be nearby would be easily frightened. "I've had enough, you bastards can stay here. Be carrion for the crows for all I care," he shouted.

Icy fingers clawed at the nape of his neck, it was his fear worsening as he glanced back over his shoulder aware of something tangible at last; something unseen and deadly was stalking him. He stood as still as he dared, holding his breath and listening. But he could not control his heart's treacherous hammering, surely loud enough to betray his presence. Again there was only silence but the sense of a malevolent presence grew stronger, closer. He pulled a long knife from his belt and gripping the rifle even tighter, he continued to retrace his steps back to the makeshift camp, striding boldly at first then as he lost the battle against panic, breaking into a run.

With no discernible path, thorned clawing branches and trip-wire tree roots conspired against his escape as they took on a spiteful life of their own. With his chest vice-tight from exhaustion and terror, he slashed and stamped frantically at the hate-filled plant life, holding him, trapping him, and giving him up to the malevolence relentlessly pursuing him. Even the faint comfort of the moonlight abruptly deserted him, hidden by a shroud of cloud. In the deeper blackness, he gave in to blind panic, oblivious of the deep gashes from racking thorns across his face and hands, tearing the knife from his hands, forcing him to push through the tangle with just the butt of his rifle.

Azrar followed him, loping through the darkness, guided by the scent and sounds of the man's fear.

Deliberately, he hung back, prolonging the pleasure and excitement of the chase, revelling in his mastery of the night-cloaked woods and his own swift, powerful body. But the blood lust and the hunger grew too urgent and tiring of the game, he used his greater speed to circle around and move ahead of the terrified man. And only then he allowed the human to see him.

At the sight of a black-clad, pale young man suddenly appearing before him, the human went into a murderous rage as fear turned into anger. He had run for his life from some savage beast, some demon from Hell itself and was confronted instead by this damned, accursed Isolanni – all that pain and fear for one unarmed young man. He wiped the blood from his eyes, his face contorted with anger.

"Make a fool of me, will you? I'll kill you for this!" he shouted, still badly shaken from his panic driven flight. He lifted his rifle to his shoulder, taking aim. Azrar looked up, his face lifting slightly to give the full impact of his green eyes, his lips curving into a humourless, mocking smile. Horror shivered through the human as he recognised the total lack of humanity in those eyes, the rifle forgotten as terror returned to paralyse him. He tried to speak, swallowing hard as fear had constricted his throat to a painful dryness. "What in damnation are you?"

Azrar's voice was a low growl, "You already know."

The man fumbled in his clothing with fear-clumsy fingers, to pull out a wooden crucifix pressed on him earlier by an old woman from his own village in Svolenia. An old crone he'd cruelly mocked as a feeble minded old hag. Yet he had still thrust the crudely carved cross into his pocket – just in case.

To Azrar's pleasure, the fight had returned to the man's mean small eyes. He stood defiantly with the gun raised again and the rough-hewn cross clenched in one fist, brandishing it as an additional weapon. Azrar paused, savouring the moment before succumbing to the now intolerable need. In a fluid, powerful movement, he leapt forward, effortlessly wrenching the rifle from the man's hands before he fired a single shot, throwing the weapon far into the undergrowth. Azrar pinned down each wildly flailing arm with a vice-like grip, shoving him against a tree for better purchase. Startled by the unexpected strength and speed of his assailant, the human fought back with the desperation of the damned, not knowing that his angry thrashing only laced the blood with more adrenaline and thus more pleasurable for the blood lust of the Dark Kind Prince.

Azrar's razor sharp, scimitar fangs dropped down and tore through the human's neck, the flesh at first soft and yielding. Then the best part, the next bite into hard muscle and sinew beneath, the ecstasy of reward as his mouth filled with the first hard pumped gush of hot, human life blood. Desperately, the man fought on, kicking and thrashing, adding to Azrar's heightened pleasure. But it was a battle that could have only one conclusion. His victim's death.

Sated, Azrar threw back his head and howled in a perfect imitation of a wolf's successful hunting call. Blood hot enough to steam in the night air stained his mouth and the rich fabric of his black garb. He dropped the body heavily onto the ground, indifferent to his victim—the man was no longer of any use to him, and sought out the nearby stream to cleanse himself in the tumbling snow- melt water, the blood briefly darkening the silver water as it tumbled down on its journey from the mountains to distant Lake Beral. He walked away to find his stallion, without any thought for the human he had killed. He was not human, he had no conscience; he lived untroubled by any moral dilemma or self doubt. The Lord Azrar, High Prince of the Dark Kind, was a predator who thought no more of his human prey then a wolf's concern for a slain hind.

Jendar Azrar strode back to his stallion, patiently waiting, cropping the thin grass struggling to grow through the leaf mould. The horse whinnied its relief at its master's safe return. Azrar gently stroked the animal's coal black satin, well-muscled neck. "There is no need to fret, my Caridor. Our unwelcome visitors have been dealt with."

Azrar waited until the wolf pack he had summoned appeared, sinuously winding through the trees like amber-eyed wraiths. They paused, respectfully awaiting his signal. Only one was brave enough to step forward, a rangy, scar-faced male, the pack's leader. Azrar walked towards the animal and gave its dark grey, brindled head an affectionate caress. "Feast well tonight my friends, as I have done. Many moons may wane before we have such strong game to hunt again."

He left the wolves to devour the three still warm corpses, as part of the pact he made with their kind long ago. Before the baleful light of dawn slipped over the forest edge, all visible signs of his night's hunting would be gone. This was the forest's contribution, for his protection from the trespass of human hunters.

Azrar sought out and found the one man he had captured and left alive; throwing the unconscious human over his horse's withers he rode back to his stronghold. He would keep this intruder through the long winter months, to release him into the forest, to hunt and kill in the fierce bloodthirsty way of the Dark Kind when the hunger became unbearable again.

As he rode, his whole being shimmered with the electric charge of renewed energy and vibrant life. The wolf cub awoke, crying pitifully again. Azrar took it from the saddlebag and holding it in the crook of his arm comforted and stroked it into relaxed quietness. The little creature would make a fine gift for Khari.

Chapter Two

Azrar's Stronghold

A gentle, rain-scented night wind moved through the child's room bringing to life the kaleidoscope of gemstones hanging from silver threads above her bed, jingling and sparkling in the flickering candlelight. Tonight, she was oblivious to the pretty sounds and dancing lights. Instead the young girl sat on a wide window ledge of cold, damp stone, waiting. Her entire being was focused, intently looking down at the rain glistened courtyard so far below her. When would he come home? Why was he not home, safe already?

It would soon be dawn – a time of danger. She could hardly bear the anxiety, the slow, long hours of waiting. How could she return to her bed and slumber knowing he was not back within the stronghold's solid walls? Back to the place where no sunlight could ever enter.

She longed to hear the sound of hooves clattering across the cobbles, to see the Prince ride his prancing war horse back through the main gates of his keep. Then she could be happy again, knowing he was safe. If she was really fortunate, perhaps he would glance up and see her looking down from her balcony, scrutinising her with his cold, imperious emerald eyes. Best of all, he might even raise a hand in greeting. Then she could go back to bed, falling asleep with a smile on her elfin features.

A savage cry echoed from the pitch-black expanse of rain-lashed woodland; an eerie, wild howl that was not from any wolf or bear.

"Come to me child, come away from the window."

The woman bustled into the room, firmly lifting her charge back from the windowsill, pulling off the sodden wool blanket from her slender shoulders. She settled the child back under the billowy goose-down bedcover, its snowy whiteness a stark contrast to the black granite of the bedroom walls. The woman, Ileni, sighed. Yet again the little one was out of bed; oblivious to the damp and cold, staring out over the forest below. And if she didn't catch her death from chill, the child seemed unaware of the very real danger of a fatal fall, perching so precariously close to the sheer drop to the courtyard. Ileni had only seen forty summers but this child was making her an old woman before her time with worry!

Ileni shuddered again, as another piercing howl echoed across the night shrouded valley to stop her heart and freeze her blood to ice. She turned back to the child, at last snuggled warm and safe in her bed. The smile of relief spreading across the girl's pretty face more chilling than that wild cry of savage triumph.

In an instinctive gesture Ileni touched the amulet hung around her neck, then with an indrawn breath of concern checked the child wore hers in an obsessive, almost neurotic gesture that she had repeated every night of Khari's seven short years of life within this stronghold. It mattered not that even without wearing the wolf talismans she and the girl would never be in danger, it did no harm to be sure and certain.

She was grateful that Jendar Azrar, the Dark Kind Lord she served, proved to be a good master. Though his manner was brooding and stern, often unpredictable, he was always generous and just. But the knowledge of what he was – the dark secret at the heart of all Isolanni life – was heavy for Ileni to bear. Her previous carefree life, wandering with her nomadic tribe high in the black granite mountains had made it easy to pretend that Jendar was no more than an ancient, imagined myth: the ageless protector who preyed on their enemies' blood, and kept them safe from invaders. Here in the stronghold the reality of his existence was inescapable.

Ileni walked to the window to pull the thick wooden shutters across, blotting out the damp night air. She flinched as wind driven rain lashed at her face; the scattered showers of the early part of the night had now turned to a torrential downfall. The clatter of a shod horse slipping awkwardly on the slippery stone cobbles made her look down. Despite the rain, there was enough torch light around the courtyard to let her see the Prince give his mount a reassuring pat as it found its feet again. Even so high up the stronghold, Ileni could make out his opalescent eyes blazing down in the darkness. She frowned, trying to make out the shape of something large lying across the horse's withers before the servants rushed out into the lashing rain to carry it away.

Ileni shuddered, not wanting to know what that heavy, awkward bundle was. She waited till Khari was asleep then slipped out of the child's room and headed back to the kitchens. As the girl's human carer, she had a room next to Khari's in the main stronghold but never slept there, preferring to sleep on the floor by the large iron range that was always lit, night and day. The kitchens were her sanctuary where sunlight was allowed to filter through, and by night, candlelight gleamed from the arrays of copper pots and pans, a warm haven full of human laughter. There Ileni could live the pretence of a normal existence.

But not in the sepulchral labyrinth of the stronghold's corridors. Before Khari's arrival, the Dark Lord dwelt content in his domain of cold and darkness. Even the great hall, where a hearty fire always roared in a hearth wide enough to take a whole oak trunk, was a desolate and frightening place. The high sheer walls hung with ornate heavy armour and barbaric weapons as were fitting for the lair of a Dark Kind warlord. Only Khari's room, brightly lit, cosy and luxurious, fit for an enchanted princess, reflected the fact a human child dwelt under the night-black wings of Azrar's protection.

Ileni's existence had changed so much from her old life: the forty summers spent as an Isolanni nomad wandering with her tribe through the harsh Arpalathian valleys and down to the briefly lush summer grasslands below their dour peaks. She'd been wed at thirteen and widowed by nineteen, giving birth and successfully raising four strong sons to adulthood. Tribal life was harsh and frequently cut short. With sudden rock falls and ferocious wild beasts, avalanches and ice storms, Isolann had a thousand ways to die young.

It all changed for Ileni one late spring morning when she searched for firewood at the forest's edge, and found an abandoned girl child. With her silver blonde hair and pale skin, the child was obviously not Isolanni but must have come from the neighbouring land of Svolenia. Ileni's heart was full of pity and compassion, she realised that this tiny, helpless child was so feared by her own people that they had risked entering Isolann to leave her for the wolves – or worse. One glance at the child's wondrous golden eyes was enough explanation. Ileni could see this little scrap of humanity could reach beyond this world and wander deep into the minds and hearts of men. Ileni's people would reject her too.

Taking every last reserve of courage, Ileni bundled the child under her cloak and walked deep into the wild beast infested forest, searching for the one being who might give the child safe sanctuary – the inhuman Dark Lord of Isolann.

Now five years passed and she remained in the stronghold, caring for the girl, unconditionally loving her as the daughter she'd never been blessed to bring into this world alive. Her sons, grown men with lives and families of their own, cheerfully accepted her new role and were infrequent but welcome visitors. The frailties of old age and infirmity came early for the mountain nomads, Ileni knew her boys were grateful she was safe and warm within the sheer walls of the Jendar's castle. She was one less mouth to feed when the snows closed in.

Ileni moved through the gloomy, ill lit corridors as she tried to slip back to the safe, cosy haven of the kitchens without attracting the Jendar's attention. The years of protection did nothing to allay her fear of the Dark Lord; it made no difference to her anxiety that she knew Dark Kind never preyed on women and children. Keeping to the shadows, Ileni stayed close against the walls but the Prince's sharp hearing and heightened sense of smell, he was aware of her passage, skirting the edge of the great hall.

Ileni stopped, stood quite still, holding her breath. She felt the ice of his close proximity – a muted coldness, a good sign he was not angered. She had never felt the full brutal frozen blast of his ire. Not did she ever want to provoke it.

"Is the child Khari well?"

The Jendar's voice, a curious mixture of velvet and growling harshness sounded concerned. Ileni stepped out of the shadows into the flickering light from the fire, dropped to her knees and bowed her head low, struggling to control her body's instinctive trembling.

"I caught her out of bed again, my Lord. She is always so anxious for your safety when you ride out alone." She spoke quickly, never raising her head, almost abruptly, her nervousness obvious and understandable.

The Jendar nodded gravely, his severely handsome, features marble-pale despite the warm, dancing glow of a whole birch trunk blazing in the cavernous hearth. He unfastened his cloak, swung it from his shoulders and with a curt nod dismissed the woman who clambered to her feet, bowed low again and ran from the room without looking at his face. Azrar shook his head. Still she feared him. Had none of her years spent in excellent service looking after his human ward made her understand he would never harm her? Could not harm her. He was bound by honour and duty in a way no human could comprehend. Humans had choices, he had not.

Ileni, once out of the Prince's sight, paused to calm her pounding heart and stop shaking before returning to her kingdom, the stronghold's kitchens where she ruled supreme. It would not do to show her weakness in front of the serving girls who worked for her.

But not before she tried to force the memory from her mind of the trace of fresh gore glistening on the Prince's shirt as he threw open his rain soaked, black wolf skin cloak. This tell-tale ribbon of freshly spilt blood showed the stark truth, the dark heart of the pact all Isolanni held with their Prince. She knew exactly what he was, how he had survived for so many countless centuries. But what of Khari? It was clear the child adored her unearthly guardian, like the unswerving devotion and unquestioning love of the most loyal hound to its master. Or maybe something even deeper, more profound—the love of a daughter to a father. What would the sight of Azrar's blood stained clothing do to such a tender and gentle mind?

Chapter Three

Azrar's prisoner awoke with a groan, his body stiff and sore all over from lying all night on a stone floor. Though groggy, disorientated and aching, at least he was alive. He looked around nervously, waiting for the inevitable threats and blows from his unknown captors. But there was no one in sight, he was alone in a large warm stone room. A well stacked up fire crackled away cheerfully from a deep hearth, the best food he had ever seen lay on a rough hewn wooden table. There was a haunch of smoked bacon, cheeses, fresh baked rye bread and a full flagon of foaming, amber sweet cider.

Such a feast would not be meant for him. If he touched just one morsel of the tempting fare he would be severely punished, so instead he began to explore his surroundings on unsteady legs. He was securely locked in and despite his great strength, pushing and kicking for many frustrating minutes, there was no yielding movement from the heavy wood and iron door. He gazed out over the courtyard through a small high window, where the pale light and still ground level mist told him it was not long after dawn.

Outside he could see a large circular, paved courtyard ringed with many neat buildings. The area was empty but there was evidence of people stirring from their slumber by the flickering of firelight and candles through their windows, out of which the tantalising scent of new baked bread wafted.

Sandor pulled across a sturdy stool and stood on it to gain a better view of his surroundings. He made out the biggest, heaviest wooden gates he'd ever seen. Through them, he could make out some peacefully grazing mares and foals in a well tended grassed paddock with some plump poultry scratching contentedly around their slender legs. Above, soared what he first thought was a craggy outcrop of the Arpalathians, but was in reality a vast fortress with sheer walls of black stone. It was a powerful, brooding edifice and it scared him.

He knew the hunting party had met with something terrible in the forest. Something very bad had happened to his companions, but they were nothing to him and he did not mourn their loss. He was alive and they were not.

He looked across at the food again as hunger gripped angrily at his stomach. Could he dare to take a piece of bread? Was it worth enduring a beating or worse for just one small mouthful? He ran thick, work callused fingers through his coarse blonde hair. Perhaps he'd been spared for a reason – he was young and strong, surely he could work hard for his keep? Hunger overrode any more thoughts, punishment was in the future, the food was there now, and he began to eat. It was so much better than anything he had tasted in his entire thirty years of living with hunger and hardship. Then he waited in placid contentment for something to happen.

Khari awoke sighing with pleasure as sunlight dappled her white bedspread. The rays streaming through her window caught the diamonds the size of robins' eggs hanging above her bed and sent rainbows flashing around her room. The day before it had rained all day, confining her to the castle. But today was going to be far more fun. One of the Jendar's grooms told her a new litter of stable kittens was due and she was eager to see if there were tiny new borns nestling in the straw. As usual, her carer, her 'umma' Ileni was there to greet her with a hug and helped her wash and dress. She pulled on the rough woven, heavily embroidered woollen tunic and trousers of the Isolanni people ,eager to please. Later when the sun warmed up the courtyard and Ileni's back was turned, she planned to change into one of the floaty dresses her 'umma' had made from the luxurious material they'd found in old wooden chests in the Prince's stronghold.

Ileni did not approve of her dressing up in such beautiful clothes out on the courtyard, they were only for her meetings with the Dark Lord. Khari loved the silken feel of the clothes, it was like wearing a star spangled cloud, but for now cheerily endured the itching wool of the red tunic, especially as Ileni had embroidered the complex and ancient floral decorations herself, during last winter's confinement in the castle from the blizzards and ice storms.

Khari's mouth was watering long before reaching the kitchen as the tantalising aroma of sweet honey and cinnamon bread straight from the oven wafted up the back stairs. But before she could start her breakfast she discovered a surprise waiting for her. A wicker box on the flagstones suddenly rustled and shook, a pitiful whimpering arose at her approach. Ileni shook her head with disapproval as Khari opened the box and with a cry of joyful surprise discovered the brindled grey wolf cub. To the child's delight, the cub squirmed and licked her face, bonding instantly.

"Wolves belong in the forests," Ileni muttered with a disapproving frown. "This one must go back to the wild as soon as it can fend for itself."

Ileni had no reason to show compassion to wolves, too many of her people had lost their lives to these menacing vermin. The nomads could shoot them to protect themselves down on the summer grazing plains or high up in the mountains, but never in the Jendar's forest. And never black wolves, they were always sacred. No Isolanni would touch a black wolf, even if it was ripping out the throat of a prized she goat.

"Don't get fond of it, child. It's a dangerous wild creature that will soon grow up to turn on you."

"Wolf will never harm me," Khari replied simply and with the complete certainty of a trusting child. Ileni shuddered, her precious little girl trusted her life to yet another vicious predator. She knew better than to fight with Khari over this helpless scrap and fetched a bowl of warmed milk for her new pet. It was a gift from the Jendar and must be well cared for without question.

As the early morning sun warmed the courtyard, everyday life began to return. Above the bustle of men and horses, Sandor heard the pretty sound of a child's song echoing around the rugged stone walls. He pulled across a wooden stool to the window and climbed to the narrow window and looked out to seek the source of the gentle, happy sound. Down in the courtyard he saw a fey little creature skipping towards his prison. Back home in Svolenia, villagers enjoyed frightening him with horror stories, especially when they heard he'd been forced to join Tark in the hunt for wolf pelts and venison. They told him that the Isolanni forests were full of strange and evil creatures, soul trapping tree spirits, werewolves and ogres. They said a terrifying Vampire Prince ruled over all these frights, a reign of blood and death to all strangers.

Now what had sounded at first to be just a child approached him. Her hair was a soft cloud of silvered gossamer lit by the morning sun. She wore a delicate dress of green and silver silks star dusted by tiny diamonds. Her curious golden eyes were huge with dark, long lashes. The man backed away from the window; suddenly afraid, for this must be a fairy or other supernatural spirit of the forest.

"Hello, who are you? My name is Khari, I'm eight."

Her voice was reassuringly human, as was her warm friendly smile of greeting. She spoke his language too, which gave some comfort so far from what passed for home.

"My name is Sandor. I don't know how old I am," he replied hesitantly. Then he felt a curious sensation passing through him. As if gentle fingers caressed his mind, the sympathy and compassion in this strange contact overwhelmed him and he began to cry.

"Please don't worry Sandor," the girl said, her voice concerned, soothing. She stretched her hand down towards him, her small, slender fingers reaching to touch his face through the iron bars. "You are safe here. Everything is going to get better for you now."

A furious woman crossing the courtyard, hands on hips abruptly interrupted any further contact with the child. The woman was small and dark, with yellow skin, slanted dark eyes, and a heavy plait of black hair down her back. Khari's mother? Her servant, perhaps? She looked nothing like the golden haired child.

"Oops, I'm in trouble again. I'm not supposed to wear these pretty clothes out in the yards."

The child gave him a rueful but impudent smile and skipped towards the woman, pausing to turn back and give Sandor a friendly wave. She was just a girl but Khari had seen into her new friend's gentle heart and felt his pain. It was good to make things better for him.

Chapter Four

That night Khari waited until Ileni was napping after dinner, before sneaking out to seek an unofficial audience with the Jendar. She found the Dark Lord in his battlement observatory studying the moons of Jupiter through a large, gilded telescope. The air high up above the Keep was blustering with icy gusts cutting like knife edges. He threw part of his voluminous black wolf fur cloak around her as she sat beside him in silent, happy companionship.

Khari thought back to the night before as he continued observing the wonders of the solar system. She remembered sitting on the rain dampened window ledge, listening for the black stallion's staccato hoof beats prancing across the courtyard. It was something she did whenever Azrar left the stronghold, needing the reassurance of seeing his safe return for herself. Many times she'd sneaked out of her room to observe him stride back into the great hall, full of power and electric energy. She knew when his hunt had been successful – his clothing was sometimes darkly sticky; once she'd seen him wipe away a thin trickle of red blood from his mouth.

Khari would then return to her bed, relieved Azrar was home and his well being and survival assured after a successful hunt. No one had told her directly about her Dark Lord's true nature or his particular needs to survive. She had gathered scraps of knowledge from the overheard chatter of Ileni's family and from clues she'd read in the libraries, but mostly from their unguarded thoughts. She loved him too greatly to condemn him. What was there to condemn? Could an eagle or a wolf help being what they were created to be? She waited until he stood back from the telescope and Khari was able to gain his full attention.

"My Lord, I saw there was a man in the barracks, a stranger from beyond our borders. Did you capture him last night?"

Azrar nodded gravely, unsure where this conversation was heading.

Khari took a deep breath, preparing herself. This was going to be a risky conversation. The prince had never been angry with her before, she never wanted to see his eyes grow stormy and dark with displeasure from something she had done.

"I know he was wrong to kill your animal, but I have spoken to him. He is just like a child. He has had such a horrible life and only knows being hungry and homeless. He has no family and works for whatever he can. He has practically broken his back working on farms, enduring horrible beatings and people laughing at him, just for a lump of stale bread and a hard bed on a cold, filthy floor."

The girl paused to catch her breath and to look up at Azrar's stern, sharp planed face. His eyes still glittered with their green fire. Emboldened by his calm manner, Khari carried on. "He could stay here and work for you. I know he will be loyal and hardworking. He can cut wood, tend the horses and keep the place clean. Please, my Lord, spare his life and let him stay?"

Azrar thought awhile before answering. Though the stronghold was already well staffed, it would be useful to employ the placid strength of the big man. "I agree. But with a warning. You must not get too fond of this man, he cannot be another pet to fuss over like the wolf cub. If he betrays my trust or harms you in any way, I will turn him loose in the forest."

Khari nodded assent, she knew this was not the harmless sounding punishment it first seemed. Azrar would only release him for the savage pleasure of hunting him down. But she sensed this would never happen. Sandor's simple loyalty would be steadfast.

"He will not betray you, my Lord. He just wants to be safe from hunger and belong to a family."

With a slight, distracted nod, Azrar dismissed her and returned to his study of the mysteries of the universe. He gazed in wonder at the awesome panorama, not as a scientist or theological scholar but as a being becoming newly aware of its majesty. He had let so much go unnoticed in the past millennia of turmoil and warfare.

The last two centuries had been the strangest period of his life. Created for war, the lengthy decades of peace had lured him into a downward spiral of dangerous inertia, existing in a bizarre dream-like state, alive but not fully living. It was only when the increasingly rare incidence of strangers invading his land briefly lifted the life draining torpor, but the trance-like state returned again when the thrill of the chase and kill had passed.

For millennia Azrar held this harsh land and kept its people safe by the relentless force of his fierce will, by his military genius and by an implacable bond of honour to his subjects. As a Dark Kind warlord he had no other life but this. But what was once held by bloodshed was now sinking into the morass of obscurity. Isolann, a backwater realm, was peaceful because it was forgotten by the world. Though it pained him to admit it, only this demeaning obscurity had saved the last Dark Kind Jendar.

Azrar looked away from the stars and held out one arm, opening and closing his fist as if trying to pull down a handful of the coldly glittering backdrop of indifferent stars. His sword arm should not be empty. It was a wrongness. His whole being yearned for battle, to feel once again the brute weight of his broadsword, to control the wild excitement of his war horse plunging beneath him, snatching impatiently at the bit.

Yet he sensed subtle change to the indolent life of his lands; an awareness of transformation that began with a most unlikely source for his salvation, from the threat of a long slow slide into eventual non-existence. The arrival of Ileni and the Svolenian child. Showing incredible courage, the nomad woman braved the perils of the deep forest to bring the abandoned little girl to his stronghold, to plead for his protection. He had been reluctant at first. This was a human matter, one of their vulnerable offspring had no place in a Dark Kind warlord's keep.

He would never forget that first meeting with the child. His guards had found Ileni collapsed outside the outer gates of the stronghold, they brought her, exhausted and bedraggled from her ordeal traversing his forests, to stand before him in the Great Hall. She stood, straight-backed and proud, the child carried protectively in her arms, ready to defend the foreign born infant with her own life. The little scrap of humanity awoke and pulling away from the protection of the nomad woman, toddled boldly over to him. Fearlessly, she reached up to put her small fingers into his hand and smiled, innocent and unafraid of the non-human Prince. He saw then her extraordinary golden eyes and looked to Ileni with the question that would resolve his dilemma. The child indeed had the *Knowing*, the gift of reading human minds. As such she would be a useful tool for his survival and she would stay in the keep under his protection as his ward.

Khari kissed the wriggling cub on its wet button nose and giggled as it licked her face in return with its tiny pink tongue. "Wolf, stop that now. We have something important to do."

She tucked the playful, squirming cub, still licking her hand, into a wool lined leather pouch on her hip. As comfortable in the world of darkness as in sunlight, Khari happily scampered back down to the courtyard, eager to tell the big man he was the latest addition to their household.

There were now two more unwanted foundlings finding shelter and safety at the Dark Lord's keep.

She found him still locked up in the make-shift prison in the compound barracks. Khari waited, toes tapping with impatience as the impassive but inwardly disapproving guards opened the heavy oaken door. Their inner thoughts told of their distrust at having a Svolenian let loose in the Stronghold. These foreigners were the enemy, always had been and always would be.

At the welcome sight of Khari, Sandor cried again. When she told him of Jendar Azrar's decision, the tears flowed even faster. This time in sheer joy as the realisation he did not have to face starvation this coming winter sank in. Instead he would stay here, safe from his tormentors in a comfortable warm home with plentiful food. In his slowness he did not grasp the irony of his situation: he was now to be appreciated and cared for properly for the first time in his life not– by his own family or countrymen, but by an unearthly creature of darkness and his strange little human ward.

Sandor was large for a Svolenian and would have been good looking if nature had been kinder. His features were just a fraction too heavy, his pale blue eyes too close together and not enough light behind them. His hair was roughly cut and a shade between straw and ginger. Though slow, he was always diligent about his work. Once a simple task was assigned to him he would methodically go about it in his own time until it was finished.

Sandor heard snuffling and whimpering from Khari's bag and held his hands out.

"Can I see what's in your bag?"

Khari smiled and carefully handed the wolf cub to the big man, sharing his big innocent smile of sheer pleasure as he felt the wriggling creature's soft fur and she joined his laughter as it tried to chew his thick skinned hands with tiny white teeth.

"So you think you are fierce, little one! " Sandor said, grinning at the show of infant ferocity.

"He will be one day," an indignant Khari replied, in the cub's defence.

"Maybe, or he could be another friend."

Khari sighed with happiness. Though she never complained, life in the Dark Lord's stronghold could be lonely. There were no other youngsters living within its confines. Ileni's sons rarely brought their children here, if Ileni wanted to see her grandchildren she had to travel to find her tribe, using her knowledge of their seasonal routes from mountain range to plains.

Now Khari had two new playmates, both arriving on the same night, both gifts to her from her Dark Kind guardian. She watched with a happy sigh as Sandor tickled the cub's fat pink stomach; life had become much less lonely.

Another hour passed, Khari had left to attend her lessons with the Prince as Sandor waited patiently. Guards arrived and he was escorted by silent and stern faced Isolanni men out of his confinement and led across the compound courtyard through an ornate high carved stone arch and into a side door of the central keep, into the heart of the Dark Lord's household. A guard pointed to a set of steps leading down to another large wooden door, from where Sandor smelled the tantalising aromas of cooking. The Isolanni guard spoke to him in his own tongue, his tone abrupt and heavily accented, laced with unhidden contempt.

"For some reason the Dark Lord has spared your life. You are to report first to the keep housekeeper, Ileni.

Behave and you will live and thrive. If not, the forest awaits you."

Sandor nodded his head gravely, unable to believe his good fortune. This was a strange, frightening place but the inhabitants were treating him better than his own people ever had. Downstairs he found a large complex of kitchens and storerooms. He also found the fey child Khari, again. He was certain his presence here had something to do with her and met her smile with a warm greeting of open gratitude and joy.

Khari gave his large work callused hand a gentle squeeze, "I told you everything would be good from now on. You are safe in the Jendar's household. Now, hurry down to the main kitchen. Ileni has a bath waiting for you in front of the range. I promise I won't peek but I need to stay close by as no one else in the kitchens speaks any Svolenian."

Half an hour later Sandor found himself comfortably immersed in a large metal tub of scented hot water, passively and unselfconsciously submitting to a hard scrubbing from a small, severe Isolanni woman.

"Ileni says the Svolenian never wash," Khari ventured with curiosity. "You are all too poor to spare the firewood to heat any water up. Is that true?"

Sandor nodded, it was certainly true for him and the villagers he worked for.

"Ileni says if you work hard and show complete loyalty to the Jendar, you will be fed and protected for the rest of your life. But you must try to learn Isolanni. Ileni wants to know if you can do this."

"Tell her I owe the Jendar my life and I will never, never betray him. And I will do my best to speak like her, though I am a bit slow with any learning."

And again the tears began to flow down the big man's face, a free unselfconscious flow of hot salty tears of heartfelt relief as years of pent up fear and anxiety ebbed away. Someone more sophisticated may have questioned what exactly was the Dark Lord and why did his people hold such unswerving and fierce loyalty to him. Sandor's lost comrades had teased him cruelly about the dangers in the hidden castle and from its blood drinker, the monstrous Prince. Sandor did not care what the Jendar was. Like all the people of Isolann, like the beautiful child Khari, he too was under the Dark Lord's protection. He belonged here now.

As he dressed in clean new warm clothes, Ileni handed him an amulet on a copper chain, it was made of carved shining black stone in the shape of a wolf.

"Khari, tell him if he values his life, he must wear this always. He is part of the ancient Pact now. He must never tell any outsiders about the Jendar, or disturb the Dark Lord when he is hunting."

Sandor nodded, he would be loyal to the Pact. He knew the Jendar was responsible for the deaths of the others in the hunting party, a fate he so narrowly missed himself, but a lifetime of violent abuse from men like that had left him unable to care about their fate. He had survived and he would live a new, happier life among these dark-haired strangers and their inhuman Prince.

As the days turned to weeks and then months, he discovered the Prince was the best employer he had ever known. Sandor was no longer taunted and beaten or worked until he dropped with exhaustion, but treated with friendship and respect. Despite this new regard and provision for his well being, Sandor had enough sense to be in respectful awe of his dangerous protector and would never risk provoking his anger.

Sandor stayed in the smallest of a row of sturdy dwellings beyond the main courtyard. It was his first home and was soon filled with his first belongings, such as his collection of interesting shaped stones. On the main wall hung a big painting of this year's new foals – a treasured gift painted by Khari. He preferred to maintain some distance from the keep, which always frightened him especially after sunset when the Dark Lord rose from his Rest. For in this, the warnings from his own people, told mainly in mocking jest, had been right, the stories designed to frighten him had a base in truth. The Land of Secrets and Shadows did have a monstrous prince at its heart.

Sandor sometimes relived the first time he saw the Prince in person, remembered the leg weakening terror of that marble-white sharp featured face. And the eyes –what terrible eyes, all green fire, pitiless and cold. Summoned to an ante-room off the Great Hall, Sandor dropped to his knees and waited in abject terror as Jendar Azrar studied some documents, the Prince briefly looked up and fixed the big man with an inscrutable direct stare. Sandor dropped his head and focused on the complex pattern of a rich ruby red, purple and gold rug, anything but meet those eyes with his. The Prince's deep voice added to Sandor's fear; if a wolf could talk, it would sound like Lord Azrar. "Serve me well and your life in my stronghold will be comfortable and safe. Displease me and it will not be the wolves who first taste your blood."

Sandor struggled to reply but his throat had constricted painfully and his mouth was as dry and dusty as a cave floor, but before he could speak the Prince dismissed him with a slight nod and a grateful Sandor was able to escape from the unearthly cold of the blood-drinker's presence.

Azrar had little need to speak to him again after that first night. Yet for all this natural and understandable fear around his master, Sandor had never been happier. This was a good home, he belonged here. He soon came to love Ileni, her stern demeanour breaking often into easy, warm smiles, lit by merry near black almond-shaped eyes. The warmth of her smile reminded him of the few happy memories he had. Some were vague recollections of his mother who had been so fiercely protective of her son. She had died in childbirth when he was eight, leaving him to fend for himself in the homes of a succession of indifferent relations before being cast out to fend for himself.

And he loved the strange little girl whom he knew saved his life. Though she spent all her days with Ileni and him, wearing the same rough-hewn clothes and eating their simple fare, she would always be his princess. To Sandor, the child was magical, with her golden eyes and silvery hair. He had no concern if she touched his mind with hers, in fact he welcomed the mystical contact. He was enchanted with her– like all the many wild animals she tended and tamed.

Khari would raise each forest orphan then teach it to return to the wild when it was old enough to fend for itself. The one exception was the wolf cub that had been brought to the keep by Lord Azrar on the same night as himself. This creature grew fast until he was long and lean, grey pelted and amber eyed. He refused to be reunited with his wild family but loped along beside Khari, protectively sleeping at the foot of her bed. As Ileni pointed out, the child had two wolves to protect her, a grey and a black one. This referred to the ancient name for Azrar, now forgotten outside their country, 'The Black Wolf of Isolann.'

Sandor found a niche for himself, restoring the neglected growing area in the outer compound. He dug a sizeable vegetable garden and found the remains of an abandoned orchard. The trees were neglected but still producing fruit, with plenty of help from the other keep staff, they cleared the overgrown jungle and brought it back to life. Sandor also had a secret project and the help of one of Ileni's sons. As a special gift of gratitude to Khari, he created a walled secret garden full of sweet smelling flowers. Prince Azrar even contributed by sending abroad for some glacial-white roses. Her reaction on finding the garden was one of great joy and amazement.

"This is wonderful, so beautiful! Thank you so much." Khari reached up and kissed Sandor in the cheek, "You always treat me like a princess but I am just an ordinary person like you."

Sandor smiled with relief that she was pleased with his gift. He could never accept Khari as a simple peasant like himself. She could speak and write several languages and had knowledge of other lands and far off times. She belonged in the keep with the Dark Lord. Her clothes should only ever be bejewelled silks and the finest furs. She dwelt in another realm to him but was happy to share her with that domain for as long as possible.

Chapter Five

City of Vienna, Austria, 1927

Garan examined the man with wry amusement, as transparent thoughts of low animal cunning shifted like squirming shadows behind the human's small mean eyes. The Dark Kind commoner needed a change of identity. Urgently. As usual, he had been careless, littering the back streets of the graceful old city with his victims. It was time to move on.

Life as one of the few surviving Dark Kind commoners had settled into a familiar routine, a chameleon existence. It was one the other survivors scattered through Europe and Asia loathed, but one he relished to the full. A lifetime in the shadows, constantly moving on,

It suited him well. Now it was time to alter his name and nationality again and so begin another stage of his long adventure, defying the fate that had decimated his kind.

Garan, forced to feign blindness, wore dark glasses to disguise his eyes amongst humans, reached out for the forged papers. He ignored the smirk of contempt from the weasel-eyed human. These were precious documents: scraps of deliberately aged and distressed paper to change him temporarily into Nikolas Urlov, a white Russian exile of considerable financial means. Behind the protection of the dense black lenses, he studied the forger again with the relentless, predatory gaze of a seasoned killer. The man was young, strongly built and well fed, with the accumulated wealth created by a black market in forgeries. He had grown rich on the tide of human misery that had swept across Europe in the wake of the Great War and the social upheavals that followed in so many societies as the old order crumbled.

This century's toll of human suffering was little different from any other Garan had experienced; though the changes were coming faster in this increasingly mechanised era. He was content to ride along, taking advantage of humanity's endless turmoil. When humans fought each other, it was easier for nocturnal predators to slip past, unnoticed, in the darkness.

The forger wafted a slight but unmistakable scent of fear as his blood surged with adrenaline. Garan recognised the hidden signs of impending treachery. Undoubtedly, the criminal planned to engineer an 'accident' for him after the exchange of money. From the forger's point of view, Garan must have appeared a perfect subject for a double cross. A young man apparently hampered by blindness with his impermeable black lensed glasses and cane. Hardly more than a boy, secretive, without papers or connections in Vienna. Just another desperate refugee with plentiful ready cash and a secret to hide! Life was good, there were so many of the fools to fleece.

By his people's standards Garan was not tall. As a commoner, he had a slighter build then the warrior or the nobility caste but shared their innate natural elegance of movement. His hair, cropped short to blend into the style of the new century, was a shade of dark metallic copper, his features were sharp boned as all of the Dark Kind. Though not as obviously beautiful as the others, he remained curiously compelling with his lustrous dark violet eyes.

Garan, with his well cut expensive sombre-hued clothing, looked out of place in the dingy squalid basement beneath a back street Viennese slum. The stench of decay, foetid and heavy from the rotting timbers and crumbling brickwork, clung to everything. The forger, whose own fine clothes looked like an ill fitting veneer, disguising the low life criminal that lay beneath, grew impatient.

He had grown rich preying on the desperate casualties of a world gone mad. Among his victims were whole families who had lost everything and who only asked for the chance of a new life. Jewish families fleeing Cossack pogroms, white Russians nobility reduced to homeless exiles – all were fair game. Murdering some blind foreigner was nothing more than easy money. He snatched the proffered notes from Garan, counting them rapidly by the greasy light of one flickering tallow candle. Satisfied, he grunted a curt dismissal to his customer.

Garan turned to walk away, footsteps eerily silent as with his night-tuned eyes, he confidently entered the darkness beyond the dingy cellar. His Dark Kind senses attuned to another fresh surge of adrenaline from the forger. The man moved surprisingly quickly, pulling something from beneath his coat, rushing forward, his arm raised ready to strike his victim in the back. Garan whirled, a mastery of controlled reflex and immense power. He drove the forger's face hard against a mould-slimed wall, one hand clamping around his mouth to silence the screams, the other forcing his arm at near breaking point up his back. Terrified, the man's violent thrashing was futile against his superior inhuman strength.

"Well, little man," Garan mocked. "Your greed and treachery has finally killed you. Still, it is not every day that you get sent to Hell. Give my regards to your devil. "

He felt the man begin to collapse with shock and horror at the sight of his killer's fangs dropping from their scabbard in his upper jaw: curving scimitars of razor sharp death. Regretfully, Garan had no time to prolong and enjoy his kill, lunging instead fast and hard into the unyielding neck muscles, quickly rewarded by the gush of flowing lifeblood. Its heat flooded his senses with pleasure, every cell celebrating the life renewing power of hot human blood.

Garan was a pitiless killer. Unlike the more cautious members of his species, he never waited until the hunger was too intense to bear. He took whatever he wanted from life as and when he desired it, often killing for the sake of it, out of pique and boredom.

There was plentiful lowlife prey readily available — specimens like the now dead and drained forger, the body slumped in a forgotten heap. But Garan was indiscriminate in his predation, using all the lessons learnt from millennia of survival. High risk, high profile prey was far more fun, to Garan provoking danger was a celebration of life, of survival. He was a renegade among his species, with no respect for the rigidly enforced and inborn caste system that underpinned their scattered society. But he did obey without question, one set of inviolate rules that had origins in their basic genetic design. He would only kill healthy young human males for their blood. A rule obeyed not from any sense of scruple, in his particular case it was the only substance that could sustain him.

With the night nearly over, Ha'ali Eshan made her way across the city, seeking Garan. She sighed in despair as she recalled the long funeral procession that had passed her just after nightfall; her heart sinking lower with every gleaming black carriage pulled by plumed high stepping black stallions. Over the metallic clatter of their iron-shod hooves on the ice bound cobbles came the mournful drone of a brass band. An extravagant, flashy affair; to Eshan so typical of Garan's capricious and reckless nature to arrange such a send off for his most recent human companion.

She felt no comfort knowing she was not the only Dark Kind survivor to despair of him. They all watched powerless and outraged as he ricocheted around Europe throughout the centuries, often with a human 'pet' in tow. His adventures were always dangerous, flying hard in the face of all common sense. Yet somehow, miraculously, he had survived when other more cautious Dark Kind had perished.

Occasionally, Eshan found him bearable company—such was the high cost of loneliness, but more often than not, he was just a dangerous nuisance. As a commoner, he found it easy to adapt to each change in human society. He had already come to terms with the new century with its political confusion and social uncertainties. Eshan's exact title in her people's language was' Ha'ali', which meant she was in the lower order of the nobility, above the commoner and warrior caste but below the warlord Jendars. Eshan had to work harder at blending in amongst humans then a Dark Kind commoner. Her struggle echoed that of European human aristocracy especially in the shock waves that followed the upheavals of the revolution in Russia.

One common thread ran through Dark Kind life however, whatever the caste: the need for absolute discretion. Eshan sighed, there was no sign of that a few hours ago! Garan had arrived alone in a smoked glass carriage at the head of his dead human companion's funeral cortege, but had disappeared soon after the pretentious ceremony. No doubt bored already with the charade.

Why did he risk his life provoking humans and their insatiable curiosity? Surely so worldly-wise a creature would know of their insatiable love of solving mysteries? Especially in this age of newspapers with their reporters desperate for the latest intrigue and scandal. The humans had police forces now, with increasingly better information gathering and sharing. Life in Europe was an ever-tightening net, one that would close hard and fast with knowledge and proof of the Dark Kind .

Eshan despaired. Who would not witness this lavish and spectacular ceremony without wondering exactly who Elize Rowley was, and what she had done to earn such devotion and expenditure? Who was the chief mourner? The spectators caught a fleeting impression of a pale, strange featured hidden-eyed boy of no more than seventeen. A well-dressed young man who had sat in his carriage during the church ceremony, alighting from it only to drop a single red rose onto her open grave. Then he'd strode away in silence, vanishing into the night, fuelling wild speculation, vivid rumours and outrageous intrigue in his wake.

Eshan sensed he was very close, possibly watching her from the shadows in the confusing maze of narrow, sleet lashed streets. She stifled a low growl, angry at being coolly observed, she felt toyed with by this impudent commoner. Grateful for the current human convention for widows to wear heavy veiling, it gave her a convenient and unremarkable camouflage from any human passer-by. But not from the fine-honed senses of another Dark Kind. A metallic click of cane on pavement, the faint trace of something similar to sandalwood, then Garan stepped out of the darkness. A mournful cold wind moaned through the winding dark streets; this did not chill Eshan as much as the gleam of raw blood lust in Garan's inky eyes.

Her despair grew heavier as she watched him focus on a passer-by, a man hurrying home aware of the threat of heavy snow. This was so wrong, dangerous to them both. The wind's low moan could not drown out any screams or sounds of struggle from his victim, nor could the shadows hide the kill from any witnesses. She ran across the street but was too late to stop Garan tearing open the man's throat, drinking deeply from the fountain of blood, steaming in the cold air. It made no difference that he'd made another recent kill, no other surviving Dark Kind was as rapacious and indiscriminate a predator as Garan.

His violet eyes flashed with impudence at her discomfort. His blood filled mouth widened with a grin of feral triumph. "What good timing, Eshan," he said provoking a growl of outrage at his lack of respect. "Please be my guest, there's plenty left."

This was torture for Eshan who had spent so many years in rigid self denial without killing. She forced herself to combat the overwhelming excitement created by the close proximity of fresh blood. With her hunger so great and the sweet, coppery smell of blood so close, she had no reserve of willpower left to control her powerful instincts. With a low groan of self loathing, she submitted and fed.

Later she would rationalise to herself that the man was already dead with Garan at his throat. For the first time in a century, blood straight from a living victim poured down her throat in a life-giving flood of intoxicating pleasure. Her additional appetite quickly hastened the man's death, and Garan with callous ease, threw the emptied body behind a pile of street rubbish.

Garan gave a vulpine grin, "Come Countess, or whatever you call yourself these days, you cannot tell me that was not infinitely better than carrion — that cold lifeless blood in jars from your pathetic 'research' clinic that you survive on."

Eshan snarled, her she-wolf voice laced with self-disgust.

"Of course it is, you manipulative bastard. It is madness to prey so openly on these humans. Why must you risk yourself?"

Garan licking the last of the blood from his thin lips gave another insolent grin, one of pure malice.

"That is the point. Danger is so wildly exciting. I know I am alive. I know I am one of the living Dark Kind, an ageless vampire with all my power and strength intact."

Eshan gave a shudder of intense distaste. "I abhor that filthy term from the mouths of foolish humans, why must you use it?"

"You nobility are always so fastidious. It is a meaningless human word. I actually rather like it."

He approached her to belatedly give the customary Dark Kind embrace of greeting. Despite their occasional disputes, their species prided itself on strong emotional ties to one another. In all their long history, no Dark Kind had ever harmed another.

"Ha'ali, listen to me," he addressed her by her correct title, but with no respect in his tone. "You live in a constant state of abject fear, dreading discovery as you attempt to subdue your nature, trying so hard to be like these infesting, clever apes. Each day must seem like a little death, waiting for one of your human friends to betray you." He clamped his hand on her arm, adding with a snarl, "Yours is a pitiful existence for a high born Dark Kind. You are a superior life form, take what you need and enjoy your life again. We do not have their weakening emotions of pity or remorse so why must you simper along and wring your hands at my perfectly natural behaviour?"

Eshan pulled away from him abruptly, finding his presence an increasing and dangerous irritation.

"Because I have learnt to respect humans! And more importantly the risks you take endanger us all. They have forgotten we exist, that could change the minute you get caught on some superfluous killing spree."

Garan shrugged with complete indifference to her opinion. No weary and faded noble woman was going to tell him what to do.

"You are a very sad excuse for a vampire, Eshan," he remarked with a smirk of ridicule. And with that final insult, he began to prowl away.

Though his steps were silent, the rhythmic click of his ebony and silver cane marked his passage from the alley. But before he disappeared into the night, he turned to address her again.

"Oh, I nearly forgot why I summoned you to Vienna! Are you still besotted with that brooding Balkan prince? It seems his neighbours to the south want to make a big move on Isolann. Someone should warn him. I would send a telegraph but the deluded fool is still living in the Middle Ages."

Garan was gone before she could question him further. She needed more information— damn him for his impudence! His lack of respect only stretched to minor aristocracy like herself, he would never dare insult a ferocious high prince warlord like the Black Wolf of the Arpalathians, Jendar Azrar. She sighed, there was nothing more to be done, Garan had melted into the night like a shadow.

Eshan saw herself reflected in the dust-smeared window of an empty shop as the sleet clouds briefly cleared to reveal a wan half moon. She lifted up the heavy veiling to talk to Garan and could see her face, pale and beautiful as if carved from flawless white marble. Her eyes were huge orbs of lavender, now flashing with renewed fire and power. All vestiges of imitating humans had vanished with those vibrant eyes, far more tellingly then her sharp gore-stained canines. What had that bastard done to her by bringing back the fearsome creature she had once been? Then with a stab of self-disgust, she realised it was wrong to blame Garan. He had not forced her to share his kill. She could have refused, walked away.

She found a silk kerchief and cleaned off the last of the blood around her lips and pulled back the veiling, hurried out of the alley and the scene of her return into Dark Kind ways. She could not deny the wonderful feeling of power surging within her, nor the greater speed, agility and sharpness of her senses. She had not felt so vibrant and alive for years.

Returning to the bright, bustling and elegant streets of Vienna, Eshan merged into the mass of humanity. She became lost within the crowds yet would always be apart from them. At times like this, especially having just shared a kill, she marvelled that people were not aware of her dangerous presence among them. Her kind had always preyed on humans. Why did they not turn on her and tear her limb from limb in a righteous frenzy of self-preservation? Had they really forgotten there was another species higher in the food chain besides themselves? Or was this thing closer to the reaction of a herd of gazelle grazing peacefully close to the lion pride once the big cats slept off their kill? Whatever the truth was, she passed through the streets unnoticed to return to her apartment, to await the next sunset. But this day's seclusion from the light would hold no peace. Her anxiety grew with each step home, lashed by needle points of frozen rain, oblivious to the growing storm.

Once within the warmth and safety of her apartments, she set her intelligence-gathering machine into motion. Eshan's considerable wealth had bought more than a network of havens in many European cities; her medical institute in Vienna employed some of the finest scientific minds in the world — to research the creation of artificial blood. Finding a viable way to survive among humans for all the last of the Dark Kind, even a maverick like Garan, was now her life's work. Her uphill and dispiriting crusade led to the establishment of a complex and far reaching intelligence network. It was designed to give early warning of any potential danger to any of the scattered remnants of her people still living in Europe and Asia.

Her system had failed. Azrar and his loyal army of nomads could never withstand attack from a modern force, even the ramshackle, poorly equipped Svolenian army. The prince therefore was in grave danger. Despite the huge risk to herself attempting to openly cross Europe, she had to go to him. She had no choice.

Chapter Six

Svolenian Northern Plainlands 1927

  Ha'ali Eshan slipped a foot out of the stirrup and gave her instep muscles a much-needed rub. Stiletto-like stabbing cramps shot through her feet as too many centuries of soft living in the human capitals of Europe took their toll. She had not ridden much beyond the occasional light hack after dark in London's Rotten Row or the Bois de Bouloigne in Paris. Now she rode for hours each night with a morose, near silent gang of well-paid mercenaries traversing the desolate plains that eventually led to Isolann.

  The journey seemed endless, a swift, furtive crossing of hostile territory under the cover of night, using horses and keeping well away from the main routes through this depressed and surly land. As if to emphasis Eshan's unease, a low, whining wind stirred up the dank night air, promising yet more teeming rainfall. Svolenia was suffering its worst ever spring, already meagre crops rotted in the waterlogged ground. Livestock came down with foot rot and other often lethal infections. Travellers were no longer made welcome in the countryside, but seen by the desperate as a source of easy gain by banditry and murder.

  Eshan handpicked her team, tough ruthless men whose only loyalty was their bank balances. Accounts now well padded from her down payments. Their leader nudged his horse forward to ride alongside Eshan to address her. "Are you all right, my Lady? We can make camp if you wish, there is enough shelter in that little spinney. The skies are about to open again."

  The burly mercenary rubbed wind-blown stinging mud from fatigue-reddened eyes; travelling only by night at his client's strange insistence had played havoc with his sleep. Clothing covered with travel grime and dried horse sweat, broad features hidden by three weeks dark beard growth all added to his unsavoury appearance. His toughness masked an innate chivalry, surely it was time for the slender woman who paid him to escort her over such wild and remote terrain to have a rest?

Eshan shook her head, setting her still painful feet back in the stirrups. A cardinal Dark Kind rule— never show weakness, any weakness, however fleeting in front of humans. Chavez grunted and shrugged, waving the others on with a heavily scarred hand. He would not openly question this Isolanni woman's insistence on travelling only by night though it meant a longer, difficult journey over rough terrain. She paid the gang an emperor's ransom to help get her to Isolann, enough to take a comfortable early retirement. Chavez already spent the money in his mind on this journey, dreaming of the olive farm nestling in the foothills of the Sierra Nevada he would buy after this trip. And the wide-hipped, dark-eyed beauty he would find to share his good fortune.

The Isolanni woman's need for heavily armed and professional assistance was no surprise to Chavez. It was common knowledge in the Upper Balkans, that there was no love lost between Svolenia and Isolann. The only mystery was the woman herself. Only appearing from her tent after the sun set, wearing incongruous dark glasses, she always rode ahead, finding her way through the darkness with an uncanny sureness, even during a pitch black, starless night. She never used maps, yet followed a route of unswerving accuracy through the most confusingly featureless landscape. She wore plain male apparel in a heavy duty brown cloth, a broad brimmed felt fedora covered her head and of course the strange dark glasses which always hid her eyes. All of it added to her eerie, mysterious aura, but if the men had any doubts or curiosity none spoke out openly. There was too much money at stake to risk offending their weird benefactor.

Isolann, even thinking the name made Eshan shudder in trepidation, what might she find there? What must she face? She knew from contact with Garan the Jendar Azrar was not only alive but also still ruling his remote mountain principality but that was all she knew, nothing more.

Although this journey was all her own choice, it was no easy task to seek him out and warn him of the looming peril ahead. First she must survive crossing this seemingly endless enemy terrain, undiscovered and unharmed. And never mind the peril from the locals, what if her human protectors discovered what she was? Would the money she paid them be enough to protect her?

If she reached Isolann in one piece there was more danger in confronting the Prince. She had incurred his fearsome wrath once before, trying to warn him of imminent danger. She had tried to save him from his own reckless fury that had bordered on the suicidal, Azrar's obsessive love for an insane, scheming bitch called Zian had put him in the gravest of danger. He had not listened; mindful that Eshan had loved him too, wrongly assuming her desperate pleas were nought but raw jealousy. That her warning eventually proved right meant nothing. Azrar's anger had been a blaze, a fury even the passing of so much time, would not have dampened.

Now she was making this long, perilous journey to give him another warning that she knew would enrage him. Even armed with so much evidence, how was she to tell Jendar Azrar he could not rule Isolann for very much longer? And the past was no longer a safe haven.

For two weeks, Eshan's company made their slow journey through the most remote region of Svolenia. They had made little contact with the locals, one useful advantage of travelling by night. The sophistication of Svolenia's cities to the far south did not stretch so far into the empty countryside, a depressed and poverty-ridden wasteland, thanks mainly to the new regime's ruinous agricultural policies. Banditry was rife, most peasants retreated into their crude mud and stone homes on nightfall— barricading themselves in fortified villages bristling with weapons—guarded by ever vigilant lookouts. It was easy to avoid these villages, always giving them a wide berth in case their own horses betrayed their presence with the clink and jingle of their harness or by calling out to their fellow beasts in the villages.

Even in the darkness, Eshan could smell the muddled collection of hovels and unkempt sties a mile away. It was always the same stench, rotting vegetation, pig shit and human fear-tinged sweat. These were a sad, lost people, defeated by their long history of poverty, disease and warfare and by a long succession of useless kings and now the burden of zealous communist rule, promising the people so much and delivering yet more misery.

Soon Eshan's senses would be rewarded for enduring this arduous journey. She could not wait to reach the Isolanni border, there she would be happily sated with the sensations of Isolann, the clean sharp wind that always smelt of winter snow coming straight from the Arpalathians, the aromatic scent of pine forests. The sight and sound of the inner keep with its wondrous Dark Kind artefacts. All were poignant reminders of a much mourned past when her species ruled the world. Supreme and unchallenged masters of the planet.

The thought of reaching Isolann gave her strength to endure the dangers of the journey and the uncomfortably curious glances from the men she now trusted with her life. She had spent so long hiding in the human world, how she longed for sound of her own language, the soft, luxurious touch of bariola velvet against her skin. She yearned to throw away these accursed dark glasses, to walk, head held high and openly live as a Dark Kind noble woman again. And best of all, whatever reception he gave her, even the hostile one she was expecting, she would be in Azrar's company again.

Chapter Seven

Azrar's Stronghold, Isolann 1928

"A curse on that creature!"

Ileni's strident voice rang through the corridors leading from her kitchen and echoed through the courtyard beyond, scattering the fowl scratching amongst the cobble stones.

"Oops, I think Wolf's in big trouble again." Khari made a rueful grimace and dropped a handful of apples into a stout willow basket and handed it to one of the kitchen staff. "I'd better leave helping with the fruit harvest and make my peace with Ileni."

Sandor nodded gravely, putting down his own basket of fruit. "And I'd better look for Wolf. I bet I will find him with tonight's dinner in his mouth."

Khari left the small orchard that nestled outside the keep, growing small, hardy apples and pears against the inner compound walls which gave some protection from the harsh mountain winds. She ran through the open inner gate and back into the keep. The warm autumn breeze playfully teased her silver-blonde hair worn loose around her shoulders. She was twelve, grown to a slender beauty that had lost none of the fey quality so enchanting to Ileni and Sandor when she had been a small child. They had become a family, with Ileni as the formidable but big-hearted matriarch and Sandor becoming a protective older brother figure, although intellectually Khari had long outstripped the man. It did not matter, they were a team, with ties as close as any blood family.

There were times it seemed the quiet rhythm of life for the mismatched but content residents of Azrar's fortress lair would remain unaltered forever. The cycle of the seasons measured time's progress and the inevitable process of ageing—a thing not shared by their inhuman benefactor. Occasionally, in the bright glare of the mid day sun, it seemed they could be anywhere in the world, ordinary people getting on with everyday lives. Once the sun set and the world of deep shadows and secrets returned, there was no escaping the truth. A brooding dark presence ruled the keep, the lands beyond, and their lives.

Supper was a bowl of steaming lentil and potato stew. It was meant to be punishment as the rest of the human retinue dined on honey cured ham and fresh vegetables. The two conspirators were unconcerned, anything Ileni prepared was delicious. Banished from the kitchen, Wolf whimpered pitifully outside the door.

"What a pathetic sound for a grown up wolf! That creature would not survive five minutes in the wild," muttered Ileni, still not forgiving the brindled creature's earlier thieving foray into her domain.

Khari managed to keep a straight face, just. Unfortunately for Ileni the girl knew that deep inside, her carer was amused by the wolf's audacity and ingenuity in stealing a haunch of salt bacon that morning, convinced it was well beyond the creature's reach.

After her dinner, Khari walked with Wolf loping at her heel to the stables then out to the paddocks hoping to see the Dark Lord. He had not been seen by any of the humans for over a week. When Khari had last spoken to him, he was preoccupied and abrupt, his voice more harsh and growl-like than usual. Perhaps it was a result of a brief visit from hard-riding messengers from a southern tribe who had ridden in at the start of the week. Khari had missed them, as she had been with Sandor and a high spirited group of the younger members of the household, gathering wild berries in a nearby valley. It had been a good excuse for singing and merriment around the camp fires, the last chance to sit under the stars in warm night air, to be free of the claustrophobic confines of the keep before winter set in and all movement beyond its walls became difficult and perilous.

Khari could not help notice an uneasy atmosphere on their return ; sweeping through the minds of those who stayed behind revealed nothing beyond a nameless anxiety with no solid, explainable cause. Before dawn Khari was awoken by Wolf tugging at her covers and the sound of hooves clattering across the courtyard below her window. Opening the wooden shutters, she shielded her sleep-laden eyes against the bright glare of burning torches.

A group of about twenty men arrived, apparently escorting a visitor into the stronghold. Khari was intrigued and nervous, these were the first outsiders besides Sandor that she had ever seen. They looked swarthy and tough, all carried weapons as they glanced around them with wary and suspicious eyes. Although she could not understand their language, she was able to detect a sense of growing unease from the newcomers, but not of any imminent threat from them. They dismounted at some hidden command and waited until the Prince's household, roused from their beds by the keep guards, rushed out to tend to the visitors' needs, stabling the horses and guiding the men to sleeping quarters.

Khari hastily pulled a warm robe of dark red wool lined with russet squirrel fur over her night clothes and sneaked down the back stairs to be near to the action. She got close enough, undetected in the shadows, to scan one burly visitor's mind. She could not understand his language but sensed only nervous curiosity and exhaustion.

Sudden brightness from candles being lit in the great hall refocused her attention back to the inside of the castle. Azrar had a guest. Khari crept in through the towering main doors and crouched low, hidden by the stairwell, and peeped through a gap in the carved masonry, curiously studying the newcomer. The visitor sported a khaki, shapeless long coat worn over breeches, laced up brown riding boots and a large brimmed hat that annoyingly hid the face from Khari's view. She tried to scan the person's mind but to her consternation met with the same solid wall of non-communication as when she futilely reached out to the Prince. It must be another being like Lord Azrar!

As Khari watched, the visitor dropped down to her knees in a low bow, head touching the granite floor in complete submission, then arose to stand in silence before the Prince. The two Dark Kind stood facing each other with the complete stillness of their kind. Although she could not read their thoughts, the bristling tension between them was obvious. An uneasy pause lingered in the silent Great Hall for an uncomfortably long time. What would happen next? Khari saw with growing anxiety that the Jendar's eyes had darkened to storm cloud grey, a warning sign of danger from his fury. Azrar sighed heavily and held his hand out to his visitor who stepped forward, then they kissed with an emotion bordering on ferocity.

To Khari's astonishment, the visitor finally threw off the hat and she could see it was a female, despite the masculine, military-style attire. She had an incredible, hard beauty with a feminine version of Azrar's sharp-boned elegance of feature. Her hair, worn up in a tightly pinned plait was a rich mahogany, her eyes shone with a lustrous lilac iridescence. As they held each other, Khari felt overcome with an intense, new emotion—one she had no name for and had never experienced before now. One that caught in her throat and heart, crushing, vice-like and almost unbearable when Azrar, his arm around the visitor's slender waist, swept her down the stairs to his vault, as dawn threatened to break across the horizon.

Khari returned to her bedroom, crawled into her now cold bed but could not sleep, the intense crushing sensation refusing to release its wicked grip. A carillon of birdsong celebrated a bright, rosy dawn but the morning's joyous beauty was lost on her. Puffy-eyed from lack of sleep, Khari's thoughts were confused, her emotions tumbling, helter-skelter, round and round. The only way to purge herself of this choked and churning nausea was to ride it out in a break neck gallop.

The Jendar would be furious with her for leaving the sanctuary of the forest paths unaccompanied, but in a flurry of unwarranted pique and hurt, she decided he would be too involved with his Dark Kind woman to enquire where she had been all day. Anyway, she would not be alone, she reasoned to herself with the ever-loyal Wolf loping beside her.

She was the only one awake as she crossed the dew sparkled yard, with Wolf scattering the bold old chickens crowding her ankles, demanding food. The horses stirred in their thick dry bark beds and whickered gently in greeting as she entered the ornate carved stone stable block. Some blinked as if in surprise as she opened the doors, letting a stream of dawn light through. The wood-clad stalls, designed to be warm in winter and cool in summer, housed Azrar's three black stallions and her new equine treasure— a well mannered dappled grey stallion brought to her from the herds kept by southern plains nomads. These horses were bred from the Prince's war-horse stock, larger and finer-boned then the mountain ponies. The Jendar gave these magnificent beasts to the brave young men who patrolled Isolann's borders and were a status symbol in Isolanni peasant society. There was always great competition to earn the right to ride them.

Khari kissed her stallion's dark grey velvet nose in apology, then ignored his snorts of protest as she tacked him up without feeding him any breakfast. She left the stable block and crossed the yard as quietly as possible, practically dragging the sulking horse away from its friends and morning routine that it knew always included a hearty feed of grain.

Once they were clear of the stronghold's outer walls and into the woodland, following a familiar and well-worn track, her horse forgot its grudge and trotted forward in a skittish and high-stepping prance. The narrow path through the woods could be dangerous, especially for an over fresh horse and Khari needed her full concentration as they negotiated the low branches and gnarled twisted old tree roots.

Once clear of the overhanging trees, she had to fight to hold back the impetuous, plunging stallion, now eager to run free. This open stretch of grassland was a favourite place for a gallop but first she needed to check there were no strangers in the vicinity, no easy task as the horse whirled around on the spot, snorting with excitement.

"Steady up Clarion, we must be safe, look at Wolf, he is waiting quietly. Just whoa there now."

Her soothing words were lost on the horse, all sensible thoughts driven from its head with the anticipation of a good fast gallop. Just as she thought her arms would be pulled from their sockets, she felt all was well and dropped the tension of the sweat-slippery reins. The stallion leapt high in the air with a squeal of delight and landed with a single huge buck that nearly dislodged her, then they were pounding across the springy turf in great, ground devouring strides. Like a grey brindled streak, Wolf loped beside them, at first easily matching the horse's gait. Khari leant forward, low over the powerful animal's neck, her face whipped and stinging from the passing of the wind and the horse's wiry long mane, which wiped away her free flowing tears.

For a while her problems at the keep and with its inhabitants were forgotten. Life was all in this moment, the fresh green smell of crushed grass rising from her stallion's hooves, the excited pounding of her heart. Every part of her being was focused on keeping her balance in the stirrups, staying relaxed and at one with the exhilarating pace of her galloping horse. But even a fit, enthusiastic young animal like Clarion had to draw breath and tire eventually. As his breathing began to sound laboured, Khari eased him up and allowed him to walk out on a long rein, the air becoming misted from the steam off his sweat drenched grey coat. In the quiet that followed her headlong gallop, Khari's thoughts began to wander back to the keep.

With a sudden clarity, she realised the reason for her distress. Why would Azrar have any time for a human child's company when a beautiful female of his own kind was sharing his bed in the darkness?

Deeply embarrassed by her thoughts and the images they conjured, Khari snatched up the sweat-slippery reins and drove her heels into her horse's sides. They carried on across the plains in another gallop, bounding across the open land, until total exhaustion slowed the horse from a flat-out run to a disunited and wavering canter, then to a bumpy jog trot. Gently, she reined the sweat-drenched animal to a halt, nearly falling off from her own fatigue.

Her tears now were not from the wind or the whiplash from the horse's mane but from deep within. From an utter, desolate inner place of bewildering loneliness. She felt a hot tongue lick her hand. In her self-pity, she had forgotten Wolf, so valiantly trying to keep up with her break-neck gallop across the yellowing grassland. The wolf was panting so hard his long narrow body shuddered with every tortuous breath. Khari dismounted and taking his brindled head in both hands kissed his forehead above the amber eyes.

"I am so sorry, you are such a wonderful loyal friend to me. And so is Ileni and Sandor and even you Clarion, I don't deserve any of you. I am just being a spoilt little idiot."

But the knot of pain had not gone; it was Azrar's love she wanted and realisation of the impossibility of this felt like a jagged knife in her heart.

Khari was not to know that the apparently passionate kiss beyween the Jendar and the stranger was nothing beyond a polite greeting between all Dark Kind. A welcome with no meaning beyond good manners.

Chapter Eight

Statue-like in their stillness, Azrar and Eshan sat opposite each other before the roaring hearth in the great hall of the keep. The Prince had dismissed all his human retinue and poured large golden goblets of warm, richly spiced wine for his guest and himself.

Eshan accepted the wine with a respectful bow of her head towards the Prince. She felt relaxed, relieved to be out of her travel-stained clothing. It felt so good to dress as a high born Dark Kind lady again. No longer in the disguise of human style clothing, instead she wore a floor sweeping dark violet bariola velvet gown, intricately worked with abstract designs in fine pure gold filigree. An extravagant waterfall of amethysts, also set in gold adorned her slender neck, with her long dark red hair falling loose down her back. She was beautiful in the hard, fierce, way of her species and for the first time in centuries she felt attractive again. A useless beauty for it could not melt Azrar's ice-bound heart.

"I take it this is not a social visit?" Azrar finally announced. There was no sign that he felt any pleasure at her arrival and Eshan's heart sank at the jagged ice in his voice. He had always been austere in manner but did an ancient disagreement between them still fester in his heart? His initial greeting at her arrival at the gates of his stronghold had been undeniably passionate but that was the way of all Dark Kind encounters, nothing more than ancient custom. She looked into his emerald eyes; they were as fierce and implacable as ever. She yearned for some way of extinguishing this hopeless love for Azrar; was she condemned to spend a wasted aeon-long life, pathetically wanting the warlord for her own? He had no interest in her, never had. Taking a long sip of the ruby wine, she calmed her thoughts before answering. This was going to be difficult.

"My Lord, you must understand. Even at the risk of earning yet more pain from your anger towards me, everything I say to you will come from my undying devotion to your well-being."

She paused briefly, there was no trace of softening in his implacable eyes — she did not expect it. She took a deep breath and plunged on,

"I have made this difficult journey for one reason alone — to warn you of great dangers."

"My life is always facing and fighting danger. What is this sudden new peril?"

Azrar's reply was even and controlled but in truth he was shocked at Eshan's weak appearance. It had clearly been a long time since she had fed.

"This land of yours is a lost world,"Eshan continued, trying to find the right words to make him listen without firing up one of his notorious rages.

"With respect, it is considered by the rest of the world to be a forgotten backwater, remote and unimportant. But this is about to change. The world of modern humans and their astonishing technology will be at your door very soon, battering down and destroying the secluded protection of your stronghold."

With a harshness she had not intended, she concluded, "You have spent too many lost centuries rattling around this vast, decaying old mausoleum to a long dead past."

Eshan took a deep breath, she had never put herself at such risk, against Azrar's wrath and scorn but he had to be forced to face the stark truth of his perilous situation.

"This stronghold was once the centre of your power but you had command of a large army then, Dark Kind warriors and battalions of professional, loyal human troops. What have you now, my Lord? A handful of nomadic peasants armed with bows, your Dark Kind warriors all slain. You are alone, Prince Azrar and in great danger."

Azrar remained outwardly calm and still but the growling tone in his voice grew lower and more threatening, "I marvel at your certainty that humans will prevail over me. I have never been defeated." His answer was caustic, his anger dangerously close to erupting.

Eshan sighed; she knew this would be the toughest, most difficult thing she'd ever attempted. The warning signs of Azrar's growing fury were blatantly obvious —the storm-darkening of his eyes, the slight tightening of his features. She had no choice but to press on however, to continue to ignore the danger from his volatile nature.

"My Lord, with the very greatest respect, you have no idea how much human civilisation has progressed. The population is growing at a phenomenal rate; their technological prowess is astounding. We are the primitives now; we are the prey cowering in the shadows, not the humans."

"Never! I hide from no man!" Azrar leapt up, fangs bared in fury, his black eyes ablaze with flashes of green fire.

Eshan fell on her knees again, dropping her head to touch the stone floor in a gesture of homage and supplication; he was a warlord, only understanding the ancient traditions of their kind. But she had to find the courage and force herself to speak more; she just had to get her warning through to Azrar before his ire became beyond control. With her head still down in the dramatic gesture of submission and obedience she continued,

"There is still time, Jendar Azrar, time to learn how to dwell with humans. Time to prepare your people for change. But if you want to survive, then I must somehow drag you and Isolann into the reality of the twentieth century."

Eshan took a courageous risk, raising herself from the floor to look him directly in the eyes. "This modern world will come here like an unstoppable, rampaging beast and there is nothing, absolutely nothing, you can do to prevent it."

"And what is the alternative? To live like you? A pathetic nothing, cowering in the shadows?"

Eshan winced at his curt words. They had struck deep into her heart, they hurt. Azrar's mind had filled with the memories of blood-soaked battles of past millennia. "I have faced and defeated all the great barbarian hordes, the military brilliance of Alexander, the full might of the Roman and Ottoman empires were all crushed by my armies. I am Jendar Azrar, High Prince of Isolann. I will not hide from apes!"

"My Lord Azrar, you are the greatest warlord of our kind. To have kept this land unconquered so long is a glorious achievement. But you have never left the Three Kingdoms; you have no concept of how powerful mankind has become! When was the last time you led an army into battle? When was the last time you actually had an army? Your only hope of survival is to blend in with humans. To live as I do."

"If that is indeed my only hope, then I will die, here, with a sword in my hand. There can be no other honourable fate for a Jendar."

Eshan's heart filled with tearing pain, as if already mourning for the proud warlord whom she loved so much. Yet she pressed on, desperate to persuade him to see sense as the successful surviving commoners had done.

"What have you got to fight with, Prince Azrar?" she challenged with boldness driven by desperation. "Archaic weapons and a handful of untrained nomads? Just this against machine guns and bombs that kill dozens with one blow. You have only horses to pitch against tanks and warplanes-the sheer might of numbers of their armies."

She hoped he was taking in the urgency of her words – she was pleading for his life.

"And when they come to break down the gates of this fortress, what will they find? One of the greatest discoveries of all their time; a living specimen of a terrifying creature feared by humans since the dawn of time — one that has long been considered a myth of primitive, superstitious peasants! These new people will not cower in fear of you, Prince Azrar. They will not try to destroy you with crucifixes, stakes and flames. The children of this new era will find you fascinating, an object to be studied, probed and experimented on — whether you be dead or alive."

"When they discover you exist, that you are not a thing of stories or nightmarish dreams, they will come for us also, the scattered survivors. Are we of less worth than your human peasants? Can they not thrive well enough without you?"

Azrar could take no more. With a low warning growl of his rising fury he strode out of the hall, seeking the sanctuary of the highest battlement of the castle. For once, the vastness of the star studded velvet night gave him no pleasure. A wind, ice-barbed, straight from the encircling mountains came blasting through the night air, a too early harbinger of the mighty iron fist of winter to come. It battered against him in angry gusts; tearing at his long jet hair and billowing wolf skin cloak. He threw back his handsome, sharp boned face and with fangs bared howled above the voice of the wind. The night echoed with the chilling cry of the Dark Kind warlord; his proud challenge to this new world of men, to all the fast breeding, short-lived but clever apes that overran his world.

The mountain wolves took up the vampire's cry, answering through the night clad, deep valleys. Then the forest packs added their ferocious and eerie call of defiance. Their kind too were hunted to near extinction, pushed to ever more remote desolate margins. Unaware of it, man was about to relearn an ancient wisdom-bound lesson. There is nothing more dangerous than a cornered predator.

Azrar, recovering his composure, decided to return to confront the Ha'ali again. He needed to show her that not all his weapons were of alien-forged metal, that his greatest weapon was made of human flesh and blood.

"Hurry child, you know the Dark Lord has no patience." Ileni sighed with exasperation and sat down on the edge of Khari's bed.

Khari had not left her place by the fire in her room since returning from her wild ride. The day's warm autumn sun was a memory; outside a bitter ice-laden wind lashed the old stone walls, wailing like a lost soul. In an unconscious gesture, Ileni shivered with fear and touched the wolf talisman around her neck. Her people once believed such winds were the souls of Dark Kind victims, returning to seek revenge. All nonsense of course, but the wind's lament was an eerie sound. She glanced across to the girl who showed no sign of discomfort at the sound of the wind's doleful wailing.

Khari sat on the floor, arms hugging her knees with Wolf lying curved around her protectively as if sensing her inner misery. Normally a summons from the Prince would have left Khari giddy with excitement, throwing off her daytime nomad clothes to quickly bathe then dress in the jewel coloured shimmering gowns she loved so much.

Ileni was puzzled, what could be vexing the child? She knew Khari had forgiven her for the brusque scolding she'd given her earlier for riding out alone. For pity's sake, the child could read minds and could sense only the understandable concern for Khari's well being that lay behind the cross words. They had already hugged and put the incident behind them. Was Khari also scared of what the Prince might say about her reckless outing? She had brought her horse back in a terrible state, sides heaving and dripping with sweat. This was a heinous crime in the Jendar's eyes — nothing was too good for his horses.

"What is the matter Khari? You can tell me."

Khari looked up, her eyes swollen from crying and attempted to smile.

"I am fine, really, I am just being foolish."

"Are you frightened to face the Jendar's anger at your little adventure today?"

Khari shook her head, "I doubt if he even knows or cares. He has an important visitor to entertain, a Dark Kind visitor."

So that was it. The child's nose was out of joint because the Prince had a beautiful female guest of his own species. Ileni always had serious misgivings and growing concern over Khari's emotional attachment to the Dark Kind Prince. This reaction added more fuel to her anxieties. Somehow, with a mixture of cajoling and demands, she managed to coax Khari out of her riding clothes and into the tub. She even resorted to helping her change into a favourite gown of jade green, silver spangled gossamer-fine voile anything to hurry her up. Khari quietly but firmly ordered Wolf to stay in her room. He stank to high heaven, his brindled coat was soaking wet, filthy and stinking with lupine and other rolled-in odours from his foray beyond the forest.

Khari and Ileni walked together in uneasy silence down to the great hall, pausing only to wait by the entrance for the Dark Lord's summons to Khari to approach. Only then did Ileni slip gratefully back into the shadows; she had no desire for close contact with the two Dark Kind. She could keep herself busy getting that smelly creature of Khari's clean but only with Sandor's help. He had an exceptional gentle way with all creatures including the notionally tame wolf. Ileni could never fully trust the beast.

She was no longer so sure of the Dark Lord either. Could a human ever trust any creature with sharp fangs that existed only to kill?

Khari approached the beings slowly as they sat on either side of the wide hearth where pine logs crackled cheerfully scenting the high vaulted hall with aromatic smoke. They held golden goblets in their hands, the female dazzling with golden jewellery set with amethysts. Azrar was as ever in sombre, plain black garb.

"And what is this creature, all decked out in the finery of the Dark Kind?"

Azrar's guest spoke in a strange language, a growling harsh tongue with no human resonance. Khari had a little knowledge of Azrar's language, but the visitor spoke too fast for her to follow. There was no hiding the creature's cold hostility towards Khari's presence. And as Azrar replied in Isolanni, his voice a controlled even monotone, Khari was also aware of the tension bristling between the two Dark Kind.

"This is my ward, Khari."

"Zaard! What are you playing at, Prince Azrar?" replied the Dark Kind woman, again pointedly in her own language, *"What is a human child doing here?"*

"Look at her eyes, then berate me for my decision to keep this human close at my side," Azrar growled in reply.

The creature's lavender eyes locked on Khari, who felt transfixed by their hypnotic power. She trembled, frightened. The icy aura that felt so familiar when coming from Azrar, felt alien and threatening from this being.

"Come here, child. I will not harm you," the being commanded. Her voice was feminine and more honeyed then the Prince – but no less alien.

An anxious Khari looked to Azrar for affirmation. The Jendar nodded gravely and swallowing back her fear, she stepped reluctantly nearer to the Dark Kind female. Close to, Khari was aware that her power waves, though similar to those from Azrar, were not as strong. She became uncomfortably aware of the female's scrutiny; the intensity of her examination more disconcerting than the energy waves.

The visitor held Khari's face with her long, ice cold fingers to examine her closer.

"Golden eyes, extraordinary! Just like the original Khari. Does she share the same gift?"

"Even more so. She is but a child yet her powers already far outstrip those of Dezarn's human queen."

"Then you have gained an invaluable weapon against your enemies. This child is truly a wonderful discovery."

At Azrar's bidding, Khari took up her favourite place, sitting on a bear skin rug before the fire, nestling happily by his feet, his hand occasionally straying to stroke her hair. Eshan was aghast, in the past she had seen the warlord show affection for his war horses but never for any human. In her opinion, there was something very wrong with Azrar. Where was the volatile fire that made him so dangerous yet such exhilarating company? This domesticated, tame creature was not the Azrar she had fallen in love with.

Eshan's visit and her doom-laden message disturbed Azrar; he became increasingly restless and agitated – even the daylight refuge of Rest held no peace for him. That night he was due to tutor his ward in the stronghold library but as he waited for the child to appear, his inner turmoil grew and grew. The dangerous tension began to build in strength within him, sending flashes of electricity from his power waves arcing across the room.

The library, the stronghold, even mountain-girdled Isolann itself felt claustrophobic, crushing him. He longed to be free of all of it, free of the shackles of duty and honour, to ride alone across the steppes on a good fast horse, feeling the stinging winter wind on his face.

Darkness and blood, they were the two powerful forces that shaped his existence. A lifetime devoted to conflict and killing left no room for anything else. Even the overwhelming driving force of Dark Kind desire had been sacrificed to his single-minded pursuit of warfare. Had he changed so much, that Eshan could look at him with such a curious expression — one that looked like the weak human emotion of compassion, of pity?

Though he was loathe to admit it to himself, Azrar's horizon's had expanded since the human child, Khari appeared in his life. He had thought nothing of the world, beyond his duty as a warlord and defender of Isolann. He existed for warfare, little more. By taking on the task of educating the child, he awakened a dormant sense of wonder. His great library, once of interest only to human scholars resident at his court at the height of its power, now became a treasure house of discovery to the Prince. Until now.

He waited with rising impatience in the library, sitting before a desk piled high with ancient documents in preparation for Khari's history lesson. But all his new-found pleasure in finding new treasures was gone. Again he recalled his meeting with Eshan the previous night, when she had looked at him with a curious expression that had no place on a Dark Kind face. This was intolerable.

Did she think the child's presence had changed him, made him soft and vulnerable? Or was it the erosive effect of too many centuries of peace as his principality lay in the deep slumber of obscurity?

He remembered with his kind's sharp clarity of recall the night when an exhausted nomad woman carried Khari into the great hall of his stronghold. The woman Ileni knew the child was gifted or cursed by the *Knowing* and was in danger of harm from her own species. The Jendar's grim fortress, built in the shadow of the Arpalathians to keep it in perpetual near darkness, was no place to raise a child. As the lair of a blood drinker prince, it existed to provide quarters to his warriors and their weapons. Yet the child was happy and content, she thrived amongst the long shadows, a tiny sprite adding her own silvery light to the dark enchantment. Could it be he too was touched in some way by this child's innocence and beauty?

Azrar snarled in self disgust, such musings angered him, as his volatile nature stirred to action. He stood up, scattering the pile of vellum documents in front of him and strode out of the library and through the stronghold to his armoury. Here the high vaulted chamber walls were hung with row after row of Dark Kind weapons. Fashioned by some unknown and non-human hands, each of the mighty broadswords had an innate barbaric beauty and character of their own. Most were his own, distinguished by the black metal and wolf designs. A few were even more treasured, they once belonged to long dead Dark Kind warriors. The Prince walked over to a bronze and jet inlaid sword that the great warrior Mahdial once wielded.

Azrar removed it gently from its honoured place on the wall. He ran his hand carefully down the glistening metal, even after over a thousand years the blade had lost none of its lethal sharpness. He thought fondly of Mahdial; he had been a strange, otherworldly being, a member of the warrior caste and a great favourite of King Dezarn. Mahdial had been an honoured warrior of fathomless raw courage and unswerving honour. Azrar missed him.

His sad reverie was broken by the gentle touch of female Dark Kind power. The Prince was no longer alone. He glanced up to see Eshan enter the armoury. She saw the bronze sword in his hands and her heart twisted with her own grief for so many lost ones. Eshan's desperation for Azrar to change and survive this new century made her find some deep reserve of courage. She needed every ounce of bravery to voice out loud a theory she had held for centuries.

"You still blame yourself for surviving."

Azrar kissed the blade in homage to the memory of its long dead owner and reverently returned the broad sword to its place of honour on the wall.

"My army may have made the difference; saved them all from treachery and the dishonourable death that awaited them."

"Dezarn wanted you to live. Maybe it's time to stop blaming yourself for his death."

Azrar's eyes darkened to dangerous stormy basalt. "You are so wrong, Lady. I blame humans."

Azrar strode past her, not curbing the rage that threatened to overwhelm him. He needed to kill, bring down a strong human and rip out his throat with all the unrestrained savagery of his being. His route through the castle was clear as his subjects felt the full force of his power waves and fled to safety — all but two. Accompanied by Sandor, with her wolf padding at her heel, Khari still made her way to the library to keep her appointment with the Prince.

Khari knew something was terribly wrong as the first shock wave hit her, battening through the corridor like a blast of winter wind from the mountains. Azrar appeared. His eyes had lost all their iridescent emerald gleam and were now all black, like two windows into the perpetual night of deep space, or the maw of Hell itself. He saw Sandor and saw prey, a strong healthy young male, brimful with life, with blood, so hot and sweet. Khari could not read his mind, but knew Azrar was consumed with bloodlust. His fangs dropped to their full vicious length. Khari shuddered, for the first time, she was afraid of him.

She knew she was not in danger but Sandor's life hung in a precarious balance. He was an outsider, a Svolenian from beyond the Pact borders. Khari calmed the wolf whose hackles had risen, a warning protective growl rumbling in his throat, then stepped forward, putting herself between the Vampire Prince and the big man. She spoke to Azrar haltingly in the harsh vampire language; she had only recently begun to learn, "He looks like a grown man but he is just a child, my Lord Prince, a child like me."

For what was just seconds but what felt like time frozen to stillness, Khari stood her ground, defying her beloved master and guardian. Breaking the impasse, she stood on her toes and stretching out her arm reached up to Sandor's neck to exposed the carved stone wolf talisman he always wore as sign of his fealty to the Prince. At first Azrar heard nothing, saw nothing beyond prey close enough to kill, then the novelty of hearing his language from a human child began to sink through the killing rage. Khari and Sandor hastily stepped aside, as the Jendar strode past without a word, the wolf slinking back against the wall in a submissive cringing stance before a far superior predator, the Dark Kind leader of his pack.

Khari sent Sandor down to the sanctuary of the kitchens and ran to her room, shivering with the aftershock from her act of defiance. Something had changed in her relationship with the Prince that night, something that had no name. She worshipped Azrar, he was the dark heart of her life, her protector, her greatest love. Running to the window, she threw back the wooden shutters and leant out onto the narrow ledge dangerously slick with cold rain. Down below, she could see the grooms running to prepare their master's stallion, and watched as he mounted the fiery, whirling black horse and ride away in a clatter of iron against stone. She yearned for the Prince to pause in his flight from the stronghold, just to rein back and look up at her window, to give her a sign that all was still well between them. But there was nothing, the courtyard fell silent and she felt a sense of loss like an aching pain in her heart as she watched Azrar ride away to be lost to the darkness.

The following night, to everyone's relief, the Ha'ali and her entourage of burly, taciturn mercenaries left the stronghold, and an uneasy peace returned to the human inhabitants once more.

As the days turned to weeks, Khari was left to come to terms alone with her Prince's murderous intent towards her gentle friend Sandor. She had long known that Azrar was Dark Kind, a blood-drinker. It had been an abstract concept, something far beyond the castle boundaries, his victims were anonymous outsiders. Accepting the reality was hard. Her only relief was that poor Sandor had no idea how close he was to having his throat ripped out –and never would. Sandor's blind loyalty to the Prince was absolute, as was his innocent love for her. Breaking that trust would be cruel and unnecessary. And despite the horror of that night, she also realised she still loved Azrar and missed him. When he returned, she knew she must do everything in her power to make things right between them. After all, the Prince had Sandor's throat within easy reach and he could easily have sent her flying across the corridor with a bolt of angry power. But he had not.

Chapter Nine

New York, USA, 1928

A warm yellow glow from an old brownstone apartment spilled out onto the street, gilding the sidewalk shining from recent rain. The soft light was evidence at least one member of wealthy New York society still had not joined the unstoppable rush to light the modern world with harsh electric light.

Jay Parrish tipped his misshapen felt hat in support for this unknown rebel. He too preferred the soft glow of gaslight and candle. He gathered up his wits, preparing to struggle across the road through the twilight traffic, a vulnerable contestant in the jostling battle for space between heavy horse-drawn trade carriages and the more numerous trucks and private automobiles. To Parrish, they were smelly, noisy monstrosities. As he survived crossing the road he gave a wistful sigh for a past time when the rhythm of hoof-beats and the creaking turn of wooden wheels defined the pace of travel.

He knew his colleagues would gently mock such musings, a recently qualified professor of history, Parrish had unfortunately earned an eccentric reputation for his passionate admiration for the ways of the past but he was unrepentant. And as for eccentricity, the man he was hurrying to see was the true oddball— so much so, his association with him could easily affect Parrish's burgeoning academic career. Parrish decided to discover what was exciting the old man so much before passing his own judgement.

His old mentor, Professor David Colgramm had within the last month returned from a gruelling expedition to Rumania and Hungary and the Upper Balkans, probably his last field trip due to increasing age and infirmity. It was sad but the old boy must be past such arduous adventures. Parrish had received a curtly worded command to meet Colgramm at 9 p.m. at his home in Manhattan. Such was the respect Parrish held for the man who inspired him so often during the gruelling years of university; he had no hesitation rescheduling all his appointments to head immediately across town. What had he found to generate such a summons?

Parrish arrived exactly on time outside an elegant brownstone, noticeably darker than its more welcoming neighbours. He was not alarmed, Colgramm was no doubt deep in study over his new finds and had not noticed the rest of the house was unlit. As he walked up the stone steps, he heard someone call his name. It was Eva, the professor's long suffering and endlessly patient housekeeper, a stout, merry-eyed Polish woman, almost as old as Colgramm himself. She bustled down the street to join him at Colgramm's house and they walked up the stoop together. Eva fetched out a set of keys from her battered carpetbag.

"Now don't you worry Professor Parrish, I will soon have the house lit and warmed up. I'm serving a spicy sausage stew tonight; your job is to make sure the old man eats it."

Parrish laughed, knowing too well Colgramm's habit of self-neglect, especially when deeply engrossed in his studies. "I will make it my night's special mission."

"You could do with a good feed too, by the look of you," Eva scolded, holding up one of Parrish's long arms. He was a tall slightly stooping young man, naturally rake thin. He came from a wealthy, well connected Boston family, but this was not apparent from his mode of dress: he wore a shabby, moth eaten and faded green tweed suit, with worn brown leather patches at the elbows.

Superficially he looked a typical fusty academic type but one with the adventurous spirit of a young conquistador hidden beneath the ill-kempt tweeds.

Eva led him through the dark, cold corridors to Colgramm's study –his sanctuary, every wall lined from floor to ceiling with bookshelves that were crammed tightly with much loved tomes; every inch of floor space was piled high with papers and yet more books. The only nominally clear space was an oak rectangle table in the centre of the room over which hung one of the new electric lights; its bright illumination compensating for its harshness. A metal lampshade directed the light downward onto a very old map. Impatient as ever, Colgramm brusquely dismissed the woman and beckoned his pupil over to see the map. Parrish recognised the thing as a sixteenth century depiction of the Upper Balkan region — the vast, remote, rarely visited mountainous wedge between Rumania and the Ukraine.

"Amazing – this is quite a find, Professor," he said with appreciative enthusiasm.

"Pah, it's a trifle, foolish boy. It's nothing compared to what I found in a ruined monastery near Satu Mare."

He began to bustle about the room, muttering angrily to himself. Colgramm had aged considerably since their last meeting over a year before; the waxy grey of his skin a bad sign. Only his brown eyes glittered with life and a worryingly manic enthusiasm.

"I take it you remember our study of the works of Aubrey Weingar?" he asked Parrish.

The younger man groaned inwardly, his spirits plummeting. Colgramm was obsessed with this obscure seventeenth century explorer and scholar. It had ruined the old man's academic reputation and labelled him a crackpot. This was one fate Parrish did not want to share, especially with a whole glittering career before him.

"Not this again, Professor," he said carefully. "Are you still chasing Weingar's myths and legends?"

"I have my proof at last, documentation that gives us a head start in uncovering the truth. Weingar believed in an old conspiracy to suppress the truth. It cost him his life."

"Can I see it?" Parrish replied simply with as much patience as he could muster. Colgramm emphatically shook his head, bundling Parrish out of the door.

"It's too precious to risk here. It's safely locked up in the library vault at Challon University. Let's go."

The two men bustled past Colgramm's startled housekeeper. Parrish had the presence of mind to pick up the old man's coat, he was too excited to think of such practicalities and the earlier rain was turning to wet sleet.

"What about the sausage stew? You have not eaten at all today, Professor!"

"There are things in life more important than stew, my dear." Colgramm shouted back at the exasperated woman, standing on the stoop, ladle still in her hand.

The mismatched pair of academics caught a cab after only five minutes but not before Parrish noticed an increasing nervousness in Colgramm, his fearful eyes seem to dart about as if scanning every passer-by for some unnamed threat. Classic paranoia symptoms, the old boy was definitely losing his mind. Parrish felt like kicking himself very hard. Why the Hell was he getting involved with this man's insanity? Colgramm's anxiety level did not recede until they had passed through empty, dark oak-panelled halls of the university, pausing only to give a curt nod to the indifferent janitor at the main door. Colgramm ran down some stairs to a locked private room beneath the main library. He beckoned Parrish down, still nervously glancing around to see if they had been followed.

Parrish reluctantly entered a poorly lit vault-like room, which added to a growing sense of claustrophobia. What was he doing down here, late at night, alone with this demented old man? He once respected Colgramm, now he feared getting dragged too deeply into his mentor's fantasy world.

"I know what you are thinking, young man, but I am not mad. You are my best student, a bright star among so many dull-witted drones with no imagination, no fire."

Parrish coughed with embarrassment, dropping his head to avoid the Professor's eyes; even in the gloom; he could see their maniacal gleam. Colgramm handed his protégé a glass-covered frame protecting a small fragment of badly torn and yellowed vellum. On it was a Svolenian inscription written in a wavering, barely legible copperplate script.

In a gesture repeated many times a day, Jay Parrish wiped his steel-rimmed glasses clear of fluff from the pockets of his baggy old cardigan, and read the original, ignoring the English translation provided for his benefit by the Professor.

> Do the Dark Kind weep tears of blood
> When they lose sons to the Light?
> An ocean of blood tears could not wash away
> One salt tear of ours.

Parrish read the fragment of ancient verse over and over again. A strange poem, what did it mean?

"It's certainly a mysterious piece from every viewpoint," he agreed reluctantly, running a hand through thick brown hair that framed a thin, aesthetic face. Colgramm, in idle moments of fancy thought he looked like a monk crossed with a troubadour-part-scholar-part-romantic. This in truth was the very essence of the earnest young American.

With his heart sinking with the inevitably of where he conversation was heading, Parrish looked up at the old man. "Does it have anything to do with the old myths of the

Vampire Kings you are exploring?" Somehow he already knew the answer!

"It may be everything or nothing," the older academic replied. "That is the infuriating thing about having so little to work on. We know Weingar was a scholar who explored the Upper Balkans extensively in the late 17th century. The nomadic Dholma race fascinated him. They were a scattered remnant of an ancient people whose kingdom was swallowed up by the Svolenian migrations. Proud but tragically doomed, the Dholma were persecuted to near extinction as worthless gypsies. Weingar tried to capture as much of their vanishing culture as possible — their folk tales and songs, some of an astonishing antiquity."

"But surely most of Weingar's work has been lost to us too?"

"Indeed it has, my boy, it is a sorry tale all round. Maybe I am being too fanciful, but I think Weingar got too close to the truth. There is no doubt records of his work with the Dholma were destroyed before his planned return to the university at the Svolenian capital. Weingar himself met with a fatal accident as he fled towards the Svolenian border."

"By some incredible miracle –or the hand of fate, I found some fragments of his work under the floorboards of the inn he stayed in prior to his flight. Most are illegible scribbles and odd words of the Dholma language... but there was this amazing scrap of translated verse."

Parrish had too much respect for the professor to dismiss him as a crackpot like so many of his peers. Yet he found it hard to sustain the same enthusiasm as the old man for these controversial theories. Colgramm believed mankind once shared the planet with a race of ancient predatory beings, creatures that once ruled kingdoms and commanded armies of human warriors. Did the long-lost Dholma know of these beings? Were they the Dark Kind of the verse fragment? And why were the Svolenian authorities of the time so determined to destroy all Weingar's research? After all, they were unlikely to have any guilt over their persecution of the Dholma— it was so far back in their history. So what other motive was there?

The old man's excitement level was growing, drops of sweat now beaded his worryingly grey features, and Colgramm began to pace up and down in an agitated manner. Parrish found him a chair but he refused to settle.

"This is where it gets more intriguing. On my last expedition I discovered there are some areas to the furthest and most remote eastern region of Svolenia that may have been the last refuge of the Dholma survivors. I visited it and there is some possible genetic evidence that they may have intermarried with their conquerors. In a predominately Slavic people, I saw the occasional dark eyes, or an almond eye shape, even the more broad features of the Asiatic Dholma."

"I wrote down the words of every folk song or tale I could. I found mostly tales of lost love or the joys of a good harvest –the usual peasant stuff. But then one night I heard a curious song. It was an eerie lament sung by the women of the village, unaccompanied. An astounding sound, dark, primeval and haunting. I made them sing it many times before I could decipher the words, I admit I became so lost in the visceral impact of their singing."

Colgramm handed the younger man a copy of his translation.

> Beware the Land of Secrets and Shadows
> Keep your men-folk safe from the black woods
> Tangled woods that hide the black wolf
> Tangled woods that hide the Dark Lord
> Keep them home, keep them safe by your hearth

When darkness falls,
For Night is the kingdom of the Dark Kind.

The old man's face became wreathed with triumph, an excited glitter lighting up his watery grey eyes as he announced, "The land of Secrets and Shadows is what the Svolenians call Isolann!"

Parrish swallowed a sigh of exasperation. The old man had gone too far. "You want me to go there, Professor Colgramm. I can see that eager glint in your eye."

Colgramm laughed, triggering off a series of wracking coughs. Parrish felt a twinge of sadness, the Professor was not long for this world.

"Jay, you are a fit young man. An arduous journey across the Upper Balkans will kill me long before I reach Svolenia. Besides, you have excellent contacts out there from your exchange days at the University. Your knowledge of their language is far greater than mine."

'Why in all Hell am I going along with this nonsense?' Parrish thought, but voiced his concerns more tactfully. "And what exactly am I looking for, Professor?"

Colgramm's face grew solemn as he handed all his research notes to the lanky young man he'd groomed to be his successor. "Vampires; living or dead. I want solid evidence of the existence of the Dark Kind."

Parrish nearly laughed out loud as visions of himself as some sort of modern day Professor Von Helsing complete with wooden stakes and crucifixes sprung to mind. He paced the small room, his unease making it seem to grow even smaller. He picked up a tired old book, some forgotten philosophical treatise. "If you are right, Professor, then everything we know is wrong." He raised up the dusty tome and in a theatrical gesture dumped it noisily in a bin. "Everything. All the knowledge we hold precious, our history, science, deep held religious beliefs, all will be false. Can you comprehend the consequences, Professor?"

Colgramm tut-tutting at the young man's thoughtless sacrilege retrieved the book from the bin and with reverence, replaced it on the shelf. "Of course I do, such knowledge is dynamite, literally. What if it was true, these things did once exist? It would put a bomb beneath the structure of our modern society. That is why I have kept my latest finds so secret. That is why I have only confided in you."

Colgramm walked over to his protégé, and put his hand on his shoulder. "Can you look me in the eye and tell me with complete honesty that you are not intrigued? Can you walk away from me now and never know the truth?"

His old mentor knew him well, too well!

"I will have to think about this. Let me have a few days to decide."

Colgramm nodded assent, quietly confident. He had seen the sparkle in Parrish's eyes at the very mention of an expedition to the remote, barely explored Isolann region. Beneath the bookish exterior, this young man had an adventurous soul.

Parrish was in turmoil. 'Why am I listening? Why am I risking all I have now and all I may have in the future?' he thought. He looked again at the Weingar vellum and at the words to the song Colgramm had translated. Why had he not just walked out? Because a small illogical part of him believed it could be true. Wanted it to be true. Finding out about the Vampire Kings was a challenge fraught with risks – to his career and reputation, maybe to his life. An expedition to a turbulent and often lawless region would be exciting and dangerous. That was why.

Parrish spent the next few days torn between his own intrigue and curiosity coupled with loyalty towards

Colgramm, and understandable fears for the direction of his career. He was helped by a delaying factor beyond his control, the seemingly insurmountable difficulty in arranging travel to Svolenia. He had visited the country six years before as an exchange student but it had then been a sleepy kingdom, content–at least to outside eyes– to drift along the seas of time and history as a quiet backwater. A revolutionary fervour, fired up by the success of Bolshevik Russia had transformed the country and made it unwelcoming for American travellers.

Parrish was partly relieved; difficulties beyond his control solved the unanswered question in his mind. Should he be chasing myths believed by his old but frankly loony friend in favour of gaining a niche in the American academic hierarchy?

A frantic knocking at his apartment pushed aside any meandering thoughts. Outside in the pale, early spring sunshine was Eva, Professor Colgramm's housekeeper. She was clearly in great distress, her eyes red and puffy from crying. Parrish took her arm and ushered her in.

"He's dead, Professor Parrish. I found him slumped over his desk this morning. He looked terrified. I think someone has murdered him!"

Parrish gently took the distraught woman into his apartment, setting her down on a sofa and fetching them both a large brandy. He needed it. All his contempt for Colgramm's paranoia came back to haunt him on a wave of shock and guilt. This was not happening. He fought to rationalise the situation, to bring back some sense of normality. After all, the old man was clearly ailing; it was obviously a death by natural causes. It had to be.

"What do the police say?" he asked as he poured himself another drink, this time a generous triple measure.

"They think he died of natural causes. They are certain his poor old heart finally gave out. I know he has not been well for some time. Professor Parrish, I think some of his papers are missing. I know he'd never let that old map go out of his sight, and it is not there."

Parrish finished his drink in one swig. It did nothing to stop the dread and chill that had now spread through him. Eva was right. This was not sounding good. The woman reached into her voluminous old carpetbag and pulled out a well-wrapped brown paper parcel. Parrish opened it carefully, almost knowing what to expect. Inside was the fragment of ancient poem, the one discovered by Aubrey Weingar.

Parrish returned with the housekeeper to Colgramm's home. With no sign of any police activity and the body removed to a down town morgue, there was certainly no sign of foul play: no broken locks or forced windows, no signs of violence. It was just an echoing empty house, a hollow place that once resounded with Colgramm's abrasive character, boundless energy and limitless enthusiasm. There was no sense of Colgramm's presence, in fact there was something uncomfortably tomb-like about the house emphasised by a hall full of fresh flowers sent by the first shocked well wishers from the University. The smell of the lilies, sickly and overpowering triggered bad memories in Parrish of his own father's funeral.

Parrish did not linger in the hall but hurried down to the study; eager to do what he had to and get away from this oppressive place. No ancient tomb he had ever excavated held this intangible but very real atmosphere of unknown threat. Quickly and efficiently, he searched through Colgramm's papers. Superficially everything seemed in place, a bad sign taking into account Colgramm's normal chaotic untidiness. He could see how the police thought nothing sinister had occurred, with the neat bookshelves and carefully filed documents appearing undisturbed. Parrish searched for anything left about Weingar or the legends of the Vampire Kings but there was nothing. The study seemed as if it had been picked clean with surgical precision.

He took his leave of the housekeeper with a hug of sympathy; she had been very fond of the old reprobate, then made his way to Challon University, trying not to let his imagination play warped games with his perception. Nobody was following him, no hidden eyes watched his every move, but yet his skin felt clammy and icy, crawling with uncontrollable goose bumps. He caught a crowded bus heading towards the university and jumped out of his skin when someone accidentally touched his elbow. Cursing himself for his own paranoia, Parrish got off the bus early and briskly walked the last three blocks to the Challon Library.

A cacophony of alarm erupted around him with the scream of sirens and strident peal of bells. He felt no surprise to see the police and fire service speed past him, nor was he amazed to see the library engulfed in a ferocious inferno. Paranoia? Superstitious fear? What the Hell! He had the Weingar fragment safely under his coat and had no intention of returning to his apartment. He had enough paper money to get home to Boston, from there he was going to somehow get to Svolenia — with or without a visa. There was no doubt in his mind now that Weingar had been murdered for getting too close to a truth. And so had his friend David Colgramm. It was Parrish's last service to his old mentor to discover just what that truth was. And why it was worth the lives of two men.

Chapter Ten

Svolenian/Abhajastan Border, 1929

Some things in Svolenia never changed. When talking stopped, exchange of hard cash was the only meaningful dialogue, thought Jay Parrish as he reached deep into the crowded depths of his overstuffed leather valise. He was certain a financial sweetener would soon settle his protracted difficulty with Svolenian border guards. For some unfathomable reason, they neither recognised nor accepted his recently acquired visa.

He offered a handful of local currency but this was brusquely knocked from his hand by a red faced border guard who then trampled the cash under his heel with surprising vehemence. It was only when Parrish spotted the exiled king's face pulverised into the mire did he realise his folly. The guards began impatiently manhandling him back towards the Abhajastan border.

"I am sorry, so very sorry. I meant no disrespect."

He fished frantically into his bag again and produced American dollars which were readily accepted. His first opinion had been right — things in Svolenia had not really changed after all.

He found out later from a frostily polite country doctor travelling with him on a rickety train to the capital city of Talish why his visa was invalid. It bore the elaborate signature of Comrade Protector Ween, now deposed as a bourgeois recidivist a full month past. If Comrade Protector Gussen had signed it he would have passed through without hindrance. Well, maybe.

Parrish installed himself in his old student digs at the Bluebell Inn. Superficially at least that had not changed either. The hug of welcome from its buxom landlady was the first gesture of hospitality from the land he had known so well as an exchange student some ten years past.

The landlady sat him down with a plate of thin, gristly broth, with a grease laden scum of mutton fat floating on top. At the side of the plate lay a leaden lump of grey bread. She shrugged ruefully in apology.

"Our farmers need time to adjust to the new regime's agricultural methods. Things will be better soon, much better than before."

Her tone was firm and convincing, but a fleeting anxiety in her eyes told a different story. Svolenia's flat farmlands, all reclaimed from ancient steppes, were never very fertile, with a short growing season and a seemingly constant harsh wind stripping the soil bare. Parrish accepted the food with a smile of gratitude and feigned enjoyment. Svolenians were a proud people with a bitter legacy of many past conquests and constant social turmoil. Manners cost nothing but gained much. The country was no place now for a loud-mouthed American to throw his weight and money around. It never had been.

The next morning, he politely declined breakfast and on a wave of nostalgia sought out his favourite coffee-house and its fragrant, hot cinnamon bread.

Superficially Talish had not changed since his last visit. The same narrow, winding streets tightly packed with a jumble of wooden framed medieval houses jostled for space with later built more imposing stone buildings. The biggest noticeable change was in Talish's citizens. Every person he encountered wore plain, shoddily made clothes in the same shade of drab grey. None would meet his gaze, but hurriedly crossed the road to avoid him at his approach. Nervous tired-eyed mothers gathered their children to their skirts to rush away from him, as if afraid of some form of contamination. These were not the content, hospitable and proud people he once knew and loved. As he crossed a rain slicked cobbled main square, he saw a familiar round race in an unfamiliar grey uniform.

"Deret, old pal – I can't believe we've met up so quickly on my return to Talish!"

Jay Parrish held out his hand in greeting to his old classmate from the university. The burly Svolenian turned and fixed him with a cold, unblinking gaze, pointedly refusing his handshake.

"I cannot believe you have bothered to return from America. This is no place for a capitalist lackey."

Frowning, Parrish searched his former friend's face for signs of jest but found only humourless sincerity. It saddened him; he and Deret had shared many nights of ale and laughter in their student days.

"I don't know if I am a lackey or not, but I am a fully fledged professor of history."

"And I am a commander of the People's Army of Socialist Svolenia. It would be best if our paths did not cross again. When are you leaving my country?"

Parrish again looked for signs of Deret's renowned dry humour but found none in his grim, thin-lipped, florid face. His grey eyes, once lively with coarse student humour were as flat as small circles of dry slate.

"I've just arrived. I am on my way to the university to follow up some research."

"Don't bother. I had it burnt down."

Parrish reeled, as if punched in the stomach. His mouth went dry, his knees buckling. Deret smiled as the Yankee fool went deathly pale. With a satisfied smirk, Deret could see the man looked close to fainting, such was the weakness of the elitist fat cat society Parrish came from.

"Please, my friend," Parrish stammered, "tell me this is one of your old pranks. What about the archives, all your people's history?"

"Our history began on the first day of the Glorious Uprising of the People. All else is ashes." The answer was bitter in its arrogance.

Parrish could barely look at Deret again as a strong new desire spread through him; a very real need to flatten this dangerously irresponsible imbecile, this poisonous philistine, to pulverise him for the crass destruction of his own people's heritage. Somehow Parrish's Old Boston high society upbringing gave him back some self-control. In a voice, flat and clipped with repressed anger he stated,

"I am going to Madame Lena's for coffee— unless you have burnt that down too."

"The coffee house is still there — for now." Deret replied with his dead-eyed humourless smile.

If he had not clenched his fist tightly and walked swiftly away, Parrish would have wiped that smile away with one blow. A strong sense of self-preservation had overridden his fury. Anyone who could burn down a university with pride and impunity was a powerful man indeed in the new Svolenia. Parrish had to take great care.

Parrish spent the rest of the day in shock, berating himself for his naiveté. He knew Svolenia had undergone a revolution yet he still believed they would preserve their cherished heritage landmarks such as the university. The extent of the loss was incalculable. So many ancient, priceless manuscripts, of a turbulent, fascinating past now just steppe-wind blown dust.

At least the precious fragment and other irreplaceable evidence of the Vampire Kings were safe. Parrish did not know why he had so carefully hidden Professor Colgramm's legacy before departing for Svolenia. Now he was deeply thankful for his own paranoia. The documents were safe in a family vault in America, far away from such destructive philistines as Comrade Deret and his grey garbed goons.

He returned to the inn, there was nothing here for him now. No one would be interested in an archaeological project. He sat down heavily on the old iron bed; his frustration and disappointment strong enough to be a physical sensation like a crushing pain in his throat and chest. Anger rose above the suffocating feeling and he threw his belongings forcibly back into his carpetbag.

Full of self-important duty, Deret rushed straight to the People's Parliament building-once the Royal Palace of their deposed and unlamented king. He marched to Comrade Gussen's luxurious offices, situated in the king's private quarters. The rooms had, in better days been decorated with delicate chinoiserie silk hangings in delicate pale blue and gold sinks. They had long since been torn down but tattered traces still remained on the bare dirty-pink, ominously stained plaster. Above soared a high vaulted pale blue, gilded ceiling with its gold moulding nearly intact — bullet holes peppered this mute and defiant reminder of a more opulent past.

Gussen appraised his comrade's angry face and rose to offer him a nerve steadying drink; one he knew the man would refuse. Deret was nothing but predictable.

"With all respect, Comrade Protector, why did you let that American into the country?"

"Please sit down comrade, calm yourself. I have my reasons. This man is a colleague of yours, is he not? He is an expert in the region's ancient history?"

"He is an acolyte of that old fool Colgramm who has spent years filling his head full of specious nonsense."

Gussen finished the drink Deret had refused, no point wasting the last of the late king's wine cellars. He held up a letter of introduction sent to him by Professor Colgramm.

"Our American friend knows about the far northern region and has studied many ancient maps. Something we can no longer do, thanks to your revolutionary zeal. I do not condemn you for burning down the university and its library, for you were under orders from the late Comrade Ween. All the same...."

Deret carefully studied the thin, slightly cadaverous-looking man, staring into his small icy-blue eyes that gleamed behind rimless glasses for warning signs of impending danger. Deret had enough sense not to remind the Protector that burning the university down had been entirely his own idea; that their last leader, Arik Ween had been despised and discredited. That Ween was now dead and not deposed and imprisoned made Deret's position with Gussen precarious. The last Protector was an ageing man, from peasant stock, with a gruff bear-like manner; this younger one from a now defunct middle-class intelligencia class was somewhat sleeker, more sinister. A polecat perhaps?

"I want you to utilise your considerable skills by taking this American on an expedition to the north. It is about time our most distant comrades realised they are liberated. That they too are part of the glorious revolution. Assemble an advance party of troops, take what you need. Armoured cars, machine guns, you know what to arrange."

Deret stood to attention and saluted. As he was about to leave through a bullet-scarred gilded door, he heard,

"Oh, and by the way, Comrade Deret, you need not bring Professor Parrish back with you."

Parrish returned to the inn, despondent. There was nothing for him now, no one would be interested in his cover story, an archaeological project to search for the remains of an ancient, pre-Dark Age palace that he believed still existed under St Alaric's Cathedral.

He sat down heavily on the creaking iron bed; his frustration and disappointment strong enough to cause a physical sensation, a crushing pain in his throat and chest. Anger rose above the suffocating feeling and he threw his belongings forcibly back onto his carpetbag, muttering curses under his breath. A light, hesitant tap on his door halted Parrish's assault on his laundry. Outside his landlady stood, anxiously wringing her hands, all colour drained from her normally rosy complexion.

"You have a visitor. It's the People's Comrade Deret."

Guessing his fearsome reputation among the ordinary citizens of Talish, Parrish tried to reassure her. "Don't be concerned. The Comrade and I were exchange students – we were friends. No doubt he wants to reminisce about old times."

Parrish reluctantly went down into the inn with a heavy heart. He found Deret seated, holding up a glass of water in a mocking salute. Water was apparently the only refreshment he would now accept from an innkeeper. Deret believed alcohol was a symbol of decadence and that inns encouraged working men to waste productive lives in dissolution and brawling. Parrish allowed the landlady to pour him some weak lemon tea then sat down with the Comrade who immediately challenged him, "I demand the truth, why did you come back?"

Parrish paused, unsure of a suitable answer. His once affable student companion had become a very dangerous man. Suddenly, he felt very alone and vulnerable in a country that had once been a second home.

"I wanted to organise a dig to benefit your university and museum. Colgramm found some old documents in Northern Hungary that might indicate the site of the lost Dholma Palace."

"Colgramm is a deluded fool."

"That he might well have been but Professor Colgramm is dead. He had a heart attack six months ago."

"Then the world is less one more fool."

Deret's attitude appalled the American. Colgramm was their genial mentor at Talish University and had been Deret's hero.

"Is there anything left of the man I knew and respected?" Parrish asked. "You were a brilliant archaeological scholar. Why are you turning against Colgramm's memory?"

Deret took another brief sip at his frugal refreshment, his slate eyes gleaming with fervour, knowing his utter conviction was right.

"Listen well to this, Yank," he sneered, "Colgramm was not a scholar, he was a deluded romantic, pathetically clinging onto archaic legends that even our peasants are finally rejecting as the nonsense they truly are. Our country is not forever cursed by some ancient atrocity that our ancestors did to some old nomad tribes. And there were no Vampire Kings."

He sat his glass down on the table, sat up straight and folded his arms.

"I have been assigned by the Protector to take an advance party into the furthest region of our domain. My mission is to bring the word of the glorious revolution to our most northerly citizens."

Parrish was puzzled. Why was Deret telling him this?

"You have studied this region intensely," Deret continued with some distaste — this clearly was not his idea. "You have knowledge of the old maps. You are to accompany me."

Parrish's mind reeled as the implications sunk in.

Deret was not talking about Northern Svolenia. His troops were going to trespass into Isolann!

Curiosity over the remote Land of Secrets and Shadows overrode any sense of moral outrage. But if history was any sort of pointer, Isolann would ably repel any would-be-invaders, it always had. All the same, Parrish answered with excitement and relish,

"Count me in."

Chapter Eleven

Village of Tubrul, Svolenia, 1929

"So, we are liberated now!"

The village patriarch snorted with derision, spitting in the thick mud outside his farmhouse for extra emphasis of sheer contempt. A big man, broad as an ox, he stood gripping a pitchfork, fixing Deret with a fearless glare. Behind him, his brood of children, wide eyed with curiosity, were being pushed forcibly back into the farmhouse by a whippet-thin, worn-looking woman, anxiety making her face pinched and old.

"You are free," Deret insisted," You no longer have to toil as serfs, bound to some fat aristo. It is a time for rejoicing and celebration"

By now, Deret was thoroughly heartsick of every encounter with these stubborn, morose peasants. Weary of every muddy, mean spirited village. He had had enough of stone-hurling urchins and wizened, curse wielding crones. He loathed the stench of pig shit and the taste of stale rye bread. He swore once this baleful expedition had ended never to leave the capital city again.

The village headman guffawed loudly, a bitter sound with no humour. "If you can find a fat aristo, bring him to me! I'd be curious to see what one looks like. If we have a lord, we've never seen him. He probably lost interest in us three famines and the plague ago."

The headman smiled in satisfaction at the perplexed expression of this pompous, grey uniformed southerner. Word had spread rapidly about these troops travelling up from the city in trucks. Like a plague of locusts, they had raided villages for food the peasants could ill afford to lose.

Forewarned, this village had hidden its supplies well, leaving only the most meagre and oldest provisions.

"What about your priest? Surely a village this large must have a holy man?" Deret persisted.

The headman laughed again, enjoying the discomfort of this southern imbecile as a waft of fresh ordure passed across his florid face. He had hidden all the fat, healthy livestock but had left behind the flatulent and bad tempered mule.

"We lost the last one forty years ago. Old age. No one replaced him. Perhaps our souls are not worth saving living so close to that."

He nodded in the direction of the Arpalathian Mountains, a jagged silhouette darkening the horizon — Isolann.

"My men will need food and shelter, we have journeyed long and have far to go."

"Of course you do," the headman grumbled, knowing what was coming next. "And what payment will we receive? As you can see, we are poor peasants with little to spare now winter is approaching."

Deret patted the man on his hefty shoulder, it was easy to be over-familiar with thirty rifles guarding your back, "The satisfaction of helping your brave soldiers of the glorious revolution is payment enough. We are all comrades now, working together to build a free Svolenia."

The headman glanced at his 'liberators' huddled in the mud-plastered trucks. Wisps of steam rose from their sodden uniforms, drawn by the warmth from an ever-strengthening morning sun. Some faces looked as pinched and grey as their uniforms, undernourished city-bred youths, no doubt missing the comforts of home. Others were more obviously country lads from their broader frames and ruddier complexions. The man standing behind Comrade Deret though was a mystery. He stood taller then anyone else and looked too pitifully skinny to be of any use to the military or any farmer. His brown eyes, slightly magnified by wire rimmed glasses were sharp and curious. His clothes were a strange, foreign design in a heavy woollen fabric, a sort of close woven green and tan tweed.

"Can I thank you in advance for your hospitality," said the stranger with a broad unidentifiable accent. He held out his hand to the headman in the first polite gesture since the arrival of these unwelcome visitors. The peasant leader reluctantly took it; surprisingly, the stranger's grip was strong.

"You can make yourselves comfortable in my barns, they are the biggest in the village. There's little food to be had, but you will find the shelter clean and dry."

Later when the men were comfortably billeted, Deret and Parrish met with the head men and the male villagers in a timber and daub meeting house at the centre of the village. The sense of curiosity and suspicion was strong and the peasants sat on wooden benches in an alert and hostile silence.

"I have already told your leader of the wonderful changes that have happened for all Svolenian citizens since the glorious revolution. He will explain things to you later in greater detail. My expedition is not solely to spread this good news. The extreme far north of our region has to be liberated from the old illusion that it is a separate country. It is not."

The peasants exchanged puzzled glances.

"By the far north, I mean the so called Principality of Isolann."

This sparked a more dramatic response. They all made superstitious gestures to ward off evil, many also touching shamanic-looking amulets. An old man stood up and angrily spat on the floor, alarmingly close to Deret's feet. He fixed the comrade with a gimlet glare, "Nobody but the very foolish ventures willingly into the Land of Secrets and Shadows! Only death awaits them in its dark heart."

Deret ignored the spittle and responded tersely, "We do not tolerate superstitious claptrap in the New Svolenia. No more greedy muttering priests, no more village so-called wise women, who are in reality poison peddling crones."

Parrish was incensed yet again by Deret's brutal and clumsy handling of his country's peasants, especially in a village so close to the Isolann border. How much vital information was now lost by making enemies out of these simple living but far from stupid people? The villagers shrugged dismissively and rose to leave. Their priority was protecting what little they had from bandit raids and now it seemed also from these state sanctioned marauders. They cared nothing for these idiots courting death in Isolann. They made their choice. They had done their duty, the imbeciles had been warned.

The American watched the villagers leave, quietly satisfied at the comrade's impotent fury at the indifference to news of the revolution and the future annexation of Isolann.

"They are nothing more then swine, grubbing in the soil with their filthy snouts! Liberation is wasted on them!" Deret spluttered, his broad face reddened with anger.

Parrish sighed. His friend had not been such a fool during their student days. What had changed him?

"They want plentiful good food in their bellies and shelter in the winter for themselves and their livestock. They need freedom from persecution and disease. They want to live long, happy lives free from fear. Can you guarantee your regime will give them all that? Until you show you can, I share their natural and understandable cynicism," Parrish said to Deret.

Deret's expression looked murderous enough to become physically violent with the American but he retained his self-control, pushing past the professor to stride out of the meeting house.

Parrish waited patiently until he could get the headman alone, seizing his chance later in the evening with most villagers and troops settled down for the night to eat and sleep. He found the big man checking the defences, a sharpened wooden palisade that surrounded the village in a bristling ring. It was a balmy warm evening, under a night sky streaked with sunset's last deep salmon, then purple-tinged clouds.

Vigilant and distrustful, the headman patrolled the village perimeter, ever-present pitchfork in his hand. Parrish offered him a cigarette, which the big man readily took. The American then produced a large pewter hip flask from a deep pocket in his jacket.

"Care to join me? I would really appreciate the company. That priggish bore, Deret doesn't drink."

Still wary, the headman grunted, took a large swig of the excellent port and brandy mix. "Where are you from, stranger?" he asked, taking the flask with a solemn nod of assent and taking a long swig.

"Word of warning, my friend," Parrish smiled." It goes down sweet and smooth but has a hidden kick. I brought it from my home in America."

Ignoring the warning, the big man took another mouthful. "You have come a long way to die, stranger."

"You seem very certain this could be the only outcome of our expedition."

The big man gestured for Parrish to follow, leading him to his home. The professor ducked low to enter the dwelling, a sturdy construct of stone, timber and daub. A shamanic talisman was nailed above the entrance, a gruesome construct of raven feathers, bones and dried blood.

Once inside, it was dark, lit by one flickering, acrid squat tallow candles. Despite the gloom, Parrish made out a spotlessly clean, simple home, and though redolent of dried herbs and smoked bacon, the hooks where the meat would normally hang were empty. Also empty were the rush baskets where normally root vegetables and apples were stored for the winter. The headman's large family nervously watched the stranger; the children in particular wide-eyed and curious- no outside had visited their village in living memory.

The headman bade Parrish sit down and handed him a large stone flagon. "Try this, then you will know what a true kick feels like."

Parrish had tasted enough village brew to know what to expect, a rough potato vodka so potent that the fumes alone could knock a horse unconscious. He felt honour-bound to defend his American manhood and took a long draught from the heavy flagon. He controlled the urge to fall down and swear as the powerful, throat-burning liquor hit the back of his head like a sledgehammer. He noticed with satisfaction the headman's respectful nod as he handed the flagon back with a smile of feigned pleasure.

"I am not like the others," Parrish explained as he began to relax, the heat of the potent liquor burning through his veins. "Especially that pompous, dangerous fool, Deret. I am a visitor to your land. I come on a quest for knowledge. For many years, I have studied the history of your land. I want to learn more. Especially I want to learn more about this remote, northern region."

"Study our history by all means, we are an ancient people, but do not go to Isolann. You are an educated man; I do not care what happens to that fat fool, but you must stop him from murdering those young troops. "

Parrish frowned. "What exactly is so dangerous about Isolann? Is it the people? Are they so very dangerous and hostile?"

The headman snorted with dark humour at the list of questions.

"People have never been the danger in Isolann."

The headman drank from the flagon again, and called for his thin, timid wife to bring food, the conversation obviously ended.

"Please," Parrish urged, touching his hand against the man's sleeve. "You can't make such a provocative statement then change the subject. What is so frightening in Isolann? What can endanger a well-armed and equipped troop of experienced soldiers?"

The big man's eyes were steady, his expression grim as he sat looking directly into the fire. "If you decide to enter Isolann, then you are a dead man. You will travel deeper and deeper in, unchallenged by beast or man 'til it is too late. Go back home now and live. Return to your family in the land of weak liquor."

Infuriatingly, the headman refused to speak on the subject any more, saying only,"You are welcome to stay and eat or to go as you please. I will not say anything more."

Parrish sighed, recognising a stone wall and knowing better not to beat his head against it. He rose slowly to leave, nodding a respectful farewell to the headman's wife; this family's big- hearted hospitality by offering a stranger food would have made their children go hungry. He had seen too many families robbed by Deret's marauders on this expedition already to add to the misery they caused en route to Isolann. The moment he left the farmhouse, Parrish heard the bolts shot home behind him and the window shutters rattle as they too were secured.

He had walked no more then a few hundred yards, when Parrish sensed he was not alone. From out of the deepening night shadows a sandy haired woman approached him fearlessly, despite the darkness and her people's unease with strangers. She was sturdy and proud, beautiful in the ripe, earthy way of Svolenian peasant women. He could not guess her age, youth and ancient wisdom had blurred together to confuse perception. She wore the basic peasant garb of the region, a long dark woollen skirt, dark chemise, the upper body wrapped in a bright coloured, heavily embroidered, floor sweeping shawl. Married women pulled this over their heads, often obscuring their faces as well as their hair but this woman was bareheaded.

With interest, Parrish observed the many shamanic talismans around her neck; more symbols decorated a capacious leather pouch slung over her shoulder. In the absence of even the most rudimentary Christian presence, the ordinary people had readily turned back to the time-honoured ancient ways. Svolenians never tolerated vacuums of any sort in their too often desperate lives.

The woman gave him a look of utter sorrow and pity. "So young, so full of life. All will be lost if you go beyond the border and reach the forest stronghold."

Parrish had heard enough. He was heartsick of mysteries and hints of grave but unnamed dangers. He met the shaman's kohl-lined blue eyes, struggling to keep the aggression and impatience from his voice. "Tell me what is so dangerous about Isolann then. Why all this mystery and vague, veiled warnings? Why can't any of you tell me directly what awaits me over the border?"

"You ask what awaits you in Isolann? I can see in your eyes and your soul that you know already. Do not seek the lair of the Black Wolf — not unless you seek your death."

Chapter Twelve

Echoes from the Past

Suharli Region of the Steppes, 704 AD

He closed his eyes, better to drink in and savour the sharp steppe winds. The discordant screech of a hunting owl sweeping low above his war horse's head made it shy and prance about. Azrar rode at ease despite the weight of his black armour, warmed by his wolf skin cloak with the reassuring feel of his broadsword lying across his back.

Through the limited vision of his wolf skull helm, he saw King Dezarn riding ahead astride a palomino stallion. Dezarn turned, his handsome face wreathed in wry amusement,

"Come on my black wolf. Do you honestly call that beast of yours a war horse when it can be spooked by a bundle of feathers?"

Azrar and the other Jendars accompanied their king back to his seat of power; a city built in the heart of his steppe land kingdom. They had spent the past three years on a hard campaign against a coalition of enemies. Dezarn's army had been harried by land hungry barbarian tribes from the north, and the zealous followers of the new religion from the south. These Dezarn found the most dangerous.

Knowing how little time Azrar had for state craft, he addressed the warlord on the fragility of Dark Kind command.

"Never forget Jendar Azrar, the security of our reign is based on the will of our human subjects. We can never rule by force, we are too few. Humanity grows in strength and numbers by the day. We remain because our strength protects them. We can fight any army however powerful but we cannot fight men's hearts. This new religion denounces us as demon; any human who supports us are branded traitors to their own kind. We face perilous times."

Their conversation ended abruptly as a party of riders galloped to intercept them. Their safe passage past the lookouts ahead in the darkness was guaranteed by their lead rider's blazing silver Dark Kind eyes. Dezarn rode off with the messenger, returning moments later, his face graven and haunted.

"Return immediately to your lands with your army, Jendar Azrar. This is my command."

His king had never spoken to Azrar in such a curt manner and it disturbed him greatly.

"We are not safely back to the capital, there may be stragglers waiting in ambush."

"I have Mahdial and the other warriors. I do not need you. Now go."

Azrar took off his helmet to voice his protest unheeded by black metal, and his long unbraided hair fell free catching in the night wind. He gave a fang-drawn snarl of disbelief and fury. His anger agitated his war horse, it spun and plunged wildly, throwing up stones and sparks from its iron shod hooves. The Prince was in turmoil; torn between his duty to obey his sovereign without question and his instinctive awareness that grave danger lay ahead for his king. He had a stronger duty to protect him as a Jendar— a warlord prince.

"This is where I belong, my place is to be the sword at your right hand."

"You have no choice in this matter. I have already sent word for the other Jendars to return to their lands."

Dezarn's voice was pure steel; he was immovable, implacable. It was agony to see the distress and confusion on Azrar's face, the Prince was his most valued warlord, at his side through battles beyond counting over the centuries. Dezarn did not know what fate lay ahead on this journey home. It could be his kingdom, and with it his own life was already lost. It would be lunacy to sacrifice more Dark Kind nobility to a lost cause- they would be needed to protect the rest of their people and their defenceless human subjects in these turbulent and perilous times.

Dezarn rode over to the Jendar, catching the rein of Azrar's fractious stallion and stilling it with a soothing word. The King reached behind to his saddle and pulled a sword from its scabbard. It was a thing of great beauty, finely inlaid with a complex, abstract design of golden dragons, and its hilt guard a dragon with ruby eyes that caught fire from the blazing torches held by the King's human outriders.

"Take this and guard it well for me, I will take it back when I visit Isolann in spring."

Dezarn waited until Azrar had taken the sword, then he leant across and kissed the Jendar with an intensity of emotion that left no doubt it was a final farewell, and without a backward glance, spurred his horse to gallop away. They were soon lost to the darkness and the melee of his army on the move again. Only Azrar stayed motionless, his face stark, sharply carved white marble, a howl of despair rising uncontrollably into his throat.

By the third night's march, Dezarn's army reached the outskirts of their city. Leading from the front as always, the King raised his arm to signal a halt and lightly reined in his horse. He paused to breathe in the clear night air, sharpened with an early frost. The scent from flower garlands wafted over from the city walls and gates, the traditional welcome to the returning army at summer's end. There was nothing sweet about the smell; it reeked of the pungent odour of decay. The blooms had been put up too early and not replaced, just left to rot on the walls.

Mahdial rode over, his robustly elegant Dark Kind warrior's face taut with anxiety. He drew his sword and pulled down his bronze horse skull helmet, leaving only his gold flecked black eyes burning fiercely in the darkness.

"My Lord, this is all wrong. I sense a trap."

Dezarn dropped his head in assent. "And what would you have me do, beloved friend? Enter my own city with an attacking army?"

The sorrow and resignation in the King's voice shocked Mahdial.

"At least let us be ready to defend ourselves."

Dezarn agreed and sent Mahdial to prepare the Dark Kind. He did not wish to alarm the human troops. With luck any treachery would only affect his own people.

He rode through the city gates, feeling his horse begin to skit and shy beneath him, despite its fatigue. He ran his hand down its once bright golden neck, now darkened to ochre with sweat. Townsfolk lined the streets, but many were outsiders from their garb. Many gasped in awe at the sight of the King in his gilded armour astride a golden stallion.

The Dark Kind warriors urged on their powerful war horses as they curvetted through the wide clean streets; their hooves beat out a staccato rhythm, iron shoes firing sparks against the stone cobbles. They made their way through a city made safe and prosperous by trade and inhabited by a confident populace well protected by their Vampire King.

Tremors of conflict and dissent spread through the crowds, many could foresee their future destruction with the betrayal of the Dark Kind. Others seethed with hatred for the demons, fuelled by their fervour for the new religion. Many were merely frightened and confused.

Dezarn realised the situation was far worse then he imagined. He glanced across to his Dark Kind warriors, all battle-ready now, with fire flashing in their storm dark eyes.

Instead of hearty cheers of welcome the people stood in uncomfortable silence as the mounted troops clattered across the cobblestones towards the palace gates. The crowd shared a sullen or guilty reluctance to look directly at Dezarn or his Dark Kind warriors. Unwilling to enter his city as an aggressor, the King unsheathed his sword, holding it lightly by his side. The stink of rotten flowers was overpowering and the stench of low treachery hung in the air like a foul cloud. There was no chance of escape, even with his army fighting like tigers they would still be overwhelmed by the sheer number of the people packed into his capital that night.

He suspicions were realised as they rounded the last corner to reach the entrance to his palace. At the bottom of the gold marble steps, a high wooden platform had been erected, clearly a place of very public execution. Beside this, at the very gates of his palace stood a large and resolute reception committee of prominent Christian leaders, surrounded by heavily armed militia –made up from his enemies from neighbouring countries. It seemed his enemies had conquered from within while he was protecting the remote borders of his kingdom.

One, a gaunt tall man dressed in imperial Roman purple raised his hand and the majority of men in the seemingly passive crowds turned into combatants. Hidden weapons, mainly crude axes, knives and cudgels appeared from beneath clothing. Dezarn could see no escape possible for himself and now wanted only to protect his loyal and valiant troops from this ugly mob. It was the last thing he could do for them now his own subjects had turned to murderous treachery.

He spurred his stallion forward but could make little progress as more courageous members of the mob grabbed its bridle. It reared, boxing with its front hooves. Dezarn spurred it down and forward. The plunging and kicking horse scattered the crowds, allowing Dezarn to make more progress towards the scaffold. He demanded to be heard and at the sound of his deep, commanding non-human voice, the throng shrank back. Many were sick at heart at the betrayal of their king but were too few in number to resist the hostile crowd.

"You outnumber my army with your mob but my men are hardened warriors with the sweat of recent battle on their brows and the blood of our enemies on their swords. There will be carnage before we are defeated. There is no need for this. Let these innocent men go from the city unhindered. Let them return to their farms and families. It is me that you want."

The King's soldiers began to protest, raising their weapons high, all ready to defend Dezarn to the death but he held up one gauntleted hand for silence as he addressed his human army.

"You have all served me with loyalty and great courage but I will not take the dishonour of causing your deaths with me to the next world. You must return in peace to your families. This is my final command to you as your King. My place is here in the capital of the kingdom I founded."

Alarmed by the nobility of the creature he'd sworn to publicly destroy, the purple-clad Bishop Alaric addressed him in scornful ringing tones.

"Demon! If you were human I would demand you repent your sins in return for the salvation of your soul. But you are a servant of Satan. You are beyond redemption"

Dezarn coolly regarded his sneering protagonist glaring down from the palace. Alaric was a burly younger son of a pagan chieftain, a blue-eyed blond from the distant northern forests. Converted to Christianity, Alaric was now a zealous bishop with an army of his own to command.

"I am no demon. I am King Dezarn, sovereign Lord of the Three Kingdoms. You have invaded my lands and corrupted the hearts of my subjects."

"Silence, demon! Your foul reign of blood is at an end. You cannot deny you are a creature of darkness, that you drink the blood of humans; that you never age and have lived for centuries. All signs of the foulest devilry imaginable."

"I have nothing to do with your beliefs, I know nothing of gods and demons. I am a noble born High King of the Dark Kind, that I will not deny."

"You have condemned yourself to die by that confession."

A great roar came from the crowd, a howling animal sound mixing the bloodlust and loathing of his enemies and the great sorrow of his supporters, for many knew the secure life of plenty they had enjoyed under Dezarn's long reign would die with him on the scaffold. The human members of his army were roughly manhandled out of the city and held at bay some miles away by the conquering foreign troops.

Dezarn signalled his stallion to rear high into a levade position. It stayed aloft, motionless on its powerful haunches, giving the King a better view over the crowds. In the centre of the wide square, a space had been cleared for a number of tall wooden stakes piled high with pitch covered straw. With a low growl of disbelief and anger, Dezarn saw leather bound books torn up as kindling, he recognised them as the histories of his people.

His long dead human Queen Khari had ordered the Dark Kind language written down and transcribed into beautiful books. The vandals had ripped off every piece of gold and jewelled inlay before consigning the books to the pyres. So, his enemies also intended to destroy the written past when ending the Dark Kind's lives, by burning them alive at the stake. It was not a warrior's death. Dezarn nodded to his body guards to ready themselves to fight.

As his horse slipped and dropped down on its haunches, a stone was thrown at the King's head glancing harmlessly off his helm. It triggered an unplanned attack on his Dark Kind warriors. They fought hard with fangs bared as the baying mob descended in a wild melee of slashing swords and axes. With the lethal ferocity of cornered predators, the warriors made heavy inroads into their assailants, more red blood flooded across the cobbles, then purple. A city that knew only peace rang with the screams of wounded horses and men, the harsh clashing of weapons and the sickening crunch of shattered bones.

For all their courage and skill the vampires were overwhelmed by sheer numbers. Dezarn howled in fury and grief as one by one his warriors were pulled down and torn apart by the mob. Mahdial was inevitably last to go down, fighting on despite terrible wounds, before disappearing under the flailing body of his dying horse. Yet despite fighting hard, killing many men, no one attacked the King. They left him alone– either out of superstition or to save him as a prize for their leader, Bishop Alaric.

With his warriors slain, there was no time to grieve. The focus of the crowd was on Dezarn now. He vowed to die triumphantly as a Dark Kind and removed the golden dragon helm. His preternaturally young pale face, with its sharply defined, noble features showed no emotion beyond great pride and unswerving courage. His fiery obsidian eyes shone in the night, his long curving fangs now openly bared in a last arrogant celebration of his dark heritage. The crowd instinctively shrank away as he spurred his horse forward. Waves of power prevented them getting close and he rode, head held high with Dark Kind majesty towards his persecutors.

Red-faced with rage, the Bishop watched, unable to stop the carnage of his supporters from the swords and vicious fangs of the Dark Kind. As the last of the demon warriors perished, torn apart by the crowd, he was furious they had escaped their rightful fate. He had long ago planned a long, slow, tormented death in the flames; dreamed about his great triumph over this ancient evil. As he began his campaign to purify these heathen lands, he'd captured many Dark Kind. He had learned much, experimenting how best to destroy them and what method caused the most suffering. It pleased him greatly they were not immortal or immune to pain. Though tough to kill, he had found decapitating was an efficient method, burning the most agonising.

Alaric was a cunning man and no fool, he knew that there was still an abiding, deep affection and respect for the King among his supporters. There was no point in creating a focus point for rebellion now in this land so recently conquered by religious fear and treachery. He wanted to prolong the King's torture and suffering till the purifying light of dawn added its own torment. Now there were no other captured demons to suffer punishment as servants of Satan. The King's death had to be swift and without emotive speeches. Alaric had no desire to create a dark martyr for his enemies to ennoble. He also knew there was no end to the Dark Kind's courage, born of their insufferable demonic arrogance. The King would not weaken or beg for his life, it had to be done quickly.

To Alaric's added vexation, Dezarn made an impressive sight. He appeared so young, so handsome; courageous head held high in the face of certain death. The Vampire King's raw power could not save him, but it kept his enemies from manhandling him and he climbed the steps to his palace with regal disdain for his captors. With no one daring to approach him closely, Dezarn turned to address the crowd, to the bishop's horror. None of this was supposed to happen.

The human crowd fell silent; the tension became a tangible force gripping them by the throat. The hushed, strained silence was punctuated only by the stifled and subdued sobbing of subjects who now regretted their part in the planned murder of their king. Dezarn's voice was deeply resonant, unwavering in its natural authority.

"I have given this land and its people my heart and now it takes my life. Your future generations must judge this betrayal of centuries of protection. I am not a demon, nor are any of my Kind. We have no knowledge of these things although we have existed on this planet for countless thousands of your years.

"I want no revenge wreaked in my name for this crime by a craven people against a sovereign who has loved them. This is a direct order to my army and the forces commanded by my noble princes."

Dezarn stood boldly facing his people; although his armour was gore and dirty, he was still every bit a great King, proud, regal and brave. There was no doubting his magnificence even in defeat. This worried the Bishop, anxious the people did not sway in their decision to give up their vampire lord. Dezarn's fierce dark eyes briefly looked to the stars, head held high as if already contemplating a greater adventure in a world beyond. He wondered if Khari's gods would allow them to meet in the life beyond. He doubted it. What place could there be for a vampire in a human paradise?

Seizing the moment, the Bishop grasped a sword before Dezarn could speak further. Using all his considerable strength he swung wildly at the vampire's neck, severing the head cleanly. Dezarn's body dropped heavily, spraying the horrified onlookers with a high arc of hot purple blood. The bishop grabbed the head by its long steel grey hair and displayed it in triumph. A woman screamed, then silence, as the horrified crowd stood, transfixed, shaking with shock. The full impact of the unthinkable began to sink in. The people of the Three Kingdoms had only known the rule of their Vampire King. They had only known peace and prosperity under his strong protection. Their immortal souls damned by the God of the Christians or not, they knew in their hearts they had cruelly wronged Dezarn, who for all his ferocity and need for human blood had never harmed any citizen of his domain.

Chapter Thirteen

Chernok
A remote fortified outpost of the Three Kingdoms

With a feeling of increasing dread, Ha'al Czardor, one of King Dezarn's Dark Kind administrators watched as a group of hard riding humans approached the outer gates of his fortress. He could see from his vantage point on the battlements that these men had pushed their horses to near death— it could only mean bad news.

They could not have brought worse tidings. On hearing of Dezarn's death, a distraught but determined Czardor mustered his troops and prepared to ride hard towards Isolann. But first, pausing to break away from his retinue, he rode to a hilltop under a sky mocking him with its star filled beauty. He threw back his head, howling with grief, an eerie, savage sound echoing across the steppes terrifying wolf, bear and human alike. What hope was there for the Dark Kind now, with their greatest leader and bravest warriors slain?

With a heart broken forever, he rode on to carry out his King's last command. It had been given to the Ha'al days before Dezarn's last doomed journey home. Perhaps the King had some premonition about his terrible fate, told to him by a human subject gifted with the *Knowing*. Czardor was charged to give Dezarn's last orders to his remaining Dark Kind warlord. He faced enormous difficulty, for the Jendar was a violent warlord who would be desperate to avenge his much-loved King by shedding vast quantities of human blood. Urging restraint to a valiant but reckless, ferocious being like Prince Azrar was as futile as trying to harness a whirlwind.

The Principality of Isolann

Azrar did not need messengers to tell him Dezarn and the warriors were dead. He felt the King's passing in his spirit. He paused with his warriors on a high rocky promontory. Dismounting, he climbed to the highest point and howled a farewell to all the slain Dark Kind. His fierce soul rent with grief, he stared across the starlit landscape. Below him on one side, lay his mountainous Principality of Isolann wreathed in a wraith like silvery mist, the snow capped, black granite Arpalathians already visible on the horizon. On the other side stretched the more barren and arid steppes. From his high vantage point, the distant glow of many fires dotted the darkness. They marked the start of chaos and murder sweeping through the Three Kingdoms in the vacuum of Dezarn's death. With Azrar's participation the carnage was going to get much worse.

Azrar turned his war horse's head away from Isolann. His enemies would pay dearly in fang-torn throats and bodies ripped apart by his sword blows. The steppes could run red with an ocean of human blood, yet it would still not be enough to avenge Dezarn.

Czardor and his small party rode across the frontier into Isolann, marked by high poles topped with wolf skulls. The night wind brought the stench of death. With ease, he followed the foul miasma of burning timber and rotting human flesh which led him to the ruins of a border village. Once prosperous and safe within the protection of the Dark Kind, Czardor was shocked to see its destruction. He sent his human troops out to search for survivors.

After an hour they returned with one elderly woman. A traumatised, badly wounded human female, her skin was scorched and blood-stained, her clothes in charred tatters.

Czardor dismounted and threw his bariola brocade cloak over her shoulders and summoned water and salves. He let her drink deeply before questioning her. She spoke in a halting, defeated tone in the Isolanni tongue. Her voice was a dry whisper.

"The Bishop's army came one morning, I don't know how long ago. They killed anyone refusing to remove their black wolf amulet even the children, then burnt the village. I escaped but not before they did this."

The old woman opened her tunic revealing a livid brand in the shape of a Christian cross on her chest. The wound was suppurating and infected. Czardor flinched in revulsion from the smell.

"Where is your Prince, where is the Jendar Azrar?"

The old woman shook her head and began to wail, "We are lost, our lord is gone!"

Czardor called for medical aid but it was a futile gesture. The old woman was dead from her wounds by the morning. Where the Hell was Azrar? Surely even the headstrong warlord would have obeyed Dezarn's last command to him. He was a Jendar, he had no choice but to obey. In his heart Czardor knew the answer. The black mountain wolf was loose on an uncontrolled force of destruction and mayhem. How could he, as a Ha'al, a mere administrator, restrain what a great King could not?

Czardor rode across a once thriving land now turned to one vast graveyard. Even in the darkness, he could sense the suffering and devastation of its people. The cries from every widow, every bereaved mother, were caught up by the wind and turned to a desolate keening echoing across the steppes. The stench of death was inescapable. Blond invaders from the south followed in the Bishop's wake, looting villages, slaughtering livestock and burning crops. Czardor could see hundreds of bloated carcasses of sheep and oxen rotting as they lay; their owners murdered or fled. The ancient Steppe race of the Dholma were finished, destined to live as scattered persecuted nomads.

It was easy to follow Azrar's route. He left his own trail of death, guilty and innocent alike bore the violence of his grief-fuelled revenge. The only slight consolation, that even in his ruthless campaign of killing the Prince did not break was the Dark Kind code of honour — all his victims were adult human males. But it was a bitter concession, the lost were the bread-winners for so many families. More loss of innocent life would follow by the first bite of winter.

Six months after Dezarn's death, Czardor entered the Prince's camp. His guerrilla army had grown with many Dholma men joining in a futile attempt to repel the invaders. He ignored the warm welcome from the Dark Kind warriors and entered Azrar's black campaign tent. The Prince had his fangs deep in the throat of a captive enemy, another blond northerner. At the sight of the late King's aide, Azrar finished drinking, throwing the drained body contemptuously across the floor.

"Sorry, old friend, if I knew you were so close to my camp, I'd have left him for you. There's plenty more out there. Join me tonight. We will hunt together."

Shocked by his haggard appearance, Czardor studied the prince's gaunt features. His cheekbones stood out like knife-edges, glittering emerald eyes dark shadowed and haunted. Shockingly, his black armour remained uncleaned, still stained with dry human blood. The recent kill had done nothing to assuage his hunger for slaughter.

"You can kill every human on this world and it will not bring back Dezarn."

Azrar shrugged dismissively, "But think of the pleasure I'd get doing it."

Czardor sighed and sat down, pouring himself a golden goblet of robust local red wine. "You are losing Isolann. If you must indulge in this killing spree, at least do it defending your own lands."

"How dare you lecture me? I am a High Prince!"

"Then act like one."

Czardor ignored the fury blackening the Prince's green eyes. He took another deep draught of wine then continued, "Any commoner with fangs and a sword can do this. It takes true courage to rule a land with justice and nobility."

Azrar snarled with contempt, throwing back his long jet hair, still wet with gore from his most recent kill.

"And what did Dezarn's nobility and courage achieve? Murdered by the humans he swore to protect. I doubt they let him die with honour with a sword in his hand."

Czardor reached into his clothing and produced a charred and warped silver wolf amulet.

"I took this from the burnt body of a ten year old Isolanni girl. Her 'crime'? She refused to remove her amulet and denounce you as a demon. She'd been raised expecting your protection. She died in agony crying out your name, pleading for you to save her."

He threw the amulet down at Azrar's feet and strode out to find his horse. He could do no more.

Isolann, The Upper Balkans. 710 AD

Facing destruction from the blond invaders with their new religion, the tribal fighters came together under the banner of the black wolf, united by Azrar's strength and courage. A new army was formed from the scattered remnants of the defeated Dholma and their cousins the Caradani and together with the native-born Isolanni drove out their enemies, preventing them from reaching the borders of the principality. But when the battles ended, Isolann was all that was left of the once vast Three Kingdoms. The steppes were lost to the Vampire Kings forever. When his remote mountain land was finally secure, Azrar ordered a gathering of all the tribal leaders and village elders, the wise women and shamen.

The sun set behind the mountains glowing defiantly orange behind an ever-thickening bank of snow clouds. A thin whining breeze barely lifted the banners of Azrar's escort, it was cold but too feeble to make them flutter boldly. As darkness fell, the wind strengthened and became increasingly threatening in intent.

The Jendar dismounted and handed the reins to a nearby warrior. Azrar was impatient. This meeting must end soon; the people needed time to make camp and light fires before the heavy snow came. As it would, soon, he had smelt it on the air as he rode from his force's camp by Lake Beral. The war horses knew it too, they shook their heads, snorting frozen air like ice dragons and stamping, eager to be heading home to the shelter of their stables.

At first there were but a few people approaching, a ragged handful crossing the flat plains below the frozen lake. Worn out, some walking, others on stumbling, winter-thin ponies. To his growing concern, the Jendar could see more than just the tribal elders trudging through the snow; it seemed everyone from the tribes had come. As the long twilight turned to deep night, the plains filled with more and more people.

Azrar was shocked at the sheer numbers of the growing silent army of hollow-eyed humans stumbling through the darkness to the meeting place. It was dark now and the snow already had started to fall, carried on a strengthening bitter wind. Flickering flames from their torches revealed care-worn thin faces; families carrying sheepskin wrapped babies or clutching the hands of exhausted small children and frail old ones, supported by their descendants on makeshift litters. A people completely debilitated by decades of war and hunger, heartsick of living in constant fear. They did not want riches or power, nothing but a hopeful future and a long time of peace to raise their children to full grown in safety.

Azrar ordered the main body of his army to immediately disperse and collect food from his keep, and timber from the surrounding forests, as quickly as they could to prevent a disaster. His Commander in Chief rode up to the Jendar, his silver eyes shadowed with concern — the treachery of King Dezarn's human subjects still fresh in every Dark Kind mind. "My Lord Prince, there are so many. Is it wise to send the army away?"

Azrar sighed, such open questioning of his authority would normally receive a drawn–fanged and snarling rebuke but the warrior's concern was understandable. "I will keep my Dark Kind warrior elite here but that is all. These people urgently need shelter and food. My friend, there is no way forward for us but to trust. We are too few to hold this land by force, only by the will of these people."

On an open plain, in the shadow of the deep forest fringing the Arpalathians, they stoically bore the first heavy flurries of the night's snowfall. The huge gathering stood surrounding the Prince and his escort of a few Dark Kind warriors. The crowd stood in near silence with only the wail of the tired, hungry babes, their cries carrying far in the frozen air triggering answering howls from the forest wolves. Azrar strode away from his guard and drawing his sword dropped onto one knee. He lay the broadsword across his open palms and held it high before him, like an offering to the people.

"I am Azrar, Jendar of Isolann, High Prince of the Three Kingdoms. I pledge my protection to the people of this realm, I will defend you until the last beat of my heart and the last breath leaves my body."

No longer separate tribes, the now united citizens of Isolann listened as their Dark Kind Prince pledged his life to protecting them. Without prompting, as one they sank to their knees in the fresh new snow to acknowledge his leadership. Later, once the camps were set up and the families warm and fed and safe from the storm, the tribal leaders met with the Prince and agreed on behalf of their people to wear his symbol, the black wolf amulet and keep his existence a secret from all outsiders. Thus, the Pact was born.

Chapter Fourteen

Isolann/Svolenian Border 1929

There was no doubt where Isolann's border began. A line of twenty feet high wooden poles topped by wolf skulls and long, wind-tattered black banners decorated with silver wolf emblems marked the frontier. Every wolf skull had sharp fangs painted bright red, as if dripping blood from a recent kill. The wind caught in the ragged streamers of the banners, creating a low, keening cry that sounded as if the dead sang — chilling the soul and deadening hope.

"Clever," Deret muttered with a hastily veiled hint of admiration. He strode through the ranks of his muttering men to the head of the line addressing them with authority. They had followed him this far without question. The true expedition started here at the foot of these barbaric, blood-caked poles. The twentieth century had finally arrived in this remote and forgotten backwater.

"This is a backward land, lost in time. The people who dwell here show how foolish and ignorant they are by relying on primitive tricks to frighten away their enemies. Are we not tough well-trained soldiers of the glorious new Svolenia? Are we children or superstitious, ignorant peasants? No? Of course we are not. We will not let them make fools of us."

Jay Parrish stepped down from the truck, ruefully rubbing his numb backside from uncomfortable miles spent sitting on a splintered wooden seat. He walked up to the nearest pole: a primitive, crude symbol yet not without a certain visceral power. He took some photographs and glanced about for any sign of habitation, borders usually had nearby villages for trade and security. He saw nothing but the gently rolling green foothills of the Arpalathians, still just jagged outlines along the distant horizon.

Deret found the American poking about the base of one the poles with his fingers and a small penknife. He sighed with impatience, unwilling to lose any time crossing the border. Once his men saw there was nothing to fear, their morale would return and once more they would see themselves as a glorious vanguard and heroes of the Revolution bringing enlightenment to primitive northerners.

"Come away from those things, Yank. We need to press on while the light is good. The men are getting jittery. The sooner we get away from these barbarian objects the better."

Parrish nodded his agreement and reluctantly gave up his search for any possible ancient shamanic artefacts buried in the rich black earth at the base of the poles.

Stopping at the border was one thing; actually crossing it was one step too far for many of Deret's men. Those with peasant backgrounds balked at entering the lands generations of their families had feared. Many were raised with legends of Isolann's supernatural dangers. It was a place of vengeful wraiths and fire-eyed demon horses who carried off the souls of the unwary to Hell. And all this ruled by a Vampire Prince who was believed more terrifying then the most alarming nightmare creature in this domain of monsters.

Deret shouted commands to drive the lorries over the border, furiously berating and insulting the dissenters. Only fear of his authority in the new regime won over any nebulous doubts and noisily the convoy rumbled into Isolann. That they were the first motorised transport to enter the ancient land soon became apparent— there were no roads. They had expected at least to see worn cart tracks leading to outlying villages, but there was nothing, only open stretches of green, smoothly undulating foothills, interspersed with thick spinnies of wind sculptured silver birch trees.

    The emptiness of the landscape was an illusion. Parrish had never felt so claustrophobic. He sensed baleful, unwelcoming eyes watching every mile of their slow progress through Isolann's foothills. He began to believe the entire population had hidden themselves away, luring them deeper and deeper into danger. The village wise woman's words came back to haunt him, she warned this would happen. The growing sense of wrongness, of the real possibility of an impending trap affected him enough to voice his concerns to the taciturn Deret but the Svolenian scornfully dismissed his fears as the pathetic ramblings of a spineless Yankee academic. Parrish took little comfort that his thoughts were shared by most of the troopers, he could see it in their eyes.

    The weather remained fair, every slow passing day the late summer sun rose in a cloudless pale blue sky, but everyone complained of a bone numbing chill. Extra layers of clothing did nothing to dispel it.

    As the jagged peaks of the Arpalathians came nearer and grew higher, Parrish found the enshrouding atmosphere increasingly oppressive. Even the wildlife had vanished. With no sign of hare or deer fleeing the rumble of their trucks or the mobbing of brazen magpies, the place seemed deserted and unnaturally empty. They came to a densely wooded region with stands of wind bent silver birch, thick groves of rowan and ash. All was silent, with no birdsong, nor the lightest of winds to rustle the leaves. It was as if the country was holding its breath while the expedition passed by. Some miles to the left they made out the shimmer of a large body of still water and drove towards it.

    They discovered a lake as large as an inland sea but calm as a mirror. Again more mystery, such a natural resource in any other country would be fringed with settlements, fishing boats would skim over the glassy surface, such a lake should be the centrepiece for teeming human life. Parrish had the wild theory there must be something wrong with the water and climbing out of his truck, walked across a narrow beach of soft black-grey sand. He squatted down and scooped up a handful of water, hesitating a moment, then risked a taste, expecting to spit out foul salty or acidic water. Instead, it was pure and delicious, reflecting its source, the white capped peaks of the Arpalathians.

The expedition was relieved, the Yank's impulsive move meant the supplies could be topped up with this bountiful supply of fresh water. Yet as the hoses went down into the lake, the troopers on this task became increasingly jittery. None would openly admit it, but something about the smooth navy surface of the vast lake disturbed them, not what was visible but what lay beneath. More than one felt unseen malevolent eyes watching them from the depths. Normally someone would have suggested catching fresh fish but not one soldier raised the idea and as one they drove away from the lake, happy to leave the silent, haunted water behind them.

If the terrain became impassable by the trucks, Deret had planned to commandeer horses and oxen carts from the local populace. A sound strategy. Only there was no populace. Instead, he ordered his company to pack rucksacks and proceed on foot. Anger, disbelief and fear rippled through the men. Already badly unsettled by the eerie and deserted country, they were close to rebellion. The point of the expedition had long become lost to them, and Deret's reputation for spite and vengeance against anyone who crossed him too well known. His malice could spread to their families and loved ones. Grudgingly and with many surly mutters and furtive glances, the men prepared to abandon the trucks and walk towards their unknown, unseen and increasingly pointless goal.

Exhausted, hungry and disheartened after days of marching, they finally came to the edge of a dense, tangled forest that spread around the base of the mountain range like a cloak of protective darkness. Twilight fell quickly, and with it a spectral mist that wove in and around the trees, infiltrating their camp with long, thin, cold ghostly fingers. Parrish knew if he was to say, "Let's go back now," he would have received unanimous support. In fact, he mused ruefully, he would probably be flattened in the stampede. This was a bad place.

As the night slowly progressed, the deepening sense of malevolence from within the forest descended on the expedition with an increasingly suffocating force. Only Deret's reputation and force of will kept his anxious men from collapsing into downright mutiny and desertion. But Parrish believed his grip on them was becoming tenuous, adding to the men's' already frayed nerves. Both Parrish and Deret knew this was not the place to lose the protection of armed troops.

A thunder of approaching hoof beats shook the expedition from its gloom-laden lethargy. A group of riders were heading towards the forest edge at a hard-pressed gallop. The riders were small, with the black almond-shaped eyes and broad, yellow toned faces of ancient steppe nomads, but their mounts were not small, sturdy ponies, but well muscled, fine bred horses.

Deret and his men readied their weapons, expecting their first confrontations with the locals, but before the riders reached them, they turned aside sharply and disappeared into the forest. The uneasy silence returned with even greater impact. Fear was starting to take a stranglehold and Parrish's sense of an impending trap deepened.

Deret decided to follow the horses. To ride straight into the forest at speed meant two things. There was a clear route through the thorn-barbed undergrowth, and there was somewhere to ride to. Back and forward, they scoured the forest margins but no sign of a clearing or track became apparent. It was if the riders had been ghosts, vanishing without a physical trace.

"This is bloody impossible, there's nothing in here except all these damned trees and wild animals," cursed Deret. Before this, nothing had blocked the progress of his success. His part in the revolution had been the steamroller ride of dogma driven ambition. Nothing and no one had stood in his way. Until now. He had been brought to a furious and frustrating halt by a tangled forest in some godforsaken backwater. He hated this country. A city dweller all his life, Deret's discomfort had started when the track had grown too narrow and difficult for the vehicles. Abandoning them and progressing on foot had seemed like a deliberate personal insult. The old natural world, with its unpredictable and uncontrolled behaviour had no right frustrating the forces of progress and enlightenment.

Taming the wilderness would be yet another battle for Deret, a man driven by an obsessive passion for violent revolution. He had already fought hard against the twin demons of powerless poverty and ignorance; the age-old evils that his father had risen above by so many long hard years of devoted service to the Svolenian King, only to find his family thrown back into squalor and abject poverty on the hated aristo's whim, when his father fell out of favour. Deret knew what it was like to be a child sleeping under stinking rags on a dank, rat infested floor, shivering with cold and hunger. Deret glowered at the thick, thorny undergrowth, the densely planted, wind twisted trees and treacherous roots lurking like traps in the moist beech mast. There was nothing here that a good flame-thrower could not clear. If only he had one!

Parrish, too, felt wretchedly uncomfortable entering the forest as if the misty wraiths of all the old legends became more solid, more tangible here beneath the silent and unnaturally still trees. He had to get a grip on himself. It was all nonsense. Myths were made-up tales to frighten children into behaving well, not for grown men to believe in. He was a product of the modern world, not some ignorant peasant or gypsy. Despite all his rationalisation, his hair stood on end as he made the first, tentative step inside the boundary of the forest's perpetual gloom. The low, thick canopy of tangled branches depleted the light, there was precious little left to reach the forest floor. Parrish fought to control his irrational panic, and replied tersely to the Svolenian commander.

"These tracks must lead somewhere. Those locals were heading somewhere in a hurry, perhaps they are on their way to warn someone that we are coming." He had replied with more conviction then he felt. He also wanted to add, "Or something," but held back, aware of the scorn he would suffer from Deret.

A shout from one of the men brought Parrish and Deret running through the brambles. The trooper pointed up to the branches of a solid old birch. Deret recoiled at the shamanic obscenity draped across the tree—a horrific mess of human bones, raven feathers and wolf fur— stained with fresh blood. In the centre was another wolf-skull, its fangs dripping with gore. The blood was still fresh indicating the vile thing had not been there long. No doubt a desperate attempt by the riders that passed them to frighten off Deret's expedition. It would take more then this shabby, pathetic object.

"These people are insane. This is the twentieth century, not the Dark Ages. Take no notice of this rubbish!" announced Deret in disgust, ordering a fit young trooper to scale the tree and pull the shamanic warning down. Once it was on the ground, he reached for his lighter and set the foul thing alight. The raven feathers ignited first with a dramatic whoosh, eliciting a resounding cheer among the men –the first sign of recovering morale since entering Isolann.

"You are heroes of the Revolution burning away the last archaic dregs of the old world. Let us enter this forest with courage and right on our side."

The men gave a cheer, though many were still nervous and hesitant. Deret dealt with these in one chilling sentence. "Or be shot here in the forest as a deserter."

It got them in. Keeping them in however was going to be another matter, especially as nightfall was only two hours away. The forest's silence soon resounded with curses as they pressed on faster, as men had their faces slashed by branches or were tripped by hidden roots. Deret ignored the difficulty, desperate to make use of every scrap of light. Already it appeared fainter as the canopy grew thicker and lower. The men were exhausted and eager to make camp, determined to create the biggest fire possible to keep the evil spirits of this perpetually dark forlorn place at bay. If nothing else it would keep away the wolves.

Deret also relished the thought of making a huge fire, to burn away this new enemy, harshly punish it for daring to challenge him. He knew only too well the satisfaction of a cleansing conflagration. He recalled the pleasure of seeing the university that threw him out for spreading his seditious ideas, reduced to charred ruins and smouldering ash. He wanted to burn down the Royal Palace too, but the Revolutionary leaders desired it for themselves. Deret was patient. The Palace too would burn on his return to the capital.

His thoughts were pushed aside by a new ripple of fear spreading through the men. Were they being watched by unseen eyes, perhaps a skulking wolf pack? Were they tracking them, waiting for signs of weakness? One of the legends told of the terrible fierceness of the black mountain wolves of Isolann. Unlike other wolves, these creatures did not wait until desperate hunger drove them to cross an unwritten natural law and attack humans. Mankind was their preferred prey.

Deret responded by firing shots into the forest with his handgun. "Let the bastards feel the pain of hot lead, the future has arrived in Isolann and it hurts like Hell!" The men laughed uneasily though they were heartened by this feeling of power over nature and pushed onward through the forest, their spirits rising further as they found a narrow but clearer trail. Parrish made an important discovery and called out to the others.

"Over here! I've found some hoof prints –they look recent. Maybe they are the tracks of those horsemen."

"So much for our ghost riders! They can't fool us with their vanishing act!" declared Deret loudly to another cheer from his men. At first they made good progress and the expedition's spirits rose with every yard of progress along the good path. But despite this advance, disappointment hit hard as the path petered out in thickly tangled woodland. The ghost riders had done it again, disappearing into the twilight without trace. Once eerily silent, the woods now echoed with the crash of broken branches and the curses of the men as they stumbled and slashed their way through.

Deret berated his sullen, bruised troopers, "If a bunch of damn horses can get through this, we bloody well can."

Many were ready to mutiny and flee the forest before nightfall as the prospect of camping the night grew ever more likely. Then came a breakthrough of sorts, they could see the top of a man-made structure, the outline of a jagged black wall visible through the last dying rays of twilight. It was too far to reach before total darkness engulfed the troopers but it gave an objective, a goal to be reached in the morning. First priority was building a huge campfire, its warmth and light desperately needed to keep away the worst darkness of their lives. So dense was the tree canopy and the cloud cover that no moon or stars were visible, nothing to give light and hope.

Once settled around the fire, the men became aware of constant movement from unseen creatures circling their camp, the sense of things, furtive unknown things, skulking around them in the undergrowth. One young hothead, his nerves frayed to breaking, fired shots into the undergrowth.

"Stop that, you fool, you might hit one of your comrades taking a piss .If you see a wolf, shoot it but not 'til you see its long snout and yellow eyes."

Chapter Fifteen

Azrar's Stronghold, Isolann, 1929

A few rays of light sullenly filtered their way through the near solid ceiling of branches, announcing a dawn hung with leaden grey, drizzle-laden clouds. Deret's men rose, limbs stiff and clothing damp from an uncomfortable night huddled together around the campfire. Spirits rose a little once the fire was stoked up again and water put on for brewing tea. A meagre breakfast of stale and soggy biscuits was enough for the chatter to return; though the forest's oppressive gloom acted as a natural damper on any sense of well being.

After breaking camp, they pushed on hard, eager to reach their goal of the black structure soaring above the trees. They broke through the tree line by early afternoon. Below them in a wide valley surrounded by the foothills of the Arpalathians, towered what appeared to be a solid wall of black stone. Too exhausted to be amazed, Deret sank down on a log. After three weeks travelling in this empty land, he had brought his men safely to their destination. And what a destination! Parrish, too, was lost for words as the imposing size of the outer walls began to sink in.

And the astonishment did not stop with the walls. What they first thought to be the start of the mountain range was in fact the tip of an enormous tower. Overpowering in size and monumental in concept, the edifice stunned the entire expedition to an awed silence.

Parrish was the first to break the spell.

"It is so vast, we should have seen this before entering the forest. But whoever designed this was a genius. What sort of ancient architect could design something to blend into a mountain range? It's unbelievable. Extraordinary!"

Deret was equally overwhelmed by the staggering scale of the stronghold. "Have you ever seen something like this before?" he asked the professor, his voice hushed by astonishment. Parrish was pleased to hear a remnant of his student friend returning – the history scholar with a burning curiosity about the past. He shook his head. There was no known civilisation in the entire world that had produced anything like this.

The outer wall surrounded the black monolith of the central tower. The distance between the two was large enough to house a fair sized village complete with grassed paddocks. Deret ordered his troops to march down the valley and approach the stronghold but as they nervously reached the base of the outer wall, they could see no sign of an entrance.

As the men circled around the perimeter, their weapons ready for the slightest sign of hostility. They found on the far side a forty-foot iron and stone drawbridge. The gargantuan scale of the stronghold was breathtaking and fear among the men once again began rising, growing close to panic.

Deret knew he needed to show bravery and resolve in front of his men. He strode forward and hammered at the drawbridge with the butt of his rifle. A futile gesture but the only means he could find to gain the attention of any unknown and unseen inhabitants.

"I am Commander Comrade Deret. I demand you open this gate immediately."

The only response was an explosion of feathered fury as a flock of angry ravens fled the battlements to circle above them, cawing their indignation at the disturbance.

"I doubt if the inhabitants –if there are any, speak Svolenian," Parrish muttered, convinced they were out of their depth here in this alien and hostile place. They had no idea of numbers or the military strength of the Isolanni. No idea of who or what they had to face. Deret glared contemptuously at the American before resuming his assault on the drawbridge.

The sound of his hammering echoed through the forest, and reverberated away to the mountains, when he stopped there was only stillness. The world held its breath.

Oppressive and threatening, the silence was harshly broken by the scream of an eagle, mobbed by the furious, cawing ravens in a skirmish high above the battlements. A wave of nervous laughter rippled through the men, embarrassed at being spooked by an old and apparently abandoned building. The eagle was the symbol of Svolenia, both old and new. With hands shielding their eyes, heads tipped backwards, they cheered on the beleaguered predator, cursing at its smaller black assailants.

"Let's even the odds – hand me a rifle."

Before Parrish could prevent him, Deret took aim and shot a raven, the stricken bird spiralling to its death, to crash close to the troops, the avian tormentor now reduced to a pathetic bundle of blood-soaked feathers. Alarmed by the gunshot, the eagle broke free of its assailants and rose higher and higher in the grey sky to glide away to its mountain home. Parrish watched in disgust as Deret received the hearty approval of his men. It was just a bird, vermin, but what if it had some spiritual significance to the locals? Every symbol they had encountered so far in Isolann was adorned with raven feathers.

The short-lived diversion over, the oppressive silence returned, somehow far worse with evening's rapid approach. Faced with the unwelcome prospect of another night's camp in the open, Deret reluctantly ordered the men to gather firewood.

The persistent cold drizzle that had plagued them all day, now hampered any attempts at fire building. All the wood close to hand was sodden and refused to light. Though it might trigger a fear-fuelled mutiny, Deret had no choice and ordered a small group of reluctant 'volunteers' back into the forest to find dry kindling. He watched as the men walked nervously up the valley, to disappear into the relentless gloom of the canopy. A small irrational voice within told him they would never be seen alive again. Parrish thought that too, he could see it in the American's eyes. But three hours later, with full darkness fallen, a faint flickering light announced their safe return laden with dry wood.

It was enough to coax a smoky, sullen fire, so different from the brash defiant blaze they had ignited in the forest on their previous night's last camp. It was as if the fire itself did not want to draw any attention so close to the mysterious stronghold. A feeling shared by the men, who spoke rarely and quietly – almost in whispers. All sat down and lay their rifles across their laps or kept them in their hands, fearful of an attack in the night. Despite their exhaustion, few could sleep, and those that did dozed lightly for the briefest of times with comrades taking turn to keep guard.

Deret watched as the American sat down with the men, totally relaxed in their company, cheerfully sharing a cigarette from the dwindling supply and passing around mouldy biscuits from the paltry food ration.

Parrish was from a well-to-do New England family, practically the equivalent of titled aristocrats in American society. Yet ironically, this imperialistic lackey found it easier to mix with ordinary men. Deret loathed them for their wilful ignorance, their base delights such as cheap liquor and fornication with whores. With his burning zeal to build a just, free society, a nobler society, he secretly despised the working classes he'd sworn to fight to the death for. He knew if one of their old oppressors returned offering them a better deal, they would turn their back on the Revolution in a split second. But he could not turn his back on them, their descendants would be free— that was worth fighting for. That was the price worth burning down the university, soon one day the Royal Palace and the Cathedral of St Alaric would be just ash; then every church and mansion in Svolenia until every symbol of oppression was scorched away.

Deret stood up with difficulty, tiredness and damp numbed his limbs and straightening with a groan, walked away from the scant comfort of the fire. Once clear of its warmth, the drizzle soaked his hair and face with a fine cold spray, somehow more irritating than heavier rain. He wiped the wetness from his eyes and glanced up at the monolith towering above him. Did its inhabitants think he would turn his men around and return home like children pretending there was no one home? Were they afraid, cowering in silence in the darkness, hoping the intruders would leave? This was too much to hope for.

He became aware of the American approaching in the darkness. He handed Deret a tin mug of weak tea. "It could be empty. Even a building of this magnitude, could be abandoned."

Deret winced as he sipped the foul tasting brew and shook his head emphatically.

"This is no derelict. They are up there, watching, waiting to see what we will do. If there is no sign of life by morning, I am going to burn them out."

As if aware of their conversation, the light from a torch appeared on the outer wall, its flame small but immensely bright against the darkness. Under its illumination a small group of five Isolanni men appeared, accompanied by a smaller cloaked figure. The figure called down to them in heavily accented Svolenian,

"You have no business in Isolann or at this fortress. At Dawn, return to your homeland."

They realised with astonishment that a young girl was addressing them. The troops sprang to their feet, arms at the ready and gazed up at the fortress. Deret stepped forward, fingering the trigger of his handgun.

"You have no right to dictate orders to me. I am Commander Comrade Deret."

"That means nothing to us. You must leave." The girl spoke, calm but firm with an authority that belied her years.

"I am here to tell you about our glorious revolution. Your people are now free from the cruel yoke of tyranny."

Deret spoke with the full force of his conviction. The girl answered, she was polite but insistent. "The Isolanni people have always been free. We choose to serve our lord, the Jendar Azrar, Prince of Isolann but only as a free people. There is no tyranny in our lands."

"There are no more lords, no more parasite aristocrats in Svolenia."

"This is not part of Svolenia and never has been. Isolann is an independent, sovereign state, by right and by ancient treaty. You have no rights here, you are an invading enemy force with one chance to leave in peace."

If she was beginning to feel impatient, she masked it well. Deret felt no such need for manners.

"I demand to see this prince."

For the first time the girl sounded uncomfortable, her voice betrayed her shock at Deret's lack of respect. "No one can make demands of the Jendar. He will not speak with you."

"Then I will stay at his gates till Hell freezes over. Tell your master I will speak to him."

Parrish caught an intriguing glimpse of a stray blonde lock of hair escaping from the girl's hood before she turned to leave. A Slavic girl dwelling among the dark haired Asiatic Dholma nomads? Another intriguing mystery. It hardened his resolve to get into the stronghold at any cost. Blackness returned as the small party left the battlements taking their torch with them. With their departure, a tense silence fell.

"I think we have little to fear from their prince. His blood is so watered down by centuries of inbreeding, he has to send a child to challenge us!"

Deret's men were not cheered by his open contempt. Nor could they sleep. Most kept watch all night, every man's eyes trained up at the fortress, but there was nothing to see but darkness.

"You were very brave."

Khari smiled weakly at the captain of the Stronghold guard. She felt anything but brave as they returned to the familiar corridors of the inner keep. As the guards escorted Khari back inside, she was glad of their presence — her legs felt weak from her encounter with the outsiders. She felt a sense of resentment, a rising anger at the Jendar for putting her in such a dangerous situation. Though the strangers were far below the battlements, she could feel the waves of hostility rising up from them and heard the click of their rifles, acutely aware that some of the guns were trained at her.

She was just a child, why was she put in the front line? This was a time for warriors and statesmen, not children. As she reached Azrar waiting for her in the Great Hall, she chided herself for such ungrateful thoughts. His forever young face solemn as ever, the Prince held out his hand to her and with this simple gesture, she felt all the anger in her heart melt away.

She remembered that poor Ileni was only two years older then her when she was married. Barely three years older when she had to bury her first baby, a still-born girl, during a blizzard, digging through the snow and the thin frozen soil with her bare hands. Such a tough, uncompromising life. Khari knew she was thoroughly spoilt by her human family and indulged by the Prince. Speaking to the invaders was a small price to repay so much love.

    Azrar looked down over his lands from the highest point of his towering stronghold. Behind him, the black granite of the Arpalathians formed a solid wall of sheer, jagged rock, below spread his thorny, tangled forest. With no stars or moonlight to give illumination, it was a dark sea, mysterious, full of hidden peril. Yet no creature lurking within its inky depths could compare to him for ferocity.

    He held out his arms to the night sky, throwing back his head as the wild, raw, mountain wind caught his hair, turning it into jet whips lashing at the night. He howled the savage, eerie cry of the hunting Dark Kind, a sound born to stop the hearts and freeze the blood of his human prey.

    Below in the Svolenian camp, their commander was working hard to quell the growing unease spreading through his men. Although many were of naturally superstitious peasant stock, even the town bred ones were not immune to the pernicious disease of fear. The final straw was a blood-chilling howl echoing from and around the stronghold. Deret found himself facing the imminent possibility of mutiny and desertion.

    "It's just some damn wolf," he announced to reassure them. "The mountains and these forests are teeming with them. It's nothing a well aimed bullet can't stop."

    Deret and his men awoke to another grey, wet dawn. But shortly after daybreak, the drawbridge creaked downwards with much groaning of its old iron workings. Despite its great antiquity though, it worked with precision, touching down on the grass with a light bump that belied its vast bulk. A group of Isolanni horsemen rode out to the camp, holding back their fresh horses to a walk. They were armed with weapons from an era long past: spears, swords and bows and quivers of arrows slung across their backs. Deret's men went to grab their rifles but Parrish noticed a young girl among the horsemen and raised his hand to calm everything down. She rode a tall well-bred grey stallion and most curiously, a large brindled wolf loped at its side. The presence of the dangerous wild creature created a ripple of fear through the Svolenians, Parrish saw their rifles being raised to shoulder height.

"They have come to talk, not attack us," he shouted, desperate to prevent a pointless escalation into a bloodbath. The girl threw back her hood and Parrish gave a gasp of recognition. The same silvery-blonde hair, the same gentle voice speaking Svolenian in a charming accent. His theory that she was a Slav by birth, confirmed by her features. His astonishment rose as she lifted her head and he saw her eyes for the first time, Parrish had never seen such a curious yet beautiful shade of gold in any one. A fairy child, a changeling. With her wolf companion, somehow she belonged to this dark stronghold in a way the robust and earthbound Isolanni guards accompanying her could not. He saw the girl compose herself before addressing them, clearly daunted by the task.

"Jendar Azrar has provided food and drink for your men. Once you are refreshed, you must leave Isolann."

Deret's obtuseness wanted to refuse the hospitality outright but he had enough common sense to realise his men were exhausted, demoralised and hungry. With their poor quality rations nearly depleted, it would be foolish to refuse this food. But he would not thank them for something he intended to take by force. He ordered his men to receive the provisions and store them. Then he walked up to the slight form of the girl, aiming a gun at the snarling protective wolf's head. With his other hand, he grabbed her horse's reins, ignoring the angry shouts of the enraged Isolanni men, their spears pointing dangerously close to his throat. He heard the reassuring click of thirty rifles behind him.

"I still demand to see this Prince of yours. I refuse to leave. My men are far better armed then yours. Your fortress may be temporarily impenetrable, but your settlements are not."

The girl's eyes widened with distaste and she murmured soothing words to calm her growling wolf. She fixed Deret with her golden gaze, a look so strange, direct and penetrating he stepped back involuntarily, lowering the pistol. The girl did not answer back with the same tone of hostility and threat, her voice betrayed only the pity she felt for these foolish and doomed men.

"I must warn you, the Prince will not react well to your threats against his people who are unarmed and innocent. Arrogance will doom you and all your men. Remember you are few in number and far from home."

Parrish, furious with Deret's blinkered stupidity, stepped forward to save them from this increasingly dangerous situation.

"Please convey my gratitude to your Prince for his generous hospitality," he said with a low bow and what he hoped was a disarming, friendly smile. "I speak to you not as a Svolenian but as a citizen of the United States of America. I bring warm greetings of friendship from our leader. Please pass this message of goodwill to the Jendar."

The girl nodded and Parrish caught a glimpse of a slight smile on her pale, beautiful face before she turned her horse in a tight circle and calling to her wolf, galloped back into the compound beyond the drawbridge with her escort deployed defensively around her.

"Saving your own worthless hide, eh Yank?" Deret sneered.

"Trying to save all of us, actually. What are you playing at Deret? You don't exactly have a whole battalion to back up your threats," Parrish retorted, almost at the end of his tether with this dangerous man, the living proof that power corrupts and distorts perception.

Deret patted his rifle and smiled laconically. "I have all I need to see off mere peasants."

Chapter Sixteen

Echoes of the Past

Azrar breathed in deeply; the night air was redolent with fear, a foretaste of the pleasure to come. Above him, big bellied, low clouds like a herd of in-foal grey mares galloped across the sky pushed hard by a sharp wind straight from the mountains. It carried with it slivers of ice, forerunners of a greater storm brewing in the jagged heights.

He did not notice the wind-born bitter shards, even with his helm off, or the whipping of the wind through his long battle-braided hair. His heart hammered with excitement, his whole being a coiled spring of hard muscle and taut nerves. This was living; this was the reason to survive. He forced himself to stay calm and relaxed for the sake of the high spirited war horse beneath him, already sensing the battle to come. He knotted the reins and dropped them on the arched neck with its full wavy mane. He could control the stallion with consummate skill, giving subtle signals with heel, knee, and weight shift, even at the confused height of a melee in the darkness.

"Steady, old man, you must be quiet now."

He stilled the plunging horse with a light caress down its tense, taut muscled shoulder; the once gleaming black coat now filthy with dust caked sweat. Like its rider, the stallion scented the enemy camp in the valley below. Through the darkness came a sensory assault of crackling camp fires, roasting meat, the whinnying of tethered horses and weapons sharpened in showers of sparks against whet stones.

In the darkness Azrar's army waited close enough for their Dark Kind warriors to pick up the sweet coppery scent of fear heightened human blood. The Prince yearned for action with hunger burning through every cell of his being. A rider approached, instantly recognisable as Dark Kind with his silver eyes blazing in the darkness.

"Everything is in place, my Lord. The enemy are surrounded."

Azrar growled assent and the rider spun his horse and spurred it away in a brisk gallop. Now Cadri's battalions were ready the attack on the invading Ottoman army could begin. There was no sign of a trap though it was strange these fools could venture so far north and not learn that the Dark Kind army always attacked by night. The unsuspecting Ottoman army down in the valley looked relaxed and unprepared. It would be a massacre.

The Prince sent word to his stalwart human army and the tough, disciplined and resolutely loyal force pressed forward to attack in the darkness. Azrar's senses reeled with anticipation. He drew his long broadsword from its ornate scabbard across his back, creating a shiver of pleasure as its familiar weight lay in his gauntlet-clad hand.

He waved the sword high above his head, the moonlit blade flashing with silver fire. His fangs were bared, openly displaying the fearsome reality of his being. At his signal, the stillness of night exploded with the deep thunder of galloping hooves and clashing weapons. The sudden attack was like a violent storm descending creating terror and panic in the enemy camp. Tortured screams and angry bellows from men and beast alike rent the night air. Braziers and torches tumbled over, spreading an uncontrolled fire blazing through the tents adding to the sudden vision of Hell.

Azrar drove on his war horse to spin and whirl scattering attackers as he swung his sword in an indiscriminate frenzy. With uncontrolled bloodlust raging, the blaze from his green eyes lit up the darkness, creating a beacon and focus for his men.

Azrar's army faced a formidable enemy, the Ottomans fought back well, dragging out the battle for hours. Azrar's thirst grew urgent. Dropping the reins onto its sweat-soaked neck, Azrar skilfully controlled his horse by subtle shifts of balance alone. Picking out a fine strong specimen full of fight, he reached down, sweeping up the enemy soldier from the ground with his rein hand. With one scything slash of his fangs, he tore open the throat of the desperate, thrashing victim. He drank deeply yet still fought on, ignoring the flood of gore drenching his armour, his long jet hair, his black wolf skin cloak. There was no time for a neat kill.

As he dropped the body, he heard the roar of approval from his men, revelling in the sight of their beloved Dark Lord demonstrating his awesome strength and ruthless ferocity.

Azrar awoke abruptly, shaking in shock in the dark of his deep vault in the keep. How could such vivid reality disappear, so physical an experience dissolve as a mere dream? He looked down; expecting to see the red blood of his last victim still on his hands; the memory of blood taste lingered in his mouth, as did the warmth of his stallion's taut- muscled flanks. Instinctively his hand closed around a sword hilt no longer in his grip.

 He felt different. Something had happened. It was not just one day's dream he'd awakened from, but a sleep lasting centuries. A new vibrancy pulsed through his body, and with it a raw hunger, an agony of craving.

He ascended the stone stairs up to the great hall. All his human servants and Khari awaited him, their eyes wide with anxiety.

"Strangers have not left, my Lord."

"Excellent." Azrar gave a low growl of anticipation; it would take an army of humans to satisfy his need.

Ileni gasped at the change in the Prince. All of Eshan's warnings returned to haunt her now. She was afraid of the strangers but far more so fearful of Jendar Azrar. Green eyes blazing with predatory fire, he strode past them, radiating powerful electric waves of pure menace. He headed towards the battlements. Khari began to follow him but Ileni held her tightly.

"Not now my child, it is how the Lady predicted. The Warrior Prince has awoken from his long Rest. He is more dangerous then you can ever imagine."

Ileni began to cry, unable to hide her terror and distress from Khari's gentle mind probing.

"Why do you think must I leave the keep? This my home." Khari pleaded, distressed.

Ileni reached out to hug the child but Khari pulled away. "I will not leave here, I belong with my guardian, the Prince."

"Sweetness, we all love you so much, but you must accept you belong with us, your human family not with Prince Azrar. He is heartless. He is not human."

Khari did not want to hear another word. Too young, too unworldly to understand why her love of the Jendar was considered so strange, she pulled away from Ileni's concern and ran past a startled and uncomprehending Sandor to seek out a hiding place. She needed solitude and for the first time the inner keep felt claustrophobic, a vast stone cage. Khari ran to the stables, with Wolf faithfully loping at her side, she knew she could not ride out. It was night and there were hostile and armed strangers at the gate. But she could enter Carillon's stable and burying her head into his long wavy mane, her hand on Wolf's grizzled head, cried her heart out to the two friends who would never let her down.

Below in the Svolenian camp, their commander worked hard to quell the growing fear spreading through the men. Though many were of naturally superstitious peasant stock, even the town bred ones were not immune to pernicious disease of fear. Deret's control over these troopers ebbed away with every minute spent in this wretched territory, this so called land of Secrets and Shadows. Many of the soldiers were mere lads on their first mission away from home. The final straw came in the darkest hours when dawn seemed a forgotten memory. Another eerie howl echoed around the keep and out to the valley beyond, terrifying the troopers. No one believed it was a wolf. Deret faced the real possibility of mutiny and desertion.

The next day, Deret found his troops in a better mood, the previous night's fears melting with the welcome warmth of a late summer sun as it spread over the snarled tooth horizon of the Arpalathians. Their better humour came from the homely aroma of freshly baked bread. They had been left several full baskets of freshly baked rough-crusted sweetened loaves as well as large earthen ware pitchers of yeasty light golden ale.

Contemptuously, Deret watched his troops fall on the simple fare, happily devouring it all within minutes. How quickly their memories of a night spent in terror of the keep and its inhabitants dissolved! He studied again the curt note giving tacit instructions from the Prince left with the food.

"You must leave my lands once your men have had one night's rest and food."

This unseen aristo still believed he was safe from the revolution in this outlandish, hulking eyrie! Deret was so much looking forward to proving him wrong! He curtly refused a hunk of bread brought by an aide, his men needed it more then him, but when joined by Parrish, grudgingly accepted a mug of watery coffee from the American's dwindling private cache.

"So this is it. We get right up to the gates of the most extraordinary edifice I've ever seen and then we turn round and go back again?" queried Parrish uneasily.

Deret sneered, sickened by the American's suggestion of weakness at the first sign of opposition from this medieval backwater. He poured the remains of the cold, bitter coffee onto the ground and threw the enamel mug back at Parrish.

"I refuse to be dismissed by some chinless, inbred, watery-blooded prince. I will demand to see him and let him know his tyrannical reign over these superstition-ridden peasants is finally over."

Parrish shook his head at the Svolenian's blindness to practicality. Deret came from an intellectual background, with no real military training. He had no doubt it led to the comrade's dangerous arrogance. They were deep within Isolann, one small troop of foreigners against a whole nation. Against a non-Slavic people who were not interested in revolution or enforced change. People who from all the evidence Parrish had seen so far were quite happy to stay as they were.

The last thing he wanted was to see the Prince antagonised and hostile. Parrish sensed there was a historical prize beyond wealth behind these featureless walls. He had never seen architecture like it. A curious combination of camouflage, visually blending with the surrounding mountain range with its unique style, high-vaulted, bizarre, which Parrish called 'alien gothic.' There was nothing remotely like it anywhere in Europe or Asia. Not now, or anywhere in the recorded past. Where had such design come from? And how did it get built in such a backward, remote region?

Leaving his men to digest their simple and welcome breakfast, Deret strode over to the heavily fortified wooden drawbridge that barred them from the inner compound. Made of whole oak trunks with black iron supports, Deret could only guess at the size and weight of the chains needed to raise and lower it.

"I demand audience with your Prince. I am Comrade Commander Deret of the People's Army. My men will not leave until my conditions are met."

There was no sign of response from the keep apart from the cawing of circling ravens. He patted the wooden gate. "You may be solid and strong but there's nothing a good dousing of petrol and one small flame cannot destroy!"

"Are you crazy?" Parrish grabbed Deret's arm as he strode back to his men, "You don't have a conquering army, just a rag taggle of nervous young troops ready to flee at the next wolf howl, or whatever else it was last night."

Deret brushed his arm away and ignoring the professor's increasingly desperate protests ordered his men to gather dry timber and pile it at the base of the keep gates. But before the first branches were laid, the gate lowered to reveal a small gathering of Isolanni men. One stepped forward to address them in surprisingly fluent Svolenian.

"You and the tall, fair-haired one may speak to the Jendar after sunset. Return at nightfall. But be warned, none of you will leave the Prince's forest alive if you attempt any assault on the keep."

They swiftly raised the door before Deret could reply; his faced reddened with impotent fury.

"I'm going to burn the bastards out! They have no idea who they are dealing with!"

"Nor do we," Parrish shouted back in rising panic. Deret would condemn them all with his mindless arrogance and revolutionary fervour. "Why don't you wait untll we speak to this prince? You have no idea of his strength or size of his army yet."

Despite his impatient and angry outbursts, Deret was not reckless and canny enough to see sense in the American's advice. He looked up to a cloudless, dark blue sky; his face felt the increasing warmth of the early sun. The mountain air was crisp and refreshingly pure, a day's rest would certainly benefit his men. He needed them fresh and strong for taking this stronghold by force.

Chapter Seventeen

Azrar's Stronghold, Isolann

It was his time of Rest but sleep was a luxury Azrar could not afford. He waited out the cursed hours of daylight pacing the floors of his vault deep beneath the central keep in a state of impotent agitation. He was a warlord, his domain was under threat but could do nothing until the last rays of sunlight were lost behind the Arpalathians. He glanced up at the heavy brocade hangings that adorned his sanctuary with scenes depicted in rich tones of purple and gold, crimson and blue of a lost world where Dark Kind ruled unchallenged. A time of glorious, powerful and vast kingdoms of darkness, these images must mean nothing to him now, dwelling on the past was a weakness born of peace time idleness. Real life was now. To his relief, the wasted years of enforced peace and idle contemplation were gone. Danger threatened and his life had purpose and pleasure once more.

The safety of his vault was one reason for his long survival within the modern world. No sunlight had ever brightened its walls, nor could anyone enter without Azrar's permission. It was the ultimate sanctuary for a Dark Kind nobleman — impregnable, comfortable and opulent. Today it felt like a prison, so desperate was Azrar for action.

When the first intelligence report had reached him of the Svolenian's expedition approaching his borders, he had set in motion an ancient defence system. All men capable of bearing arms were mobilised and a council of tribal elders held at the stronghold, the first for centuries. One old man had advised ignoring the unwelcome visitors in the hope they would find nothing of interest or value in Isolann and return, leaving the country to its long forgotten isolation. The Prince could see why this would be an attractive option to his human subjects. But it was a suicidal plan.

Azrar knew this small troop of brash Svolenians were merely forerunners, the first invaders of the modern world. His instinct was to kill them all. It would only delay future larger and better-equipped invaders but would buy him time to re-organise his nomad army into a more modern fighting force. Khari's report of the strangers mentioned an American professor, this man triggered Azrar's curiosity about the New World, a place his people had never dwelt in. He was also the only one who bore his people no malice. Azrar would kill him last.

The Prince sat at his ebony bureau, piled high with ribbon-bound scrolls bearing his black wolf seal, all were treaties with long dead Svolenian kings. Each document attesting to Isolann's sovereignty and independence from its much larger southern neighbour.

Each had been won with much blood spilt on both sides. Azrar pushed them to one side dismissively, they were worthless, Svolenia always ignored them as new generations of humans were born to take up the challenge of Isolann's conquest. Born to fail.

A simple box that had lain forgotten beneath the scrolls distracted Azrar's eyes. It was Ha'ali Eshan's parting gift after her visit. He opened the box, with a contemptuous snarl. Inside lay a pair of platinum framed spectacles with intensely black lenses. So it had come to this. Did his survival mean disguising his eyes, hiding what he was from humans? Never! Azrar took the hateful object in his hand, ready to crush it. Dark Kind commoners survived using such pathetic disguises, dwelling among humans in fear. He would live and die openly a Jendar. It meant his death was probably closer now than at any time in his long life. So be it. He would not hide. The visitors would see him tonight as a Dark Kind warlord – such a sight would sign their death warrant, and the thought of drinking their blood made his shiver in pleasurable anticipation of the killing soon to come.

    Darkness fell with a glorious sunset of gold and pink that faded into a lush purple sky. Observing its glory was a useful distraction for Parrish, who stood away from the Svolenians, pausing for a few moments to gather his thoughts as the magnificent panorama took his mind of what was to come. Great mystery lay beyond the weighty oak and iron-clad doors, sometimes such doors were better left unopened.
    The Isolanni kept their word, and at dusk the door opened slowly with a deep groan like a dragon with bellyache. A group of Isolanni soldiers solemnly escorted Deret and Parrish through. The two outsiders were politely told to wait in the courtyard till summoned for the audience with the Prince Azrar. Left alone, Parrish immediately began exploring the vast, cobbled compound. Deret remained, seething at being made to wait, standing in the courtyard, arms folded looking like a grey statue commemorating stubbornness and pride.
    Parrish as a horse lover was first drawn to the stable block, as grand in scale and design as any mansion for human dwelling. Inside bustling grooms tended rows of fine looking horses, their polished coats gleaming in many shades of grey ranging from near black to star dappled iron grey and snowy white. One section contained shy, leggy young stock and mares with foals, all near weaning age. Another held a dozen stallions, their proud, noble heads turning to snort nervously at the stranger. The most high spirited was a well-muscled jet black horse, his arched neck

was graced with a long rippling mane that reaching down to his knees.

Parrish tried to pat the black neck as shiny as patent leather but the horse whirled away; its dark brown eyes flashing with anger. It reared, boxing the air with flailing hooves. Parrish instinctively stepped back at the dangerous display of equine fury, suspecting his soothing words would not calm such a high mettled beast.

"There, there Caridor. I am sure the man means no harm."

Parrish turned to see the young girl with the silver blonde hair. Now she was close he could see she was in her mid teens. She walked towards the horse, speaking in a strange, harsh unknown language. The animal ceased rearing but retreated to the back of its stable, glaring at both humans with haughty superiority.

The girl wore the bright woollen garb of the local nomads, the earthy green tones highlighting her extraordinary golden eyes. Somehow, disconcertingly, he seemed to feel her presence in his mind; he hastily brushed away such fanciful notions. Perhaps the strangeness of the stronghold was affecting his judgement. She spoke to him in her accented Svolenian, clearly this was a foreign language to her.

"The Prince's war horse is rarely touched by humans, and never by strangers. You had better leave him, only that will calm him down."

Parrish walked with the girl away from the stallion. She relaxed when they reached the section containing the mares with their foals and was happy to show them off to him, pride and affection making her face glow with pleasure. His gentle touch with the foals pleased her greatly and her guarded attitude towards him softened.

She told him her name was Khari and she had lived in the keep all her life as the ward of the Jendar.

"What is the Prince like?" Parrish asked quietly, watching a wary mask fall across her face but not before a tell-tale flicker of love sparkled in her amazing eyes. She answered him simply but precisely.

"The Jendar Azrar is our Lord, he protects us."

"I am not the same as the men in grey camping outside your walls. My name is Jay Parrish. I am a visitor, an American professor of history who is fascinated by these ancient lands. The Svolenian call Isolann the Land of Secrets and Shadows. They say it is ruled by a vampire Prince."

"What is a vampire?" Khari asked, intrigued by the unfamiliar word.

"An evil monster, an immortal demonic being that drinks the blood of men to survive."

Khari's face briefly drained of colour but she quickly recovered, looked up at the American and her eyes met his fearlessly, "There are no demons here, Mr Parrish."

The girl turned away without another word and walked towards a group of wary Isolanni grooms who had discreetly watched every moment of the stranger's arrival in their stables. Parrish started to return to Deret outside in the compound. A wave of unease spread through him as he looked back to where the Prince's stallion was stabled. Khari's mysterious statement came back to intrigue him, was it just a linguistic slip, for if no human rode the fiery black horse, what in damnation did?

Deret waited with increasing fury at his treatment by these primitive natives. No longer a statue, he paced up and down like a penned wild boar. Two hours had passed since being admitted to the compound. The American fool, Parrish had disappeared into the stables and no one from the inner keep had approached him.

As he watched the bustle of the courtyard preparing for nightfall, he saw a willowy and obviously Slav girl walking among the dark, short Isolanni. She was clearly relaxed and at home in these alien surroundings but what could she be doing so far from her homeland? Was she the same girl who had challenged them from the battlements and ridden out to give word of the Prince's command?

Deret prepared to corner the girl as she left the stables and walked back towards the sanctuary of the keep. Up closer, he could see it was the same girl. She moved with well-bred poise, carefully tutored light graceful steps, as girls of the despised Svolenian nobility once walked.

Her sheltered life was clearly not burdened by any morality or social strictures. He decided he would take pleasure in bringing the real world to destroy her fairy tale existence; her days of innocence in an enchanted castle were about to come to an abrupt end.

A heavily pregnant young Isolanni woman joined the girl in her short journey across the compound. Both wore the native clothing of the region, a form of nomad garb worn despite their settled existence. Khari and her companion's outfits were loose wool trousers tucked into low-heeled leather boots. A matching wool high-necked smock, over which was fitted a long tunic in a heavier material was split up the sides and held in place by an ornate wide leather belt. This was intricately worked with coloured beads and quills, all in bright dyed colours, a rainbow variety of hues in red, green and yellow. Their leather belts and the tops of their long boots were intricately worked with more finely woven decoration.

Deret spat with displeasure at their peasant clothing, as gaudy as any travelling circus, all of which he'd banned back home. The people's struggle for equality would never be achieved while such showy and divisive individuality was permitted. In the new Svolenia, there was to be fairness to all. No matter what your age or background; everyone was equal. Everyone wore the same shade of grey.

Although the young women wore the same style of garb, the physical contrast between them was startling. The native born woman was short, her long raven hair worn in a thick braid down her back, her clear skin light gold, her black, almond eyes and high cheekbones were indicative of her ancient steppe nomad ancestry. She was most likely of the Dholma race who once roamed throughout the Upper Balkans. The old history student Deret would once have found her fascinating. Now since his enlightenment, she symbolised a stubborn race who deliberately shunned progress. Such people could not be allowed to stop the glorious revolution.

Khari in stark contrast was tall and willowy in build, her porcelain white face framed by a waterfall of blonde hair. She swung a wicker basket, empty of the grooms' suppers that she had brought from the fortress kitchens.

The two young women sang an Isolanni peasant tune, to lighten their anxiety over the strangers. Khari's clear pure notes echoed around the grim old stones with a haunting resonance. Her companion sang in the ancient nomad way, an eerie primeval sound, yet stunningly beautiful. Its direct connection with an ancient past was visceral and touched Deret's spine with an electric vibrancy. The new order would ban such backward, primitive music. Already it had destroyed the country's many monasteries and with them, the monks' chants were lost. Banning old folk songs in Svolenia was harder but the people would prevail.

The women paused. Khari tried to copy her companion's singing style but failed, reducing them both to tears of helpless laughter.

"It's no use, Deema. I sound like a twittering sparrow and you sing like a bijol songbird serenading the birth of spring."

Deret walked towards the women, and watched with satisfaction as their innocent laughter ended abruptly at his approach. He addressed them in Svolenian, "In my appraisal, it would be impossible for you to sing like some primitive heathen."

Khari stared at the unwelcome invader with the full force of her golden eyes, interpreting unpleasant impressions of a mind in turmoil, a roiling confusion of futile anger and disappointed bitterness. She pulled away from his mind, his thoughts felt tainted, leaving behind a foul, contaminating aftertaste in her own mind.

"I don't know how you ended up living in this forsaken place but you do not belong here. I perceive Svolenia to be your true home. Perhaps your master wanted a little blonde ornament? I hope he doesn't get bored with his foreign plaything."

Deret watched with a satisfied smirk as Khari's happy expression turned to dismay and confusion. Deema pulled at Khari's sleeve. She only spoke her native tongue and did not understand what this grey uniformed, rude stranger was saying. "Let's get away from this horrible man. The Dark Lord will soon have his throat and we will be safe again," she urged, tugging harder at Khari's sleeve.

Khari nodded assent and hurried off into the sanctuary of the keep, holding tight to Ileni's daughter-in-law. Irrationally, Khari suddenly feared even Deema's unborn baby could be poisoned by the outsider's unwholesome presence.

She ran to her room and lay on the thick soft sheepskin bedspread, but its cosy warmth gave her no familiar comfort. These unwelcome strangers were challenging everything she understood and accepted; particularly the ugly, grey-clad one. She never felt any different from the people she had lived happily alongside and had taken her paleness and blonde hair as being of no more significance than the wide range of hues among the compound hens. In her world there were two types of being –humans and Dark Kind, nothing more mattered.

Deema's remarks about the Jendar sent Khari into more unease. She had known for a long time the truth of the Prince's existence, but it had been a somehow abstract concept, one she accepted without question. For the first time, she felt confronted by the brutal reality of Azrar's nature. She knew he would kill Deret. But this was not some anonymous, unseen, victim in the darkness but a man she had spoken to and offered food to. A man with future plans, hopes and dreams; perhaps with a loving family waiting for him? And what of the other stranger? Parrish had made an effort to befriend her in the stables. His thoughts were foreign and unreadable yet held no malice, even towards Jendar Azrar.

Horrible images crowded her mind, of the pleasant young American held in Azrar's strong grip, screaming in terror before his throat was savagely torn open by the Prince's fangs. Suddenly it all became too much for Khari and she fled to find Ileni. Blinded by tears, Khari ran until she reached the kitchen complex. In her distress, the stronghold's human haven had lost its warm heart. The normal cosy atmosphere, spice scented floors and walls seemed a thin veneer as brittle as ice.

"Child, whatever is the matter?" Ileni ran to comfort the distraught girl, shocked by her great anxiety. Khari pulled away brusquely, fixing the older woman with the full power of her golden eyes.

"Is it true, am I just some foreign brat brought here for the Jendar's personal amusement? Remember Ileni, I know if you are lying."

Ileni's eyes clouded with tears of compassion for her adopted child but at the same time, she was also furious. "I don't know what foul rubbish those Svolenian curs are telling you. The truth has never been hidden from you. It simply wasn't important. You are loved by Sandor and I, nothing else matters. Your home is here, safe in the keep. You are our little Princess."

"But I am not an Isolanni."

Ileni returned to supervising the kitchen, this was her domain and nothing, not even interfering foreigners, was going to wreck her routine. She turned to state adamantly, "Not by blood, no, but you are by the command and wishes of the Dark Lord himself. That makes you very special. You are his ward. No human of any blood, foreign or native-born has ever been so honoured."

"Their leader says I'm just the plaything of the Jendar. To be discarded when of no further use to him."

Slamming down a heavy iron pan onto the wooden table, Ileni's blood and anger rose. Khari shrank back; she had never seen the woman so furious. "That creature is pure poison! A snake! He needs stamping on like a vile, filthy worm." She took a deep breath, calming herself. "Khari, you have lived to thirteen summers now, cherished by us all for every one them. You tell me. In his own stern, Dark Kind way, has the Jendar ever shown anything but respect for you?"

"How can he? He is not human. He is a vampire. A blood drinking killer."

Ileni shuddered at the foul term of abuse coming from the girl's lips. Where had she learnt such an insult? Certainly not from any Pact respecting Isolanni!

"Never use that word, ever! Not while you live in Isolann. Jendar Azrar is Dark Kind. He is our lord and our protector. "

Khari's confusion made whirling wordless thoughts, swamping her brain. "Why am I here? Is it because I can see into men's minds, an especially useful tool for a non human ruler?" She had to know.

Ileni sat the girl down in front of the range and brought two large stoneware beakers of hot berry tea. Ileni sipped her drink then began to talk. It was a story she should have told Khari years ago.

"I will never forget the night of the great ice storm, a night when gale driven shards of sharp ice tore down from the mountains. I shivered with fear, all alone in a cave shelter as the winds howled like tormented souls escaping from Hell, my refuge clawed by their icy talons. Come next morning it was calm and clear. I will never forget the colour of the sky, a deep, washed blue. I wrapped myself in my warmest shawl and walked to the forest edge to harvest the unexpected gift of wind torn branches. They would set me well for several days.

"I found a tiny Svolenian child wandering alone, abandoned to die by frightened peasants."

Ileni paused, shook her head, her heart still torn with pity at the sight of the poor, pathetic little child.

"I realised straight away that your gift must have terrified your own people. What else could drive them to travel deep into a strange, foreign land, to the edge of a forest they knew to be full of wild dangerous beasts — and much worse. How could you ever be safe again?"

"It had been centuries since any of our people were born with the *Knowing*. So many years that I feared my own people also might react badly too towards you, so I took you to the Jendar. I knew the Dark Lord would protect you and he has, without question, for every minute of these past years."

Ileni leant forward and took the girls hands in hers, holding them tightly. "I must admit to you, at first the Prince refused to take in a human child to dwell in the inner keep, saying you must live with me in the outer compound. But you woke up in my arms and toddled over to him, taking his ice-cold hand in yours, gazing up at him with those amazing golden eyes, totally without fear. I remember the look of astonishment across his fierce Dark Kind face. Somehow I found the courage to say; 'It seems the decision has been made, my Lord and for once, not by you." Ileni paused before continuing.

"Now listen to me, Khari my child. This is really important, so heed my words well, both with your heart and your mind. Dark Kind do not feel the same emotions as us, in their world, we exist merely to be used by them, as we use horses and goats. The Dark Lord could have had us thrown back into the forest, he could have had us killed. Instead he swept you up into his arms and carried you into the inner keep, into his household and perhaps, miraculously, found a place for you in his cold, black heart."

Khari dropped her head and wept, this time with relief. Ileni's words confirmed her greatest wish, that in his way Azrar could love her. Now, the threat from the strangers seemed less fearful. As she had always known, the Prince would protect her.

Chapter Eighteen

Azrar's Stronghold, Isolann, 1929

It was time. Deret's days of frustration waiting impotently outside the artificial mountain were over as the doors to the inner keep creaked slowly open. Beyond them, a small band of Isolanni men, all bristling with swords and spears. Deret, heartily sick of the wasted time of infuriating waiting, brushed past them brusquely and marched into the keep.

Parrish hung back, suddenly reluctant to enter the bizarre stronghold by night. He'd enjoyed his pleasant interlude talking to the strange, young girl. This was different, he sensed only bad things awaited them inside this keep. Only hours before, his curiosity about the stronghold and its mysterious master threatened to overwhelm him, now the thought of turning around and going home held the most appeal. Parrish was no coward but nor was he a reckless fool either. A malevolent presence dwelt within this place, one he was in no hurry to meet. But Parrish could think of no sane argument against going in, anything he said would make him seem a lunatic. Against the judgement of all his senses, and with an icy sensation of growing unease, Parrish took a deep breath and followed Deret inside.

Their silent escort took them through a winding maze of high vaulted corridors lit by flickering torches. The corridors, though full of shadows, were immaculately clean with no sign of cobwebs or the cumulated dust of ages past. Their construction was mind-boggling to Parrish. The keep's outside walls were rough-hewn, inside the walls were smooth and seamless with no sign of any joins. How could this be done? And by whom? Parrish's mind raced as their footsteps seemed muted despite walking on smooth but not slippery granite flagstones, another sign of the skill of the unknown ancient craftsmen?

They were taken to a huge, high vaulted hall and were left there alone. On one side, a comforting fire burned in a hearth, large enough to hold a large section of beech tree trunk. The light from the crackling flames lit the walls, displaying the most extraordinary collection of armour and weapons. Parrish wandered down the hall, fascinated, marvelling at the array of broadswords, all intricately worked, some inlaid with black gems; shields were decorated with the black wolf symbol. Ferocious looking helms in the form of black metal wolf skulls and horse armour were as finely fashioned and decorated.

The girl in the courtyard had told him the term Jendar meant warlord. This hall was certainly a monument to warfare at its most brutal and barbaric despite the undoubted beauty and skill in the design of the weaponry.

Set before the hearth, a long table was laid with solid gold tableware, already brimming with a spicy scented, plum coloured wine. As for the food, generous slices of roast venison, honeyed ham, fine-grained white bread and fresh cheeses lay on golden platters. Fresh, perfect fruit and nuts, a selection of small golden plums, figs, rosy apples, plump almonds and hazelnuts sat beautifully displayed in golden bowls. A repast fit for a king.

An Isolanni woman walked briskly in, her feelings for the unwelcome visitors evident in the scorn in her black almond eyes. A huge Slavic giant followed her, bearing the last component of the feast – a hot sweet pie, scented with honey and cinnamon that made Parrish's empty stomach cramp painfully with craving. The sight and smell of such sumptuous fare made him feel the effects of every long miserable month travelling constantly hungry, surviving on dry, poor quality rations.

"The Prince bids you enjoy the hospitality of the keep."

Deret fixed the big man with a contemptuous sneer, yet another Svolenian in the servitude of this foreign overlord. "I will not partake in all this luxury while the peasants who slaved to produce it are starving in poverty."

Confused by the stranger's diatribe, the big man shrugged and stepped back to stand protectively beside the smaller, dark woman. Parrish felt a growing sense of entrapment. For all its echoing vastness, the great hall felt claustrophobic yet also curiously incomplete. As if there was a vital missing component needed to give it purpose. He dreaded finding out what was the missing link of this bizarre puzzle. The sight of the servants glancing up to a imposing stone stairway made Parrish groan in dismay. Their eyes glowed with pride as they looked to watch a figure descend into the hall.

The nightmare now began in earnest. The blaze from the hearth lost all warmth, as if a wind from the snow topped mountains had swept down, filling the hall with ice. The black clad form swept down the stairs with a silent, prowling gait; it appeared to be a sternly handsome, surprisingly young man wearing a dramatic cloak of heavy brocade that fell behind him in a long black train. As he neared, all superficial resemblance to humanity disappeared. He had a sharp planed, marble white face framed by straight, waist length jet hair. But his eyes –the eyes drove the modern world of science and reason from their minds. All emerald fire, with no white, a cold, fierce, relentless gaze burning through the visitors with undisguised menace and behind the eyes, a predatory sharp intelligence.

Parrish felt his sanity slipping into another dimension, a safer place, hidden away from the relentless gaze of those inhuman eyes. His short lifetime's work surrounded him in ancient tales of wonder, full of fabled creatures and mythical monsters. This was harsh reality. All other sensations, the coldness of the stone floors, the once welcome warmth of the great blazing hearth, the gleam of gold on the table, all faded into insignificance and meaningless distraction. His entire focus was on the Prince, his ice waves of raw power, the sharp-boned features and the terrible yet beautiful eyes glittering with opalescent flames.

Parrish felt his mouth dry to parchment with fear but he could not swallow, dared not take a breath, even blink in case those searing eyes turned to focus fully on him. Instinctively Parrish knew this creature felt no pity, no compassion, but was spawned in Hell with one purpose – to kill.

In bizarre contrast, if Deret was fully aware their host was not human, he did not show any sign of such awareness. Perhaps the protective wall of self-deluded madness or perhaps the denial of reality went deeper within him.

The Prince held out his hand and the blonde girl appeared from the shadows to stand by his side, her golden eyes glancing up at his face with obvious adoration. At her side loped the wolf, her hand reaching down to rest protectively on its neck, her fingers entwined into its thick brindled fur. Gone were the colourful peasant clothes she'd worn in the afternoon. In their place, a floor sweeping, flowing robe of jade silk, a gold voile shawl patterned with gold leaves and sprinkled with tiny diamonds draped gracefully over her narrow shoulders. Around her neck gleamed strands of fine golden chain also set with diamonds. In her hair, a filigree head-dress, each delicate golden leaf studded with diamonds cut to represent drops of dew.

Deret gazed at her in wonder, not at her beauty but at the opulence of her jewellery. He had found evidence of something worth liberating from this stone mausoleum. He was no longer thinking of the servants.

"You have met my ward Khari already," Azrar said. "Join her and the most senior members of my household for supper. You would not insult Ileni's hospitality and hard work letting such fare go to waste?"

The Prince's voice chilled their blood with its strange timbre, a rich, deep velvet sound with a harsh, growling undertone. He spoke their language fluently but with a curious accent. Parrish could tell it was not Isolanni but nor could he identify it. He had the curious thought that if a wolf could learn to speak in a human voice it would sound similar to the Prince.

Everyone sat themselves at the table with the Jendar at the head, except Deret, who remained standing apart, his arms folded, his expression disdainful. The American, Parrish, grew more afraid, not just of their eldritch host but of the sheer suicidal folly of Deret's rudeness.

To soften the impact of the Svolenian's hostility, Parrish hesitantly took a portion of meat onto a plate, glad of the distraction of the delicious food. If he could concentrate on that, maybe he could stop shaking. Relieved to be sitting next to Khari, her gentle smile of welcome also helped him forget he was in the company of something not of this world. He tried his best to ignore the Prince, who sat in chill stillness, his back warrior-straight yet relaxed. No cutlery or dishes had been set for him, although he raised a goblet of wine in what appeared to be a salute to Parrish, acknowledging his courage.

Deret steadfastly continued his act of contempt; ignoring an offered goblet of wine from the big dull-eyed Slav, he fixed the Prince with a glare of scorn. "The world beyond your walls is being purified, scorched with the cleansing flames of revolution. Your reign is over, Azrar. Prepare to feel the heat of the approaching inferno." The words spilled out, arrogance and hate filled into the room. Parrish paused, unable to swallow his food. His hands began to shake again, as horrified, he realised this behaviour from Deret was beyond suicidal. Deret would condemn them both with his runaway mouth and blinkered insolence bordering on insanity.

The Prince stood up and with his silent, prowling gait walked to a nearby wall and removed a huge broadsword from the impressive array of weaponry. He held it lightly, manoeuvring the massive unwieldy weapon with ease and a coiled muscular tension that was tempered with grace.

"This blade has run red with the blood of many would-be invaders." The Prince seemed lost in a world of his own as the firelight flashed off the blade's sharp edge. He whirled it around him, in a deadly dance celebrating the conflict of its form. It was an object of both death and beauty; an exquisite work of art and a vicious weapon. The air whirred at the speed of its passing, its weight vanished with the Prince's great skill. Whatever else he was, the term Jendar-Warlord, could not be more apt.

The Prince and sword are one, Parrish realised, the thought almost rising to his mouth as spoken words. Like the weapon, Azrar was also outwardly beautiful, yet Parrish knew that this was a highly dangerous creature. He pushed away the word 'vampire' as if thinking it would make it a reality. But the word persisted in his mind and would not go away.

"You come to my stronghold uninvited and though I offer you hospitality, you threaten me. Should a commander not put the welfare of his men above all else? You are a long way from home, Comrade Deret." The Prince's tone was pure menace, the warning snarl of a predator with its prey in sight. With a leaden feeling of inevitability, Parrish realised Deret and his Svolenian troopers would not leave Isolann alive. He had never felt such fear coursing through him in a paralysing wave.

"If any harm comes to us, Azrar," Deret countered, "You will bring the vengeance of the People's Army to flatten your principality. You will be swept away, like a piece of worthless rubbish from the gutter."

The Jendar reverently replaced the broadsword back onto its place. His voice was calm, but the velvet had gone leaving a steely growl, resonating with malevolent power. "Your threats are laughable, little man in grey. My people and I have kept the most powerful armies of the entire world from my lands for millennia. Isolann has never been conquered nor ever will be."

"You mean your ancestors and their people?" corrected Deret with a sneer. For all his pride, the prince was still just the deluded ruler of a scattered race of goat herders.

Azrar smiled for the first time, a cold gesture deliberately displaying a hint of his deadly, curving fangs. Parrish felt his whole being shudder with apprehension and terror.

"No, it was I, Azrar, Jendar of Isolann, High Prince of the Three Kingdoms."

And Parrish knew for sure he was going to die. Soon. Very soon.

Deret had already come to the same conclusion. Far from being deluded, his mind had sought to control the desire to scream at his first sight of the Jendar. Only a deep reserve of bravado and natural arrogance kept him from turning to flee the keep in terror. If at any point he admitted to himself the obvious, that the Prince was some sort of preternatural being, Deret would open a trap door and fall to madness, a plunge so deep he may never crawl back from its depths.

Mesmerised, like a rabbit transfixed before a snake, he stared at the Prince, whose marble-pale face caught no light or warmth from fire or candlelight. His eyes glowered with an inner light and his whole being emanated a power making the air around him feel charged with static electricity.

Deret tried to remain in control, consciously remoulding his fear to anger. With a mad logic of his own, he decided even if Azrar was not a human, he was still contemptible aristocracy. His mission had not changed, he was still here to shatter the centuries old complacency of the ruling class, to destroy forever this lord's stranglehold over his domain. How could this Prince of Isolann be so defiant, living in this decaying mausoleum with little more than a peasant woman, an idiot and a child for company, guarded by a handful of peasants armed with spears?

"I cannot understand your complacency, Azrar. All this is finished now." Deret pointed to the great hall in a dismissive gesture. "Your lands and keep are now under the ownership of the Svolenian People. All the wolf-ridden forests in the world cannot protect you."

His attempts at intimidation did nothing to disturb the Jendar's poise, although his emerald eyes momentarily darkened. He signalled for his guard to conclude the audience by escorting the visitors out of the keep.

"You must leave at first light. Keep your men close to your camp, my forests are not safe at night."

"Is that a threat?"

Azrar gave a slight shrug of indifference. "I have no need to make threats."

Deret and Parrish walked towards the guard but stopped when the Prince spoke again.

"Professor Parrish, you are to remain a while longer. My ward is eager to learn about your homeland of America."

To Deret's fury, Parrish made no protest, staying behind, eyes cast down unable to meet his, as the Svolenian was ignominiously dismissed and escorted away. The meal concluded, the household retinue retired leaving Parrish alone with the Prince. The American was still ill at ease, though the atmosphere had become less fraught after

Deret's dismissal. The creature made no threatening moves, but sat in his high back stone chair relaxed with the curious stillness of his kind.

Finally Azrar said, "You are a man of science, I take it you realise I am not human, Professor Parrish?"

Parrish nodded, his stomach churning with fear. Was this it, the prelude to his death? "I researched what little exists of the legend of the Vampire Kings. I know now it was no legend but truth."

"Would you like to learn more?"

Parrish agreed readily, desperate to see a chink of hopeful light in this all-enshrouding darkness.

"Khari needs to learn about this new twentieth century and I want her to learn your language. You may stay here at the keep to be her tutor; in return I will spare your life and answer your questions about the Dark Kind. But if you want to keep your throat intact, you will not betray my trust or ever insult my people again by calling us vampires. We are Dark Kind."

Eagerly Parrish nodded, "I agree, Jendar Azrar. I am deeply grateful for the extraordinary opportunity you offer. But what of the others? What will happen to Deret and his men?"

Azrar gave another slight, indifferent shrug. Parrish knew better than to pressure this deadly creature to give an answer. He tried to rationalise his guilt about the bloodbath that was to come, that Deret and his men were dead the moment they entered the forest. But he could not. If he tried to warn Deret, the fool would probably not listen anyway. Could he keep quiet and live with his conscience?

Unwittingly, Azrar helped his inner turmoil by summoning Sandor to show him to his quarters within the confines of the keep. Perhaps he would never need to see Deret and the troops again. Perhaps he would never know what happened to them. Denial and self-delusion, Parrish concluded to himself, these were not traits reserved for

Deret alone. Damn it! Isolann was an entire society based on one huge act of denial, a collective closing of minds and hearts that had endured unchallenged for millennia.

Even the girl, Khari, was not immune to this miasma of delusion, how else could she look up at this, he could still say the word in his mind–this vampire—with such open adoration?

Chapter Nineteen

Azrar's Stronghold, Isolann, 1929

With the touch of warm sunlight on his cheek, Parrish awoke in his plain but comfortable quarters in Azrar's stronghold. While he slept lost in the deep oblivion of mental and physical exhaustion, servants had opened the wooden shutters and left warm rye bread baked with dried fruit and a jug of fresh milk on the table beside his bed. They also left a big ewer of hot water and clean towels on a mirrored stand. Parrish examined himself in the mirror. No fang marks on his neck. He gave a humourless smile, in the bright light of morning such thoughts seemed fanciful and crazed. He'd obviously read too many lurid horror stories back home, he'd be pinning up wreaths of garlic next!

He took a thick slice of the sweet bread and walked over to the window. He sat on the wide ledge, watching wind-dashed frivolous clouds skim the snow-clad summits of the encircling Arpalathians. The whiteness of snow and clouds contrasted against the black granite of the mountains but did nothing to soften them. Nor did the scattered islands of green life in the deep valleys, gorges carved from the rock by ice and fast tumbling rivers of melted snow. Isolann was a hard land but it had beauty too. Parrish glanced up at raucously cawing ravens, the feathered fingertips of their black wings outstretched, glided on the warm currents. Below in the sun-dappled courtyard, the Isolanni household bustled about.

Parrish could see these people were not bowed by fear and humbled by servitude. They went about their business with their heads held high, the old walls echoing with their laughter and outbursts of merry song. If they had any fear of the Svolenian troops outside their gates, it was not evident in their behaviour. As he watched the Isolanni from his high vantage point for an hour, only one person glanced up at his window high in the keep, a young man who met his gaze with an inscrutable expression, neither hostile or friendly, just mild curiosity. A polite knock on his door announced an unarmed escort of two castle servants, who silently brought him down to the great hall where he was left alone. Though mid-morning, no light from the outside world filtered in. Torches flickered, bouncing warm light over the barbaric splendour of the weaponry hanging from the cliff-like walls. For all its vastness, the hall was warm, with an entire tree trunk blazing in the cavernous stone hearth.

He heard a soft, clicking sound and followed it to its source; it was the young girl who sat cross-legged on a thickly fleeced snow-white sheepskin rug. To his relief, the girl's pet wolf was nowhere to be seen as she studiously tumbled what looked like large pieces of coloured glass onto the floor, rearranging the glittering fragments into pleasing patterns. On closer examination, he was astonished to discover they were real jewels, an emperor's ransom of emeralds, rubies, diamonds and sapphires. She held up a flawless pink diamond, the size of a quail's egg and handed it to Parrish.

"That's one of my favourites. It's so pretty."

Parrish's hand trembled at the weight and perfection of the stone, it was impossible to guess at its value but he knew it would be right off the scale.

"Jendar Azrar says these stones have no worth. I'm sure he won't mind you having some."

The girl swept up the gems into a finely woven gold thread bag and handed them to a dumbfounded Parrish. He did not believe that the warlord of this vast keep had no concept of value. She must have misunderstood his words. He could not accept this gift; this innocent gesture could be a death warrant from a vengeful Dark Lord. Tactfully, he said, "You are very kind but it would be a shame to stop you making such pretty pictures. I would be happier if you kept them."

Khari shrugged, unconcerned. She did not bother to re-probe this stranger's mind for it was full of confusing thoughts and in a language she couldn't understand. But she easily sensed a conflict of emotions; excitement, curiosity and fear.

"It would be a good idea if you kept them out of sight when Comrade Deret is nearby," Parrish suggested. "They are not playthings to him, but objects of great worth. Great enough for him to do something rash."

Khari studiously fixed the young American with her uncanny golden eyes. He seemed kind and she enjoyed talking to him, but she did not like the other one. That one's mind was a black pit of seething hatred. She disliked reaching into that cesspool, but Jendar Azrar wanted to know his intentions towards Isolann and she had to obey her beloved Prince without question, choking back the tears and shivers of revulsion. Khari was almost glad the Svolenian would be dead soon, his hatred and bitterness would then go away on his journey to the world beyond, and perhaps be replaced with peace.

She knew Parrish would probably die soon too and she was much sadder about that. She decided to ask Azrar to spare him, after all, he had readily agreed to let Sandor live at her request.

Parrish shook his head, a slight, agitated movement as if trying to clear it of an odd sensation. He had the most bizarre notion he was not alone in his own mind, that someone else had invaded the most private part of his being. He glanced up at the girl who gazed back in return with her strange gilded eyes, enchanting yet unsettling in their candour. Could she be some sort of mind reader? The thought was frightening; the keep was a dangerous enough place, with its eerie vampire lord within and a fanatic with a small army outside. He tried to force away any negative thoughts, his mind must stay his own.

With a close approximate of a warm smile, he addressed the child.

"Jendar Azrar wants me to teach you my language and about the outside world. Would you like that, Khari?"

The girl nodded with a broad smile, suddenly relieved. Azrar wanted him to live too!

"We could start now. Where do you normally attend your studies?"

Khari took him through a twisting labyrinth of torch lit corridors, designed so that daylight could never penetrate. Parrish marvelled at her ease with so much darkness, dwelling in a shadowed realm that should leave any human child fearful.

As she pushed open ornately carved double wooden doors, Parrish's knees threatened to buckle under him in surprise. The girl had led him to a library, but what a library! A vast, brightly lit amphitheatre of semi-circular rows of stone shelves spread before him. Each shelf was neatly stacked with beautifully preserved ancient tomes and parchment scrolls.

Parrish gasped, speechless with astonishment. This was a sight far beyond his wildest dreams. Before him lay a priceless treasure house of ancient wisdom – of staggering proportions and world-shattering importance. It was unlike any library in existence–at least on this world. No overcrowded dusty bookcases, laden with musty, decaying volumes. No gloomy shadows or claustrophobic aisles. The spacious round room had no windows to the outside but was light and airy, the temperature bone dry, yet fresh and comfortably cool.

The dome's high roof was a wonder of construction. A panorama of brilliant stars glistened against the deepest blue firmament, which had no visible sign of support. Its unfamiliar twinkling constellations appeared to float– as if the roof had been removed, exposing the library to the heavens. But Parrish noted with a gasp of wonder that they were not stars that graced this planet's night sky for there was not one familiar constellation or planet in the moving panorama.

With no sign of any officious human staff, Parrish ran, wide-eyed, laughing in near hysteria along the tiers stacked high with gold bound leather volumes, chests full of papyrus scrolls of mind blowing antiquity. He came across one area with stacks of carved stone and clay tablets from man's earliest times. Parrish became short of breath, his chest tightening with sheer excitement. He could spend a lifetime studying these marvels and only touch a tiny fraction of the treasure, the lost knowledge they contained.

It was all too marvellous and too much for one man to take in. Surely the answers to mankind's most ancient mysteries could lie here! Atlantis. The origin of the Sphinx. Who built Stonehenge and why. Khari and her English lessons were forgotten. Parrish wanted to touch, smell and open and cherish as many ancient volumes as possible, drunk and careless with excitement.

As time passed from minutes to hours, Khari did not like the thoughts pouring from the stranger. His excitement at first was infectious and fun, he was like a small child at his birthing day party. But later his fevered exploration of the library became something else. She sensed unpleasant new feelings, of possessiveness and avarice. As if this library had become his alone now and no one else would be allowed to jeopardise its sanctity, most especially its unearthly owner. Khari left the American alone in the library. He did not notice her leave.

Five days had passed since Azrar allowed one of the strangers, the American scholar to stay in his keep. The man had become obsessed with his library and had not left it. All meals were left uneaten; he appeared not to have slept beyond a few snatched hours slumped over the documents. If this obsession was not checked soon, Azrar believed the Professor would slide into madness, it was apparent he had made a rare error in judgement. Parrish was not an ideal candidate to tutor his ward.

The Prince awoke from Rest to find his military chief, Miho Rann pacing the floor of the great hall, an intelligence report gripped tightly in his hands. On seeing the Prince, Rann stood to attention, controlling his nerves admirably in his sovereign's uncomfortable presence. Azrar also saw Khari sitting at the foot of the stairs, clearly in distress, her head in her hands. He met his commander's eyes.

"Meet me at the Raven Tower battlement."

He turned back to Khari obviously in some sort of emotional turmoil. He held out his hand to her and led her to their favourite place beside the hearth. Azrar sat in the high-backed stone chair and Khari nestled at his feet, wrapping herself with his wolf skin cloak. He waited, patiently in comfortable silence, until she found the courage to speak her troubled thoughts out loud.

"My Lord, I know that you may have to kill these strangers."

"Their fate is in their own hands," he replied evenly. In fact they had already sealed their own doom by entering Isolann bearing arms.

"But if I tell you something bad about one of them, it will be my fault when you kill him."

Azrar gave a low, angry growl. Death came first to anyone causing distress to his household humans, especially his young ward. "Khari, you have a duty to tell me if you have discovered harmful thoughts."

The child nodded her head, tears welled then spilled down her porcelain cheeks. The burden of guilt heavy on such a young heart, a burden no human should bear. The harsh reality of the Pact with its murderous repercussions was the true dark heart of Isolann.

Azrar's Library

Parrish had lost all sense of time; hunger, thirst even the most basic bodily functions pushed aside as he studied volume after volume in Azrar's extraordinary library, not reading, just discovering what forgotten treasures lay patiently sitting out the ages in a monster's lair. One leather-bound tome made him pause. His hand trembled as he touched the pristine vellum pages of a manuscript made by Coptic monks, a mere century after the birth of Christ. It was an undiscovered gospel written by St Matthew... beyond priceless. It was an earth-shattering discovery.

"You approve of my library?"

Azrar's sudden appearance behind him startled Parrish. His heart hammering, Parrish hastily but gently put down the precious volume to steel himself to face the vampire Prince. How had the creature entered without making a sound? As if the books were not enough, Parrish realised at this moment that the Prince himself was an earth-shattering discovery. Living proof of a superior species pre-dating the rise of mankind dwelling on Earth. Parrish bowed his head, not wanting to meet the penetrating cold scrutiny from the vampire's emerald eyes.

Parrish tried to swallow but his throat was dry, as if filled with dust. He could hear his own voice. So feeble, the squeak of timorous prey quaking before its predator as he stammered, "I thought your keep was the eighth wonder of the world, I believe your library is the ninth. I have considered your generous offer. I would be deeply honoured to tutor your ward. If I spent every day of my whole life in this incredible library, it would not be time enough."

"In that, I have the advantage over you. It is ironic, Professor that there is so much of your human history here, yet it holds little interest to my Dark Kind warrior soul."

"Then, with the very greatest respect, why is it here, Prince Azrar?"

The Prince picked up one the old scrolls, glanced at it with a slight shrug of disinterest, then tossed it back onto the granite table where it landed with a loud thump. Parrish's whole being winced at the sound, mind reeling with the possible damage to the priceless document, which he knew was an incredibly early account of the campaigns of Alexander the Great.

"Accumulation of objects such as these books is merely a by-product of my long existence. My passion is for the land and its people –not a collection of dry old tomes and chests full of trinkets."

Parrish was astonished at the Prince's cavalier attitude to the priceless treasures lying about the keep. This murderous vampire had no right to possess this library, it belonged to humanity. It needed a courageous human, a man of destiny to take it, to protect it. Nor must it fall into the destructive hands of Deret and his minions of the philistine glorious revolution. Deret the man who burnt his own university and museum down, who watched with pride as his own people's heritage, a nation's soul, was reduced to ashes.

Parrish felt like a man holding an exquisite, frail spun-glass vase, protecting it from two dangerous, destructive, warring barbarians. The actions of either Deret or the inhuman Prince could destroy treasures beyond any price. Parrish looked across to the vampire warlord, prowling through the library with his almost deliberate careless contempt for its contents, it was obvious in the way Azrar picked up and discarded a priceless pristine ancient text or pushed aside a neat pile of papyrus scrolls. It was a monstrous injustice. He should not have them!

A small, quiet and still rational part of Parrish's mind pondered on the extraordinary state of preservation of every artefact in the Stronghold, from the finely-worked tapestries on many walls to the library itself. Nothing had decayed in this man-made mountain. Man-made. That was wrong surely? No known human technology from the past could have fashioned the smooth, seamless inner walls from black granite. Nor could it have been Azrar's people. They were blood-thirsty savages, wearing the thinnest veneer of borrowed civilisation. But borrowed from whom? His increasingly fevered thoughts hardened Parrish's resolve. This library did not belong to Jendar Azrar and never had. Parrish's opportunity to reach any conclusion was brutally interrupted as the Prince spoke to the American again. "My men will now escort you back to your encampment."

The Prince's words shocked Parrish to the core, he trembled, both aghast and frightened. The thought of returning to Deret was appalling, he must not, could not leave the library or the tenuous sanctuary of the inner keep. Only death lay outside the stronghold. Any hope of survival meant staying under Azrar's protection. He grabbed the back of a nearby chair so hard that his knuckles blanched from blood loss, his legs turned to rubber.

"Surely I can stay, my Lord. I can teach your ward so much of the outside world. We have become friends already."

Jendar Azrar watched the American grow increasingly grey-faced and weak with fear. It was the reaction he expected. Earlier that night, when Khari told the Prince of Parrish's obsession with the library, he knew the American would do anything to stay in the keep and close to these tomes, even betray his Svolenian companions.

"The future is not set in stone, Professor. The presence of these Svolenian outsiders endangers my people. Comrade Deret is an idiot fuelled by dogma not reason. I need your greater sense of reality to diffuse this situation. Only then will I consider your possible place in my household."

Parrish was not insane. There was no point arguing with the Jendar; that would be suicidal. This was a creature whose every command over the centuries was always obeyed. Nor did he want Deret and his men to be victorious against the Isolanni troops and gain access into the inner keep. He shuddered at the thought of the inevitable orgy of violence and destructive looting that would follow, mindless louts rampaging through the corridors, endangering the library. He bowed his head low. "I will do my utmost, Prince Azrar. Just spare me and I will be your most loyal servant."

The warlord swept out without further comment, his departure silent and swift. Though the temperature rose perceptibly once the vampire had gone, Parrish felt his baleful presence everywhere, in every shadow, in every dark corner. Desperation flooded through him as all hope faded, not just the loss of the library; staying in the keep and tutoring the child meant staying alive. If he was given another chance to live here, it would be an ordeal on many levels but he did not care, living in constant fear was a price he could pay.

Parrish did not know how long he had left in the library before the keep guards arrived to escort him back to that damned lunatic, Deret. He made the most of it, slipping as many precious objects as he could into his clothing. If he was compelled to leave Isolann, they would be proof to the outside world that the keep was worth taking from its Dark Kind incumbent by force. He just had to keep away from that unholy child and her chilling gaze.

But deep in his heart, he knew that his life span hung in the balance, the scales weighted heavily against him. All thanks to Khari.

Trembling, Khari watched from the battlements, hiding behind a pillar, her eyes filled with tears of guilt and confusion. What had she done? The American was not a bad man. He was vain and greedy but not evil. He did not share the same hollow blackness of spirit as the leader of the Svolenian expedition.

Khari was distressed and confused. She would never have deliberately set Wolf on a defenceless hind in the forest even knowing that was the animal's natural behaviour. What she had done was far worse; she had set the Dark Lord on a defenceless human. Her tightly clenched hand rose to her mouth in anxiety. What had she done?

Trembling, Khari risked a furtive glimpse, peering down from the battlement onto the courtyard. She watched the

Jendar's troops escorting Parrish out of the safety of the inner keep. Even from her high vantage point, she could feel his terror, his awareness of his fate. It was not too late. Once before she had pleaded for a man's life and succeeded in convincing the Prince to be merciful. She could do it again. Below her, Parrish paused and looked up. Though she was well screened by the parapet, Parrish couldn't possibly see her. Yet his eyes seemed to burn through her soul, a lance of pure hatred.

Chapter Twenty

Svolenian encampment outside Azrar's Stronghold
Isolann, 1929

Every step away from the inner keep felt like a step towards the scaffold for Parrish. His legs had lost their power; fear gripped his heart in a vice-like grip. If this was not enough, leaving the library was a bereavement, torn away from so much beauty and splendour. A treasure that was destined to be his. One thing was certain, he had to find a way into the keep and win back Azrar's goodwill — or escape from the company of the Svolenian troopers before he shared their inevitable fate.

Parrish took his place by the Svolenian campfire, to an uncomfortable, hostile silence, all too aware of the ripple of distaste his reappearance caused among the men. Both troopers on either side of him, men who but days ago, happily shared their rations with him, leapt to their feet and walked away, one turning to spit at Parrish's feet, cursing openly. Parrish rose and helped himself to a tin of muddy and bitter acorn coffee and sought out their leader, who sat on a log with his back ramrod straight, as if impervious to the fear permeating the camp. The growing tension among the men was like a piece of elastic stretched by the minute to breaking point, to be released in violence and bloodshed.

Why had that fanged bastard changed his mind so rapidly? Parrish thought back hard, had he upset the girl in some way? Infuriated by his own stupidity, Parrish admitted to himself that he had neglected her in his excitement at discovering the wondrous library. Was that enough to fuel this banishment, the petulant whim of a spoilt child? Parrish's mind could not help returning to the other conclusion, the completely outlandish one he had tried hard to shake off. It was irrational, just a figment created by his fear and disappointment — the ridiculous belief that Khari could somehow read minds. Yet he could not deny to himself the horrible sensation of not being alone in his own mind had occurred many times in her presence.

If this was true, she would have known his true feelings of loathing for her beloved Azrar, would have discovered how he coveted the library for himself. If this bizarre theory was correct, all hope of escaping Isolann was gone, he was doomed to die by Azrar's raking fangs. What a little witch! He felt violated, his innermost, most private thoughts on open display to a corrupted child raised by a monster to share in his cruelty. Parrish swallowed hard as realisation hit him with the force of a steam train. If he was right about Khari's abilities, he could never go back into the keep, except at the head of a conquering army. This Svolenian rabble were hardly that!

"Fool, you are spilling that coffee, there is hardly any left. And as a Yank, you will be the first to moan about it," interrupted Deret, bemused by the American's pale features and shaking hands. The Svolenian was methodically cleaning his already spotless handgun and laughed with malicious satisfaction as Parrish grimaced at the taste of the foul cold brew. Parrish drank it anyway, seeking any strength and comfort however poor. He watched Deret obsessively polishing the weapon and suspected the man would dismantle and clean the gun many more times that night. Parrish walked over to him but his former friend did not look up but continued the obsessive cleaning. "So you have been booted out already? The high and mighty Yankee professor. You will have to share our fate after all."

Parrish shrugged and shook out the last gritty dregs from his mug onto the ground. "What the Hell are you going to do, Deret? Do you think you can fight every inch of ground back to the border? We must get out of here, tonight. That hellish creature will kill us all."

Deret laughed, the bone-dry, humourless sound of cold wind in an abandoned graveyard. "No chance, Parrish. We can take that keep. Or burn it down."

Parrish snapped. He leapt to his feet and grabbed Deret by the lapels. Around him, some part of his mind still registered the sound of rifles being grabbed and levelled at his head, of shouts of alarm and warning, but he was beyond caring. It would be a mercifully quick death.

"This madness has got to stop, Deret. You will condemn all these good men to their graves. The only slim chance is to negotiate with the Prince. To give him a reason for us to be allowed us to live. Draw up a new treaty confirming Isolann is an independent sovereign state with an inviolate border. Then, armed with that slight protection, we must leave, if it it's not too late."

Deret roughly pushed the American aside and ordered him to be physically restrained. Two of the burliest men grabbed Parrish's arms in a painful grip and shook him to make sure he remained still and quiet. Deret walked up to fix him with a stony glare. "You have a choice, Parrish. If you are here with us again then somehow you have blown your chance to toady up to that green-eyed demon. If you want to see the Land of the Free again, you had better grab a gun and prepare to fight these barbarians."

Parrish shrugged off the troopers restraining arms, perhaps Deret was right, the vampire warlord wanted them all dead, to protect the secrets of his realm. Reality with all its horrors had set in. He was naïve to believe they would be allowed to leave. The Jendar had centuries of old treaties with his neighbours. It was all just dry old paper and vellum in the end. Why should he tolerate the charade of another being drawn up and ignored by Svolenia?

Parrish knew his naiveté was born of desperation. He did not want to die in this blighted forest, or in that baleful stronghold of evil, his throat ripped open by monstrous fangs. Parrish sank to the ground; arms wrapped around himself, rocking backward and forward with a low keening sound of despair. Deret was horrified. The tenuous hold he had on his men's morale could not take this shameful display of open despair. He grabbed hold of Parrish's shoulders and hauled him to his feet, snarling in his ear in English.

"Stop this pathetic self-pity. We must all be strong; this weakness will kill us all."

Deret hauled the man away from the others, it was easy, terror had reduced Parrish to loose-limbed frailty. The Svolenian commander reached into his rucksack and produced a small hip flask of strong brandy. He had brought it untouched from the capital in case of medicinal need among the men. Deret's resolve never to touch alcohol had never wavered, even now. He watched with contempt as the American greedily tipped back the flask and gulped down the strong amber liquid. After a few minutes, his hands began to shake less and a flush of colour returned to his cheeks. Parrish's voice still wavered as he looked up to Deret to say in a quiet, defeated tone, "What exactly are we doing here?"

Deret was relieved to hear the American sounding less panic-struck. It meant one less bullet wasted as he planned to take the wretched foreigner into the trees and shoot him rather then let his spineless whimpering endanger the fragile morale of his troops. A drastic and not ideal solution, they were too outnumbered to lose another man able to fire a rifle. Parrish sat down on the ground heavily, oblivious to the damp, muddy grass beneath him and held his head in his hands. He spoke to Deret in a flat, defeated voice.

"They'll easily pick us off in the forest before we even reach the plains. I was right. The whole journey here, the strangely empty lands, the lack of any challenge from the

Isolanni, it was all an elaborate trap. We are nothing more than fresh blood for that creature."

Deret forced himself to ignore the American's last remark. He had heard enough crazy lectures from Professor Colgramm about some myth of Vampire Kings ruling the entire known world in pre-historic times, an alien race whose remnants still held sway in the Upper Balkans and central Eurasian steppes until the Middle Ages. Madness. He refused to let his mind make a connection with these wild tales and the eerie Prince of Isolann. Centuries of inbreeding gave Azrar those weird eyes; there was no other sane explanation.

Deret helped the man to his feet and took an offered cigarette with a curt nod. American tobacco was one imperialistic luxury he allowed himself, the local stuff stunk of sawdust and goat dung.

"How has it come to this, Gregor?" sighed Parrish. "Remember our university days, carefree carousing at night and an even greater thirst by day —the quest for knowledge and truth."

Deret gave his hollow, sepulchral laugh again. "I found the truth. The days you spoke of were delusion, vainglorious self-aggrandisement posing as intellect. The truth was while we studied in heated halls of privilege, in my case sponsored by an obscenely wealthy church, my people starved in countless thousands. We didn't know, didn't care, it was just nameless, faceless serfs out in the countryside, bled dry by their masters so that when the crops failed with blight there was no reserves to feed them."

"I was sent by the university to fetch some medieval manuscripts from the monastery of St Andrezh in the Hidrazy district. I found starving families waiting outside the locked gates, defeated, hollowed eyed, silently queuing for scraps, while inside the monks prayed to bejewelled and gilded icons, lit by golden candelabra."

Parrish sighed, he had no right to comment. It was not a time to debate ethics, though he believed helping the poor did not mean drastic gestures like melting down a nation's historic heritage to raise revenue. Not when the grain stores of the rich were full to bursting.

"I am sorry, your people have had more then their fair share of hardship."

Deret snorted and pointed up to the towering battlements of Azrar's stronghold. "You see why I have been sent here to scout out this land. Isolann is rich, with fertile plains and thick forests full of timber and game. And a centuries old fortune in gems and treasures in that bastard's keep. Svolenia needs this land to survive."

As Khari approached the Jendar's Vault of Rest, she picked up Sandor's fear and distress before she actually found him. The man she loved as her big brother cowered close to the entrance to the Dark Lord's vault. That in itself was strange, the big man hated being too close to Prince Azrar and would never go there voluntarily. She pushed aside all thoughts of Parrish; calming her brother's distress was the most important thing now.

As Sandor looked up on hearing Khari's approach, she was shocked. His normally weather-tanned face looked bloodless and pale with fear, red circles under his eyes showed he had been crying too.

"I need to tell the Dark Lord that I am loyal, I must tell him I am not like those men beyond the gates."

"Who would doubt it, my brother? The Jendar knows your heart."

Her soothing words, the gentle hug of support and love did not comfort Sandor. "Those horrible soldiers are from my country, from your country. Some of the tribal fighters camped in the compound said we should not be here in the keep close to the Prince, that we might betray him to our own kind."

Khari was furious. She too had felt the growing distrust among many of the human inhabitants of Azrar's keep towards her but had tried to ignore it. Fear fostered such ignorance. She hoped it would go once the Jendar dealt with the Svolenian intruders. But now poor harmless Sandor was distressed by this talk. It made her angry and more than a little frightened too. She had never felt different from the native-born Isolanni until the arrival of these intruders or felt any animosity from the people she'd grown up with either. She took Sandor's hand and gave it a comforting squeeze.

"I will ask the Prince to speak to them tonight. It is just not right, how dare they think we will side with these dangerous strangers! This is our home, the Prince is our lord too!"

Her other hand instinctively went to her wolf amulet, her symbol of belonging, torn with conflicting emotions. The Isolanni lived comfortably with the Pact, it had been part of their lives for a thousand years. Sandor and she were outsiders, adopted and cherished but still not native born. An Isolanni would have no hesitation in leaving the invaders to their fate. Could she?

Chapter Twenty-one

Azrar's Inner Keep, Isolann, 1929

"What do want us to do about the foreigners, my Lord Prince?"

The sun had just set, an early wraith-like mist insinuated down from the mountains, swirling about the stronghold in sinuous strands, softly glowing in a gathering twilight.

Azrar leant against a battlement, statue still, a coiled spring of latent violence as he read the latest intelligence report on their unwelcome visitors. The commander of his small native army waited in patient silence, nervous but respectful of his ruler. Azrar handed back the report with a brusque nod of acknowledgement.

The Prince moved forward in a fluid, power-laced movement to look down beyond the outer compound walls where the light and warmth from the Svolenian camp glowed like a beacon in the darkness. He could hear the crackle of their fires and the uneasy murmuring of the foreign troops. He could smell their growing fear rising, combining with the mist wreathed night air. A delicious, intoxicating smell stoking up his hunger to a dangerous level. He gave a low growl, control was all – curbing back his ferocious nature until the time was right to hunt and kill.

"I will not have any of my people put in danger from these would-be conquerors."

"I do not think they will leave willingly, my Lord. They have taken up a defensive position."

"They won't leave, not with that bull-headed leader. But I will not tolerate a blood bath in my keep. Their weapons will cause terrible destruction to our people. We must get them out, then attack and harry them all the way to the border 'til none remain alive. Not one must return to Svolenia."

"Miho, you must get everybody living close to the forest edge away tonight, take them up to the mountains. You must be quiet and careful leaving the stronghold, if the Svolenians realise what's going on, they will try to stop you."

The commander was alarmed at attempting such a risky move; the heavily armed foreigners had camped in front of the main entrance, the only one used to let mounted troops out of the compound. But he still bowed his head in unquestioning assent.

"We could leave them a hospitable gift, say some kegs of sloe brandy. They will soon be too drunk to move, let alone investigate any disturbance."

"An excellent idea, Miho. Take all you need from the stores. Once all my people are safe, you will return to position our fighters in the forest."

The Prince's ploy began immediately. His troops had to force open an ancient well-hidden gate in the compound wall, situated behind the large stable block. Made of ancient iron and stone, the gate finally yielded with a worryingly loud groan of protest but it was far enough from the barrack area not to alert the Svolenians. The noise was a necessary risk; the gate was vital to their mission's success. A mountain track wound through the forest beyond the gate, just about wide enough for a one led horse at a time, their hooves muffled with heavy sacking.

Azrar in stern silence watched as his elite soldiers prepared to leave. It would not be long now. Once he knew the people dwelling by his forest and its borders were safe, the harrying and slaughter of the enemy would begin. His whole being yearned for that sublime moment, for the pleasure of wielding a sword against his foes and to drink deep of their hot sweet blood.

His reverie was interrupted as his commander bowed low before leaving the stronghold. "This must be very hard for you, my Lord. Isolann has never been invaded before."

Azrar gave a grim, fang-bared smile, fire sparking in his emerald eyes. "Do not concern yourself, my friend. This is not an invasion- a temporary infestation of vermin."

Encouraged by Khari's words, Sandor steeled himself to walk up to the battlements. The dizzying height made his nervous and he gripped the granite on the edge of the parapet so hard his knuckles turned white and bloodless. Down below he could hear the voices of the strangers carried by the wind from their makeshift camp beyond the outer compound.

They spoke a language he had nearly forgotten, a familiar sound that dragged up every unwanted bad memory from his past. They were his own people, they shared the same blood, but he hated and feared them. The voices from the intruders' camp spoke the same language as those that tormented him from his earliest childhood, a life spent victim to cruel mockery and jeering spite. Khari's family was of these same people, the ones that left her to die in the wild woods when she was a helpless infant. Why wasn't the Dark Lord chasing them away with sword and fangs drawn?

What if these men were the first of many, a mighty army of invaders from the south? Sandor wanted to run to the Prince and plead with him to drive these men out, now. Keep this land safe, keep his beloved Khari safe- keep him safe. But he greatly feared the Jendar and the ice fire of his frightening eyes and would never approach him. One thing was certain, though he never found the guts to defend himself, even if the keep fell to the invaders, he would find the courage to protect Ileni and Khari; he would become brave.

Svolenian camp, outside Azrar's Stronghold

A crushing dead weight pressed down, suffocating him, draining his life's breath. He flailed out in panic, fighting for his life.

"Steady, Yank. It's only old Grubal."

Parrish awoke with a start. He was still in the encampment. Unconscious with drink, a trooper had slumped onto him while he slept. Someone roughly pulled the man off Parrish, the drunken man gave a grunt then lay on the ground, lost to alcohol-induced oblivion. Deret approached, fury blanching his normally florid features. "The bastard knew this would happen. He was softening us up. He knows we are a more powerful force than his rabble of nomads."

Deret was livid when the kegs of native-brew spirit arrived the previous night. He detested alcohol and its effect on his men confirmed his abhorrence was correct. He had considered refusing the gift but he didn't need the American to point out how low morale was among the men. Fear was eroding their resolve. Deret knew he trod a narrow line between their sullen subordination and mutiny.

He tried to compromise by rationing the highly potent sweet tasting brew but as the drink flowed, their mood became increasingly aggressive. Helpless, Deret left the fools to drink themselves to a stupor, keeping a lone watch, pistol gripped in his hand through the night.

The stench of stale sweat, urine and vomit was unbearable. Parrish pushed out of the tent and joined Deret outside to find a silent and still world. Behind the compound wall was silence. No sound of chickens scrabbled about the courtyard, no whinnying from hungry horses, nor any cheery bustle of the household about their morning chores. Even the ever-circling ravens had gone.

The morning air was motionless, without the slightest of breezes to stir the first green leaves of autumn.

"What is this?"

Deret reached for his gun. The silence felt more threatening than the previous day's wary watchfulness of the Isolanni. He ordered his men on full alert, furiously hauling the most comatose onto their feet with kicks and blows. Within minutes his sorry looking, malodorous troops were somehow mustered.

"Search every inch of the perimeter. I want answers."

It was the slim, wild chance Parrish had prayed for. While Deret and the troops scattered, Parrish grabbed his pre-prepared bag of biscuits and a water canteen and slipped unseen into the surrounding forest.

An hour later, every report back was the same. The narrow strip of open land surrounding the outer compound appeared deserted. There was only silence with no evidence of any movement of people or sounds of livestock. The drawbridge to the stronghold was resolutely barred shut. It would take high explosives to open it, of which they had none.

"Does this mean the castle is ours –have they run away?"

A ripple of hope and optimism spread through the troops seriously spooked by the deserted stronghold.

"Maybe," Deret replied uneasily. The natives could have realised the futility of standing up against the might of Svolenia and the twentieth century. It was feasible the prospect of taking on modern weaponry was too much for such backward people. Confused, Deret shook his head, anxiously scanning the brooding black mountains that encircled them like a slowly closing fist. Deep in his heart, beneath the protective wall of denial, he knew Jendar Azrar had not survived so long without adding guile to his armoury.

By the end of the morning, the still air became increasingly sultry. The Svolenians returned reluctantly to their camp having found no sign of any Isolanni after a through search of the forest close to the compound. Even Deret was reluctant to take the search up into the mountains. These primitive nomads had the advantage; they knew each tortuous mountain pass, each hiding place, they could virtually melt into the jagged landscape.

He believed to take and hold Azrar's stronghold was to conquer Isolann. To destroy that thing —what the American fancifully called a vampire, would be to possess this land forever.

Adding to the sense of increasing menace from the unknown, the sky darkened to the sullen colour of sour buttermilk. Despite the sticky heat, Deret refused the men permission to remove their uniforms. He accepted the oppressive humid air added to the men's discomfort but he feared any lapse of discipline. It would take so little to break their nerve completely.

By the end of the afternoon, a furious Deret had to admit defeat. The stronghold seemed as impenetrable as the side of a mountain it so closely resembled. It would take a large quantity of high explosives to dislodge the iron and wood gate designed by a genius to fit so tightly against the walls; it was difficult to see the joins with the rock. He ordered his exhausted, hungry men back to the camp as the darkening sky turned from an eerie green to roiling purple-tinged lead.

It was only then he realised the American was missing. No trooper recalled seeing Parrish in their search of the compound. Deret smashed his fist down onto a wooden table, scattering everything on it in a furious tantrum.

"He couldn't have got far, search the woods –you can shoot the cowardly bastard on sight."

A sudden ominous rumble of fast approaching thunder put paid to his plans, the fear and near mutiny in his men's eyes had deepened. The storm was badly timed and with reluctance, Deret had to let the American go – hopefully to his death, torn apart by ravenous wolves.

The night fell early as tumultuous storms rolled up from the south, in a series of battering assaults. Their tents took the brunt of huge, jagged hailstones and rain like high velocity needles of ice. Despite the violent blustering winds, the simple but strong canvas shelters held mainly watertight, taking on the raw power of the storms. They won the battle, keeping the humans sheltering within dry.

The warmth and security of their shelter created new problems for Deret. He wanted patrols out all night, alert for surprise attacks but getting his men to leave the safety of the camp was a dangerous risk to his faltering authority. Lightening strafed the night sky, lighting up the Arpalathians in brief, brilliant flashes. It made the mountains themselves become a new enemy, as they cowered beneath vast implacable giants of primordial malevolence. For centuries, they shut of Isolann from the outside world, and now they trapped Deret's expedition in their stony grip. There was no sanctuary for the foreigners in those harsh fortresses hewn by nature, only for the Isolanni under the black wolf banner of their unearthly leader.

Only when the last storm faded to surly distant rumbles did Deret finally get his first patrol out. It returned two hours later four men short out of twelve. The badly shaken survivors could offer no explanation. The missing men disappeared in silence as if swallowed up by the night itself.

Deret knew who took them. The killing had begun.

Still guilt-ridden, a distraught Khari spent a sleepless night in the warm cave-like kitchens. She needed to be deep in the human heart of the stronghold, far away from her room. It was so full of Dark Kind influences, the glorious bejewelled gowns, the ancient exquisite objects gathered from thousands of years of power and now gifts to a human child from a vampire Prince. Her mind was in such turmoil but there was no comfort to be found below stairs. Ileni and her staff had long retired to bed.

The crashing of the violent storms had been a relief, at least Khari had an excuse for not sleeping. But the real reason was her troubled conscience. She had not risked approaching the Jendar to plead for Parrish's life. Her mind still fought a battle. Did she do what was right? Was it cowardice or wisdom that halted her footsteps to the Prince's vault?

Parrish was doomed to die yet she could not cut off her feelings for the Prince. She loved Azrar with all her being, yet she knew he was in the forest, hunting down the Svolenian troopers. He prowled among the night-clad trees, seeking some poor terrified wretch to tear out his throat. She could no longer distance herself from this slaughter; she had all but signed the young American's death warrant with her report to the Jendar that he could not be trusted. Death had always been an abstract thing for her. She knew how food came on their table; she'd seen plenty of chickens killed for the pot over the years, but she had never known the death of any humans.

Parrish for all his faults was a human like her, a young life full of hope for his future. What right had she to terminate this life by her compliance with the Jendar? Khari sensed this was a difficult enough moral dilemma for an adult choosing to live in Isolann, honouring the Pact. She was still just a child, who knew no other life but that of the keep and the Dark Lord's protection.

She turned as she heard noises behind her; a bleary-eyed Ileni approached with her daughter-in-law, Pana. In the younger woman's arms lay her youngest child, a baby wide-eyed with fright over the crashing storm.

"Here take Shuki for a while Khari, I hear you have a lovely way with the little ones. I will make us all hot sweet milk. The storm devil hasn't finished his rampaging yet."

Khari readily took the child into her arms with a smile, instantly bewitched by the baby's huge almond eyes as black and lustrous as autumn berries.

"You'll be ready for little ones of your own before much longer, my dear. You are lucky –the keep is full of handsome young men. "

Khari flushed pink with embarrassment at Pana's words, but smiled shyly all the same. Recently, she had started noticing some of the better-looking young men visiting the keep for their military training. Ileni saw her response to the younger woman's banter and was relieved. All she wanted for Khari was a safe, ordinary life, for an Isolanni woman that meant a loving husband and large brood of happy children. The Dark Kind Lady, Eshan was right; Khari could never live a normal life sheltered under the black wing of Azrar's sombre influence.

"Hush your nonsense now Pana, the child hasn't even had her first visit by the Moon yet."

As the storm gradually ebbed and the thunder faded over the mountains, Khari could hear the scrape of a horse's hooves on the granite cobbles in the keep's courtyard. To Ileni's dismay, she handed the now peacefully sleeping baby back to her mother and ran up the stairs and out to the compound. The torrential rain had made the flagstones slick and wet, yet Khari stood barefoot, oblivious to the cold. In the darkness of the storm-lashed night, she could not make out Azrar though she heard the distinctive rhythmic beat of his proud high stepping war horse. Then a soot black shape passed her without pausing, the fierce glittering blaze of his emerald eyes showing the hunting had been clearly good for him. Khari felt the electric waves of his renewed energy pass over her, she shivered, frightened at the intensity of the power. He was growing stronger with each kill. As Eshan had prophesied – the Black Wolf was waking –and he was a stranger to her.

Something profound changed within Khari. Her innocence of her childhood ebbed away with each hoof beat fading into the night. She could no longer sit at Azrar's feet, puppy like with adoration. She realised she must still serve him as a human member of his Household but to be no different to Ileni and Sandor. The fantasy of her childhood ended. She was not a beautiful Dark Kind princess but an ordinary human. Even with her *Knowing*; the curse that was called a gift by her adopted people.

This new wisdom came at a price. Her heart was torn, jagged with new pain. Her great and constant love for Azrar could not be extinguished whatever her mind dictated. Her guilt over Parrish's eventual fate was the burden she must accept and bear in return for loving Azrar.

Ileni joined her in the yard and threw a shawl over her pale, slender shoulders and gently brought her back in from the rain. She saw the confusion and distress in the girl's eyes as the Prince rode past. Ileni assumed it was because he rode on without pausing to acknowledge his ward. This was a hard but important lesson for Khari. One that was long overdue. There was no future for a human girl who loved a Dark Kind prince. It was better she realised this now before throwing away her youth and beauty yearning for what could never be.

Khari returned to the kitchen, straight-backed and resolved, her mind already learning to accept the changes to her life triggered by the arrival of the strangers.

At the sound of the Dark Lord's return from his forest hunting ground, Pana had reached beneath her robe and touched her black wolf amulet muttering an ancient invocation.

> *"When the Dark Lord rides out*
> *Our children sleep in peace*
> *That is how it must be.*
> *Keep faith, all children of Isolann*
> *Keep faith all Sons of the Pact*
> *The Dark Lord protects us*
> *He is the Night"*

Khari looked at the sleeping baby, and she found her heart was easier and more at peace with the Pact. The infant was so vulnerable, so innocent. His life meant nothing to the invaders who wanted Isolann for themselves. It meant nothing to the young American who would willingly destroy a peaceful nation just to gain possession of Azrar's library. Minutes ago she considered her ability to look into the hearts of men as a curse. Now she saw it as the Isolanni did, it was a gift, one she could use to help Azrar protect this land and its people. She was not Isolanni born but they had taken her and loved her as one of their own. She would protect them with the same single-minded ferocity of the Jendar.

Chapter Twenty Two

Parrish ran until his lungs burned, stumbling beside the track until he collapsed, vomiting behind a thick bush. He had no choice but to keep close to the main track out of the woods; wandering too far away meant floundering, lost and starving, until death from the wolf packs – or worse. He rested for as long as he dared. Shadowing the only visible track through the forest was exhausting but openly running along it made for a swifter but more reckless progress. He listened with every pause to catch his breath for sounds of pursuit but there was none. His gamble that Deret and his troops were too preoccupied to notice his escape had paid off — so far.

Poor doomed idiots! How could they blindly follow such an obvious madman, a zealot like Deret? They had plenty of opportunity to leave him to his own delusions and flee back to their homeland. In Parrish's mind, they were already dead; it was just a matter of time before that dark creature and his minions finished off the entire expedition. He had done his best and tried to warn them. Ultimately they chose their own fate. Parrish gave them no further thought, not through callousness but to protect his own survival. He was no naïve fool; the chances of getting out of Isolann alive were pitifully slim. With a certain death awaiting from a Svolenian rifle or Azrar's fangs he had no choice, better to gamble that he could fend off hypothermia starvation and wild beasts, than to die in the keep.

How long could he live in this hostile alien land? Water was plentiful, clean and fresh with many icy, snow-melt streams tumbling down from the mountains. He had some sparse basic rations but nothing to help him live off the land with its abundant game, no guns or knives. Nothing to catch fish or gather forest berries. How long could he last on a few hard salt biscuits?

Grabbing his only chance to run away, Parrish had not thought his escape through, not even which direction to head in. Svolenia was surely a non starter, as a wealthy American, he had only survived incarceration as an undesirable before through Deret's dubious, state-sanctioned protection. If he returned to Svolenia, there would be too many awkward questions. Ones he could not answer, such as why was he the only survivor of the expedition? And what had happened to the rest? To the direct north and east was the poverty-stricken, thinly populated country of Amantzk, a possible safe haven. There was one huge drawback –in fact a whole mountain range of huge drawbacks. The vastness of the Arpalathians was as good as a solid, impassable wall for one man on foot. What chance did an ill equipped hunted single enemy stand climbing so many jagged, hostile peaks? None!

To the east was Abhajastan, another thinly populated country, there were still mountains to navigate through, but the range was not so deep in that direction. He opened a water bottle and took a generous swig, it was the one thing he had a plentiful supply of. A stiff brandy would have been more useful as he contemplated the full impact of the colossal, perilous journey he faced to escape with his life. East it had to be.

With an involuntary shudder, Parrish's thoughts returned to the Prince. He deduced Azrar would keep his people up in the mountains, it made the best strategic sense. Once they were all safe, the vampire warlord would come back for the Svolenians. With so many enemies to occupy the demonic Prince, one lone American might just slip away from Isolann unnoticed — with more than a little luck. Parrish was not a religious man, but he prayed now, to every deity he could think of, even the Devil, just in case.

To his surprise, one of them must have been listening, for he made out the rhythmic thud and rumble of an approaching cart.

Taking up a broken branch, he hid behind a dense clump of bristly shrubs as an elderly man drove along the track in a light, two-wheeled farm cart pulled by a shaggy dun steppe pony. The old man looked asleep slumped in his seat, letting the pony take its own time along a well-known route. He did not see or hear Parrish leap up from the track to swing the branch as a club at his head. He was dead before hitting the ground. Just months ago, the idea of killing a defenceless old man would have been a vile, cowardly act, totally repellent to Parrish. Now, survival overrode his conscience as he hastily secured the pony and hauled the body off into the undergrowth, throwing a pile of branches over it after stripping it of the rough-hewn clothing. As an extra precaution, he snatched the wolf amulet from the man's thin neck; Khari said it protected the locals from the wolves. Once he would have rejected this as fanciful, superstitious nonsense, but not in Isolann where the orderly rules of the modern world ceased to exist.

Ignoring the pungent odour of goat, he dressed in the man's nomad clothing and searched the cart. On the floor was the nomad's travelling fare, some small rolls of fresh bread, and a large hunk of dried meat. He stuffed them into his knapsack, nearly delirious with his good fortune. Rummaging around, he found more treasure, a useful long knife and some fat tallow candles. Someone up there or more likely after the old man's murder, someone down below was looking after him! Pulling the man's wide brimmed felt hat low over his face; he turned the pony around and slapped its wide rump with the reins. Happy to be heading home after an unexpectedly short journey, it raised its head and with pricked ears trotted jauntily back along the track. Parrish expected to see mounted Isolanni patrols beyond the forest's perimeter but encountered only one, too distant to be an immediate threat. If they saw him, they gave no sign, no doubt they were firmly focused looking for grey clad Svolenian troopers; a passing peasant was of no interest.

Parrish carried on with the pony and cart for as long as his nerve held, but when it struggled to go off in a different direction – no doubt towards its home, Parrish was forced to try another tactic. Damn the stubborn brute! He shouted curse-laden encouragement and slapped its shaggy rump with the reins in a savage intensity born of desperation, yanking hard on the bit to try to turn it but the pony refused to face away from the direction of its home. In desperation he managed to drive it a couple of feet off the track and jumping to the ground, hurriedly unhitched the pony from the cart where it immediately dropped its head and cropped greedily at the pale thin grass struggling up through the forest floor.

Tempting though it was to abandon it to the wolves, the infuriating stubborn little beast was his best hope of survival. Parrish tied the long driving reins to a tree and let it munch away at the grass. He made sure everything useful was removed from the cart and concentrating all his physical and mental energy into his left shoulder, Parrish pushed the vehicle down a gully. It rolled down through the tangle of trees with an alarmingly thunderous crash until it could not be seen from the track above. Parrish held his breath and paused but nothing was disturbed by the trap's noisy demise except a few indignant squirrels and birds. He then returned to the pony and stripped off most of the driving harness except for the bridle and reins and collar, to which he attached his sack of food. Then, scrambling aboard the pony's thin bony back, he hauled its head towards the direction of the open plains beyond the forest. Unwilling to be parted from its impromptu lunch, the stocky little animal resisted and balked at first but Parrish was too desperate and determined to give in. He reached up and pulled down a long twig of willow as an extra and effective incentive and with his long, strong legs around its yellow barrel, he kicked it hard to canter on towards freedom.

Chapter Twenty Three

Svolenian village of Tubrul, 1929

The first hard frost of autumn turned the heavily rutted track into Tubrul almost impassable as mud changed to rock-hard peaks and deep trenches filled with solid white ice.

At the sound of many approaching horses, the whole village ran out to watch in grim, nervous silence as dark haired, sloe-eyed foreigners entered driving five well-laden drays. An escort of mounted warriors rode beside the carts, the silent men armed with the archaic spears and swords of a forgotten age. Old fashioned weapons maybe but they could still kill.

Their war horses and sturdy draught ponies clouded the morning air, snorting hard with frosty dragon's breath. More steam rose from their sweat dampened sides; their journey had been long over across unforgiving and frozen terrain.

"Put it all in there," ordered the village headman curtly with his burly arms folded, unwilling to speak any more than necessary to these despised visitors. The headman watched with cold dispassion as the Isolanni unloaded the dray carts. All were piled perilously high with food, precious supplies now filling up his largest barn. He noted they had brought many large honey-cured hams, barrels of stored apples and bulging sacks of plump rye grain and barrels of potent berry spirit. He felt his wife tighten her grip on his arm. Her fear of the Isolanni nomads was waning with each muslin wrapped block of bacon fat, each wooden box of mountain honey.

The whole village would eat well this winter, no family would lose members to starvation this year. There may even be enough to spare some of their own produce to give to a desperate village stripped bare by Deret's troops. But not too much. It was unwise to draw attention to this illicit bounty from across the border — or face questions about the hard price they had to pay to receive it.

The headman's wife scurried away, as the last box was unloaded, preferring to help the other villagers store the food. There was a festive air in her barn that morning. That last box and its contents would destroy that wonderful feeling.

Her husband did not have this luxury. The headman stood rock still as the Isolanni commander approached. It was strange to be so close to the enemy, though their two peoples endured centuries of conflict, it seemed more myth than reality now.

Before him was a descendant of a long vanquished race from the steppes of Svolenia, for the blood of the nomadic Dholma ran in this man's veins. A people slaughtered or driven from Svolenia by his own ancestors. If this individual bore a grudge, there was no sign of it now, he held his hand out and shook the headman's hand with a firm grip.

"All you have to do is leave this box where it will be found by your authorities. There is no hurry; next spring will be acceptable. You need not open it."

The headman nodded brusquely. It would certainly be a sop to his conscience if the box remained resolutely sealed. He waited until the Isolanni commander re-mounted his tall, well bred horse and rode away without a backward glance, preparing to lead the teams back to their own country. Once the food was unloaded, the Isolanni drove their draught ponies away in silence, without pausing for rest or refreshment. None was offered or would be given – the old enmity was too deeply ingrained.

While his people were distracted, joyfully inspecting the food delivery, the headman dragged the chest into his home; there was no need for any other of the villagers to be sullied by knowledge of its contents. Checking he was alone, the headman pried open the iron bound wooden chest. With a shaking hand, he delved inside to find the bloodstained effects of thirty young men – none of who would be going home. He sorted through the pitiful tangle, all that was left of so many lives. Warped dog tags, damaged religious medals, scraps of diaries and torn photos, even bits of clothing with name tags intact.

The expedition met its end, weakened, exhausted and riddled with a disease contracted in Isolann. Those that survived the pestilence became lost and disorientated in the deep forests where vicious wolf packs picked them off, till all were killed.

That was the story accompanying the box of pathetic effects. It was a lie, of course. But the people of Isolann were not the only ones to make deals with their resident demon; Tubrul's headman was equally damned. He carefully replaced the items back in the box, sealing it with another leather strap and iron padlock of his own. Damn idiots! They had been warned, he suspected many times, on their foolhardy journey to that hellish land. They had been told only death awaits trespassers in the Land of Secrets and Shadows. The headman was pragmatic, nothing could stop the expedition's fate once they crossed into Isolann, and at least his own people would survive the winter with this wonderful bounty, his payment from the Devil.

PART TWO

Thunder in Spring

Chapter One

Berlin, Germany, 1935

"Damn! Zaard! This is no fun anymore!" Garan muttered to himself as he wiped a smear of fresh blood from his mouth and glanced ruefully at the gash across his arm from an assailant's knife. It had only damaged his clothing but still was too close. He glanced about, the street was empty despite the early hour. The locals had seen the brown shirt gang waiting to ambush him and had disappeared. The stench of fear rose from the streets like festering vapour, 'see no evil and survive' –that was the motto of the citizens of this city now.

This last attack confirmed Garan had more than enough of Berlin and the increasing paranoid violence among its younger inhabitants. Yet again, a gang of brown shirted youths, many little more than mean-eyed boys, had tried to jump him in a side street. The reasons varied, sometimes the sight of his dark glasses, an outward sign of blindness and vulnerability triggered their violent attacks – his perceived disability equated to genetic weakness in the deluded minds of his tormentors. Garan had also been attacked for his non-Aryan dark red hair, his clothing. Surely, they reasoned, only a filthy Jew would own such expensive suits.

The encounters, in back streets and alleyways always ended the same. Garan was too proficient, swift and strong a killer to let any brown shirt escape alive. He had enjoyed the extra frisson of danger at first but was now bored of their assaults; he was the predator, not pimply, pale-faced youths high on power! Even drinking their blood was boring, so much for their arrogant boasts of being the master race; their blood tasted exactly the same as any other human. He should know. Over the centuries he'd drank his fill of blood, sampling from ancient Egyptians, to Persians and Vikings. From Tuscan princes, Chinese warlords, French monks to Parisian male whores. Blood was blood.

But then again… there was his special delight in Andalucian blood, a feisty unique flavour from its genetic blend from three continents. The best blood he had ever tasted came from a gypsy bullfighter from Trianna. Garan recalled the night he watched the matador return in triumph from the corrida, carried high on the shoulders of his cheering aficionados through Seville's narrow streets. Proud, handsome and excited from his victory over three brave and strong fighting bulls, the glow from the many bars flashed reflected fire off his golden suit of lights, spattered with the dark brown gore of the slain bulls. Some primeval instinct made the Spaniard look sharply up to the hotel window where Garan watched his triumphal procession. Their eyes met, briefly, the matador blanched, hastily crossing himself. Had he seen his impending death at the window? Or the devil incarnate in the form of a slim young man?

Garan had taken his time with this kill, keeping his victim alive all night, a courageous, worthy prey who never lost the will to live and fight back, damning him with sinister gypsy curses. As if he cared! Garan enjoyed every minute of the handsome matador's futile defiance, savouring each taste of blood like a pampered cat lapping the finest cream. It was the best he had ever drunk. There would be nothing to compare in this mean-tempered city with its pallid northern Europeans.

Twirling his silver mounted ebony cane, Garan left the pile of brown shirt bodies where they fell in the alleyway, and strolled with relaxed, silent steps through Berlin's streets. He was unbothered if anyone saw him leave the scene of carnage – he didn't care. That night he planned to leave Germany; there was no way this hunter was going to become prey! He had not made his mind up where to go. The rest of Europe was increasingly drab in this century, a worn out, broken down playground. He'd seen it all before, killed in every major city. Only thoughts of exploring the New World excited his imagination, but were still too far for a vampire to travel safely. He headed to his car, time to move on.

As he reached his rakish red Hispano Suiza, the same glamorous vehicle that had tempted the matador to his doom, the temperature fluctuated with an icy breeze. He halted, inhaling the air; he detected a tell-tale familiar scent of a Dark Kind presence ahead of him in the darkness, too far away to identify yet. He hoped it was Jazriel, the impossibly handsome devil would make an excellent killing partner, one brave enough to tackle some high risk, high profile game. These accursed brown shirts were practically throwing themselves onto his fangs. Where was the fun in that? He did not hide his disappointment at seeing Eshan's lilac eyes glowing from the darkness.

"Don't tell me, you are going to give me another lecture. How I must not be a bad boy and single handedly decimate the Nazi Youth movement."

"You can kill as many of the little bastards as you like, just don't get caught," Eshan replied with the ghost of a smile. Garan shrugged, still disappointed. "I'm out of here. You're welcome to this madhouse."

"I must leave too." Eshan's lustrous eyes clouded over. "I have gathered the finest medical and scientific minds in the world for my research project in Austria. And what do these madmen want to do to such brilliant minds?"

Garan faked a wide yawn of boredom, a totally human gesture but appropriate to show his disinterest in Eshan's project to create artificial blood. She ignored him, too angry to stop her diatribe. "If any of my people are not of pure German descent, their lives are in grave peril. Utter madness. It has been difficult but I've got everyone out, and the clinic is safely relocated to Paris."

Garan dipped his head in an insolent mock gesture of respect and began to walk away, turning his head to ask, "Oh, while you are still here, do you know where in the world Jaz is? I feel the need to consort with a real vampire again."

"If you mean Jazriel, last I heard he was still living with Sivaya in Venice."

Garan sighed, foul smelling, damp old Venice was not his idea of a fun city. In fact nowhere was now. As he walked away, prudence dictating putting some distance from the slain brown shirts, Eshan fell into step with him, her voice, pleading, conciliatory,

"I know we have had our differences over the years but I desperately need your help. I heard you had a plane, on an airfield just outside the city. Please, fly me to Isolann. It is really urgent."

Garan raised an eyebrow in amusement, the high and mighty Ha'ali begging a favour from him — the world was truly going crazy.

"I can't see the urgency. That brooding Balkan still won't be in love with you."

Eshan curbed back her anger at his insolence, this was too important to jeopardise by alienating this Dark Kind brat. "I have intelligence that Isolann is in very grave danger. I must go to Azrar now."

"Let me think this through. Going to a cold, primitive backwater still firmly in the Dark Ages where I'm forbidden to kill the locals or flamenco bars with my choice of delicious, dark-eyed Spanish men, their blood hot and fired up from the corrida, no contest. I'm going back to Seville."

Chapter Two

Azrar's Stronghold, Isolann, 1935

A curious stillness hung in the air like an unanswered question. The cloud cover was low, an unbroken featureless blanket, bathing the compound in a silver light. There was a sense of unease and expectancy among the livestock. Even the bolshiest yearling meekly accepted being caught in early from the paddocks and seemed visibly grateful for the soft bark beds and shelter of the winter barns. By the time an eerie early twilight fell, every creature in the outer compound was safe under cover.

As usual, hardworking and resourceful, Ileni, the stronghold's housekeeper, had ensured the keep's readiness for the onset of the brutal winter to come. But thoughts of stored grain and dried meats were furthest from her mind that night. All talk around the compound was of disruptive and violent changes in Svolenia again and with these changes came inevitably the greater threat to Isolann. Damn these outsiders –could they not just leave them alone! Ileni cursed to herself as she supervised the preparation for the night's meals.

Supper around the huge oaken plank table in the main kitchen seemed quieter than usual that night. It was one of many meals being eaten in the stronghold that night. For the past five years, the numbers of humans living permanently in the stronghold had swelled. The doomed Svolenian expedition invasion had finally awoken the Dark Lord from his centuries old isolation. His people awoke too, newly aware of grave dangers beyond their border and their need for their Dark Lord to protect them. Now the keep grew busier by the day with young men living in the refurbished garrison. Some were part of a permanent army, others stayed long enough to learn all the military skills needed to defend their homeland before returning to their tribes. There were also frequent visits from village leaders. Azrar had appointed the ablest to remain with him as aides and administrators.

It was one of these aides, a normally pleasant, garrulous man, who spoke of a darkening of mood throughout Isolann. This sense of foreboding had nothing to do with the first onset of winter but the increasing rumours of grave danger from the outside world. Khari watched the young man, unable to reach through the fear-driven confusion in his mind.

Her own concerns were triggered by the arrival of three messengers from Ha'ali Eshan that day. She scanned their minds but they had no knowledge of what message they had carried from the Austrian/Hungarian border for their mistress; their minds were full of the small fortune they would receive from her on their return.

"Do you know what news those foreigners bring?"

Khari looked up at the Prince's aide with a slight shake of her head. "It's still a mystery to me. But I suspect it will not be good news."

After supper, Khari changed into her favourite gown, a sweeping extravaganza of lushly fern green bariola dusted with tiny silver stars. As she entered the great hall, deeply distracted, the Jendar gestured without looking up from his papers for her to play her spinet. Azrar had imported it from Hungary as a gift for her fourteenth birthday. Khari went to the delicate ancient instrument. She ran slender fingers lovingly over the exquisite fretwork, inlaid with softly gleaming mother of pearl, before settling down to play. She knew the Jendar's moods too well to disturb him with chatter. As the music fluttered like bird flight around the great stone hall, Azrar sat by the roaring hearth fire, his head to one side, resting in one hand, contemplating the contents of the letter from Ha'ali Eshan. There was no hiding the grim set of his finely sculptured jaw or the opal fire in his eyes, a fierce light that gained nothing from the burning logs but was a blaze from within his warrior soul.

Khari played quietly for an hour though decidedly unnerved by the disquiet in the Prince's demeanour. He suddenly dismissed her without saying a word, which added to Khari's sense of growing unease.

Ileni tenderly kissed her charge goodnight, gratefully leaving the clearing up to the many new servants who helped her tend to the needs of the growing number of human inhabitants. Her self appointed role was to supervise the domestic smooth running of the keep, though the Dark Lord wanted her to take life easier and delegate more. She had no time for such idleness. She glanced back at Khari as the girl arose to get changed into different clothes before spending time with the Prince. Khari's life was a strange mix of peasant and princess. Ileni worried constantly about Khari and what the future could hold for such a fey girl with the curse of her mysterious power. So much had changed and the years had flown so swiftly.

Khari was now a beautiful young woman and the keep teemed with people. Ileni hoped for some semblance of safe, normal life for the girl she adored and raised as her own daughter. She surreptitiously vetted all the handsome young men who passed through the keep as they prepared to defend their homeland ...perhaps one of these could capture Khari's heart and make her his wife.

A normal life, with children of her own, that was what Ileni desperately wanted for Khari. But she could see how Khari's wondrous golden eyes would shine at even the mention of Azrar's name. Khari loved him, there was no denying that. It was a dangerous, foolish, hopeless love that could only break her heart. Azrar was always as gentle as his fierce Dark Kind warlord heart could be towards Khari.

But Ileni was not naive despite her simple nomad background. She knew he kept Khari close because he wanted her special ability to give him an advantage over humans. But he could never love her, never give her the affection and comfort she deserved.

    Khari awoke to a world of near silence without the everyday sounds of early morning bustle; a pale blue crystalline light bathed her room. She threw a brindled grey fox fur cloak across her shoulders and threw open the heavy drapes across her window. The first winter snows had fallen during the night transforming the keep and the surrounding forest with dazzling white magic. The sky was a rich cobalt blue and cloudless, the early sun creating a billion tiny diamonds across the soft, thick new snow.

    It didn't matter how many times she saw the first snow of winter it always delighted her, filling her soul with a childlike thrill of sheer pleasure. Khari knew all too well the Isolann winter would not always be so benignly beautiful, such glorious gentle days were to be savoured to the full. After helping the others with the daily chores, she dressed for winter riding in sheepskin and fur. She ran, savouring the crunch with each step to the stables to saddle up her new stallion. The splendid beast, still in his youthful coat of iron grey greeted his snow-clad world with loud snorts of mock fear and excitement. With his tail high like a flag, he spun and skitted, circling at rein length around a laughing Khari untll exasperation forced her to reprimand him. Even then it took help from Sandor and a groom to still the horse long enough for Khari to spring into the sheepskin covered saddle.

    "Let me send one of the lads out with you, all the war horses will need exercising."

    But Sandor's words were lost to the slender young woman as her stallion kicked up a flurry of loose fluffy snow. She pushed straight on into a brisk canter, risking Azrar's wrath at not warming the horse up by increasing his pace gradually.

The first snow was the best to ride on. It was too soft to be slippery and did not ball up dangerously to hard icy pads in the horses' hooves in the near silence created by the dazzling thick white carpet. But Phuruz, the Prince's military chief and a small party of troopers, cut her ride abruptly short by barring her way.

"Lady Khari, it is imperative you wait for an escort before leaving the keep compound. These are dangerous days for us all. I have sworn an oath on my life to the Dark Lord to protect you."

Khari could hear the sincerity in the stocky man's words but his mind held a different story. In his view she was nothing more than a spoilt Svolenian changeling, an overindulged brat who somehow had bewitched her way into their sovereign's household. Now she rode about on a magnificent stallion as if she was Princess of Isolann instead of some enemy foreigner's unwanted bastard.

Khari stayed calm, her voice reasonable and sweet in tone as she struggled to control the wild whirling of her horse, eager for action and giddily over-fresh with the cold and new snow. It would look very bad to barge even accidentally into these stalwart defenders of the realm with half a ton of trampling horse.

"Captain, I am deeply grateful for your concern, it is comforting to know my welfare is so highly prized. But I have ridden these forests and the foothills beyond since a small child and have never been in any danger."

The captain sighed heavily, again struggling to hide the contempt he held for her. "Those were more fortunate days, my Lady... every Isolanni is preparing to defend our land from a powerful outside force. We cannot take risks with anyone's life, especially not the Jendar's ward."

The man's emphasis on the word 'Isolanni' was an ill-veiled insult, which Khari chose to ignore. Her obvious Slav origin was impossible to disguise but had never been a cause for hostility until now. She was soon to learn why Phuruz was so hostile to the Svolenian people but that morning she shrugged his contempt off, refusing to let anything tarnish the joy of such a beautiful dazzling morning. Until she spoke to Azrar, there was nothing she could do to force this matter and accepted an escort of outriders joining her ride out with good grace.

The raw cold air froze her breath, forcing her to breath through a woollen scarf to protect her lungs, but it was worth the discomfort for the sheer pleasure of the ride, despite not being alone.

As Khari turned the young stallion's head for home, she became aware of other travellers also heading for the keep. All were native Isolanni and no cause for disquiet in themselves but the large number of tribal elders accompanied by young men on the Prince's high spirited war horses was worrying. She crept through their minds and found they had been summoned to an urgent meeting with the Prince. All were very nervous, understandably, about being in the dangerous presence of their Dark Kind ruler and for the still unknown cause of their journey across a winter landscape that could change from benign to lethal in minutes.

Chapter Three

Isolann, Upper Balkans, 1936

Night creatures cowered as the still, cold winter air above the Arpalathians echoed with the monotonous drone of a small aircraft, the first ever to over fly the mountains. Despite the inky darkness of a moonless night, it needed no lights to navigate the snow-bound rugged summits, dipping and rising with insolent ease as it wove through the deeply gouged, jagged valleys.

The biplane flew beyond the mountains, to land on the deep soft snow covering the foothills close to the Jendar's fortress. Shortly after it landed, a small group of Isolanni troops rode from the forest to meet the plane, holding their horses with difficulty as the terrified beasts shied and whirled around. The night air filled with ice dragon's breath, as they snorted with wild-eyed horror at the monstrous invader from the skies.

Inside the plane, Ha'ali Eshan pulled on a dark brown sable, ground sweeping coat then paused, hesitant at the wisdom of this hastily arranged visit. Returning to Isolann and the Jendar's cold indifference to her was never going to be easy. She turned to her pilot as she prepared to disembark.

"This is crazy, Garan. Why don't you come with me to the stronghold?"

The Dark Kind youth shrugged with feigned indifference, his true unease fleetingly evident in his vulpine features. "I haven't exactly been the Prince's favourite subject over the years. As this is literally a flying visit, I'll wait for you in the plane. It's been fitted to protect me from sunlight. I'll be fine."

Eshan sighed; reunion of any Dark Kind survivors was a rare enough event. It seemed inconceivable to her that Garan would not want to savour each precious opportunity. She did not have time to argue. "Just keep your over-used fangs out of the locals. You know damn well they are all protected by an ancient pact with Prince Azrar."

"Cross my heart and hope not to die," Garan replied with a humourless, foxy smile as without a backward glance, Eshan leapt lightly from the plane to take a horse from her escort for the journey to the stronghold.

Eshan pulled the generous collar of her fur coat around her face, glad of its softness and warmth. Snowbound Isolann was in the grip of its usual bleak winter. Who would choose to live in such a brutal place when they could live anywhere on the planet? She rode in silence, once a journey towards Azrar would have filled her with excited anticipation. Now it was just dread of the confrontation to come.

The outer compound was bright and warm with flickering torchlight and large metal braziers blazing. The great gate was down in readiness for her arrival and as her horse clattered across the wooden planks her heart gave a leap at the sight of Azrar waiting on the steps of the inner keep. There was no sign of welcome in his stern expression or in the hard gleam in his eyes. The years apart had clearly not improved the strained relationship between Eshan and the Prince.

Azrar walked down the steps to help her dismount. He kissed her on the lips in the Dark Kind manner but addressed her with frosty civility. It was what she expected, but she still felt the bitter stab of disappointment in her heart.

"How is your ward, Khari? She must be a young woman by now," she asked, desperate to break the bad blood between them.

"You can see for yourself," he replied in a terse growl of impatience. He halted on the steps, unable to contain his volatile nature. "Ha'ali, why are you here again so soon? What matter can be of such great urgency and importance that you risk travelling in winter in that flying contraption?"

Eshan sighed, they had not even reached the great hall and his hostility had already flared up.

"My Lord Azrar, last time I came to you it was with a warning. Now I return on my knees, begging you to save yourself. I say this not just from the love I have always born for you."

He turned away from her with a snarl of impatience, angry enough to lower his fangs. Eshan further risked his wrath by holding his hand. "Azrar, you are the last Jendar, our only warlord Prince. There are changes rippling through human society in Europe, threatening uncertain times for every nation. Unlike the last great human conflict, the next will not pass you by."

She gestured to the lights and sounds coming from the old barracks, all signs of troops living once more in the outer compound. She'd also ridden through the many rows of tents that now surrounded the stronghold.

"I see you have mustered and trained another army. So where are your tanks, warplanes, machine guns and mortars? It's still all just swords, horses, blind courage and hopelessly stubborn pride."

Snatching his hand from hers, Azrar's mood was instantly thunderous, fangs now fully drawn, eyes all black flashed with fire and fury. "How dare you lecture me on warfare, what madness would make you question my leadership of this realm?"

"Not madness, just desperation born of love."

"I have never loved you, Eshan. This is no secret."

Eshan sighed, grateful to see his eyes return to sparkling emerald again. "It makes no difference," she replied, eyes cast down as he walked over to his armoury display with all its barbaric splendour, its uneasy union of beauty of form and deadly purpose. He ran his hand along the handle of an intricately decorated broad sword; the matte black metal inlaid with garnet and amber.

"It is a beautiful weapon, lethally powerful in your hands but it will not be enough to stop the humans. It is time to let Isolann protect itself with modern weapons. You always said the winters alone killed more enemy troops than your armies. I doubt if this holds true now."

With a deceptive, relaxed ease, Azrar picked up the sword as if still savouring the exquisite workmanship of the unknown genius that forged it. Then with a speed and violence that terrified Eshan, he swung it around his head and drove it deep into a heavy oak table, burying the hilt right up to the handle.

"Never! I will never abandon this land. My duty is only over when I am dead. Now leave my presence, you will leave Isolann at next sunset."

Eshan gathered every shred of her dignity to bow low to the Prince and then walk away slowly, her head held high. Azrar's fearsome pride would condemn him and his people to annihilation. But what did she expect? He was a Jendar, created to be haughty and ferocious. It was in his every gene to seek a warrior's death with a sword in his hand. How could she expect Azrar, the Black Wolf of Isolann, to spend his life like a craven commoner, disguising his true form, lurking in shadows hunting human vermin?

Clearly dangerously agitated, a glowering Azrar curtly dismissed his grooms and saddled up his favourite war horse, Caridor, himself. Greatly relieved, the human staff scattered into the shadows, alarmed by the all-black eyes of their master. Azrar led the high-stepping animal out onto a courtyard covered with thick snow. The warlord glanced up at the star scattered clear sky. He was not fooled by the sharply frosty night as his over-fresh horse shied and skittered around on the snow, its breath dragon-like in the bitter cold air. Azrar did not bother to quieten the fractious stallion but leapt in one agile movement to the saddle. He smelt more snow on the way in another few nights. One of Isolann's notorious heavy blizzards, raging storms that could lasting days - even weeks.

Azrar rode out of the stronghold, dismissing his escort of elite guards. He left his fortress not to hunt but to think without distraction. Eshan's unwanted visit had given him an opportunity to act on a plan. A risky strategy that could backfire or bring him greater security. The Jendar cleared the forest and galloped right to the edge of Lake Beral, its vast expanse spread before him milky and sparkling like frozen moonlight. The lake was like so much of Isolann's landscape, deceptive, serene but ultimately deadly. In summer, fed by the swift rivers of melted snow, its smooth, calm surface hid deadly undercurrents and hidden depths. In winter it appeared to freeze hard enough to support the weight of an advancing army, but as many ill-fated would-be invaders found out, the ice could fail catastrophically without warning. Down in the abyss-black, silent depths, the bones of whole armies lay forever lost on the lake's silt bed. Yet again Isolann protected itself.

Now, more invaders threatened the land. Azrar dismounted and holding his stallion's reins in one hand, walked to the edge of the lake, where he could see his unchangingly youthful reflection in the shimmering ice. A human might have fancifully imagined the ghosts of fallen enemy warriors reaching out with spectral fingers, vengeful spectres clawing their way from the icy inky depths. No such thoughts concerned the Jendar.

Instead, he recalled the distant lost nights of glory when King Dezarn ruled vast kingdoms on the steppes of Central

Eurasia and he remembered the remarkable human woman at his side. The first Khari loved the King and gave him her unswerving support and loyalty. But her gift of the *Knowing* was enhanced by her life before marriage as a Dholma crown princess, the daughter of a warrior king. She was born of a tough race, living in a brutal time. A child who learnt survival and fighting skills as soon as she could walk, who had a knife thrust into her hand and given captured enemy warriors to slaughter to practise her skills of killing in self defence.

 Azrar's ward , his Khari, could not have had a more different life, she had a quiet childhood, kept safe and cherished within the sanctuary of his keep; the only brief anxiety coming when Deret and his doomed rabble entered his realm. To be of any use to Azrar, it was imperative she learned the ways of the modern world, she would have to leave Isolann. And this was the great gamble he must face, Khari and the gift that could save his life, may not return. His country had never been a prison to its people, the borders always open to any that wanted to leave. Few did and most of those returned, the Pact still unbroken. To have Khari at his side helping his continued reign, he needed to send her away – with no guarantee she would come back.

Chapter Four

Back in the keep, a sorrowful Eshan prepared to leave Isolann. In her heart, she believed that was the last time she would ever see Azrar alive. A servant disturbed her sad reverie with news the Prince commanded her presence. She hurried down the corridors and across the Great Hall, dutifully answering his summons. No matter how volatile his mood, at least she would be with him again. With a shudder, she saw the broadsword still embedded in the table, as if to remind her of his unswerving strength and resolve. The sound of his deep wolf growl voice made her freeze to stillness.

"There is a matter I wish to resolve before you leave."

Eshan turned to face him and bowed low, openly relieved to see his eyes had returned to imperious emerald fire again, a sign his anger had abated. He escorted her to their throne-like seats before the hearth.

"I have made a decision. Khari is a useful tool to me but she has been far too sheltered living here. When strangers from beyond this region arrive, she cannot interpret their thoughts well, there is too much she cannot understand. I want you to take her with you to Europe. Teach her the ways of modern humans. Only then can I use her full potential."

Eshan was astonished by this command, "What use am I to a young human girl?"

"You make no secret of your unnatural empathy with humans. It saddens me to see a Dark Kind noblewoman betray her heritage and despise her own kind but this pitiful half-life you have chosen is useful for me now."

Eshan bowed her head in assent. She did not have a choice, his duty was to protect his subjects, human and vampire alike; hers was to obey him.

Khari could not remember a more beautiful night. She rode through forest tracks made silent and soft from recent heavy snow. Ice thickly frosted every bare branch, every twig as if encrusted by millions of tiny diamonds. The fullest moon she had ever seen silvered the snowy woodland glades, glowing on a mist entwining through the trees with an ethereal light. The silver light glistened on her horse's mane and her thick, tawny fox fur cloak. For a split second, she looked out for the familiar brindled form of Wolf loping beside her. Khari felt a choking grief rise in her throat, for she desperately missed the presence of her dear Wolf who had recently succumbed to old age.

The moon's light had no magical effect on the Prince, who rode ahead, easily finding his way through the tangled woods and the deep drifts of snow masking hidden dangers from ditches and bone breaking tree roots. It was as if his presence negated light, drawn and lost forever into his inner darkness.

Khari realised with sudden clarity why he favoured matte black metal for his weapons and horse harness; he used nothing that could reflect light, enabling him to blend into the darkness, become a silent shadow. Even deep in his own lands, Azrar was first and foremost a predator.

They came out of the forest at the start of a mountain pass and let their horses have their heads, galloping up the track in ground devouring strides. She glanced across at Azrar and she thought her heart would burst from love. He sat his spirited stallion with consummate skill, relaxed and elegant. His long jet hair streamed behind him and in the open, the moonlight prevailed over him, lighting up the sharp planes of his features. He was a creature of the night, as much part of the shrouded darkness as the moon and the stars.

Their route up the mountain startled a herd of deer that plunged away down the slopes with swift graceful bounds. Azrar's black stallion shied dramatically, plunging and cavorting with loud snorts of mock terror. Nothing the beast could do unbalanced the Prince, who merely smiled indulgently at his horse's antics, eventually calming it with a light caress down its arched, tight muscled neck. Khari reined in her horse, grateful for its docile, easy going temperament.

"There isn't a being alive who can ride as well as you, my Lord," Khari laughed.

"I've had more practise than most," Azrar replied with a slight shrug of Dark Kind amusement, gently easing his horseback as the path grew steeper. They reached a nomad camp and rode through in a clatter of hooves and a billowed cloud of dragon's breath from the horses' nostrils. The tribes people came out, shyly at first, then eager to show their respects to their Prince, they bowed low. The bolder ones cheered and reached out to touch the trailing hem of his wolf fur cloak. Azrar, his face set in a familiar austere demeanour, acknowledged his subjects with respect then rode out of the camp to a nearby high promontory. It gave a remarkable view of the moonlit landscape, silent and serene under its blue shadowed blanket of deep snow.

Azrar paused for some time to gaze across his lands, taking in the distant twinkling lights from other camps high in the surrounding mountains, the black mystery of the forest around his keep and far to the south, the vulnerable border with Svolenia. When he spoke, his tone was grave, as it had been since his renewed contact with Eshan.

"This peace will soon be a memory. More outsiders are on their way to our borders as invaders and destroyers and we will have to fight to survive. I need you, Khari. I need you by my side as the first Khari stood shoulder by shoulder with King Dezarn."

"You know I will do everything in my power to serve you, my Lord." Khari replied with a shiver at the intensity of Azrar's comments.

"There is a mighty storm coming."

The Prince stood up in his stirrups and raised one hand to feel the direction and temperature of the icy night air. "It is coming hard and fast. You must leave here tomorrow night with Ha'ali Eshan." He continued, "She will take you to Europe under her protection and tutelage."

Khari's eyes filled with tears, she tapped her heels against her horse's warm grey sides to halt alongside Azrar's stallion, ignoring its warning half rear and imperious stamp of fury.

Khari somehow found the courage to speak. "You are sending me away from my family, my home – from you?"

Azrar did not look directly at her, but continued to gaze over his lands. He waited for what seemed to Khari a tortuous eternity before replying. "Do you remember when I brought you an injured, abandoned wolf cub? What happened when it recovered and grew to full strength?"

Khari smiled sadly as she remembered Wolf, how he had always stood protectively at her side, gazing up at her with his enigmatic amber eyes.

"I set him free in the woods to be with his own kind."

"After a few months running with his wild family, he decided to return to you. As you will to me."

Azrar waited until his words sank in, that the girl must realise she was not being banished but sent on a temporary mission. "I want you to live in the modern world, learn all its ways." He continued, "Learn from the labyrinth depths of human minds and all their guile. Only then will you be able to fully scan visitors to my realm and advise me with intelligence gathered from their thoughts."

Khari knew there were wondrous things to experience in the wide world beyond Isolann's boundaries. But she had no interest in discovery and adventure. All she wanted, all she needed was here in Isolann, yet she had no choice but to give a brief nod of assent, she was a servant of the Pact, no different from Ileni and the Isolanni who'd welcomed them that night. They turned their horses' heads to descend back down the mountain track to the keep but as they rode through the dark, tangled forest, she wept silently, grateful for the cloaking darkness to hide the sight of her frail human tears.

Khari returned from her ride, throwing her horse's reins at a confused Sandor and ran away to her quarters without speaking to him. It was an unkind thing to do, but she was too wrapped in her own misery to see his eyes blur with tears at her curt behaviour.

Time became an enemy as Khari tried to pack for her unwelcome journey into the unknown. In a desultory manner, she chose some clothes then let them drop to the floor as the shock of Azrar's command set in. She sat on the edge of her bed, her head in her hands, convinced she would die from the weight of this misery, crushing her throat and chest like a vice.

Forcing herself to move, knowing Ileni would chide her for such a weak display of self-pity, she wrapped a heavy fox fur cloak around her shoulders and watched the dawn rise above the mountains from the wide balcony outside her quarters. The first rosy light from the rising sun filtered through the frost-wraith mists but did nothing to soften the harsh outline of the mountains.

There was never a gentle aspect to the Arpalathians. Even the kindest warm spring morning could change with a brutal snowstorm within minutes. Cold, hard and ageless, these black peaks reflected Azrar's nature. Like him, they remained resolute and unswerving, protecting the Isolanni people from enemies beyond in their granite embrace. Like him, they could be deadly but there the comparison ended. Azrar would never harm his people, the mountains took lives indiscriminately with their grim annual toll from rock falls, avalanches and falls caused by ground obscuring mists. Add landslides and hypothermia to the lost and unwary and it was clear how the mountains filled so many graves.

Yet she would miss their constant brooding presence around her. She had never travelled beyond their shadow and the thought of the wide open spaces of the world beyond frightened her. But no fear was as brutal as the tearing pain of leaving her human family. Her only bittersweet consolation was she did not have to leave her childhood companion, dear, loyal old Wolf, she had already said farewell to him.

Her mind filled with Ileni's caressing touch as she arrived at Khari's rooms and she held out her arms to her. Ileni joined her on the ledge and gave her a tight squeeze, "Hush, child. It is not that bad. This is just a short trip away to further your education. I knew one day you would leave the keep; it is the natural way of things." Ileni gave a rueful smile, "Mind you, I was hoping it would be as the bride of some handsome young warrior. Still, no matter, there is plenty of time for that to happen."

Khari sighed, in her heart, Ileni was deeply distressed at the thought of her leave-taking, belying her fears with lightly bantering words. Khari tried to be strong and continued in the same manner, "Who would have me as their wife?! What man would want a woman who could read their every thought, know every hidden emotion?"

"A good, loving honest man with nothing to hide. That is what you deserve for I know there is no badness in your heart."

Khari turned to watch the dawn's magnificence develop, sending long rays through the jagged peaks to flood the snowy valleys with first a pink-hued then a crisp blue light. "I cannot imagine any normal man wanting an aberration like me, you call the *Knowing* a gift, to me it is a curse," she murmured, suddenly sombre.

Ileni addressed her again, this time there was no hiding the sadness in her voice, "My precious child, we native born Isolanni have great darkness inside our souls, because we are heirs to the ancient Pact. It is like a piece of corruption welded permanently to our hearts." Ileni took the girl into her arms and held her tight. "When you return to Isolann, Khari, you must choose your lifetime's mate among our people. Then you will share the same heart and its burden of darkness. But at least beneath the Dark Lord's night shadow, you will be safe."

Ileni helped the girl pack for the rest of the morning, in a strained, uncomfortable near silence. Khari did not need to touch her mind again to know how truly distressed Ileni was at Azrar's decision. For all these happy years since Ileni first found the abandoned Svolenian child, the keep and its non-human master kept Khari safe from the dangers of the outside world. Ileni firmly believed Khari's *Knowing*, her ability to read minds would always endanger her life. What evil doer would allow her to live once he knew she could see deep into his soul, to the truth he tried to hide from the world? Ileni also wanted to protect the child from the corrupting foulness of so many human thoughts –at least until she was mature enough to understand them.

"I will try not to hate the Jendar for doing this," Ileni stated simply, there was no point in hiding such treasonable thoughts from Khari. "But at the moment, I really despise his cold, black heart. If he has a heart at all."

Ileni's strong façade crumbled and Khari held her tightly as they wept openly together; at this moment they were closer than at any other time, truly mother and daughter despite the lack of shared blood. Eventually, Khari, her eyes red rimmed and puffy pulled away. She blew her nose and sighed at the thought of the next tearful farewell, "Umma, does Sandor know yet?"

Ileni stood up and brushed away imaginary fluff from her embroidered tunic. "I'll tell him, you must pack."

Azrar walked down to his vault in a foul temper. If the outside world was encroaching as Eshan had warned, let it come. He would be ready, fangs drawn, sword in hand to greet it. Much red blood would be spilt before his own purple lifeblood would finally enrich the barren soil of Isolann.

Eshan watched him descend into the darkness beneath the keep. Such was the stormy thunder in his eyes, she doubted he would emerge until the next sunset. It was just the opportunity she needed to give Khari an important lesson but it was a dangerous move, it meant entering Azrar's forbidden rooms. Pushing aside any doubts, she sought out the girl and found her in her quarters. Khari sat on her bed, surrounded by hastily discarded clothes, head down, sobbing pitifully.

She seemed too upset to register the approach of the Dark Kind noblewoman and barely raised her head when Eshan announced, "Before we leave, I think it is time I showed you something."

Eshan led the increasingly nervous and hesitant girl down corridors the sun never touched into an area Khari knew she should not enter. "You must swear to absolute secrecy that you will never tell the Dark Lord I took you to into the Jendara's chambers."

Khari nodded a hesitant assent, keeping secrets from Azrar felt deeply wrong and dangerous, yet curiosity had taken over, who was this Jendara? Eshan took her deep into the light-less heart of the Keep. Khari followed as best she could, the Ha'ali's steps were silent, her pace brisk but the girl could hear the swish of her long gown against the cold granite floor and followed the sound.

Eshan halted and lit a torch outside a large black wooden door, the inevitable wolf symbols carved with great beauty, the eyes inlaid with emeralds and rubies. As Eshan hastily lit a torch beside the door, Khari saw her reach into her robe to produce a green crystal rod which grew painfully bright as it touched the ruby and garnet inlaid door handle.

With a deep groan of protest after centuries of disuse, the heavy door slowly opened. Khari and Eshan paused, hesitant whether to enter. Crossing this threshold was more than stepping into a long abandoned room; it was a betrayal of trust to the being they both loved. Khari broke the impasse, "It is only you who thinks this is important enough to risk the Jendar's fury. It must be you who enters first."

Eshan was now growing uncertain of her actions; impetuous acts and rash behaviour were not part of her nature. "I brought you here because I know you are in love with Prince Azrar. I have lost centuries of my life enduring the pain of a hopeless love that will never be returned. Your entire life span is measured in a few swift decades. You must not waste one single day yearning for what you can never have; it is time to see why."

Eshan walked into the room and lit the torches put in place on the walls. Khari marvelled at air still fresh and sweet in a room locked for centuries. Dust free rich brocades and tapestries in unfaded glowing jewel colours in many hues of crimson, purple and gold adorned the walls. In the centre of the room was a large raised dais of Dark Kind Rest, draped with exquisite fabrics and furs. A fabulous gown lay on the bed, a glittering mesh of woven silver, the precious metal thread woven as fine as the softest silk .Beside it was a delicate diadem with long moon rays of thinly beaten platinum, heavily encrusted with thousands of tiny diamonds.

"These beautiful raiments were to be the wedding and coronation robes of Azrar's princess, his Jendara. They were never worn."

Eshan pulled back a gold velvet cloth to reveal a large portrait. Khari gasped at the power of the image –at the cruel beauty of the Dark Kind woman it represented. Dressed in a stylised form of nomad riding clothes, she was painted astride a snow white Arabian stallion, its elegant, fine-boned beauty complimenting the poise of its slender rider. Her face was pale, sharp-boned yet surprisingly delicate for Dark Kind. A wind-tangled mane of thick dark chocolate hair blew around her face and streamed around her shoulders. Adorning her neck she wore an exquisite and extravagant waterfall of rubies, the tear drop stones lay like bright drops of blood against her white throat. The artist, a forgotten human genius who clearly lived long before his time had captured the wildness and arrogance of his subject, her imperious, impetuous nature reflected in her huge, all navy-blue eyes.

"She is beautiful" Khari sighed, overawed by the power of the portrait. Eshan too was transfixed, the old anger, the hurt returned with a force that threatened to overwhelm her. "We must leave. Now," growled Eshan, her voice abrupt from alarm. "This place is accursed."

Khari was puzzled at the sudden urgency and distress in Eshan's tone, the vampire woman could not leave the room quickly enough. "I will tell you all about her and what she did to Azrar but not in this room. I was out of mind to ever open it."

With that, Eshan put out the torches and fled the room, sealing it up again with the crystal rod. They returned to Khari's quarters via the great hall to allow Eshan to pour some strong brandy to steady her shattered nerves. They sat opposite each other by Khari's cosy fire as Eshan, her hands still shaking, took a long draught of brandy to steady her nerves before beginning her tale.

"There have been two important loves in Azrar's life. One was good for him in every way but the other nearly killed him. Her name was Jendara Zian, she was the Dark Kind female in the portrait. Beautiful, alluring but dangerously insane."

Eshan told Khari about the love affair, sparing the girl the most unpleasant details. She told of Azrar's doomed love for Zian, a creature driven by ambition, hungry only for power. When her advances were spurned by a king in Northern India, she set her sights on ensnaring a High Prince —Azrar. It was not a hard hunt, he was besotted with her from first sight. She tormented him for decades, giving just enough of herself to stoke the flames of his desire but never sating them.

"Azrar lost his mind completely over that creature. He loved her beyond all reason; he would have ridden into sunlight or taken a sword through the heart for her. How she revelled in her power, playing with the tempestuous emotions of the most powerful warlord of our kind."

Eshan paused to drink more of the strong wine, these were millennia old memories yet painful. She still bore the open wounds from Azrar's brutal rejection when she tried in vain to warn him about this creature and her wiles. A warning not fuelled by jealousy but from her love and concern. It was then his eyes hardened towards her from mere indifference to scathing contempt.

"Zian knew full well how badly he wanted her and his desire for her to be his Jendara, ruling Isolann at his side." Eshan shuddered, Zian had enjoyed tormenting the Prince too much to give in easily. It went against all Dark Kind nature to play those cruel games. "It was obvious to everyone save Azrar that she was crazy, but he was too bewitched to be told."

Eshan had difficulty recalling the next part of the story, there were things too bloody, too depraved for the tender mind of a human child to endure so she played down the gory details of Zian's doomed adventure. Her overpowering vanity led Zian to become the living demon goddess to a cult of bloodthirsty humans. They worshipped her, bringing her an unlimited supply of victims, many were missionaries of the new religion sweeping Europe from Rome. The High King of the Dark Kind commanded her to stop this folly which endangered all Dark Kind. He was furious with her for the cruel treatment of Azrar and he ordered her to stop tormenting him, to leave her perverse human followers and bond with him, or get out of his life completely.

"In her twisted mind, the choice between being worshipped as a goddess or ruling a gloomy mountain principality as a mere princess was obvious. The demon Goddess remained. The stories of Zian tearing open the throats of Christian missionaries and drinking their blood in front of hundreds of cheering followers created ripples of outrage that soon reached the Christian Roman emperor, who sent out a large vengeful army to stop her."

"Azrar discovered Zian's life was in grave danger. He rode out with the full military might of the Three Kingdoms to rescue her- only to be ordered by the High King to stand down his troops and return to Isolann."

Khari sighed, she could only imagine Azrar's torment. As a Jendar he had to be loyal to his king, yet the woman he loved beyond reason needed his swift moving army to save her life. Eshan continued, "The High King was wise. He loved and valued his black mountain wolf too much to risk Azrar committing treason. He sent a team of Jendars, the only ones able to match Azrar's strength and ferocity and had him bound in stasis where he remained in a long dreamless sleep until Zian and those who killed her were long turned to dust."

"When he was finally revived and released, his grief and rage was terrible to behold. The High King's fears were not in vain. Azrar was desperate to find revenge in spilt blood and to rampage across Europe slaughtering humans indiscriminately. Fortunately, the King in his wisdom had waited until enemy armies from the East besieged Isolann before awakening the ravening black wolf. There was enough human blood for Azrar to spill defending his realm."

"So you see, Khari. There could never be room in his fierce and forever broken heart for me, a Dark Kind noblewoman who has adored him forever. And it is physically impossible for him to love any human. Humans exist only to serve his needs."

To the girl's relief, Ha'ali Eshan left her alone to prepare for departure. Khari needed these last precious moments in her room, surrounded by so many objects precious to her and the many memories they represented. Some were simple things, the well-worn rag doll Ileni made for her, or the carved wooden rocking horse fashioned by Sandor. All objects made with love. Other things were far grander, gifts from the Jendar himself, such as the blue and white porcelain vases from China, the rich tapestries from Italy.

She pondered over what things to take with her, which small, easily portable things to help keep her hopes of a swift return home alive in her heart. One thing needed no decision- the platinum wolf amulet with its sparkling fine-cut emerald eyes; it was something she would never remove from her neck. Another was a simple wood bangle, carved by Sandor for her last birthday. So much love had gone into making the smooth mountain ash bracelet, so many careful hours polishing its surface to mirror smoothness.

Khari walked slowly around her room, caressing each treasured object, as though imprinting the look and feel of each rose-filled vase, each gleaming gem-studded candlestick into a treasure house in her mind.

Khari's eyes caught sight of a glittering mobile that once hung over her bed. Made from precious metals, it was a dazzling, bejewelled array of stars and moons, lazily circling in their own self-contained solar system. Azrar had it fashioned by an Isolanni master craftsman using precious gems from the keep's treasures and hung it above the cot himself. It was all the proof she needed, she was more than an animal to the Prince.

As a last act of farewell to her own private sanctuary, Khari sat on her wide window seat, on thick brocade cushions masking the cold black stone beneath. It was stone hewn from the mighty Arpalathians that loomed above her, encircling the keep like titanic bodyguards, protective and yet sometimes spiteful to their puny charges. The high pitched screel of a hunting night hawk winging across the valley below made her glance up to the heavens, a clear moon filled night gave the stars an overpowering rival to dim their brilliance. It was not a gentle loveliness, but Isolann was still beautiful in its own always harsh, uncompromising way. Khari put on the wooden bangle and gave the wolf amulet a tight squeeze for comfort and strength. It was time to go.

She paused on the top step of the keep entrance and the lump in her throat grew ever larger; she thought her grief would choke the life from her. She reached out to find something solid to steady herself, finding only the cold, black wall. Then she saw Sandor down in the compound. The pain on his face was unbearable. How could she turn her back on her gentle, big brother, how could she leave him? He would never understand she had no choice.

Sandor saw Khari's approach and stood with his head down, gently caressing the long silky forelock of her grey horse, its reins looped tightly in his hands. She dared not reach out to the big man's mind, so strong were the thought waves he projected of abject misery. She did not want to be strong now, but she had to be –for Sandor. She was the young adult, he forever a child. She took the reins from his hand and reached up on her toes to kiss his cheek, "Can you look after my roses and hens, my brother? I will be home soon. I promise."

Sandor began to cry, "Don't go Khari, please don't leave me!"

"You will be fine, Ileni is here to look after you and the Dark Lord will keep bad men from the gates."

Sandor sniffed with abject misery and shook his head, this was a really, really bad dream but he could not wake up and make it go away. His nightmare started when that noisy metal monster flew out of the night-borne clouds and landed near the stronghold. To his relief he was not the only one frightened by this alien thing, the rest of Azrar's household were scared of it too and all it represented. The outside world could no longer be kept at bay if unwelcome visitors could just drop out of the sky carried by monstrous iron birds. Now he learned his beloved sister was to leave him, carried away against her will in that foul-smelling flying machine. Sandor wished the Isolanni had destroyed the thing, put a fire underneath it and purged the land of its contaminating presence. But none did and he was too terrified of the Dark Lord's wrath to do it himself.

His thoughts were interrupted by a clatter of many hooves as the castle guard approached, ready to escort Eshan back to her plane. Khari gave the big man a warm, tight embrace, somehow finding the strength to say goodbye, not for the first time she had to be the strong one, the grown up. "I must go now," she insisted, peeling herself away, with all instincts telling her to stay and comfort him. He looked so lost, so alone, the man fated to live out his life with the eyes and soul of a bewildered child.

"But believe me, Sandor, I will return as soon as I can, nothing will keep me away from you and Umma."

Ileni came down the steps, slowly, anything to delay saying goodbye to her little foundling child, now such a beautiful young woman. She carried a fragrant bundle in her arms, which she insisted on tying to the saddle of Khari's patient grey horse.

"Just a few little things for your journey. Some fresh honey bread, some of Pana's special mountain violet soap; that sort of thing. Nothing much," she added brusquely, fighting back her tears.

"Thank you, Umma. I love you so much…"

Ileni let the weeping girl embrace her before holding her at arms length, "Now listen well, my child. You have enjoyed the safety and protection of the Dark Lord behind this fortress. The outside world is noisy, overcrowded, full of strangers – some will be kindly, others will mean you much harm, all will fear you if they discover about your gift. Do not tell anyone, even a friend, even a lover about your *Knowing*."

Khari nodded assent, they had spoken often about the dangers from other people, frightened and threatened by the *Knowing* and the importance of keeping her abilities secret.

"And stay close always to the Lady Eshan, she is honour bound to protect you. Knowing you have a Dark Kind guardian will help me survive this awful, cruel separation."

Khari kissed the woman she owed her life to and mounted her horse. "I will be home soon, and we will all be together again."

As Khari rode out of the stronghold, she glanced up through her tears at the battlements, looking for the one being who held her heart forever in his dark spell. But of Prince Azrar, there was no sign.

The wind had changed, it whined and moaned through the trees with a malicious biting intensity. Trees that had mutely carried their burden of heavy snow, now dumped their white mantles and clawed at the party of silent riders leaving the sanctuary of the keep. Among them, a forlorn Khari, who rode with her head down through near pitch black glades, too distraught to guide her horse. Thankfully, any danger was averted by the animal's familiarity with the labyrinthal route through the trees and its herd instinct to follow the other horses. They journeyed beyond the tree line into the open plains, where the full bitter power of the gathering storm hit them. Eshan looked up at the sky, still clear with no clouds obscuring the stars. The freshening wind told another story, she knew they would need to get away swiftly ahead of the coming blizzard and hoped both the little plane and its Dark Kind pilot was up to the task.

As the plane came into view, Khari was forced to cling on tightly to the stallion's mane as it swerved and shied away from the twentieth century monster. Nearly falling off forced her to push aside her grief and focus. Azrar had taught her to ride so well; memories of his countless hours spent patiently teaching added to the deep well of sorrow. She looked into the darkness, desperate to catch a last glimpse of a black-clad figure, imperious and aloof astride his war horse but there was nothing except the inky sea of the tree line and the screech of hunting owls through the wind-whipped frosted branches.

Khari dismounted and gave her horse's neck a hug and kissed its grey velvet nose, one more farewell to a treasured friend before handing the reins to one of the outriders. She followed Eshan to the plane, but hesitated, her courage failing. She was nervous of getting in this metal thing; how could such a heavy object get off the ground, let alone fly? She was aware of a slight figure blocking the doorway, leaning against the frame, arms folded. Wrapped in a floor length fox fur coat, the glittering dark violet eyes were unmistakably Dark Kind. Ignoring Khari, he spoke to Eshan in their own language.

"It's a good thing Azrar kicked you out so soon. I'm cold and hungry and really bored. I've had ignorant peasants gawping and poking at my plane day and night. If you hadn't come back tonight, I was going to start ripping out throats."

Eshan brushed past with a low growl of impatience. When Khari tried to get on, the Dark Kind male barred her way with a malevolent smirk that made her shudder. "No fangs, no fly."

"Stop that nonsense. This is the Prince's ward, she is my care now," snarled Eshan, her eyes darkening in fury.

"I don't care. I call the shots on my own plane. I don't carry livestock."

Eshan leapt forward and pinned him by the throat against the side of the plane, her fangs fully drawn, and her eyes now totally black. "This is the last insult I will take from you, commoner. You have no idea how bad life can be if I have you denounced as a pariah. It is the same threat I used to force you to bring me here, one I have no hesitation to use. You think you already live a lonely existence as a Dark Kind survivor? You are so wrong. It will be stepping into a void, a living Hell."

Eshan released her tight grip on Garan's throat and continued, "I am an Ha'ali, therefore I demand respect and also for this girl, Khari, who is under my protection."

Garan nodded curtly with a low growl of grudging assent, "Okay, I'll allow Azrar's little pet to come on board, anything to get me away from this frigid dump."

Eshan studied the human girl who had a steady stream of tears running down her cheeks as she stared out of the biplane's window. Dark Kind could not cry but did not need any outward sign of grief.

What could any human know about the intensity of real emotion? Feelings so powerful they sustained the few remaining Dark Kind to survive centuries of persecution and destruction. Humans could only experience a pale reflection, with their pitifully brief life span, their hearts so fickle and easily swayed.

The small plane flew across the seemingly endless snow-bound bog lands and flat plains of Northern Svolenia, unseen beneath the cover of darkness and cloud. The girl had not spoken throughout the journey but curled up in a tight ball of desolation. Her face was swollen and puffy from crying as she pined for her home in the forests, for her adopted family and for the Dark Lord who ruled her heart.

"If I was a human, we would be about the same age. It's a big world out there, you will love it." Garan made an attempt to draw her out of her gloom. He spoke of the wonderful things she would soon see once they left the Upper Balkans. But he gave up with a shrug of annoyance; Khari was inconsolable, only speaking to Eshan when she had no choice, perhaps in some way blaming the vampire woman for her exile. Eshan knew she had to be patient, this was just a young human after all. She had to take into account that her existence was so frail, so easily destroyed by accident and disease, her natural life span so short, that even a year away from Isolann would seem an eternity. Eshan learnt from bitter experience to temper her emotions with much caution, knowing great joy or unbearable sorrow would stretch on for centuries.

As they traversed the flat lands, overcast and starless, Eshan's mind went back to the first time she saw Azrar. Back to a time when the earth was still a verdant paradise, the unpolluted air pure as sparkling crystal and the only artificial structures on the planet were the towering palaces of the Dark Kind nobility.

Eshan had lived in her own marble palace built by the coastal region below what was now called the Pyrenees. It was a quiet region, very green with a plentiful supply of strong healthy game. She harboured an ambition to make the long and arduous journey over her mountains and across what is now Europe and the Middle East into the sub continent of India, to visit the High King's fabulous palace on the roof of the world.

One year her request was granted and the High King sent a small party of warriors to safely accompany her over the long distance to his domain. The escort was normally a formality made out of respect. Any danger from the small, scattered human tribes was minimal but the passage of time had brought strange changes and there were more and more reports of humans getting bolder, more organised and aggressive towards the Dark Kind.

She could barely contain her excitement when the ornately armoured riders first clattered into the palace courtyard, heralding the start of her adventure.

She swept down to meet them, running ahead of the rest of her equally excited household, her feet barely touching the snowy marble stairs. She watched with her heart pounding with excitement as the lead rider, clad in night-black armour rode a spirited high stepping black stallion across her moon-silvered courtyard. As he removed his helmet crafted in the shape of a stylised wolf skull, Eshan thought her whole being would explode with an overwhelming rush of intense desire. All the Dark Kind were perpetually young and beautiful, but this austere, jet haired nobleman with his imperious green eyes was the most fascinating male she had ever seen.

Now some fifteen thousand years later, the intensity of that first rush of emotion, the hot physical desire that had turned to love, was as strong as ever. What human emotion could compete with that?

Khari in turn was lost in a deep well of misery. She watched through a blur of tears every hated foreign mile leading her further away from home. Azrar's will was absolute, his wisdom unquestionable, but high above the clouds under a cold, star crowded night it was human warmth she most craved. She did not want to dwell with the icy hauteur of the Dark Kind but to be back in Ileni's gentle arms again, in her cosy kitchen, deep within the protective black granite walls of the keep.

"I will return," she said out loud with a sudden determination, addressing the unknown world below the clouds.

"Return to what? Across Europe, humans are about to go crazy again with their usual wasteful bloodshed. Isolann will not survive this time." Garan's remark seemed disloyal and callous.

"I am just a human girl but I have total faith in Prince Azrar; he will prevail over all his enemies. Does he know you doubt him, is that why you hid in this machine rather than face the Jendar?"

Garan gave a humourless grin, giving a brief warning glimpse of his fangs. "Azrar's pet is a feisty little thing. And either brave – or very stupid. Not many humans would be trapped in a tin box hundreds of feet up in the sky with two vampires and dare call one a coward."

Eshan gave him a low, threatening growl, also furious at his use of the insulting human term for Dark Kind in her presence. "Leave her alone. She is little more than a child, but very precious to Azrar."

"Then she has an advantage over you, my lady!" Garan replied with a foxy grin, enjoying Eshan's anger at his usual disrespect.

"Just fly this damned plane," Eshan muttered, desperate to get back to her home in Paris and away from this irritating commoner. Garan bowed his head with an insolent grin, riling the nobility was always an amusing diversion when there were no humans to hunt and kill.

The dense cloud cover dispersed as the plane cleared the Upper Balkans and headed for its first stop-over in Northern Italy to avoid the sunlight. Khari peered out of the porthole in growing alarm as the featureless darkened landscape changed and she could make out twinkling lights from human settlements. Though she was too high above them to make actual contact, a tidal wave of thoughts reached up to her, an unbearable chaos and confusion from millions of minds, crowding to get into hers. How could she leave her sanctuary, her secluded haven in the mountains? The clamour from all these minds will surely drive her insane! How could she leave Azrar, whose mind was forever closed to hers and who kept her safe? And the one whom she loved, regardless of Eshan's words of warning. She cared not for tales of Azrar's past loves. Even the memory of Zian's image, burning any hapless spectator with the raw power of her compelling eyes did nothing to change her feelings. Khari loved him. Not as a guardian, or mentor but as a man with her whole heart, mind and dare she admit it even to herself, her body.

Chapter Five

Vermont, New England, North America, 1935

Harlequin drifts of fallen leaves, a vibrant tapestry in many hues of russet, crimson, green and gold lay before Jay Parrish's feet. The carefree beauty gave him no pleasure. He walked briskly through the piles of dry leaves, kicking at these new enemies, stamping down hard on the mute reminders that he was in America. To Professor Parrish, the gaudy Fall leaves were too potent a symbol that he was back in America. Not by choice, but as a prisoner of his powerful, wealthy family.

The Parrish clan acted fast when news reached them that their errant son was languishing in a poor way in some remote backwater with an unpronounceable name beyond the Upper Balkans. With the help of the American Embassy, the family's agents found him in a pitiful state, dirty and emaciated, barely coherent in the Abhajastan capital, Khoukar. He refused to leave, ranting about his discovery of a vampire prince and a castle full of priceless treasures. With force and heavy sedation, Parrish was bundled into a car and eventually brought to this sanatorium in a quiet location in rural Vermont.

Sanatorium, that was a joke. A madhouse – for all its kindly doctors, gentle nurses and spacious grounds. Many fallen sons and daughters of the powerful and wealthy languished here, addictions, mental health problems or worryingly a number were just opinionated misfits. Thorns in the side of their influential families. Parrish was not unique in being incarcerated for telling the truth. His prison looked like a gracious large country house with a tall pillared grand entrance, pristine white weatherboards and typical New England wide, sweeping lawns. He'd tried to walk across those manicured green swards to his freedom many times; the swift restraints from burly white-coated men soon shattered any illusion that this was anything but a nut house.

He had to grudgingly accept the enforced rest and good care had brought his body back to full health. He needed to recover after his arduous and extremely perilous journey across the Arpalathian Mountains on foot as he escaped cursed Isolann and Azrar's raking fangs. The sanatorium had not cured his febrile mental state.

Each minute he spent trapped impotently in America was a corrosive torture. He had to get back to Isolann, to lay claim to the fabulous library and its treasures beyond all value, beyond the measurement of mere wealth. He could think of nothing else, vivid visions of the high vaulted library haunted his dreams and preoccupied all his thoughts through every waking hour. What if other explorers found it while he was a prisoner? Steal what was his, snatch away all the contents of that fabulous treasure house of history and cover themselves with stolen glory that was rightfully his. Or perhaps an even worse scenario; a larger force from that philistine nation Svolenia, better armed and in greater numbers. The thought of more vandals like Deret smashing into the Keep made him physically sick. These were people who readily burnt their own heritage to ashes on the whim of an indoctrinated madman.

"Mr Parrish, what are you doing out here without a coat, sure, won't you catch your death of cold out here!"

A new young nurse scurrying across the lawn, bearing his navy cashmere coat over her arm interrupted Parrish's reverie. A gift from his mother who had not deigned to visit. The haughty Parrish clan matriarch would not grant him an audience till he was considered normal and acceptable to New England society again. Parrish rudely shrugged off the young Irish nurse's kindly attentions and stalked further away from the sanatorium.

"It's *Professor* Parrish to you. And I don't need that ridiculous coat. Do you know how cold it gets sheltering from ice storms in bear-ridden mountain caves in Isolann? Of course not. I survived those brutish mountains; I will survive a mild Fall afternoon in goddamn Vermont."

Parrish watched the young woman's cheeks flush red at his snapping retort with no sympathy or remorse. She chose the wrong profession to be upset by the ravings of lunatics. Once he would have been charming and flirted with the dark haired colleen. Once he had been a reasonable looking young man, with a future full of great prospects. He needed no mirrors to know he had become gaunt and haunted in appearance, his skin pale and sallow, his sandy hair thinning and lank. His life would all change soon, once he got back to Isolann and claimed his rightful possession of the library. Then he would be even richer and feted by the world's intelligencia, he would have his pick of lovely young women and his outward appearance would be of no importance.

"You have some visitors, Professor Parrish."

Parrish followed her back to the home with little curiosity, no doubt it was just his sisters coming to fuss and fret over him. One day he would care about them again but they meant little to him now, there was no help coming from his family. Nobody believed his story, at least not to his face.

With his body fully recovered from its ordeal, Parrish realised the only way out of this benign prison was to give them exactly what they wanted. They needed to know his mind had healed too. To buy his freedom he had to deny his entire experience in Isolann, to disclaim his idea that Jendar Azrar was a blood-drinking near immortal, a non-human monster that never aged and had lived for countless millennia.

Only then would be able to gather up his own considerable resources and head back to Europe. Parrish now believed he stood a better chance of being taken seriously in the Old World, where knowledge and experiences of the Dark Kind still existed, and real folk memories were transformed into myths and legends.

With little interest, he walked into the main drawing room where informal meetings with visitors were held but instead of his family, he found two silent, dark-clad men standing protectively beside a slightly built man. He was in his early forties with the aesthetic lean face of an El Greco saint; his dark hair shot with badger stripes of silver. As the stranger stood up to offer his hand in greeting to Parrish, he noticed the dog collar and purple of a clergyman. He also wore a heavily jewelled antique crucifix around his neck. Parrish recognised it as an ancient Eastern European treasure, a priceless museum piece. He forced his eyes away from the exquisite object as the priest introduced himself as Monsignor Alejandro Reyes.

"This is a wasted visit, I come from a strict Episcopalian background, but frankly I do not believe in any such nonsense."

"The purpose of my visit isn't about your personal faith. Is there anywhere we can speak alone in private?"

Parrish looked hard at the Catholic priest with a gasp of astonishment. He could swear his appearance changed for a split second, a slight shimmer in the very fabric of reality. He did not doubt the strange experience, not after what he witnessed in Isolann but swiftly pushed such thoughts aside...he was trying to get out of this nuthouse.

The priest waited for Parrish to nod his assent to a meeting and with a few words of swift Spanish dismissed his two aides or bodyguards; the purpose of their presence still uncertain. The monsignor's visit sparked off Parrish's curiosity and he led the man to his comfortable private room. It was large enough for a sofa and a set of easy chairs, one of which he offered to the priest.

"I will not waste your time with small talk. I am here to speak to you about your experiences in Isolann, to talk about your encounter with Jendar Azrar."

Parrish was torn. Was this all an elaborate trap set by the Sanatorium medical committee to test how far gone into insanity he was? To see if he was still hopelessly lost in his delusions. Or was the East European crucifix a sign that there were authorities that believed him, who knew the truth? Who better than the ancient European Catholic Church to know about vampires at first hand. Did not the fires of their brutal Inquisition take many Dark Kind lives?

Parrish did not answer but studied the clergyman's thin, pale face for signs of guile but saw only an earnest interest in his answers in the man's soulful brown eyes.

"I'm sorry, you have had a long and pointless journey. I did not meet Isolann's prince in person. He would only receive the Svolenian Commander, Deret."

Reyes produced a sheaf of notes from a slim black leather valise, "I must challenge that statement. I have your personal reports of the ill fated expedition here. They clearly state you did meet the Prince and that you know that he is 'Ganiszhi'."

Parrish was startled at the use of this early medieval Svolenian term for Dark Kind; it had not appeared in any of his reports. This mysterious cleric knew a lot and Parrish suspected the use of the obscure term in an archaic language was deliberate. This shrewd looking man could be a vital ally or even a possible foe but talking to him now would jeopardise Parrish's bid for freedom. If need be, he would track him down at a later date.

"I was a very sick man when I returned from Abhajastan. Starvation, exhaustion and cheap native narcotics can create a pitifully poor state of mental health. That is why I am here. Nothing in that report is worth the paper it was written on, Monsignor Reyes. Now please leave, it is time for my medication."

Reyes sighed and with an elegant gesture of assent, stood up. "You have been through a considerable ordeal Professor Parrish. At some point in the future you may change your mind. Have my card, I will always be ready to speak to you."

Parrish took the card and put it into his pocket without looking at it in a show of indifference and watched in silence as the Catholic priest left. Once alone he took the card out. There was no name or phone number, just an address in Rome.

"The man may be an intellectual but he is a pitifully poor liar."

Reyes addressed his aides as they drove away from the sanatorium. One of the men removed his dark glasses and rubbed his eyes, grateful for the warm sunlight and to be free of their gloom. " Is he going to be a problem?"

Reyes shrugged. "He showed courage and initiative to escape Isolann alive. He also has considerable wealth to back him, especially when his mother passes on and he inherits his share in the Parrish fortune. One to watch I suspect."

Chapter Six

Paris, France, 1937

As the citizens of Paris hurried about their business, Khari took her seat at her favourite boulevard café. Though it was a working day, the atmosphere seemed festive as the first warm Spring day put everyone in a buoyant mood. The welcome early sunshine gave an extra enthusiasm to their smiles of greeting and added energy to their steps.

Khari was dressed in the latest and most expensive couture day attire, a crisply tailored creation in soft grey-green, her silver blonde hair pinned up under a jaunty little hat adorned with a discreet cockade of pheasant feathers dyed a matching green. Her gentle beauty and immaculately chic appearance triggered many admiring glances. She ignored them all, and sat back in her chair, taking a tentative sip from her hot black coffee, smiling to herself as the taste and aroma flooding her senses with pleasure. That annoying Dark Kind, Garan was right about one thing, the world beyond Isolann was exciting.

What once she feared would be a terrifying experience proved instead a great adventure. But not from the start, the early days had been very hard and not just from the inevitable culture shock and homesickness. From dwelling in a remote castle with a handful of familiar people, Khari had been taken to a country teeming with strangers, so many minds crowding into hers. It was an onslaught that could drive any human insane. It was this urgent need to keep her sanity which forced her to control her *Knowing*, learning quickly how to shut out unwanted thoughts from other people's minds. It had been an arduous process but survival was an efficient taskmaster.

She was far away from the sanctuary of Isolann and Khari often despaired, believing she would die from sensory overload, so many strange new sights and experiences, so many people. Her Dark Kind companion, Eshan had done her best to minimise the danger and wisely chose to stay at first in isolation, a rented large country house on the outskirts of a quiet village, until the girl learned to control her *Knowing*. Only when Khari's own confidence in keeping her ability under control was established did they eventually settle in one city, Paris. Eshan believed this preferable to dragging her around an increasingly dangerous and unstable Europe and she already had an established home there near her scientific research clinic.

Now two years had passed since leaving Khari's Upper Balkan home, years that had flown past in a dizzy blur. She had endured many moments of homesickness, but they passed with surprising swiftness. She was not in a permanent exile, she reasoned when struck with pangs of guilt from just how much she was enjoying herself. She would return home – soon.

Khari shivered as a single dark cloud passed slowly over the sun, momentarily bringing with it a brief reminder of the chill winter just past. She looked up as a friendly waiter; an elderly Armenian exile brought her favourite breakfast, a warm freshly baked almond and chocolate croissant. She did not need to reach into his mind, his open anxiety was obvious enough for the world to see.

"What is it Yuri, you look so sad and troubled," Khari inquired, giving his hand a gentle squeeze.

The old man shrugged and sighed deeply as if the troubles of the whole world burdened his thin shoulders. He looked up at the offending cloud, that marred the perfection of the Spring morning with a sour scowl. One dark cloud was always the forerunner of many more.

"I am foolish, instead of enjoying this pretty morning, I listen to the radio. More bad news. I am convinced the filthy Nazis plan to devour Europe like a monster with an appetite nothing can satisfy. I am worried France will be invaded again."

Khari shivered again, this time with her own growing unease. What the old man said was nothing new, it was a view shared by many Parisians. But perhaps the surge of fear rising within her was another part of the *Knowing*, not idle speculation but a premonition of very real danger to some. Khari wished it was not still daylight so that she could relay her thoughts straight away to Eshan, but the vampire woman was deep in Rest back at the spacious luxury apartments they shared in the most fashionable part of the city. She would have to wait until sunset.

Khari's anxiety was not the danger she and Eshan faced from any future German invasion, but of the immediate peril it would bring to Eshan's team of scientists and their families, most of whom were Jewish. She hastily paid her bill and rushed back through the crowded streets. Evacuating so many people again was time consuming and difficult, even for someone with Eshan's considerable resources. The sooner they started the better, but where would they go to now? Where in the world was safe now?

Khari walked quickly, but her progress became hampered by interference invading her mind. She became increasingly disturbed as her defences against the *Knowing* faltered and failed, allowing nearby people's thoughts to intrude into her mind against her will. She tried to stay at a calm walking pace but she wanted to break out into a panic stricken run as the shored up mental wall of her mind's defences buckled under the assaults.

Fleeting snippets of thought from passing strangers, some trivial, others in considerable mental turmoil broke into her mind. Khari stopped and raised her hands to her head, now crowded with a clashing cacophony of other people's thoughts. It became harder and harder to shut them out. It was not just her own growing anxiety that triggered the break down –it was the weight of accumulating fear from the citizens of Paris. The gaiety of the morning had been an illusion. Despite their outward light-hearted enjoyment of the spring day, like old Yuri, they were deeply afraid, with good reason. With a grim inevitability, the Third Reich and its murderous land and power hungry leaders had seen the whole of Europe as theirs by birthright.

    Somehow, she gathered herself together, desperately seeking some deep inner reserve of self control. She could not live her life like this, her mind and sanity assaulted by the crushing weight of other people's thoughts. She had to go back home, to safety and protection behind the sheer walls of black granite of Azrar's Keep. To Azrar.

    Back at Eshan's fabulously luxurious fin de siecle home overlooking the Seine, Khari could not wait until nightfall and began to pack her clothes. Panic was a dangerously negative feeling and it did not subside as each suitcase was closed shut, fully crammed with her modern French clothes, symbols of her new life. When sunset finally arrived and Eshan arose from her Rest, Khari had already completely packed.

    Eshan did not need to be a human mind reader to know something was very wrong. The girl was dressed in travelling clothes, her suitcases packed and left by the main door. "What is going on, Khari? What has happened?"

    Khari tried to keep the rising panic out of her voice but failed miserably, "My lady, I must go home to Isolann. My mind can no longer shut other people's thoughts out. It has got so bad, that I fear for my sanity, even for my life."

    Eshan sighed, "You have been doing so well for such a long time. Has something triggered this setback?"

    Khari explained about the premonition of danger she'd experienced that morning. "It is not just speculation, we know the situation with the Germans is worsening. I am convinced they will invade France one day soon."

Eshan nodded, fully understanding the girl's anxiety. She too had received accurate intelligence from her agents confirming the human girl's fears. Eshan had already started evacuating her scientists again, this time across the Channel to England. It was a damp, dour little island but it enjoyed a courageous and high principled democracy that would not give into the Germans without a fight, despite the unpopular move for appeasement from their current Prime Minister, Neville Chamberlain.

"Khari, we must stay calm. There is no immediate danger right now. Because of the logistics, I have already started to move my people to England. I thought we could stay here a little longe, but perhaps it is time for us to move on too. We must also leave for the British Isles."

Khari stared at the vampire woman in surprise. Why England? She had to get back home. Eshan saw the girl's face grow pale; her golden eyes widen and become tear rimmed. Eshan was expecting this; she fetched a letter from her safe and handed it to the girl to read for herself. Khari gasped at recognising the black and silver wolf seal, the familiar sight made her heart beat faster. It was a letter from Jendar Azrar himself, written in his usual impatient style in the Dark Kind language. Khari read its contents with a sinking heart, taking in the command to Ha'ali Eshan that if the route back to Isolann was too dangerous, she was to keep his ward protected from harm. No attempt must be made to return until it was safe. With Svolenia under a new fascist regime in league with Hitler's Germany, it was clear she stood little chance of getting home. Khari was furious with herself, she had enjoyed her stay in Paris so much she had left it too late to get home.

"We are on the run from danger, child. I have had more than a few millennia to get used to it. And so will you. It is

Azrar's will that I do not put you at risk. I must obey him without question. We will go to London."

Khari dropped her head, signalling assent but she was far from compliant. There had to be another route home, there just had to be. She wondered where Garan was, the youthful-looking vampire had his own plane and a huge disrespect for any authority – Dark Kind or human. He might accept the challenge of flouting Azrar's iron will and annoying Eshan in the process. Part of her knew this was all just wild speculation. Tracking down an illusive vampire commoner with the whole of Europe, Russia and Asia as his playground was difficult enough for a Dark Kind noblewoman, it was beyond impossible for a young human girl.

But Khari was determined to try. She had to, already in her heart, she was home in Ileni and Sandor's warm, loving embrace. She was back up on the stronghold's towering battlements surveying the black depths of the surrounding forest; she could hear the high cry of a circling eagle gliding through the Arpalathian peaks far above its frozen gorges. She could smell the short-lived but pretty spring flowers growing in the grassy foothills fed by tumbling snow melted water. And as the night fell and stars took their rightful place in the heavens, she could see the emerald green of Azrar's fiercely beautiful eyes turn their unfathomable gaze towards her.

In turn, Eshan saw the girl's wistful gaze and knew she must be extra vigilant. Getting back to Isolann was impossibly dangerous now and she was grateful for Azrar's sensible and pragmatic orders. But her charge, Khari, for all her gentle manner and quiet ways was a very determined young human. One that might put them both at risk trying to get back to Azrar. Eshan could see difficult times ahead.

Chapter Seven

Vienna, Austria, 1938

With a snarl of disgust, the Dark Kind being known as Jazriel wiped a gobbet of spittle from his lapel with an ivory silk kerchief, swiftly throwing the offending object to the ground. He sighed; his exquisitely cut, iron grey cashmere suit was now ruined, defiled. He would never wear it again. He lit up a cigarette and glanced towards his lover, Sivaya, in the shadows, as she tore open the human's throat, watching with cold detachment as her victim's violent thrashing weakened to feeble flailing then complete stillness.

"There's no place to put the body," he remarked quietly, anxious not to be detected. The calm of the Viennese back street was just a momentary lull, one that would abruptly change to noise and bustle when a nearby theatre finished the night's performance, disgorging high-spirited crowds onto the streets all around them. Sivaya shrugged, unconcerned, though still angry at the verbal and physical abuse the now very dead youth had subjected her beloved Jazriel to. The human's mean little eyes had been crazed with hatred as he spat out the word 'Yuden', aiming his bile at Jazriel's face but hitting his chest instead. She would have understood the young Austrian spitting at Jazriel for being Dark Kind but not for mistaking him as a species of human. The end result would have been the same; no filthy primate defiled her lover with spit and lived.

With ease, Sivaya lobbed the body down some steps leading to a basement, making no attempt to disguise the deep fang slash on the man's throat. It was long past time to leave Austria, but the escalating human conflict had dangerously hampered their normal escape routes. Jazriel took her by the arm and strode away into the night, trying to put aside his annoyance over the suit; his vexation fuelled by the knowledge it was irreplaceable. The genius of a tailor who made it for him had completely vanished, along with his entire family.

Jazriel genuinely hoped they had escaped, they had been courteous and gentle people who deserved to reach safety far away from these Aryan madmen. Had they come to him for help escaping, he would have given it unreservedly. Instead the family were gone, leaving behind a vandalised shop and empty apartment, still furnished and full of their personal belongings. By now even these mute witnesses to tragic, ruined lives would be gone, looted by the mobs terrorising so many of the city's peaceful citizens. Jazriel's enquiries to the family's whereabouts were met with a suspicious, hostile wall of sullen silence from their neighbours.

"We must get out now, this country is a tightening noose," he muttered. In a subconscious reflex, he touched his neck, the light golden skin now smooth and perfect, his throat undamaged. Narrowly escaping the centuries of inquisitions and witch fires had come at a price. The scars had long since healed but memory of the pain would never leave him.

As they strode together in silence through the back streets, keeping to the shadows, Sivaya noticed this slight, unconscious gesture and her mind flew back to the first time she had seen Jazriel, in Prague in 1760. Though she had lived mainly in the Far East, she had already heard of the fabulously handsome commoner who had once been the lover of a high ranking member of the Dark Kind nobility and had dwelt in palaces and castles. Lover! Hah, that was not the right word, Jazriel was a used and abused plaything!

Now instead of a life of indolent luxury, he was filthy, torn and bloody, dragged by horses through the baying mobs filling the city's cobbled streets with their hatred and fear.

Unwittingly, her mind went back to those horrific first moments, the screams of hatred and anger from his captors, getting ever more loud and menacing, urged on by the mob. No amount of passing centuries could erase that sound from her mind. She recalled that despite their rider's flogging and cursing, the horses dragging his broken body were hampered by the crowds and made slow progress. Their nervous shying and jibbing helped Sivaya to catch up and push her way through to his side. Heavily veiled in widow's weeds, she made the pretence of dropping down and wiping a handkerchief on Jazriel's face and what a face! His pain-darkened eyes had looked up into hers, flashing with surprise and the flicker of hope and her heart lurched, already in love from that first fleeting contact. She had to save him.

Her gesture with the handkerchief went unnoticed by the crowds, many were trying the same thing, the thin purple blood of the Dark Kind was supposed to have medicinal powers —such nonsense! Instead, she used the darkness and confusion to cut through a rope tearing into his neck, not able to break it right through but weakening its stranglehold to buy him some more time.

The execution rabble halted at a wooden frame with a noose already strung up, next to a fiercely burning pyre hastily constructed in the centre of a square, with large blunt axes lying on the cobbles close by. With horror, she learnt from a mad eyed crone pushing past to her to get a better look, that they planned to hang and dismember him with the blunt axes before throwing him into the fire. " I hope the blood drinking demon will still be alive to feel the flames, I'm told they are hard bastards to kill," muttered the old woman gleefully, "Hang around, you might get some bits of black bone as souvenirs; they will bring you good fortune. Maybe a new husband!"

Sivaya's hand went up to check her heavy widow's veiling and moved quickly away from the crone. She must not be discovered, she did not want to die, torn apart and burnt to death by a human mob like so many of her kind. And she was Jazriel's only hope.

The horses already badly spooked by the noise and the jostling press of the mob, began to panic when their riders halted them by the furnace-hot blaze of the crackling pyre. Sivaya took her chance. She reached into a leather pouch hung on her belt and lobbed several small grey pellets into the flames. Instant chaos; the night exploded into mayhem as the fire erupted into a thunderous fireball which instantly killed many of the crowd closest to the flames, injuring many more. More importantly, it created complete pandemonium. In the resulting panic and confusion, she was able to cut Jazriel free and drag him to safety. They had been virtually inseparable ever since.

"I saw you touch your once broken neck. You are thinking of that night in Prague, the night I nearly lost you," she ventured, stroking his face with her hand. Jazriel shook his head and kissed her, tasting the human blood still on her lips, "When I think of Prague, I think only of finding you."

They walked swiftly with silent steps through the streets towards their hotel, and escape in his hand built Bugatti Atlantic. It must be their last night in Vienna. Jazriel focused on staying undetected. The taint of human fear lay heavily in the air of this uneasy and hostile city, hanging like a rank, sour miasma. The nights were always tense, sudden and bloody violence never far away. Unlike Garan, Jazriel was not attracted to epicentres of human turmoil. He had come to Vienna for a fitting of a new wardrobe and to obtain some of the highest quality narcotics in Northern Europe. He did not bother seeing out this particular source of his gratification, he was sure the cocaine dealer had disappeared too. He had Sivaya, her golden beauty a pleasure more intoxicating than any human-made drug.

Sivaya caught his loving glance and gave his hand a little squeeze in return. Her heart grew heavy, 'You think of me with fondness, my beloved, but do not really love me, not with fire, not with passion,' she thought fighting back the wave of inevitable sorrow. They were together, she should be grateful for that. But how much of his affection was based not on love but on gratitude, on some sense of honour bound duty? She had saved his life, nursed him back to health, fallen in love with him when his beautiful face was still torn and battered. The questions tormenting her mind would remain unspoken. It had to be enough just being with Jazriel, the nights spent travelling the Old World, hunting together and days spent making love. Even after over five centuries together, she still craved him with every atom of her being. It would have to be enough.

Her reverie was abruptly halted as Jazriel grabbed her arm tightly, preventing her from rounding the corner that lead to their hotel. He quickly pulled her back into a shop doorway. "It is what I expected, that vermin you killed was tracking us. His friends are waiting for us at the hotel."

From their vantage point, they could see from the reflection in a glass shop window opposite that a large mob of youths in brown shirts, all armed with clubs and knives had gathered at the hotel entrance. "Zaard!" Jazriel cursed under his breath in the vampire language. They had nothing with them but their latest forged identity papers and some Austrian money. But with no sign of the gutless local police, he had no intention of taking on the mob himself.

This was not cowardice, he and Sivaya could easily hold their own against an undisciplined gang of human youths, but it would bring down too much dangerous attention. In this increasingly paranoid society, it was getting harder to survive in the shadows. They turned away, abandoning their hotel suite, there was nothing left behind but clothes and jewellery; all could be replaced. More worrying, they could not reach Jazriel's beloved car, making their escape more perilous.

Where was safe? Europe was a hornet's nest, fearful and deadly to all who did not conform to the genetic pattern set by a madman. Too many dangerous borders hampered the route to India and the East. Jazriel yearned to explore the New World but the Americas were too far for Dark Kind to reach, in the future maybe but not now. Jazriel glanced at the cloud filled night sky, just three hours left of darkness, how far could they get in such a short time?

"What about the station, could we get to the Hungarian border before dawn?" urged Sivaya, her lover's obvious growing unease adding to her own rising anxiety. "We must try," he replied tersely in agreement. At least Hungary was in the right direction. With a sinking heart he accepted that in this time of human madness, there was only one safe haven for the Dark Kind. Isolann.

"Zaard!" Jazriel swore again. "I am going to get my car. Those Nazi maggots have killed or driven away my tailor, they are not getting their filthy hands on my Bugatti!"

Chapter Eight

Chess Manor, The Chiltern Hills, England 1938

A rosy new day dawned, joyously noisy with birdsong through a dark tangle of bare branches, greening with the promise of new born leaves. The early morning light shone in Joe Devane's eyes and he groaned as waking made him aware of painful stiffness in his back and neck. He had fallen asleep slumped over his desk – again! This was getting to be an unwelcome habit. He got up, limbs creaking and stiff and walked through a set of French doors to have the first cigarette of the day in an old flagstone courtyard. Beyond the stone square, the Chilterns burst into the hesitant glory of an English early spring morning. Today it was mild, with watery sunshine rising over the patchwork of gentle undulating farmland and woods. Tomorrow it could be a snow-clad winter scene again.

Chicago-born Devane loved this ancient landscape and its fickle but temperate weather. A confirmed Europhile, he readily accepted his posting in Britain to set up a new covert intelligence and combat agency. The joint British and American team that set up the squad had given him the rather melodramatic code name 'Shadowman' and spacious headquarters in a neat Georgian mansion hidden deep in the Buckinghamshire countryside. The setting was an unexpected bonus. Its calm beauty felt detached from the tragedy tearing the world apart, but he needed complete privacy to make plans for the new agency.

Devane pulled on a grey great coat and pulling up the collar, strolled around the still nascent gardens, the lush lawn scattered with the nodding white heads of brave snowdrops, bright yellow catkins fluttered in the hedges.

He did not miss the fierce ice storms and sharp winds across the great lake back home. He glanced up at the horizon as if he could see the other storm raging over the English Channel –one that could so easily sweep over and destroy this quiet landscape and peaceful people. He was just one young Yank, but his entire being was dedicated to stopping this German madman's war—whatever it took.

"What do you make of that report I sent you, laddie?"

Devane looked up at the sound of a familiar soft Highland burr. His choice of second in command approached, carrying two blue and white enamel mugs of steaming strong tea. He was Colonel Archie MacCammon, the scourge of many an apoplectic military bureaucrat. Devane took the mug with a smile, warmly shaking the huge hand of the first British rep on his new team, already nicknamed the 'Spook Squad' by the very few people who knew of its shadowy existence. Both men were appointed on the ethos that the Nazi menace must be defeated –using any means. Devane's spooks were certainly any means.

Like his boss, MacCammon was an unusual man; he had to be on the team of the most secret of covert squads. A tough professional soldier, he also had a thirst for arcane knowledge and a very open mind. His Celtic blood clearly evident from his thick black hair already streaked with a badger stripe of white, and vivid blue eyes. It also came through with his extensive knowledge and love of the mystic; he was a true son of the Celtic Twilight.

Six months had passed since the two men had concentrated on recruiting genuine psychics for the squad, but found only two so far of sufficient consistent power. Now the search for living weapons against the Nazis had a whole new and potentially mind-blowing direction. It started with a report anonymously sent to the big Scot. It told of another more mainstream, allied intelligence group who had intercepted an American called Professor Jay Parrish. British military authorities had rejected the man as a complete lunatic when he had made a nuisance of himself, demanding that the British army invade a distant Balkan principality called Isolann to rescue a fabulous library from its vampire ruler. In Parrish's view the allies could then use the country as a barrier to stop the enemy advancing beyond the Upper Balkans. Stopping the Nazis getting through Europe's forgotten backdoor, using their latest ally, the now enthusiastically fascist state of Svolenia.

Furious at rejection and ridicule from the British, Parrish was arrested trying to flee to Berlin, to ask Hitler himself to organise an invasion of Isolann. In his possession were copious notes and ancient documents stating that he proved Prince Azrar of Isolann was not human, but an ageless blood drinking monster. It was dismissed as deranged nonsense to every authority. But not by the newly formed Spook Squad. Their entire recruitment policy depended on listening out for crazy stories and paranormal-based rumours.

"So, Mac, what do you think of Parrish's material?" Devane asked as he finished his cigarette and stubbed it out on the flagstones. He ran a hand through his close cropped brown hair.

"The man has produced a fine work of imaginative fiction. What if it is true?" MacCammon replied evenly.

Devane's dark grey eyes began to sparkle with the slightly manic fervour that was part of his complex character. "My God, Archie, it will be too much to take in. It will force us to re-write all our history, our science. Let's face it, this will put a bomb beneath everything we believe in."

McCammon nodded agreement. Outwardly calm, inside he was brimming with excitement, daring to hope the wretched Parrish was telling the truth. Like Joe Devane, MacCammon also needed to live in a world where magic and mystery still dwelled, where new discoveries lay waiting for the brave and the bold to find.

Where is this Professor now?" Devane asked eagerly.

"Languishing at his Majesty's pleasure."

Devane slapped the big Scot on his back, his voice almost shaking with impatience. "Let's get him here straight away. We must know more. If these beings exist, we must recruit them before the Nazis get hold of them. Hitler has enough monsters working for him, let's have some of our own."

Chess Manor, The Chilterns, England.

"I think we have left our guest to stew alone long enough."

Joe Devane announced to his team as they waited in the dark oak panelled hall of Chess Manor, the home of the Spook Squad. He decided to play the sympathetic approach to the prisoner waiting in the drawing room. He reasoned that Professor Parrish tried to defect to the Nazis because no one in Britain believed him. He was more likely to open up to an earnest believer in his cause.

As Devane entered the room, the prisoner flinched as if struck. Devane pulled up a chair and sat opposite Parrish, who squirmed in discomfort, trying to avoid his gaze. Though both men were of similar age, around their mid twenties, fear had prematurely aged Parrish. Despite his height, the Professor looked unsubstantial —a living ghost. His sandy hair hung thin and wispy with the maggot-hued scalp showing through; his thin face had an unhealthy grey pallor. Only his pale blue eyes showed any animation, angry and fearful by turns.

"Relax, Professor. I only want to talk to you."

Parrish's eyes widened at the unexpected sound of an American accent; what was another yank doing in his nightmare? He spoke in a bitter, worn down voice, "Do you know what your Limey friends plan for me? Some of their military guys want to string me up as a spy. You are in league with these bastards. Why should I speak to you? Why should I trust you?"

Devane sitting opposite the man, noted how his eyes darted frequently to the room's large leaded glass window, as if considering whether to jump to his freedom or death. After three months imprisonment on a treason charge, it was probably the same thing to Parrish.

"Do you consider yourself a traitor?" Devane asked in a quiet voice, offering the Professor a cigarette.

The man accepted it with a shaking hand. "Of course not," he sighed, "I am an American patriot, always will be. But our boys are not involved with any future European war."

He took a deep drag on the cigarette and began to cough violently, he had not smoked until caught up in this damn war. "I went to the limeys for the sake of all humanity. The threat of war in Europe has created an emergency. I need to get that library in safe hands as soon as possible." Parrish looked up at his countryman, his eyes pleading. "Why doesn't anyone see how important this library is? The answer to every ancient mystery in human history could be there."

"So why would you let the Nazis get their bloodstained hands on this treasure house of knowledge?" Devane asked, genuinely puzzled at this bizarre and foolhardy move.

Parrish sighed and took another deep drag on the cigarette, hacking away wretchedly before answering, eyes watering, his voice hoarse from coughing.

"I know it sounds crazy now. It made sense at the time. I wasn't thinking straight; going to the Germans was an act of desperation, but I will never consider myself a traitor. That library belongs to all mankind, not locked away in the lair of an inhuman monster. We can get it back off the Germans if there is a war."

Devane handed the man a glass of water, then pushed some papers around his desk, giving the man time to settle and recover from his coughing spasm.

"There is no need to be on the defensive with me, Professor Parrish. I believe every word of your report on the Dark Kind. That is why you are here in this beautiful old house and not rotting in some prison cell in London."

"So what do you want from me?"

"I need to know everything about the Dark Kind. My mission is to track them down and make contact."

"And what of the library?"

"There is every chance of war breaking out, Professor. Isolann is surrounded by hostile fascist states and Nazi occupied territories. We know the Jendar is preparing to defend his little principality against them. Just pray he is as good a warlord as his long survival suggests he is."

Three productive hours later, Devane found MacCammon outside the door.

"Our jailbird is singing away," Devane informed him. "I think he wants to be part of the team."

"And is he going to be a new recruit?"

"Absolutely not. The guy's a fanatic with only one objective and that's getting his hands on Azrar's library. He wants all Dark Kind wiped out; hardly the sort to recruit for working with them. Mind you, I don't blame the guy, from what I understand Azrar had earmarked him for a quick bedtime snack."

MacCammon nodded towards the heavy oak panelled door, "So what is going to happen to our worthy Professor?"

"We'll pump him dry of information, then let the Brits have him back."

MacCammon nodded in approval of his new boss's cold hearted approach. Devane outwardly seemed relaxed and amiable, a reasonable, kind hearted career soldier and student in his spare time of languages and European art. The big Scot knew that he had to be much more to have achieved his status as chief of an allied security corps at such a young age. He saw the ruthless core of the man, one that never stopped fighting this war. One who would not let anything or anyone prevent him from fighting it his way.

The American prisoner did not have his sympathy. In MacCammon's eyes, Parrish had put his own head in the noose by seeking out Hitler's help. He may not have intended treachery but the road to his own personal Hell was paved with so called good intentions. He would find no mercy here.

"But some good news, we have two possible new recruits in London! " Devane and his second in command walked back into the Manor's spacious hall. " Parrish has given us an amazing lead." Devane continued, "We already know a mysterious Isolanni countess has brought her laboratory to London from Paris and Berlin to escape capture by the Germans."

"You mean that bunch of blood research boffins? I read about them, but what has that got to do with our project?"

"Parrish believed that the Countess is Dark Kind and the young girl with her is Khari herself."

MacCammon's lean, dour features broke into a broad, enthusiastic smile," "My God, the golden eyed mind reader!"

Devane was equally delighted and clapped his companion on the back, "We could get two for the price of one, Mac! The fact our shadowy Countess fled twice from the Nazis is a good sign that she has no sympathy for the Third Reich. I am going to track them down."

MacCammon shook his head, this was dangerous new territory. Recruiting human psychics was one thing, tackling vampires another. "And what makes you think this she-devil will leave your throat intact?"

"It is a chance I must take. If the Countess kills me, you must keep going Mac. Recruit the girl, she will be invaluable. Then try again looking for a co-operative vampire with Khari's help. Promise her a security pact from the British government for Jendar Azrar after the war. Parrish told me the girl adores her blood drinker guardian."

MacCammon shook his head in admiration, he thought he was the toughest son of a bitch in the intelligence corps but Devane's single-mindedness was on a higher level of dedication. "You forget one important fact, Devane. This wee lass is supposed to be a mind reader. She would see right through that blatant lie."

Devane laughed and gave a rueful shrug of acceptance. His life grew more bizarre by the day! He had willingly entered the world of the strange, embraced and encouraged its weirdness. Soon if his plans were successful, he would be working with mind readers and clairvoyants and deadly inhuman creatures of the night. It sure beat his last job in Intelligence, stuck in offices deep down in a dank cellar pouring over scraps of secret messages from covert operatives within Germany. He patted the big Scot on his broad shoulder. "Oh boy, Mac, are we in for some interesting times!"

Chapter Nine

London, England, 1938

Eshan pulled the sable collar of her coat tightly around her neck, the feel of the sodden soft fur was unpleasant but it was preferable to the sting from lashing horizontal rain. She hated London. Many centuries of constant travel around the capitals of Europe and Asia had hardened her opinion of this bustling, grey city. But it was the safest haven in a war torn, dangerous world. Not for her... nowhere was truly safe for the Dark Kind; but for her people, her team of the brilliant scientists.

Eshan had survived so long by making the most of her wealth. It paid for privacy and an efficient intelligence network and therefore she had plenty of warning of the danger from Nazi Germany, evacuating her laboratory in Paris long before the storm troopers marched in.

It wasn't the equipment that mattered; she had that completely destroyed long before the Germans invaded France. It was the minds of her scientists that needed protection. She was relieved when they arrived safely with their families in London; most were of Jewish origin. The British authorities welcomed her talented contingent with open arms. Her laboratory's ground breaking research into blood and its diseases was world famous. In particular in this time of global conflict, the research into creating artificial blood and successful transfusions attracted great interest from allied military medics.

Eshan considered her own options as she hurriedly crossed a darkened city towards her hotel. She felt bad about uprooting Khari again. The girl had begun to find her way in the frenzied modern world beyond Isolann. She was just beginning to enjoy the frivolities and delights of Paris when they had to flee to this more staid and dour city. Had Eshan still been predatory, London's blackout would have been a vampire's dream. Khari and her scientists were safe; the laboratory back working at full strength; did she need to be here in London? And if not, where could she go?

Europe was a seething maestrom of anarchy, a charnel house. She had considered returning to Isolann but the journey was now far too dangerous. Azrar now fought a guerrilla war, battling hard against the Nazi's ally, the newly fascist state of Svolenia, from his high mountain eyrie. Her heart was torn with fear for his safety but she could do nothing to help him. She also knew he would be revelling in the conflict as he became a warlord again.

Her reverie was interrupted by a human's approach in the rain lashed gloom. The tall young man was alone and no threat to her but his hesitant manner suggested he knew she was dangerous. He addressed her in fluent Hungarian in an accent she recognised as American.

"My lady, I apologise for the impudence of stopping you in the street, but I have something to discuss that may be to our mutual interest."

"I very much doubt it," Eshan replied in an even but firm tone, keeping the low Dark Kind growl of warning from her voice.

"I am sure Dark Kind also have a sense of curiosity. If my suggestions displease you, you can always kill me."

"You are either a very brave man or the world's greatest fool"

"A bit of both, I suspect," the young American replied grinning, tipping back his rain drenched felt fedora. Eshan made a swift judgement; he had what appeared to be a genuine and honest smile which lit up his otherwise rough hewn features. His grey eyes shone with intensity and candour.

"I will give you ten minutes to intrigue me. Meet me at the Dorchester in an hour. And you must come alone"

"I will be there, Countess."

The man bowed low and disappeared into the bitterly wet night. He called her Dark Kind. She had no choice. She must meet with this man, find out all he knew –then she would have to kill him.

Eshan found her ward, Khari back at the hotel listening to show tunes on a radio in the suite. "You should go out. There is a new production at the Apollo opening tonight." Khari smiled at the Dark Kind woman's suggestion. She had the same idea herself but a porter told her the night's cold wind threatened snow and she felt too warm and settled to leave the suite.

The past four years living with Eshan had altered her beyond recognition; her slender figure now comfortable in modern Paris fashions reflected her ease with the world beyond Isolann. She was no longer a child in homespun peasant garb, but a sophisticated young woman in her pale jade silk suit, her hair up in a chignon, fastened with a jade silk flower.

"I wish you to go out, Khari." Eshan's voice had the hard imperious edge of a being used to being obeyed. "I have business to attend to."

Khari switched off the radio. "Maybe I can help?" she suggested, unbothered by the hardness in Eshan's voice; she had been raised in a Jendar's stronghold and was used to brusque Dark Kind commands. Eshan paused. She had wanted the young woman out of the way in case she had to kill the young American but there was no doubt Khari's gift could be useful, she could learn far more than he would say openly. She nodded assent and told Khari about her unexpected encounter in the street.

Khari waited in a side room as Eshan received their visitor. She peered through a gap in the door and was pleasantly surprised at the sight of an attractive young man. In his mid twenties, Devane was not tall but had the confidence and presence that made his lack of height an irrelevance. Khari looked beyond the intelligence and good humour shining from his eyes and searched his mind for clues. She liked what she found. It was also clear he was understandably frightened of Eshan – who wouldn't be? To know she was Dark Kind meant an acute awareness of the danger she presented.

Khari stepped out of the side room and walked towards Devane with her hand extended in greeting. "Good evening, Mr Devane. My name is Khari and as you can see I am quite human. I hope this will help you relax."

Devane took her hand and kissed it, his heart doing somersaults of excitement…this actually was the golden eyed girl of Parrish's ranting. She really did exist. And she was lovely, no, more than that, she was breathtakingly beautiful. Devane forced his mind away from the strong attraction he felt for the young woman and when Eshan bid him, sat down and explained in great detail his plans to recruit what he described as people with useful talents to fight the Nazi menace.

Eshan saw no need for disguise with this particular human, and she removed her dark glasses giving Devane his first glimpse of Dark Kind eyes. He could not control the loud gasp of astonishment as he felt her cold penetrating gaze on his face from her all lavender eyes, eyes that were both beautiful and chilling.

"And what 'talents' do you think Dark Kind will bring your little gang?" she questioned in a voice that was curiously husky and velvety at the same time. "Other than the ability to rip out human throats."

"That will do for a start." Devane laughed nervously. "But I think your survival abilities, fine honed over millennia will be damn useful too. You are fast, agile and have perfect night vision in the darkest situation. That will do for me."

Eshan's voice took on a harder edge. "And what makes you think any Dark Kind will have anything to do with a human agency? We have never concerned ourselves with any human conflict. Why should we care if you want to kill each other?"

Devane leaned forward in his chair, and with a surge of courage, dared to look directly into the vampire's eyes. "You don't care. But you do care about surviving. This must be getting harder with each decade of human progress. The world is changing, perhaps too fast for the Dark Kind to adapt to."

Eshan gave a dangerous growl, her eyes darkening at this human's impertinence. "You go too far, Devane. You have a reckless disregard for your own throat."

"Hear me out, Lady Eshan. I offer your people protection and a new sense of purpose. You will no longer be hiding in the shadows but a vital part of worthy cause. The scourge of the Nazi must threaten you too, why else did you flee first Berlin, then Paris?"

"My humans were in peril, I am not."

"Fine, go back to Berlin, see how long you last."

Eshan started to growl again but Khari put a comforting hand on hers before addressing Devane.

"Mr Devane, thank you for your intriguing offer. It is a lot to think about. You must understand, The Dark Kind have prevailed so long by not getting involved with human issues. Ever. Please leave a number where you can be contacted and leave now."

Devane stood up and gave an old fashioned respectful bow to the two women, leaving the apartment in silence. Eshan stood up, preparing to follow Devane and kill him before he made contact with anyone. Khari took a calculated risk and blocked her way. She knew the dark wings of Azrar's protection would stay Eshan's hand against her.

"Don't do it, Lady Eshan," Khari pleaded, her liking for the American stranger adding to her anxiety. "This man is sincere and I think he could be useful to us."

Eshan's eyes darkened, how did this human know her intent? She could not read Dark Kind thoughts.

"I know he means the Dark Kind no harm. I have entered his thoughts. He has an honest soul, a brave man without guile," Khari continued with rising desperation in her voice. She hoped her flustered initial reaction to Devane did not show. She must make Eshan spare his life, but it would weaken her case for his survival if the vampire woman thought Khari's attraction to Devane was the reason for such heart felt pleas. From her journey into his mind, she also knew the young American was attracted to her. Unbidden, her body gave a shiver of excitement, just knowing the feeling was shared. This man must not die by Eshan's fangs. Or disappear forever after a visit from one of her many shadowy agents.

With difficulty, she continued struggling to keep her voice calm and level, "I searched deeply for any hidden motives but found nothing dangerous to the Dark Kind. Devane was like an open book to me. His new agency does exist and he has been given carte blanche to use anything and anyone to fight the Nazi, and that includes us."

Again, she omitted telling Eshan she found the American very attractive. It was trivial, an irrelevance in this volatile time. Ha'ali Eshan raised a quizzical eyebrow. She could not work out how Devane found out about her and Khari. Worse, none of her people had prevented him accosting her in the street. What was that human expression? Heads will roll for this.

"It would be better if I finish this tonight," Eshan insisted, her duty to protect Khari lay heavy in her mind. She would not let Azrar down, killing some human was a paltry price to pay for the girl's safety. "This is a situation we should avoid. We must take greater care and move again."

Khari walked to the heavily taped window. With the hotel room's lights out, she could see the dark, rain slicked streets of a frightened city below her. She worked hard perfecting her extraordinary skill, she'd made the greatest advance learning how to switch off; to enter a room full of people without being overwhelmed by the clashing clamour of their thoughts, their emotions. But she learned enough to know fear, to relive horror stories from the growing flood of refugees from the relentless, brutal Nazi advance across Europe.

"I want you to let him live. Because I am joining his team."

Eshan turned with a low growl of surprise at the girl's simple statement, spoken with complete and unwavering conviction.

"It seems I have unwittingly made it my lifetime's quest to enrage Jendar Azrar. I will not do it again. He appointed me to take care of you. I cannot allow you to risk your life embroiling yourself in this crazy war."

"You cannot stop me, Lady Eshan. But you can join me."

Eshan shook her head and paced the floor. She had spent the last centuries of her life looking for some direction, for some purpose to her near immortality, a way of dwelling peacefully alongside humans. Had she been alone, she would have given Devane's offer more serious thought. But she had been charged to educate Khari, to protect her – not give her up to such grave danger from reckless adventuring.

"According to human convention, I am now an adult. I can make my own decisions. I will write to Prince Azrar, tell him you tried everything possible to stop me. But I will not be swayed on this. This is a human war, it is nothing to do with the Dark Kind."

Eshan admitted defeat. She had never seen Khari so steely, so determined. "Don't bother to write, Khari; nothing can get through to Isolann now. It looks like I will have to join Devane's little enterprise as I am bound by Dark Kind honour to protect you. I am not so easy to shrug off."

Khari smiled, she sensed the Dark Kind woman wanted to join this team as much as she did. The alternative was to live a hunted life on the run, constantly seeking out safety in an increasingly dangerous world. The decision made, Eshan relaxed a little and poured them both a small glass from the last of the cognac they had brought from Paris. The two women raised their glasses in a silent toast to their uncertain future.

"I just wonder how your dashing Devane will react when he realises he has hired the one vampire who won't kill for him."

It was Khari's turn to raise an eyebrow in surprise, Ha'ali Eshan using that hated term to describe herself – the world had truly turned upside down.

Khari saved his life. Devane had no doubt of that. He staggered to a small park opposite the hotel, his whole being trembling with the adrenaline rush from his confrontation with the deadly creature, Eshan.

Devane sat on a bench, and with a shaking hand attempted to light a cigarette as he relived the meeting in his mind. His gamble that Khari would keep him alive had paid off, a risky strategy but a successful one, at least so far. He gave his neck a reassuring rub, it was still intact by the narrowest of margins.

Before confronting the vampire, he had waited, patiently, letting hours turn to days, watching the hotel where the two women were staying from a discreet distance until he was confident of their movements. If Parrish was right about her abilities, the young Slav woman Khari, could sense he was genuine, that he meant them no harm and thereby keep Eshan's fangs from his throat. He doubted few if any modern day humans were allowed to know about the Dark Kind and live.

His senses reeled. The Dark Kind were real. Fear and fascination merged into one powerful, nameless emotion. Nothing could ever be the same again. If this wasn't complex enough, he felt a strong attraction to Khari. If she truly could read minds, she already knew this but somehow it did not matter. He felt enchanted, as if under her magical spell; lured in by her wondrous golden eyes, and it felt good. She had gazed into his soul and not finched away. He walked towards his hotel through the narrow strip of park, it was impossible to ignore that this was a country at war. Earlier as he passed through the icy drizzle-damp streets of theatre land stripped of their gaudy gaiety from the black out, the city's stalwart citizens passed him, hurrying home, clutching gas masks.

He needed to focus on his team and their efforts in the battle to remove the threat of invasion. It was not a good time to fall in love. He paused to listen to a robin, high in a plane tree, its joyous song rising above the drone of the city traffic. Maybe it was the best time to fall in love after all he mused, as the bird and its carefree song in its small green oasis defiantly ignored the dangers around it. Love, like the bird, was a reaffirmation of life amid so much destruction and death.

He decided to keep his feelings to himself. A bemused Archie MacCammon, for all his toughness, a hopeless romantic at heart, would no doubt lecture him on the strange workings of destiny and the importance of following intuition. He didn't want lectures, just to see Khari again. As soon as possible and without her Dark Kind guardian.

Chapter Ten

Azrar's Stronghold, Isolann, 1939

With the mutual respect of one predator to another, Prince Azrar watched a hunting owl swoop low from the battlements, its wings briefly silvered by the light of a full moon. It dropped suddenly from sight, having found its prey somewhere in the thick shrubs surrounding a walled garden within the outer compound of his stronghold. The Jendar wandered into this oasis of tranquil beauty, so at odds with the encircling harsh military world of his keep. It was an alien place to Azrar, a gentle, feminine and totally human haven.

A single white rosebud remained in Khari's garden. Frosted by the glacial touch of the night air, its frail beauty would be lost by morning as the warmth of the autumn sun would trigger its inevitable decay. But now, for one more night it was perfect; the last flower in a midnight garden.

Azrar reached to feel the pearly softness of the petals, his touch as cold as the frost that silvered the rose. He lingered a while in the garden as if to savour the last moments of peace and serenity symbolised by the flawless white rose. Then he put aside all thoughts of peace without a moment's regret. As he crossed his courtyard, he could sense the coming danger, a threatening shock wave of human fear and turmoil blowing in on the wind across the mountain peaks. This was good. Azrar's being was vibrant with fiery energy, taut-wired, ready for action. It was how it was meant to be, he was created for combat and his fierce warrior's spirit stirred, eager for battle.

The Jendar paused again, to watch a team of young Isolanni men train in the compound. Surely no enemy would mistake these hardened, well disciplined warriors as mere nomadic goat herders now. Azrar had no idea when the attack on Isolann would begin, his own existence and the lives of his people had never faced such grave peril but Jendar Azrar finally felt truly alive, the unnatural torpor trapping him for three lost centuries lifted forever.

He touched the rose to his lips, saying goodbye to the serene years of peace his people had enjoyed for so long and returned to the inner keep where his tribal headmen and generals awaited. He needed to plan for the arrival of the British and Russian emissaries.

From the shadows, Ileni watched the vampire Prince kiss one of Khari's roses, only to throw it on the compound cobbled floor. She held her breath, unwilling to confront her master. When he was gone, she ran from her hiding place to rescue the bloom. She gently lifted the rose from the ground, carefully avoiding the barbed thorns. How dare that creature treat this lovely thing so callously? She knew she was foolish to expect anything more from Azrar, after all it was his inhuman heartlessness that had sent her daughter away. Now he trampled something so beloved to Khari with equal cold indifference.

"Are you all right, Umma?"

Ileni turned to see her eldest son approach. She pushed aside her bitterness and her face was lit by a warm, loving smile of welcome, allowing him to envelope her in a bear hug of greeting. Faraz had become an important general in the Isolanni army. Tall for an Isolanni, Ileni reached up to stroke his hair in a familiar gesture of affection, sighing as she saw so many silver hairs now mingling with the coal black. Only yesterday it seemed, he was a dark-eyed, smiling babe she'd lovingly cradled in her arms. Time was the real enemy, it had turned her tiny, helpless babies to warriors and changed her to an ageing woman, stiff with arthritis. Time was a cruelly implacable foe, one that could never be thwarted unless you were fortunate to be born Dark Kind. Time did not heal the pain of separation; would she ever see Khari again? Ileni forced away these gloomy thoughts, what good did they do? It was so good to see Faraz again. She should be celebrating his safe return from a scouting expedition perilously close to the Svolenian border.

"I am fine, you are back and all is well now. I am also missing Khari and can't help worrying about you all. Are the rest of our family all right?"

Faraz gave his mother another bear hug. Like all her sons, he had nothing but love and respect for the tough little woman who bore and raised them in the mountains of their tribe's wanderlands.

"Dobruz has taken them all to the mountain hideaways. Khari is probably the safest of us all, the Germans and Svolenians will make a joint move against us soon. She is better off away from Isolann." Faraz spoke without rancour. The danger from invasion was just one more thing to face in the ongoing battle for life in such a harsh environment.

"The Prince must be really missing her now," he added. "I have heard some important strangers are on the way, seeking an alliance with Isolann against the Nazis."

Ileni touched the rose to her lips, this at least gave her a glimmer of bittersweet satisfaction. The Prince for all his lofty pride had made the biggest mistake of his long, long life sending Khari away. A mistake, she prayed, that would not bring death and destruction to the ordinary people of Isolann. It was right that only the Prince should pay for his folly and arrogance.

Ileni's plan to avoid the Prince failed miserably later that night as she unwittingly encountered him as she rushed through the corridors towards the kitchens. She paused to bow very low, her eyes lowered. She stayed on her knees, ignoring the excruciating pain in her knees from the cold flagstones. It was more tolerable than the harsher cold emanating from him.

"Get to your feet, Ileni," Azrar commanded, "You are still angry with me for sending Khari away. If it is any consolation, I meant her to be back long before now."

Ileni kept her head low, the Jendar was too close, the waves of ice too powerful. And he was right, she had never forgiven him for Khari's long absence. Of course the Prince wanted her back with the allied emissaries arriving soon. Khari was just a tool to the Jendar, another human to be used. To Ileni, she was a treasured daughter.

"I trust the Lady Eshan. She feels it is far too dangerous to attempt to cross Europe now. Khari's long absence is a hard burden to you and Sandor, Ileni. I wish she was here too."

Now, his words made Ileni feel bad for her continued ill feeling towards the Prince, a resentment that now dissolved leaving her heart less burdened. The prince continued to address her, "I will meet with these outsiders and form an alliance with them. If I can help end this war quickly, Khari will be able to return soon."

Ileni reached into her tunic and kissed her wolf talisman, praying the Dark Lord was right as she watched him stride away into the keep. Maybe Khari was just a useful intelligence-gathering device to Azrar but it meant she was important to him and would always enjoy his protection. If she was here.

Azrar walked to his war room to study the latest intelligence reports. He had a radio transmitter now, finally bringing the outside world into his stronghold. Again it was his southern neighbour, Svolenia that jeopardised his country. No longer communist, the Svolenians embraced the new creed of fascism with customary enthusiasm. The

Prince knew this meant his own country had been catapulted from a remote and forgotten state to one of high strategic importance. His mountain home was seen by the allies as a barrier to the Nazi advance from the South. If he prevailed, he would protect many remote and vulnerable regions of Eastern Europe. It was a heavy responsibility for such a tiny, technologically backward land, but one he would not back away from. Free Europe's enemies were his enemies too. His people, descended from ancient tribes of Steppe nomads, were deemed by the Nazis as racially inferior. The Svolenians would eagerly take this genocidal belief to further their own ambitions for the principality, fuelled by centuries of festering hatred.

Azrar had no illusions how terrible his people's fate would be at the hands of these powerful murderous lunatics should he fail to protect them. Even the landscape of Isolann was under threat. The mountains were rich in valuable ores; the foothills and plains lush and fertile, rapacious invaders would destroy the harsh beauty and its delicate natural balance.

Despite this seemingly hopeless scenario, Azrar knew Isolann had ways of protecting itself beyond the physical barrier of the mighty mountain range. He knew how to enhance the natural assets to form another natural line of defence. His first and most urgent task was to organise his people to alter the course of the two main rivers, to massively enlarge Lake Beral. The lake then became a virtual inland sea; totally blocking the southern approach to Isolann for land based armies. In winter the ice covered lake was unpredictable and treacherous, seemingly strong enough to tempt a crossing. King Darius lost tens of thousands of his invading Persian army to the ice without Azrar having to lift a sword in defence of his realm.

His people had already moved to inhabitable caves in the deepest valleys in the mountains, they would be well protected by near impenetrable sheer walls of jagged rock.

Only someone with local knowledge could find a way through the narrow and tortuous mountain paths. No mechanised transport could negotiate the confusing labyrinth of winding trails, many deliberately leading to sudden chasms and dead ends, perilous with rock falls and avalanches.

He began the gradual preparation of his people after Ha'ali Eshan's first visit – the rude awakening to danger he needed after so many wasted decades of torpor. Now every man, and most of the women without small children, were well trained in modern weapons and mountain warfare. There could be no direct assault on the enemy; this was a tiny principality with a small population of scattered nomads. But they had a deep well of courage and unswerving resolve; Isolann had never been conquered. It would not be now.

Chapter Eleven

Sir John Lowden-Dunne, the chief of the allied diplomatic mission gave a gasp of awe and astonishment as he surveyed the chilling grandeur of Jendar Azrar's stronghold. It overwhelmed him to silence and on shaky legs, he stepped down from the Russian military plane that brought him and three other diplomats with their aides to Isolann. After circling what they first assumed was a small mountain, one of many lesser peaks at the edge of the towering, black stone Arpalathian range, the craft had landed on a makeshift runway. This had been created in a wide, lushly green valley, its outer edges sheltered by dense forests to the south and the rest encircled by the mountains.

Despite the warmth of a late autumn sun, Sir John shuddered, strangely chilled, as he took in the brooding presence above them, for it was only on disembarkation he realised the mountain was in fact a purpose-built stronghold. Carved from the living rock, its uppermost battlements were so high that clouds encircled them.

Along with the other members of the delegation, the polite but mainly silent and reserved Isolanni showed him to comfortable quarters. Sir John sat on the edge of a heavy carved wood bed. What had he let himself into? Over forty years serving his country, first in the army, then in the diplomatic service had not prepared him for the dark dreamlike world that was Isolann. A land locked not just by the high mountain range that encircled it, but frozen in a distant, barbaric past. He'd already noted with rising concern mixed with curiosity the collection of bizarre armaments that adorned the walls of a great hall the party had passed through en route to their guest quarters. This labyrinthal journey through twisting, shadowy corridors was taken in near silence from their escort of Isolanni soldiers.

These obviously Asiatic people intrigued Sir John. Few in his department of the British Foreign Office had ever heard of Isolann. He had assumed it to be a remote and barely inhabited province of Svolenia. He was amazed to discover it was a separate principality and its indigenous population were not Slavs but descendants of Steppe nomads, a people unchanged from ancient times. Now he could see them at first hand, as an amateur anthropologist, these proud, almond eyed, dark haired people fascinated him.

Nothing in their little known history could explain the bizarre and spectacular stronghold of their Prince. What manner of culture could design and build such a fantastic edifice? The Isolann were a nomad race with no recorded past of building anything, not even a large town. And why was it designed to prevent any daylight seeping through its dark, shadowy corridors? He wondered about confiding his thoughts to the other delegates. Understandably two of the party were Russian ambassadors; if Isolann fell to the Nazis, the southern most states of the Soviet Union would be threatened. But strangely, one of the diplomatic party was a senior emissary from the Vatican. What was this Spanish Monsignor doing here? The churchman had been pleasant enough on the flight from the Ukraine, courteous and good humoured, but reticent to speak beyond making polite small talk.

The Russians though serious and aware of the importance of their mission, were still more outgoing and gregarious. They spoke freely of their belief that this tiny country was the key to success or failure in keeping this little known back door into Europe and Russia firmly closed to the enemy. A pragmatic decision had been made many years before to tolerate this tiny island of aristocratic rule as useful to the socialist regime. Svolenia had always been distrusted, believed to be too fickle, too treacherous to be allowed close to the Soviet border, whereas Isolann was steadfast and unchanging, an aristo-ruled state maybe, but one who would never threaten its neighbour.

    Azrar allowed his visitors a full day to rest in their quarters, and as night fell, sent them a summons to a lavish feast in their honour in the main hall of the keep.
    Unused to any indecision, Azrar grew angry and restless alone in his war room. His uncertainty over how to deal with the humans of this new era kept him back from meeting the diplomats in person. It felt wrong to be skulking away in his own stronghold, while the prince remained upstairs in his war room, his generals entertained the guests. Racasi, Azrar's most senior military chief — once an astute tribal headman, now a general, knocked discreetly on the wood and metal door to await Azrar's next command. The Prince called him in. Racasi saw with dismay that the Dark Lord was in a dangerous mood, his eyes noticeably darkening.
    Azrar gave a snarl of contempt as he picked up a pair of rimless black metal spectacles, their black lenses seeming completely impenetrable. Brought to him by Eshan on her last visit; he studied the object with loathing. Had his survival and maybe that of his people come to this? It was a matter of great pride that he had always ruled this land openly as Dark Kind. But this was a strange new century with constantly changing rules as Eshan had taken such risks to warn him. Yet donning these hideous glasses seemed a defeat, a concession too far to these invasive humans that had stolen his world.
    General Racasi shifted uncomfortably as his lord pondered over the issue of the dark glasses. The outsiders were very keen to address the Prince in person, but the

military leader was all too aware of the dangers to his master of such close exposure.

"My old friend, I have had uninterrupted dominion over this land since before you humans had a name for it. Has it all now come to an end? Or will these things make such a difference?"

The man, his lean face wizened to tough yellow leather by forty decades wandering the barren, wind blasted mountains, shook his head, uncertain how to address the Prince in such a volatile mood. The Pact meant his throat was safe from Azrar's fangs but there were many other ways to die in Isolann.

"My Lord Prince, it seems such a very little price to pay. These men will go away to their own lands and the war will descend like a terrible storm. But when the storm clears you will still be Jendar of Isolann."

Azrar sighed, the man was right of course. His explosive pride was a trait he struggled to control and it was only this pride that held him back from donning a disguise. Racasi was correct – it was a very small price to pay.

"I will be with them shortly." He replied, dismissing his general. He returned to his papers for a last study of the intelligence Eshan's agents across Europe provided for him. There was no doubt the gravity of his position; Isolann had never been so threatened.

An hour later, Azrar descended into his great hall, using the full force of his steel will to hold and control his powerful natural force field. His hair loose to the waist, he wore a version of the Isolanni native costume of loose, belted tunic and trousers tucked into knee length riding boots but in a black, luxurious fabric. Over this he wore a floor sweeping and dramatically voluminous surcoat in richest black bariola velvet studded with black metal and trimmed with black wolf fur. He did not need Khari to tell him the effect of his dramatic appearance had on his guests; even diluted by his repressed icy aura and hidden eyes.

He bade them return to their seats and sat at the head of the table on an imposing throne-like chair, the black stone carved in the fantastical alien gothic style of the inner keep. He accepted a gold goblet of damson coloured wine from a nervous manservant and raised it in a silent toast to his guests.

For Sir John, the descent into nightmare took a further plunge at the sight of the Jendar. Forcing unwanted and outlandish thoughts of demons and vampires out if his mind did no good. This was not a human. There was no disguising the inhuman malevolent gleam behind the creature's dark glasses or his uncanny icy aura. His sepulchral white face, though undeniably sternly handsome had a sharp planed bone structure that could not be based on a human skull shape. What Azrar actually was remained a mystery. Sir John was not going to ask him. In fact all he wanted to do was open his eyes and be back in his Chelsea home again, far away from this creature and his light-less lair. Instead he faced an uncertain future, would he be allowed to look at the true face of this handsome demon and still leave Isolann alive?

It took some time before any of them found the courage to speak. Urmanov, a stocky Russian diplomat ventured a nervous and hesitant thanks in broken Svolenian for the Prince's hospitality, it was enough to break the stunned impasse.

Azrar replied to him in fluent Russian and greeted Sir John in a word perfect but curious, old fashioned English but to the British diplomat's increasing dismay the words were spoken in a strange and inhuman timbre. He looked around for the comforting sight of Monsignor Reyes, armed with his large gold crucifix and the ancient spiritual might of the Roman Church, but there was no sign of the Vatican's emissary. Somehow the absence of the churchman was most chilling. Sir John could not fight his belief he was in the presence of something dark and demonic, that the supernatural world really did exist, embodied in Jendar Azrar.

Yet again, it was the Russians who kept the meeting on course and thereby preventing Sir John in fleeing the table in panic. Courteously, the Soviets agreed to use English as a common language. The Prince addressed them at length and gave an obviously sincere and firm commitment to the allied cause.

"I can understand how difficult this meeting is for my honoured guests from the Soviet Union. Dealing with a foreign aristocrat to plot against an old ally, a fellow Slavic nation, must pain you, especially as Svolenia has so totally rejected its socialist regime."

"Indeed, Prince Azrar," Urmanov agreed with a sigh, any sign of discomfort at addressing the Jendar well muted. "But it was their choice to reject their own glorious revolution and become the fascist running dogs of our mutual enemy. They must take the consequences."

Taking courage from his Russian counterpart, the British diplomat signalled his equally frightened aide to bring a wooden crate to be brought as a gift to the Prince. Avoiding eye contact, he signalled to an aide to crowbar it open — revealing a cache of machine guns. Azrar controlled the urge to recoil from the unfamiliar and unpleasant smell of machine oil and new metal and took a weapon from the case. It was as light as a child's toy.

"A small token of the esteem His Majesty King George and the British government holds for you and your valiant people," Sir John ventured, horribly aware of the nervous tremor in his voice. The Russians had played a far better hand; somehow it felt a safer strategy to treat the demon Prince as normally as possible.

Azrar addressed his guests in his rich, wolf growl voice, "I am not naïve to the grave peril this land now faces. Yet many things comfort me, the sheer brutality of our winters, which protect us so well, and the impossibly difficult terrain of this mountain-girthed land."

The Prince's eyes flared with a fierce light the glasses could not hide as he continued,

"But most of all, Isolann is kept free by the indomitable will of my people to resist all invaders for many thousands of years. The Nazis will not prevail here."

The other Russian emissary, Leonid Sergiov, nervously wiped his hands of sweat with a fine white linen napkin, fighting back the irrational fear he had of this strange nobleman in his bizarre lair.

"Jendar Azrar, with the utmost respect, no one doubts the great courage and resilience of your subjects. But because of the strategic importance of this region, you may face the full force of Hitler's war machine."

He made a gesture towards the outer compound where earlier, the diplomats had watched Azrar's army train with rifles.

"You have no modern large armaments, no tanks or warplanes. But we can give you weapons and teach your people how to use them."

Only the nervous breathing of the humans around the long stone table punctured a tense silence. Azrar picked up a golden knife from the table, running a strong slender finger along its edge. Somehow the sight of the Prince handling a more primitive weapon, albeit only a blunt utensil, caused a collective intake of breath from the visitors, so potent was his aura of strangeness and menace.

"You will give us nothing, gentlemen."

Azrar waited until the ripple of nervous murmuring from his guests abated, then continued, "But I will purchase from you whatever I deem necessary to protect this land and my people."

Azrar turned abruptly to leave the hall, bidding his guests enjoy the rest of their meal– no difficulty to a group of tired and grey faced men enduring rations and hardship back home. He returned to his war room to mull over the evening when a tap on the door revealed a nervous Racasi again.

"One of your guests, a Monsignor Reyes, has asked for a private audience with you."

Azrar raised an eyebrow in surprise; he had no intention of entertaining a representative from the same church that so brutally decimated his kind for two millennia.

"The Monsignor expected you to refuse and asked me to give you this." Racasi handed the Prince a small gold badge in the form of a dragon's head behind two crossed keys. Reassured by this potent symbol, he handed it back to his general. "Show him straight up."

The Monsignor entered the room, giving a slight nod in a polite but muted gesture of greeting between two equals. He was a wiry, rail thin man, little more than five foot six in height. His hair was a halo of lustrous black shot through with streaks of steely grey. Gentle brown eyes, combining great intelligence and compassion light up his thin, aesthetic face from within.

"It's good to see you still with us, Prince Azrar. The years have been kind to you."

"I wish I could say the same for you, Ma'alore."

A bright golden shimmer in the air turned night into day as the war room became bathed in a soft golden light with a curious yet beautiful light scent of flowers. A much younger version of the same man stood before Azrar. He spoke, his manner urgent and pointedly less respectful.

"We have much to discuss vampire, and very little time."

The room resonated with the bright shimmer again before disappearing to return back the room to deep shadowed gloom. Monsignor Reyes was back to his original, older appearance.

Downstairs, the near unbearable tension had lifted noticeably as the Jendar left his hall. Sir John's knuckles were white and bloodless as he had clenched his hands so tightly throughout the brief audience with Isolann's unearthly leader.

"What in Hell's name was that?" his aide Jenkins managed to whisper. 'What in Hell, indeed?' concurred Sir John to himself. Only the two Russians seemed completely unfazed by Azrar's eerie presence. The bear-like Urmanov put a meaty arm around Sir John's thin, bony shoulders.

"We have lived at peace on the borders with this ancient darkness for many centuries. We don't bother it and it in turn leaves us alone."

"But what the Hell is Jendar Azrar?"

"If you don't know, it is not for us to tell you. But go back to your King, to your Winston Churchill with one message — that Isolann is a tough little land that will prevail against the Nazis – with some help from us all. Of course," the big man gave a humourless chuckle before continuing in a conspiratorial tone. "In return we insist on your discretion. Isolann is ruled by a brave and resourceful Prince, no one need know any more than this."

Sir John nodded his head gravely, fully accepting the wisdom of this, for who would believe him back home?

Chapter Twelve

London, England, 1939

Click, tap, click, tap, click, tap, tap. Eshan could hear a curious, metallic, rhythmic sound coming from her private office at the blood research clinic in Belgravia, London. She gave a small sigh of exasperation as she felt power waves from a Dark Kind coming from within her inner sanctum. Only one Dark Kind could be that irritating – Garan. She opened the door to see him slouching back in a thickly padded leather swivel chair, spinning it around while impatiently tapping the floor with his platinum-tipped cane.

"About time, your ape lackeys said you would be here at six." His youthful, foxy features were marred by a petulant scowl as he put his feet up on her polished mirror-topped mahogany desk. Eshan winced, this elegant eighteenth century piece was precious to her for its graceful beauty, the desk was reputed to have once belonged to the doomed French queen Marie Antoinette. "It's bad enough to be hanging around in gloomy old Fogtown in Dampland. Even the locals have grey, watery blood."

"Watery or not, you've drunk plenty of it", Eshan muttered as she pushed his feet off her desk with an outraged growl. His utter lack of respect for fellow Dark Kind, especially the nobility, was legendary but must he also wreck her fine antiques? "What do you want, fool? I am extremely busy."

"Now don't be nasty, Eshan," he replied in mock hurt. "I've heard word among the survivor grapevine that you are seeking out Europe-based Dark Kind for some sort of project."

"It's still Ha'ali Eshan to you, commoner. I know it will not interest you. You've never obeyed a single command from a Jendar or an Ha'al all your life. You certainly won't take orders from a human."

"You've got that right." Garan yawned, allowing his stiletto-sharp fangs to descend to their full curving length. Like all the chameleon survivors, Garan wore the human garb of this decade. With his dark red hair styled short and wearing a sober charcoal wool suit, he looked almost respectable and therefore at his most uncomfortable. Only the ebony cane was an accessory he felt at ease with, an elegant sword stick he'd stolen from a victim. He stretched out in the chair before rising to leave. "What shall I tell anyone I meet?"

Eshan explained the details of Joe Devane's covert squad. She hated divulging this information to an unpredictable maverick like Garan, but others would be useful for the team. Having someone like Jazriel onboard could swing the difference from possible failure to sure-fire success. Brave and co-operative, the stunningly handsome commoner, Jazriel, would be a wonderful asset. Having his lover Sivaya on the team was potentially less beneficial, she did not have his effortless ability to get on with humans, but she was courageous and much quicker witted then Jazriel. Garan's response to her scheme elicited the expected response. Dark Kind did not laugh but his scornful amusement was obvious. And anger.

"You have always been a sorry excuse for a vampire, Eshan but this must be the ultimate betrayal of your kind. And so hypocritical! All these years of berating me for risking exposure when all I was doing is being Dark Kind, enjoying to the full my predator's birthright. Now you want to work with humans, as openly Dark Kind. And what do you think this ape Devane and his cronies will do with their pet vampires once their little war is over?"

"Devane respects us. We will not be harmed," Eshan relied evenly though the same thoughts had occurred to her. She relied on Khari's gift to see deep into the hearts of the humans she now worked with. Garan slammed his cane onto her desk, sending a cut crystal carafe of fine ruby wine smashing to the floor, the shards on the floor spread like diamonds mixed with fresh spilled blood. The unexpected violence of his gesture shocked Eshan to silence. Garan stood up slowly, cleaning his wine-spattered cane on a white Irish linen kerchief. It too was now ruined. "Do you really think I will risk any Dark Kind life, especially one so beautiful and easy going as Jazriel by mentioning this madness?"

"Co-operation with the humans is the only hope for our survival, Garan."

He walked towards the door and turned back, his violet eyes now a stormy dark purple. With fangs bared he replied, "Killing humans, as many as possible –that's the only way for a vampire to survive. But perhaps you have forgotten what you are. Look in the mirror, Lady Eshan." How could she forget? She waited until Garan had gone and looked long and hard into the mirror. Her beauty had not diminished but what good was beauty when it left the one she loved so indifferent and cold to her. And how could she ever forget what she was? When every night she arose from Rest with the terrible, unending hunger, the gnawing, tortuous craving for human blood. How she could not pass a healthy young male without fighting back the urge to tear out his throat with her fangs and drink deep. She was always hungry, always weak yet she battled on and on every night against her true nature. For she knew if she succumbed to killing even just once, she would be lost forever to the dark world she fought with such hardship to distance herself from. Not from any self-loathing or rejection of her kind but from the instinctive need to survive in this human world.

Chapter Thirteen

St Tarod's Cathedral, Gerain, Amantzk, 1939

He knelt, praying, succumbing to a state of despair beyond the pain in his knees from hours spent on the cold rough flagstones. Time had lost any importance. All that mattered was the burden of his knowledge, so heavy, far more then a cloak of solid lead across his shoulders. The oppressive pall weighed down his soul.

He sighed with a sorrow bound into every cell of his being and glanced up at the light streaming from the glorious thirteenth century stained glass, bathing the cathedral aisle with ruby and sapphire and emerald light. Naively he once believed light was the all powerful symbol of goodness, that evil could be defeated with light, both spiritual and physical. He knew better now.

Much fear came from ignorance. Alejandro Reyes' own personal terror came from very real experience. He knew all too well what waited in the abyss, in the darkness, the hunger for pain and destruction that could never be sated. There was only one cure to his heartache, the pain from a lifetime where every moment was a living nightmare. That was victory. Total and complete victory against the enemy. And he knew that the first casualty in this war was already dead, the first victim was hope.

"Monsignor. Are you alright?" Reyes was brought back from his trance-like meditative state to everyday life by the worried voice of his young assistant, another priest of his secretive order. Greatly concerned, Father Gerry Mackie put a hand on the senior clergyman's shoulder. It was then that the Irishman noticed the thin stream of blood seeping across the flagstones from the Monsignor's broken knees. The sun had set more than five hours ago – it meant that Reyes had knelt and prayed in the Cathedral for twelve hours without moving. Father Mackie helped him to his feet.

"There is no need for concern, my friend. This is just a superficial graze," soothed Reyes with the ghost of a smile. He was exhausted; every fibre of his being ached or worse.

The young priest looked uncertain as he took Reyes' arm and helped his mentor to the nearest pew to sit down. The cathedral was in near darkness, save for the small, perpetual sacred light burning in a red glass by the high altar. Father Mackie walked to the nearest sconce and lit the largest candles he could find. As the warmth of the softly golden candlelight reached Monsignor Reyes, he seemed to revive quickly and smiled to reassure his anxious assistant.

"I needed some time in a place of purity and grace after my visit."

Then Gerry Mackie understood the reason for the priest's long painful vigil; he had not long returned from Isolann and its monstrous Prince.

"Did Azrar have any news?" queried the younger man, "Or anything to help us?"

Reyes sighed. He could never be close to Dark Kind without feeling contaminated. "We must continue to be patient my friend. The Blood Drinker received me with courtesy and respect – far more than I could give him. But he knows nothing."

"How can we be sure?" Mackie questioned, "We are dealing with something that is not human after all."

"The Dark Kind are many things, all of them vile, but lying is unknown to them. Deception and treachery are it seems traits of purely human weakness."

Monsignor Reyes struggled to his feet, wincing, but the muscle cramps and stiffness persisted. "I need to take a walk around the cathedral gardens, my night-scented stocks will be at their best now. Walk with me, Gerry. Perhaps we should temporarily put aside our mission and concentrate on how we can help alleviate suffering here in Europe. Forget the future, there is a very real flesh and blood monster threatening the world's innocents now; one that is all too human."

Chapter Fourteen.

Chess Manor, 1939

   Fragile beams of moonlight silvered a woodland glade on a warm midsummer's night; the English countryside at its most serene. A harsh report of handguns shattered the peace, scattering forest creatures in a panicked flurry and flutter through the undergrowth.

   They were in no danger, they were not the targets of the guns. Joe Devane's Spook Squad wrecked their peace as they shot at practice targets deep into the woodland surrounding Chess Manor. The squad was now a small but cohesive force, despite their bizarre abilities and widely varying origins.

   Their headquarters was this remote country house in the Chiltern Hills encircled by its own two hundred acres of fields and woodland; close enough for easy access to London but well away from prying eyes. In just a few months Chess Manor had been transformed from an empty redundant country house to a centre of intense activity by its strange community; all arriving with a common sense of commitment and purpose. The first to join Devane and MacCammon was Anna Vandenberg, a Dutch born empath and psychic. Soon after came Lenny Dawn, a circus performer with latent telekinetic abilities. After Khari and Eshan came two tough British career soldiers; Major John Raker and Colonel Alan Fitch-Brown who fitted seamlessly into the team. Both had clairvoyant ability— which they had spent a lifetime suppressing. And both men welcomed this extraordinary opportunity to use their unwanted skills as weapons against the Nazis. To be welcomed and valued as having useful talents, not shunned and mocked as freaks, was a liberating experience.

Inevitably, there was one very major problem for all the humans on the team, with the exception of Khari — the very real difficulty overcoming their shock at finding a vampire female in their midst. It was a monumental concept to take on, shattering their belief systems to not only discover that such creatures existed, but to be expected to live and work alongside one.

That night, an extra nervous tension in the group made concentration difficult for both Khari and the empath Anna Vandenberg. The women waited until MacCammon paused to help Fitchie with a jammed pistol, then walked away to the edge of the glade to take a break from the shooting. Khari refused a cigarette from the Dutchwoman with a warm smile.

"Thanks, Anna, but I don't think it will help."

The dark haired older woman nodded in rueful agreement and put the packet away unused in her khaki overalls. "We will all be less nervous when Devane gets back."

Khari didn't want to add, "*if* he gets back." He wasn't just the leader of the squad, she really liked him. Hell, who was she kidding, she had fallen in love with the American commander. Due back any day, Devane and Eshan were on a high risk mission to Sofia to recruit two more Dark Kind, Jazriel and Sivaya. If the anxiety created by having two members of the squad in deadly peril in occupied Europe was not bad enough, the prospect of two more vampires at Chess Manor put everyone on edge.

Joe Devane spent the journey back to the Manor in a darkly contemplative mood, driving through the winding lanes of Hertfordshire in uneasy silence. His anxiety was not surprising as he shared the journey with three deadly creatures, any one of which could tear out his throat if they so desired, with no human conscience to trouble them.

Devane would never forget the alarm yet excitement in his human team when he presented them with Eshan for the first time. In the months leading up to discovering her, he suspected his even more shadowy superior authorities indulged him as he chased fairy tales. The reality that he had found a genuine vampire was dynamite. All pretence at humouring his eccentric whims disappeared and the project was truly operative. He was granted full co-operation and access to the resources of the allied intelligence network to seek out more Dark Kind.

The result now sat in the back of the blacked-out shooting brake, a male and female, both beautiful, the male spectacularly so and so far eager to join the squad. Devane recalled the male, Jazriel's handsome features break into a dazzling smile and with his velvet, languid drawl agree to return to England with him.

"There's only so much fun to be had here outwitting these tedious creatures. Nazis are such humourless brutes. Joining your squad could be an intriguing venture."

The female had not spoken but fixed Devane with a ferocious, defiant glare from her all-forest green eyes, holding her lover's arm in a tight, possessive embrace. There had been too many dangerous moments getting out of Europe and Devane had to utilise the swift, silent killing skills of his weird new recruits on several occasions. With a combination of sheer good luck, razor sharp fangs and courage, they had miraculously got back to England unscathed.

As he crossed the invisible border into a moonlit Bucks landscape, Devane's thoughts turned inevitably to Khari. He knew now that he loved her, the past months absence from her had been awful. Was it possible to have a relationship with a telepath? What future was there when your loved one knew every thought, every unwitting betrayal?

He was jolted out of his reverie by the approach of an army vehicle. "Not now," he groaned, he needed time to train these new recruits. It could destroy the squad if they attacked British soldiers. Ever astute, Eshan could see Devane's anxiety and turned to speak to the new vampires in their harsh, snarling language. Sivaya gave a grudging growl of assent. Jazriel spoke to Devane in richly accented English,

"Relax, my friend. We are not savages."

But you are, mused Devane to himself. Dark Kind are wild creatures with the thinnest veneer of borrowed civilisation, their vicious predatory nature curbed only by the need to keep a low profile to survive. Devane glanced into the mirror, not fooled by the carved golden perfection of Jazriel's features. 'You are still a monster for all your good looks,' he thought grimly, 'but with luck you will be my monster, a living weapon against the human monsters I swear to defeat by any means'.

The shooting practise finally over, Khari and Anna linked arms to walk with the others through the winding forest paths that lead back to the Manor. Khari enjoyed her relaxed and easy friendship with the Dutch woman. Before leaving for Europe, Devane entrusted Khari's care to Anna, grateful that she combined matronly warmth with considerable inner steel. Cassandra-like she had warned her Jewish husband and family to flee Holland but they had dismissed her as 'Josef's crazy gentile wife'. With a breaking heart, she had bundled her three children into the back of a fishmonger's lorry and fled to Britain. As she crossed the storm lashed English Channel in a tiny fishing boat, hugging her children close to her ample form, she knew they would all be safe, and they would survive. She also knew her husband and family would not.

As a natural empath, Anna taught Khari how to control and strengthen her formidable powers. She helped her protégé protect herself from taking in too much unwanted input, guarding herself from the danger to her sanity from the disturbing effects of other's nightmarish thoughts. It was not an exact science. Khari was haunted for weeks by the Major's terrifying memories of the Great War; his sheer Hell in the slaughterhouse of the filthy, terrifying, blood-soaked trenches. The indescribable horrors would never leave her, but Anna taught her how to lock them away in a mental strongbox. But sadly, not how to throw away the key.

In return, Khari had tried her best to prepare the human team members for the arrival of the new Dark Kind. In reality there was little she could do to lessen the shock. Now there was no time to help them any more. With a shiver of excitement, she saw the squad's shooting brake parked outside the Manor's main entrance. Though still some distance, she reached out with her mind and caught the faint but definite presence of Joe Devane. She wanted to run to the Manor and throw her arms around him in joyous, loving welcome, but held back her desires with self-discipline. Her act of cool detachment did not fool the empath.

"You two are quite insane," Anna chided gently, "absolutely everyone on squad knows you are crazy about each other and that has nothing to do with our spooky powers!"

"Darling Anna, you cannot be serious! We are at war and he is my commanding officer. Maybe when it is all over…"

Anna grew serious, her heart forever broken by her beloved husband's loss to the Nazis. She interrupted Khari's meandering by taking her shoulders and turning the young woman to face her. "Listen to one who knows. Even tomorrow may be too late. This is a time to seize love with both hands and hold it close."

Back inside the Manor to Khari's disappointment, there was no sign of Devane who was no doubt settling in the new recruits. The squad went to their rooms to change out of their camouflage combats for dinner. Once all reassembled in the drawing room, Lenny tried to lessen the tension with hilarious stories of his life on tour with the circus.

At first, Devane's entrance accompanied by two others a beautiful women and a stunningly handsome young man was an anticlimax to humans expecting to see monsters. Until they removed their dark glasses.

"May I introduce our newest team members, please make them welcome."

Khari had never experienced so deep a silence, such tightly wired-in emotions. Then Jazriel stepped forward, a tall elegant figure in an exquisitely tailored suit. He held out his hand towards the nearest human and gave a dazzling, disarming smile artfully designed to weaken women's knees and defuse hostility in men... It worked and the tension level dropped noticeably. Devane was immune to the vampire's charm, he correctly saw it as a well-used survival ploy, and knew there was a calculating, fierce, cold mind behind the handsome face. He glanced over to Khari, anxious for signs she was taken in by Jazriel's good looks. Of course she sensed his concern, what else could he expect from a mind reader! Though they had never openly expressed their feelings for each other, her loving smile of reassurance was all the answer he needed.

The punishing schedule at the Manor continued. In charge of training, MacCammon was relentless, pushing the team hard. The squad's shadowy founders were insisting they were given missions as soon as possible.

Lives would be lost unnecessarily if they were not ready. That night he silenced their groans as he announced another night target practice. Firing at objects in the darkness was no problem for the Dark Kind, but the humans had to be as accurate as possible.

"Does the Commander know what a brutal slave-driver he left in charge before starting his trip to London?" an exhausted Lennie moaned.

"There's a full moon out there, laddie, what more do you need, a spotlight?" the big Scot chided, ushering the reluctant team out of the games room, where they had settled for an evening of much needed relaxation. MacCammon had pushed them hard on the assault course all morning and without a pause, tutored them in intelligence-gathering techniques all afternoon.

Only the Dark Kind seemed eager for the training session, with the prospect of spending time in their natural habitat, the night. Where had time gone, mused MacCammon. Had it been two months already since the arrival of Jazriel and Sivaya? As their trainer, he had been all too aware how hard it was for all the squad to take on two more vampires. The team struggled to pull together, to dovetail their strengths and abilities. Inevitably, it was the human males of the team who found this time the most difficult. It was an understandable and expected fear; they knew how the vampires survived. They had just about coped with the reality of Eshan. Her power was so muted, so weakened by her reassuring vow not to kill humans. There was no such assurance with the newcomers, who were still cold blooded killers with all their speed, strength and ferocity. The concept of Dark Kind honour was an abstract one to the human members of the team and few would admit to trusting them.

Of the newest Dark Kind, Jazriel was the easiest to work with. Uncomplicated and focused, he won them all over with his indolent charm. It helped to calm down the atmosphere in the Manor, but no one was taken in. He was just as dangerous as any other Dark Kind.

His partner Sivaya remained aloof and hostile. She clearly only tolerated being at the Manor while Jazriel remained interested in the squad. Too besotted with him to leave, too distrustful of humanity to enjoy the situation, she remained a loose cannon, the most unpredictable team member.

MacCammon was not naïve. He knew these unearthly creatures were volatile and lethal. They had no loyalty to humankind and would stay only while it suited them. Handling them was like playing with active nitro-glycerine, and he was indebted to Khari's insights to their behaviour. Now the night creatures stood bathed in the ethereal moonlight. He could see how much they belonged to the silver light, how it lit their beautiful yet sharp, fierce features, how it sparkled in the glitter of their opal eyes. They embodied man's darkest fantasy, beings from the most ancient fairy tales where beauty and death were dangerously intertwined. MacCammon sought the familiar weight and cold metal of his handgun to drag him back to reality – his new, strange version of reality. He steadied Jazriel's icy golden hued hand as he helped him aim at a target.

"Get the balance right and this gun will all but find the target for you."

The tall, blue-black-haired vampire nodded with a slight smile, enjoying learning new skills and the adventure. Already adept at swordplay and old duelling pistols, it was his first time using modern handguns.

"Come on, Jazzman. I got a score of forty at my first attempt. Let's see if a Dark Kind can beat that on a first go," Khari teased gently, her arm and shoulder aching from her handgun's recoil. She ignored the steely glare from Sivaya's forest green eyes. Khari had become good friends with Jazriel from day one. It was nothing to do with his incredible good looks; they simply got on well. She already knew the pointless folly of being emotionally involved with Dark Kind, and more importantly she was in love with Joe Devane. She tried hard to befriend Sivaya but the golden haired being distrusted humans too much to relax her guard.

"There's a vehicle approaching from the west."

No one, even the Dark Kind with their sharper senses could detect anything. But they trusted the Major's sixth sense, and ten minutes later, a truck without headlights on drove into the clearing. MacCammon watched the truck lumber and lurch up the rough dirt track, and felt a forgotten part of him kick into being, his long buried conscience. When he started this squad, he was grateful he'd long lost his faith. For what he was about to do would surely condemn him for an eternity burning in Hell.

"Everybody, could you return to the house. Except Jazriel and Sivaya. I have some more practice for you."

Mac's grim tone brooked no dissent. When all the humans and Eshan were clear of the firing range, he turned to the two vampires, "This is all yours. I will clear up later."

At exactly 6:00 a.m. the previous morning, Horace Brook had been hanged for a series of six violent rapes and murders, his youngest victim only twelve. The atrocities had shocked a country already reeling from the horror stories filtering in from the war-torn continent. No one mourned the passing of the Monster of Surbiton.

Brook was not dead. During his execution, as he dropped through the trap door, blindfolded with a tight noose around his neck, Brook was caught by an intelligence agent and cut down. He was then bundled blindfolded from the death chamber. All that remained was a false death certificate and a weighted, sealed coffin to be buried in the prison's grounds.

Brook had no idea why he had been spared. No one had spoken to him throughout a long uncomfortable journey, rattling around the back of a truck, heavily shackled and gagged. He was cold and bruised and in shock. Brook was not intelligent, but had enough low animal cunning to realise he had not been spared as an act of kindness. The truck finally came to rest after bumping violently down a heavily rutted track and the door was unlocked. His blindfold was roughly pulled off and he blinked as bright moonlight streamed into his face. Brook looked beyond his burly captor but saw nothing but night cloaked woodland.

"Hanging was too quick and merciful for scum like you, Brook. Now you can go to Hell slowly, screaming in vain for help like those poor wee lasses. Rot in Hell, Horace". The big Scot, who knew exactly what awaited the man in the forest, roughly hauled Brook out of the van and threw him to the forest floor. Without another word, he joined Devane in the cab and drove away, leaving the astonished prisoner alone in the silent glade. Hope of escape began in Brook's heart and on unsteady legs. He blundered heavily through the trees, grateful for the strong moonlight. He did not question why he had been spared – just concentrated on getting through the tangled, barbed undergrowth that impeded his escape.

After some minutes of crashing about aimlessly, falling over many tree roots and the talon-like low branche swiping him in the face ripped his face, Brook rested on a log, bruised, cut and exhausted. As he slowly recovered he became aware of another presence in the clearing, something silent, still and menacing. He looked up to see no monsters but a beautiful young woman standing in the moonlight. She had long golden hair, not actually blonde but spun metallic gold falling down her back and framing her sharply defined pale features –beautiful but too knowing, too worldly to interest him sexually. There was no child-like innocence here.

Brook knew there was something terribly wrong with her presence in the woods. She wore modern clothes, a plain dark wool dress and jacket, and she did not look lost or distressed, but poised as if in her natural element. She smiled, angel-like, with her golden hair and glowing dark green eyes, holding out a slim elegant hand towards him. On the brink of madness since the hangman's noose tightened around his neck that morning, Brook's already shocked and exhausted mind raced. Perhaps he had died in prison after all, and this was an angel guiding him to Paradise. He approached her weeping softly in relief and gratitude; the whole world believed he was going to be tortured in Hell for what he did to his victims. He was within feet of the golden haired angel when he saw the fierce cold fire in her unearthly eyes, the imperious, predatory stare of a hunter. Her smile lost all illusion of sweetness; with a low whimper of horror he saw her long curved fangs descend.

Delirious with terror, Brook swerved, stumbled into the darkness, into the arms of a tall young man. A saviour?

"Help me, there's something after me, something evil."

The young man put his arms around the quaking Brook whose legs had failed him in his terror. The man smiled, he had an unearthly beauty far beyond that of the female pursuing him. With a low groan of defeat and despair, Brook realised the man's eyes were all opalescent turquoise fire, that he too had long curving fangs glistening in the silver light. Brook mustered his last pitiful reserve of strength and with an animal-like high-pitched scream, broke free, plunging into the undergrowth in blind panic. Freedom and safety lay beyond the forest, if only his prison-weakened muscles would keep going. As he crashed and blundered through the trees, he saw the moon-silvered fields beyond. He clutched his chest, his heart hammering, and oxygen starved lungs burning. If only he could just reach the open ground...

A vice-like grip on his shoulder spun him around and grabbed him tightly as the beautiful, deadly male held him out as an offering to his golden companion. Brook knew he was going to die; he flailed and thrashed as the female creature stepped forward growling softly, her fierce eyes glittering with anticipation. Brook's body arched in shock as her fangs sung into his neck. She began to drink, pausing only to watch her lover do the same on the other side of their victim's neck, swiftly draining Brook of every drop of blood. Within minutes, Brook was dead, another victim of the voracious bloodlust of the Dark Kind.

Beyond the woodland, Devane waited with his second in command by their van. As Brook's first scream of terror echoed beyond the trees, Devane hastily grabbed a cigarette, taking in a deep lungful of acrid, burning smoke.

"You feel like a complete shit, I can see it in your eyes, Laddie. Well I don't. The bastard is getting the punishment he deserves. I can show you the pictures of what was left of those poor lassies after that animal had finished with them. Being nutrition for our Dark Kind agents gives his miserable life some meaning. I will sleep easily tonight."

It was one of the longest speeches Devane had heard from the taciturn Scot. But he still felt uneasy about leaving a defenceless human in the woods to be hunted as prey. If only they would survive like Eshan with occasional drink of blood from anonymous donors, he could sleep easier. But these ferocious killers would not consider touching what they called 'carrion'. He could not order them to drink it, commanding them was walking on the thinnest ice.

"Go back to the house, Joe. I'll clean up after our friends."

Devane nodded, grateful for MacCammon's lack of squeamishness. Thoroughly evil though Brook was, it still felt too close to cold blooded murder. Taking life in combat was a grim necessity of war that he did not shirk from. Feeding humans to vampires was a big step towards a dark new place, one he was not really ready to take. Yet he had sanctioned throwing Brook to his death by the sharp fangs of his agents. Like Mac, he was grateful for his lack of faith, his moral turmoil was problematical enough without the fear of divine retribution.

MacCammon gave the matter of Brook's fate little thought. He respected the Dark Kind as a big game hunter admired big cats and wolves. To him, they were beautifully crafted living weapons, to be used and discarded as need be. MacCammon had already offered to be the one to kill the Dark Kind agents if the need arose but Devane believed it was his duty, he recruited vampires, and he alone would deal with the consequences.

Chapter Fifteen

London, England, 1940

"You don't have to do this, Khari."

"Of course I do, that is why I am working here with you in England and not living with my family in Isolann." Khari's unexpected terseness with him was understandable. Confronting a hostile ghost from her past was always going to be a gruelling assignment for her. Joe Devane took her arm protectively as they crossed a busy London street packed with shoppers. It was an illusion of a normal Monday morning in Regent Street, reality was the taped up shop windows, the gas masks slung on everyone's arms, the odd uneasy glance at the clear blue skies. There was an unspoken question on everyone's lips, as if saying it aloud would bring the nightmare to reality. It lingered, a tangible, very real threat, like the electrically charged prelude to a huge storm, brewing and brewing, ready to break. Just when would the Germans come, bringing their storm of death from above?

Devane and Khari walked together through the streets of London, assigned to interrogate Professor Jay Parrish. Devane was surprised when he heard the man was still alive. Parrish had narrowly escaped his fate at the end of the hangman's noose as a Nazi spy after last minute intercession from his family. Influential, powerful and wealthy, back in the USA, the Parrish clan of New England obviously had friends in all the right places. For his part, Devane was pleased the man was alive. He doubted there was any further evidence of espionage to interest his bosses but he welcomed the chance to find out more about Jendar Azrar, the strange being he had to share Khari's heart with. They paused before descending into the Underground. Khari was nervous about entering this claustrophobic network of tunnels, reeking of the press of humanity – it was an overwhelming assault on her mind, too many people with too much emotion, too much pain.

"It's okay, we can turn back now," Devane said soothingly, unwilling to compromise his team's greatest asset on this trivial mission. Khari glanced up, her wondrous eyes huge and fearful. She looked like a slender, graceful forest creature – a startled doe perhaps, paused for flight. She took Devane's arm and gave it a tight squeeze, desperate for reassurance. Khari had dropped her self assured barrier, her need, her vulnerability broke through Devane's reserve and he took her face in his hands and kissed her, no longer holding back the strength of his desire for her, his very real love. To his relief, Khari responded with equal fervour and the bustling London street, the war, everything disappeared. For a few moments the universe was theirs alone.

The steady push and shove of commuters and shoppers moving down the stairs to the station finally broke the spell but for Khari and Devane, their relationship was in a new place, from which there was no turning back. Devane started to speak but Khari hushed him with another, more light-hearted kiss. "Let's get this thing over with."

Devane nodded and once again apart and businesslike, they walked down into the station concourse, slipping into a side door that led to a secret corridor that wound for miles deep beneath the city. There they met with Dougie Halshott, a British army major and Devane's chief agent in London. In appearance, he looked like a bluff country squire more at home on a horse in the hunting field than in the city, Halshott was in fact a highly intelligent, astute covert agent with many missions behind enemy lines. He shook hands warmly with Devane and Khari but she was not taken in by the hearty mannerisms. She saw the cold steel behind the twinkling grey eyes and was relieved he was so adamantly on their side.

"Our guest is in room 32, old chap. And not in the happiest of moods."

"His mood is about to get much worse," Devane replied grimly. He was certain that Parrish would welcome the devil himself before speaking to him. Halshott ushered them to a locked, guarded room, the dank walls reeking of ancient damp. The dim lighting picked out a pitiful figure. Stick thin, maggot-pale, Parrish sat perched on a chair, his arms around his knees, rocking backwards and forwards with the rhythm of despair.

"I'll leave the two sergeants with you," Halshott stated, gesturing to the taciturn armed men in civilian clothing guarding the door.

"There is no need, I will speak to him alone," Khari replied quietly, visibly shocked at the change in Parrish. Last time she saw him in Isolann he was a lanky, but strong and vibrant young man. Now most of his hair had fallen out, what remained lay in grey, greasy strands, his face was skeletal, eyes shadowed, haunted. "I won't be in any danger," she continued, aware of the ripple of disapproval around her.

"No, I will stay. That is an order."

Devane was adamant, and Khari knew better than to argue with the American; he was her commander.

Parrish glanced up briefly, his eyes the flat, dead glare of a shark, shooting Devane a look of pure loathing before dropping his head and settling back to his rocking motion. He muttered beneath his breath, his voice cracked and dry as if unused to speaking.

"I'm still here, Devane. You and your limey friends think you can murder an innocent American citizen. You are so wrong."

"I'd drop the innocent nonsense, Parrish. You were caught on your way to a cosy tea party with Adolf Hitler."

"So? I have committed no crime, America is not at war with the Germans. Get out, Devane, you are stinking out the room with your hypocrisy. I'm not the one trying to recruit a team of murdering bastards. Vampire vermin. At least the Fuhrer is a human being."

"Watch your mouth, Parrish. You are in no position to throw your weight about," barked Halshott, raising his hand as if to strike the prisoner in the face. Khari stayed his hand with an angry glance, could they not see this man was already deeply traumatised and frightened, he'd faced the hangman's noose and was now hidden in this secret underground prison, far away from the rules and conventions of decent society.

"If you won't leave me alone, I will just have to speak to him in Svolenian."

On hearing the unexpected sound of a woman's gentle, compassionate voice, Parrish looked up again abruptly. With a quiver of shock, he recognised the extraordinary golden eyes, the silver blonde hair, Azrar's fey ward had grown into a beautiful young woman.

"What in damnation are you doing here? Why aren't you with that filthy, throat-tearing creature in Isolann?"

"Finding a way out of this mess for you, again. I saved your life in Isolann, it's becoming a habit," Khari answered in Svolenian. The faint light of hope raised a spark of life in Parrish's eyes.

"There must be a price to pay."

"Just your co-operation, tell them everything they want to know. They already know Jendar Azrar is Dark Kind, there can be no secrets any more from Devane and his team."

"That thieving bastard Devane has all my papers, there's nothing more to say."

"It's your knowledge of Svolenia they want. Tell them the layout of the capital city, where their military bases are located. You are one of the few people in Western Europe to know this land intimately."

Parrish fixed the woman with a long stare of incredulity; they had met so briefly in Azrar's stronghold, she had been a child. Why was she so determined to help him?

"Old feelings of guilt, I told Azrar about your plans to steal the library and unwittingly gave you a death sentence. That's far too much guilt for a child to bear," Khari answered quietly, as the echo of childhood feelings returned to haunt her. Parrish's suspicions that she could read minds were now confirmed, how else could she have known what he was thinking? No wonder Jendar Azrar had turned so swiftly against him. Parrish had plotted the vampire Prince's overthrow and death many times in his mind. All completely justified, the library was a fabulous treasure, too great and important to be held in the bloodstained hands of a Hell-spawned monster. He looked at Khari with a new respect, a new fear. Beautiful as she was, her kindly manner and gentle voice were illusions – her power made her a far greater monster than her guardian Azrar, that accursed, be-fanged creature in his remote mountain lair.

"I will tell you everything you want to know," Parrish muttered bitterly. "There's no point holding anything back; that little witch will steal it out of my mind."

Chapter Sixteen

Chess Manor, The Chilterns, England 1940

A discordant clash of steel on steel bounced off the oak panelled walls of the old manor. It was a familiar sound to the ghosts of the house, a bloody skirmish of the English Civil War once made the same walls resound to swordplay. Then it was a matter of life and death. Now the swords clashed for honour alone. At least that was the idea. That night after dinner, a new recruit to the squad, John Raker, a highly skilled fencing master before the war, challenged Jazriel to a friendly bout in the Manor's well-equipped gym.

The pressure of training had got to Raker, that and a restless desire to get away from the confines of the Manor and get on with fighting the war. His restlessness was also aggravated by the stress of close contact with the Dark Kind operatives. He had loathed the male vampire agent on sight. If Jazriel had been born human, Raker would have hated him as an indolent playboy, trading on his looks and easy charm. As Dark Kind, Raker despised him even more, Jazriel was without argument a cold-blooded killer who destroyed innocent lives without a flicker of remorse or pity. This hatred had become an unbearable burden, a physical pressure that lost him sleep and wrecked his appetite. Exhausted by this turbulent, negative emotion, he realised he needed to purge his feelings. With most of the squad still out of the Manor, he took his chance and called out to Jazriel.

"Eshan told me you were handy with a rapier. Dare to challenge an Olympic gold medal winner to a few bouts? Or is a mere human too puny a foe for a vampire?"

Khari picked up on the man's dangerous mood and reached out to gently touch Jazriel's arm, speaking to him in the vampire language, "Find an excuse, Jazzman. He's in a filthy, unpredictable temper. And remember he will be more dangerous than a normal human opponent; his special gift is ultra fast reflexes with latent precog skills. "

Jazriel flashed her one of his most disarming smiles. "Don't concern yourself, little one. He is still just a human. I will let him wear himself out. I'll even let him win a few bouts to save his pride and self respect."

The two men walked to the gym, and fetching down the rapiers from the wall display, began to swing their weapons ready to fight, not even bothering to change into the protective whites and face guards. Seeing this reckless act of madness, a horrified Khari ran out to find Mac and Devane, still out in the grounds with the rest of the squad deciding the next day's exercises.

At first the two combatants parried and sparred cautiously, quickly getting the measure of each other's skills. Raker sensed the vampire was holding back, he knew the creature was faster and stronger than any normal human. It seemed Raker's heightened abilities made little difference. He decided to provoke his opponent into a more challenging attack but Jazriel was aware what Raker was doing and held back with restraint. He was honour bound not to hurt this human, even if meant taking a few cuts or worse himself.

Raker battled on, fighting the onset of fatigue. Jazriel was indeed a brilliant swordsman, elegant and spare in technique but with an astonishing finishing speed. Raker felt his opponent's blade tip touch his clothing many times but such was the vampire's astonishing control of his rapier that it never damaged the cloth.

"It's a good thing your kind don't compete in the Olympics," Raker laughed humourlessly through clenched teeth, his lungs were agony, his sword arm turning to lead.

"Got better things to do, old man," replied Jazriel evenly, flashing a wicked smile.

"Like lurking in filthy, dark alleys waiting to tear out unarmed men's throats," Raker spat, lunging forward to attack with the last resource of energy, giving his sword the extra edge of hatred.

"Stop this madness!" Devane's strident voice managed to still the vampire with his prenaturally swift reflexes, but it was too late to stop the impetus of Raker's lunge. The rapier cut through the flesh and muscles of his shoulder, to become embedded in the black bone beneath. Jazriel gave a low gasp of pain before pulling out the blade, leaving a fast flowing stream of thin purple blood in its wake.

"Oh, Hell, what have I done? I'm so sorry." The sight of blood draining from the creature, an ally and fellow squad member shocked the madness from Raker. Horrified at how far he'd gone, he rushed forward to help.

"It's nothing really, this will be healed over by the end of my next Rest," Jazriel reassured the agent through clenched teeth, the pain bringing his fangs down into view. Raker fell back, horrified at his first sight of the stiletto-sharp blades of curving silver white bone.

Sivaya ran in, her forest-green eyes now totally black with fury, "What have you done, human?" she snarled. Unaware of how much his life hung in the balance Raker moved towards Jazriel, his hand held out to help. Hastily, Jazriel muttered to his outraged and dangerous lover in their language, in an urgent attempt to prevent her attacking Raker, controlled his pain with sheer will power. He had experienced much worse in his long lifetime. "It's nothing, sahma'a. Just a sporting accident. No harm done."

"Get the wound seen to, Jazriel, I'll speak to you later," snapped Devane. He had seen only a few brief moments of the fight; it had little to do with sport. When the two vampires had gone, Devane turned to Raker.

"Do you feel better now, got it all out of your system? Was it worth damaging our best Dark Kind operative and alienating another? For what? Human pride? Or is it the start of a one-man crusade against vampires? Do we have a budding Van Helsing in our midst?"

Raker dropped his head with remorse. What if he had killed Jazriel, or provoked the vampire into killing him?

"It was as Jazz said, a sporting accident," Raker muttered. Devane glanced up at Khari who quietly nodded her head. The man's remorse was genuine, what good would it serve the squad to tell Devane that Raker had wanted to kill his Dark Kind opponent in the heat of the fight. Jazriel's injuries were superficial and would soon heal, nor would he hold any grudge against Raker; it was not the Dark Kind way to harbour resentment.

Devane was still not convinced, but had to be guided by Khari's unique insight. "Ok, that's the end of it. But I insist on no more fencing without full safety equipment and no more bouts between humans and Dark Kind. What were you two idiots thinking off? It had to end badly."

Soft rain speckled a leaded glass window, creating glistening rivulets racing each other downward in a wayward shimmering trail. Khari sighed, how gentle the weather was in this country which grew more beautiful with each day's journey into spring.

Feeling restless, she grabbed her coat and stepping through a set of French doors, walked across the old stone flagstones of the Manor towards the now tangled, overgrown formal garden. At least it was still a garden; neglected and forlorn but not dug up to grow vegetables like so many others in Britain. Unbowed by the rain, the jaunty heads of daffodils nodded in a light, mild wind. The still winter sodden mossy grass brushed by her footfall smelt fresh and new. Beyond the garden, new lambs bleated on the rolling Chiltern hillsides.

Khari raised her head to let the gentle rain run down her face like a welcoming caress from her new home. In her own land, the weather was an enemy, always harsh and confrontational. The wind could hammer down laden with ice from the mountains, or roar with hot dragon's breath up from the southern plains, scorching the earth bone hard, desiccating crops to brittle skeletons. In Isolann now, winter was still holding the country in its ruthless grip and would do so for at least two more months. Khari tried to imagine what her human family and the Prince would be doing now. It would not be the old, timeless and quiet rhythm of their lives. That had gone forever. Isolann was now a country under siege with neighbouring Svolenia a land hungry fascist ally of the Germans.

Khari surprised herself how quickly she had adapted to life beyond Isolann's protective mountainous walls. Eshan had spoken of the world of wonder waiting for her to discover. She had been right, but her discovery of the delights of human society and Europe's technological marvels had been short-lived, all due to the depth of evil spreading from Germany like a fast growing disease.

Living at Chess Manor, learning to be a covert operative felt the right response. She could no more turn her back on the war than Azrar could turn away from defending his realm. She was just an ordinary young woman but she had been blessed –or cursed with a unique gift. Not to use it to help fight evil seemed a grave insult to whatever deity had bestowed it upon her.

Khari's reverie was interrupted as she saw Joe Devane approach; the transparency of his feelings for her needed no mind reading to know. They walked together across the lawn in comfortable, companionable silence, to pause by a low stone wall, beside which a little brook tumbled, its clear water flashing with baby trout. Khari's delight at the sight of the darting fish brought home to Devane just how young she was. She looked more elfin than ever, with her rain soaked blonde hair tightly framing her face, accenting the delicacy of her porcelain pale features. Devane decided to shelve telling her his feelings, wryly observing to himself that she probably already knew from probing his mind. Instead, he opted to surprise her with a kiss but her face was already rising to meet his – a relationship with a beautiful telepath was a challenge for any man! They enjoyed the precious moment of intimacy but the spectre of war was always too close, an unwelcome stranger forever glaring balefully behind their backs. Last evening's dangerous incident between Raker and Jazriel had given Devane a sleepless night.

"I am worried about ever getting humans and Dark Kind working together," Devane sighed, running his hand through his close-cropped brown hair. "Of course I expected problems for our people. It's a mighty tall order for them to accept vampires without fear, but the hostility is holding up our training schedule. Last night's madness could have ended with a tragedy."

Khari gave Devane's hand a comforting squeeze, knowing the success of the squad meant the world to him. "Don't be angry with Raker. It is only right for humans to fear the Dark Kind. You cannot wipe away millennia of instinctive behaviour overnight."

"And I can't form a squad of humans and Dark Kind without some trust on both sides. I need your help on this, Khari."

She smiled, then spotted the turquoise, brilliantly iridescent flash of a diving kingfisher. To Khari it was a fantastical creature, belonging more to the world of myth than reality –like the Dark Kind.

"What you are asking is no different to expecting those little fish to relax in the company of that hunting bird, or those lambs over there to lie down with a hungry fox. Get everyone together. Let the humans voice their fears, make them feel comfortable and normal about their hatred. Only understanding can bring some form of acceptance, then perhaps a form of trust will grow."

Khari dropped her head, this conversation was heading towards difficult ground for her; how would Joe feel when he knew about her feelings for Azrar? The American believed her to be compassionate and humane. Would this view change?

"Joe, you know that I was raised by humans but with a Dark Kind guardian. I will always love and respect Jendar Azrar, but I have no illusions to how dangerous he is. Our Dark Kind operatives are equally lethal. They are predators; we are their prey. We are asking a lot of our human team members, you might have to buy more time for the squad."

Devane shook his head. Time was a luxury even rationing could not preserve.

"Khari, I know you show respect for us by staying out of our minds. This may be distasteful to you but I want you to do some exploring, find out what exactly each human team member is thinking about the Dark Kind."

Khari moved away from him and walked slowly down the riverbank, she needed time to think this through. It seemed like a gross violation of trust. The same trust Devane had just stated the team was lacking. She turned back to him.

"It's too drastic, it could destroy the team. Let's try to talk it through first. Once the rest of the guys realise I've been into their minds, it will destroy far more than trust. They will start to hate and fear me too."

Khari prayed her plan to get everyone talking openly about their fears would work. The fight between Raker and Jazriel brought a new urgency. Sivaya was on the verge of quitting the squad, thankfully Jazriel had lost none of his enthusiasm. Khari didn't like the undercurrents in Raker's mind; meandering, formless but murderous thoughts buried deep in his subconscious that briefly surfaced the night before. Khari decided to chat to Anna about her concerns; the Dutch woman's empathic abilities were better than hers at interpreting the more subtle human emotions.

Her discussion was put on hold as ribbons of sweetly sad music caressed Chess Manor's oak panelled rooms. Anna and Khari met in the hallway and descended the main stairs together arm in arm, eager to seek out the source of the haunting sound. In the main drawing room, they found Jazriel playing Lenny Dawn's battered old saxophone, the vampire's strong but slender fingers completely at ease with the instrument.

Anna clapped her hands with delight at the thought of a musical evening. What better way to release the tension than sharing the pleasure of music?

"It's so beautiful –it sounds like an ancient folk piece. I had no idea Dark Kind could be musical," sighed Anna, it had been so long since she allowed herself any joy in her life.

Khari smiled gently, sharing the woman's delight in the music. She realised how much she had missed the melancholy songs of her homeland as she listened to Jazriel recreating one deep in the English countryside. She walked to his side, took a deep breath for courage and joined in, singing the age-old story of a lost love, not in the primeval, almost spine chilling manner of the Isolanni nomads but in her own sweet, honeyed tones. Recognising one of the old songs of Azrar's people, an appreciative Eshan entered the room and sat in front of the fire. When it was over and the enthusiastic applause died down, Eshan addressed the gathering, "That was delightful. I see Lenny has taught Jazriel well."

"You have a beautiful voice, Khari. And Jazriel, you play very well. Where did you learn to play the saxophone?" asked Anna. The vampire smiled, genuinely pleased with the compliment and gave a light-hearted bow of acknowledgement towards Lennie. Eshan took up the conversation. "Jazriel is an excellent mimic. He can imitate the style and phrasing of human musicians. But he is unable to interpret the music for himself, nor can he compose any of his own. Creativity is a precious gift of humankind. You must always treasure it."

At their prompting, Jazriel began another Isolanni love song, this time Khari sat back in a chair and closed her eyes as she allowed the music to take her home. Once again, she was astride her dappled stallion as she rode through the mountains of home, her brindled grey companion, Wolf padding silently by her side. Above her two courting eagles soared and spun together in an elegant aerial ballet. An ice wind, fresh and clean as if on the first day of creation blew over the valley and through the jagged peaks. The sun was setting in a glory of pink and gold, soon Azrar would awake from Rest....

Anna shook her head in wonder, entranced by the beauty of the music and the handsome vampire that played it. The firelight flattered his extraordinary looks, highlighting the perfect features and light golden skin, the glittering glory of his turquoise eyes. It also showed up highlights of strange iridescent blue-green in his black hair. Jazriel glanced up at Eshan and an enigmatic look passed between them. It was not missed by Sivaya who gave a low growl of contempt, breaking the spell of the music.

"Isolanni peasant music; how I hate all that human wailing."

She sneered in the vampire language, flashing warning fire from her darkening green eyes at her lover. Jazriel merely shrugged, unconcerned, instantly changing the music to a soulful American jazz number. Khari was fascinated. There was clearly an interesting history here but knew not to pry into Dark Kind lives.

The rest of the squad entered the room, instantly changing the atmosphere. None of the male squad members were comfortable about being close to vampires. Their fear was understandable and reasonable. Khari knew it was imperative to quickly build bridges between the two species; without trust the squad was doomed to failure. She spoke directly to the whole squad.

"Last night's accident showed us how far we have to go before we can work together as a team. Why don't you guys speak openly to the Dark Kind tonight? Ask them all the questions filling your mind. They will not take offence at your curiosity or your candour."

Joe Devane nodded his approval, smiling at Khari with gratitude. As with Eshan, she had proved a vibrant, hard working and courageous member of the new squad. Ffitch-Brown spoke up first. "It's no secret; I am scared of you vampires. I have great difficulty living under the same roof as inhuman things that live on human blood. Can you not find something else to drink?"

Jazriel put the instrument down and turned to face his questioner with a rueful smile, "I do like an excellent old cognac and never say no to good champagne. But they won't keep me alive. I have no other choice."

"So it is human blood or die?"

Jazriel nodded assent.

Raker took a long swig from a tumbler full of whiskey before stating,

"Then we are all in danger from you vampires."

Eshan took up the discussion. "Not while we work together. Dark Kind understand loyalty and honour in a way no human could comprehend. We would never betray or harm an ally."

Sivaya stood up to wrap her arms protectively around Jazriel, kissing his forehead as if asserting her partnership in front of the human females. She had endured centuries experiencing the effect his looks had on them. When she spoke, her voice had a low growling undertone, clearly an undisguised threat. "We do not enjoy that certainty from you. Betrayal by humans has already cost too many Dark Kind lives. One hint of treachery and our co-operation ends and with it any protection from our fangs."

"That will not happen," Joe Devane insisted, unhappy at the tone the female vampire had introduced to the discussion.

"It's okay, Joe," MacCammon replied, handing his commander a glass of pre-dinner sherry from the last bottle in the now empty wine cellar. "We want to know exactly where we all stand."

Eshan continued the discussion, uneasy that Sivaya's eyes were still darkened. Seeing her lover injured by a human had upset her badly and this made her dangerous and unpredictable. "The history of our two species is written in spilled blood, both purple and red. But once we did openly co-exist – not exactly in peace but with mutual respect. That is all we ask for now."

Eshan spoke with her usual serene wisdom and a more comfortable silence fell across the room. Joe felt better about the squad's prospects of working together. There was still much bridge building to do but he was sure the foundations had been laid that night.

While Sivaya continued to glare angrily at the humans, a guarded and cautious Jazriel continued to field questions from the human squad members. Khari followed Eshan onto the balcony, carefully pulling the blackout curtains closed behind them. Danger from German bombing raids was very real even so deep in the Chiltern countryside. Eshan felt stifled by the intensity of their interrogation and needed a brief respite in the fresh air. Outside the night air was sharp with a slight sweet scent from the brave spring flowers left in the neglected gardens. The earlier rain clouds had disappeared and Khari caught her breath in delight as a vivid bright green shooting star flashed across the sky.

"Please tell me if it is none of my business, but is that protectiveness of Sivaya's normal for Dark Kind couples?"

Eshan shook her head with a deep sigh of exasperation. As ever, she was comfortable being candid with Azrar's ward. Raised by a Dark Kind warlord, the girl had a unique insight into their lives no other human had shared, since the long distant days of the last Khari.

"It is not normal, but sadly understandable. Jazriel loves her well enough and will never stray or hurt her like a human male. But Sivaya knows she is not the greatest love of his life, that there is another still living whose hold on Jazriel's heart will never be broken. When two Dark Kind are meant to be together, during lovemaking, their souls reach out and briefly merge. Sivaya will never know this ultimate intimacy with Jazriel and it tears her apart.

"That is so sad. But why isn't Jazriel with his one true love?"

Eshan looked up to the stars. She understood Sivaya's pain only too well. Sometimes she envied the casual and fickle way humans could love and their emotional ease as they changed partners.

"That is a question only they can answer. Nobody else can understand why."

Only two days had passed since Khari's sterling efforts to breach the tensions seething beneath the surface within the squad. With no announcement from Devane on any forthcoming missions, life returned to its old uneasy pattern of training sessions and tentative inter-mixing between the two species. That night Devane took a call in his office. He put down the telephone with surprising force and sat back on his chair to calm himself and focus his thoughts. Despite his misgivings, he no longer had any leeway to stall his superiors. He now had the full details of his squad's first mission.

He walked into the Manor's music room and to catch MacCammon's eye. The entire Spook Squad had gathered in there for the evening pre-dinner get-together. He was pleased to see them all relaxed for the first time, chatting together with no noticeable undercurrents of the previous animosity. It had been an uphill struggle to get this far. But was it far enough? There was no more time to find out.

Earlier that day, Lenny had dusted down and re-tuned an old grand piano and with dusk fallen and everyone there, he was ready to take requests, delighted at having an audience again. The atmosphere in the room was light hearted. It looked like any elegant gathering in an English country mansion, a group of smartly dressed people, faces lit by the glow of candlelight. With a long mahogany table set for dinner, a cheerfully crackling fire chased away the November chill, as a sharp wind whined and scratched against the leaded windows like a peevish banshee. But it could never be a normal setting– not with the presence of three vampires.

"Sorry, Lennie, could I borrow Mac for a few moments. You will just have to do without his splendid baritone!" Devane quipped as he took his second in command out to his office. This created a ripple of laughter as MacCammon was renowned for a singing voice like an out of tune foghorn. Once seated, Devane's mood became sombre and ignoring rationing he poured two generous measures of an old single malt.

"Steady on, laddie, anyone would think there is a war on," MacCammon mock-chided, the twinkle in his eyes a give-away. His commander, used to his open irreverence with officialdom of any kind pushed the tumbler over to the big Scot.

"One we are about to get pitched into headfirst. What do you think Archie; are they ready yet?"

MacCammon took a long swig of the whiskey. "Something tells me, it doesn't matter whether they are or not!"

Devane nodded gravely as MacCammon ran through the progress of each agent's training and development of their special abilities. "And what of Sivaya? You seem to have the best rapport with her."

"Ah now, don't worry too much about our blonde spitfire, she'll be fine, at least for as long as the Jazzman is still on the team."

Devane's mood became serious and he fixed MacCammon with a steady gaze. "I want to form a squad for our first mission. It's a Hellish one to start with but we have no choice. We've been given a make or break baptism of blood and fire by our higher powers."

MacCammon was more than ready for some action. "I take it we will be using the vamps, do you want me to stay close to Sivaya?" he questioned. Devane nodded again, amazed how well he worked with Mac in the ten months since the squad was formed. They had such different personalities yet could dovetail their thoughts with ease till they appeared to work with one mind. "You seem to have the measure of her."

MacCammon gave a wry smile of amusement as he explained to his commander about the strange bond he'd formed with the most difficult member of the squad. "She reminds me of a wild cat kitten I once found, a tiny badly injured and bedraggled bundle of fury. I saved the little scrap and looked after it but it never stopped fixing me with a fierce green-eyed glare of sheer hatred." MacCammon held up his hands, criss-crossed with thin white scars. "As you can see, it rewarded my care with scratches and bites. Once old enough to fend for itself, it just disappeared into the wild without a backward glance. She'll do the same one day."

Devane agreed before noting in a casual tone that was unconvincing even to a non-empath like MacCammon," I have noticed Khari and Jazriel work well together."

MacCammon laughed, a rare sound that made the American raise a quizzical eyebrow, "You have nothing to worry about there, laddie. He is a handsome devil and charm itself, but I have seen the way the bonnie lass looks at you. You are the one she wants, not some attractive but black-hearted, blood drinking creature of the night."

Joe dismissed the Scot's banter with a rueful grin but deep down was grateful for his shrewd observation. MacCammon usually said little but missed nothing. He made up for any lack of special powers by acute observation. That combined with a level headed approach and a ruthless streak made him so invaluable to the team. For the next hour Devane discussed their first mission, and was aware how MacCammon's mood darkened with each detail.

"It's a real bastard, we did not form this team to become a suicide squad."

"You haven't heard the best bit yet, Archie. The boys upstairs want us to go in with a team of regular agents. It seems we are just too strange, too green to be trusted yet."

MacCammon sighed deeply and pushed his glass over to his commander for a large refill. "I need another stiff drink, it seems there is a war on after all."

Chapter Seventeen

Outskirts of Leuven, Belgium, 1940

Khari shivered, shifting her weight slightly as the first twinges of sharp cramp threatened her calf muscles. She could not give in to this weakness or make any sound as she crouched down low in a heavily wooded copse, silently enduring stinging rain turning to sharp sleet as the wind changed direction. Around her, hiding low in the undergrowth, waited her companions in adversity, a group of dark clad British agents. Heavily armed, their faces blacked up, two of them wore dark glasses despite the soot black, freezing night.

Fear held her in a close grip, it tightened around her throat and pressed down on her chest, her heart hammered too fast, too loud. Surely the Germans could hear such a pounding drumbeat. She tried to swallow quietly, terrified even to breathe but her throat felt full of jagged grit. Instinctively she looked over to the Dark Kind agents, needing their fearless strength but they were too focused to see the dread in her eyes.

What appeared to be a long deserted, derelict farmhouse lay ahead of them, the surrounding land neglected and overgrown, filled with rusting and broken machinery and farm implements.

"This is a sick joke, some chinless wonder in Intelligence has sold us a pup. There is nothing in there but rats," Banks, the leader of a group of covert forces muttered in cold fury. Already in grave peril so far beyond enemy lines, he was uneasy with the strangeness of the other agents on their first mission. Khari wiggled forward on her stomach to get close to Banks, bringing with her the earthy scent of the forest floor and crushed wild garlic.

"Our target is in there; don't be fooled by the quiet. It is packed with Gestapo officers and a squad of crack storm troopers, all in the main building and on full alert. They are vigilant, expecting the local Maquis to try something."

Banks shook his head in disbelief, how could this slender girl—a refugee from some remote Balkan state, possibly know? "In that case it is still a wasted mission. We can't take that lot on with a handful of agents."

Khari's anxiety level rose alarmingly, bombarded by the waves of negativity from all the non Spook agents who were suspicious and hostile. They were clearly unnerved by the presence of the Dark Kind on the mission without really knowing why. Perhaps it was a deep rooted, primeval instinct, a survival mechanism every human was born with.

Khari's alarm was shared by MacCammon. He glanced across at his people, knowing they alone stood a chance but only if allowed to operate unhampered by the outsiders. Khari picked up his thoughts and went to find the Dark Kind agents, ignoring the irritating prickle on her belly from dank, pine needles on the forest floor. Using only his mind, he sent a message directly to Khari. Inching forward, biting her lip to distract herself from the sharp pain of a broken tree root sticking through the pungent sodden leaf mulch, she approached the two Dark Kind and spoke rapidly to Jazriel and Sivaya in their harsh, wolf growl language.

"I can tell you exactly where they are holding our target. He is bound up in a loft room, the one on the right with a cracked skylight window. They are expecting any Resistance move to come from the perimeter; not from above so he has not many guards close by. I'll get Mac to keep our unwanted new friends out of your way."

Jazriel gave a brief, humourless smile of assent and the two vampires slipped away silently, instantly lost to the darkness. The sudden disappearance alarmed an already jumpy Banks who grabbed Khari's arm.

"What the Hell is going on?" Banks whispered through gritted teeth," No one authorised this move."

Khari was anxious not to talk any more; anything could alert the enemy – a snapped twig, an involuntary cough. The quietness and lack of activity in the farmhouse could change within a split second with the guard dogs the greatest worry. Once the German troopers released them the British agents' cover would vanish and survival could depend on a messy and suicidal fire fight in the darkness. Hastily, she made up the story the vamps were surveying the perimeter of the farm under MacCammon's orders, stifling any protest from the more experienced operative, who were stunned by the speed and silent stealth of hidden eyed ones.

The hostility and suspicion did not leave Bank's eyes or his mind. Along with his own band of experienced operatives, he had marvelled at the two Spook agents. It was not their first time to be amazed by them. The journey from the remote drop zone had been made in a black van left hidden by the local Resistance. Sivaya drove it without any headlights. It was an eerie, unreal experience, to be driven at high speed by a silent young woman wearing dark glasses through winding, unlit lanes and across fields in complete darkness. Yet she drove with uncanny accuracy. Later, as they moved closer to their target on foot, the regular agents marvelled at the speed and strength of the eerily beautiful couple who made no sound as they confidently prowled through the tangled woods.

Who the Hell were they? Or as Banks began to wonder, *what* the Hell were they?

As Dark Kind, Jazriel and Sivaya were at home in the gloom like no other creatures on earth; their nocturnal created eyes had perfect vision even in the darkest night. So silent, their approach was not detected by the Germans waiting in the farmhouse. With their cat-like agility, they easily climbed the farmhouse wall and found the skylight described by Khari. It was jammed tight after years of neglect and disuse but Jazriel's strength was far greater than any human and he prised it open slowly and quietly without great difficulty.

He saw the target beneath him, a slight middle aged man tied to a chair in a bare, filthy room. He was slumped forward, unconscious, bruised and bloodied from many beatings and torture from interrogation. The team's orders were to get him clean away or kill him. Both Dark Kind agents decided it was possible to get him out alive. Not that they had any qualms about killing the prisoner but they agreed it was a better morale boost to the human team members to bring Hitler's defecting astronomer back to England alive.

In one silent lithe movement, Sivaya dropped down into the room and cut the prisoner free but left his gag on in case he regained consciousness. She could sense the guards dozing outside the door from their strong blood scent; they were fearful, expecting an attack from the local Resistance eager to get their hands on this unusual prize – a man the odious Nazi leader had confided in. Sivaya had to move fast before all Hell broke loose. With her superior vampire strength, she easily lifted the man up to Jazriel before leaping to join him on the roof. They leapt down and ran for the cover of the woods, the prisoner slung over Jazriel's shoulder.

Their swift return with the prisoner caused a furore among the hiding agents, how could two people pull of such an audacious liberation without alerting the Germans, who were expecting a rescue attempt at any moment?

"I don't like this, it stinks of a set up," Banks snarled, eyes frantically darting about in the darkness as fully expecting to be surrounded by storm troopers.

"We don't have time for this, they'll be onto us any minute," MacCammon snapped back, his own team already slipping away towards the well hidden van. His relief at the success of the vampire agents had to be muted for now despite justifying Devane's faith in them. Risking his own throat, the Yank had taken a dangerous gamble in recruiting them; but judging by tonight's performance, it had paid off.

"We must go, now, one of the guards downstairs is thinking of taking a coffee up to his friend guarding the prisoner," Khari snapped. Wy hadn't they moved out already?

Banks did not argue and as one, the team ran back through the leg-breaking tangle of tree roots, following the route of the hidden-eyed agents in their element, swift, silent and unhampered by the night. Jazriel still carried the prisoner over his shoulder with nonchalant ease, unburdened by his weight. Khari suddenly raised a hand and everyone stopped in their tracks, scarcely daring even to breathe. She whispered in her soft voice,

"A patrol of four troopers have just crossed ahead of us to the right, close to the clearing and the van."

Sivaya and Jazriel exchanged excited predatory glances, then the male vampire passed his burden to the nearest human, slipped away into the darkness again. Banks was still deeply suspicious and sensed betrayal. He dropped back from the others and tried to follow the couple with great difficulty as the darkness enveloped him. He hid at the heavy tramp of the German patrol approach, crashing through the woods in a noisy progress. He raised his handgun, fully expecting to see the spook agents make contact with the patrol and betray the mission.

What he saw made his mind reel with shock and revulsion. The two spook agents attacked the patrol from somewhere in the darkness. The female snapped the necks of two troopers as easily as dry twigs with her bare hands. The male disarmed the other two and grabbed them by the neck in a tight, choking grip, tight enough to silence any screams. Now shivering with shock, Banks watched in horrified fascination as the two removed their shades and kissed passionately despite the frantic thrashing of their victims. The male handed one of the troopers to his companion; both doomed men fought back furiously, arms flailing and kicking out at their attackers but still in silence from the vice-like grip on their necks.

Then Banks's mind fell headfirst into a nightmare. Both glitter-eyed beings grew curving scimitar shaped fangs; long, silver- white, vicious. With low growls of animal excitement, they plunged them in a tearing motion deep into their victim's necks. Silently, they drank the gushing blood, their bodies shivering with intense pleasure.

Banks bit into his hand to stifle his scream of terror as the creatures drained their prey dry of blood, dropping the bodies into the undergrowth and kissing each other again with a wild, fierce, snarling passion. The lovers were bloody vampires! Banks mind span, delirious with horror. No wonder MacCammon spoke of his spook agents' special abilities, they had somehow recruited undead monsters; the age-old, horrific myth was a reality.

The nightmare deepened as now fully sated with human blood, the two vampires prowled over towards his hiding place. The male glanced with his cold, beautiful eyes at the bush where Banks crouched, shivering with terror. He spoke with a heavily accented voice, like a predatory growl, a dangerous, humourless smile on his features still handsome despite his lowered wicked long fangs.

"Be grateful we are on your side, and your throat is safe, Banks. We must rejoin the others quickly before this patrol gets missed."

Somehow Banks managed to get up, and on legs barely able to hold him, reluctantly followed the vampires back to the rest of the team. He had no other choice so deep within enemy territory, but sat in silence, shivering in abject misery, in the rear of their getaway van. Again Sivaya was at the wheel, driving at reckless speed from the farm. They could hear the first sirens wail, and saw searchlights rake the sky. They could sense the humiliated fury of the Nazis break free and pursue them like a maddened monstrous beast. Seemingly unconcerned, Sivaya accelerated harder, pushing the van beyond its limitations, driving at a faster speed than was safe in full daylight.

Despite bouncing off a few high earth banks, they kept on course, with Khari up beside Sivaya, scanning the road ahead for minds to read. Occasionally she snapped a warning in the vampire language and Sivaya would pull over into the fields to let a patrol pass them.

The regular operatives were puzzled and amazed by the spook agents' abilities but were also grateful for the edge it gave the mission; they might just get home alive. Their mood noticeably lightened as admiration for skills of the two blonde women grew. Only Banks sat hunched, in shocked silence. MacCammon did not need Khari's mind reading to know the man had seen too much in the woods, perhaps even witnessing the vampires making a kill — something no human should ever see.

It was the worst case scenario he and Devane dreaded when forced to work with these regular operatives. His mind raced for a solution, he wished Jaz and Sivaya had silenced Banks in the forest but he knew they were honourable beings and would not turn on their temporary compatriots.

By some miracle and Sivaya's breakneck driving, they reached the narrow, heavily rutted fallow cornfield where their plane waited. The sensation for the regular agents of being thrown into a dark fantasy, a living nightmare deepened. Unlike any other escape from occupied or enemy territory, they could see no Resistance fighters ready to light make shift runway lights. The plane painted black waited in silence until everyone was safely on board. Then without any use of internal or navigational lights, the unseen pilot let the plane's propellers whirr noisily into life and it taxied straight as a die down the pitch-black field.

Once in the air, MacCammon resisted an urge to 'accidentally' push Banks through the briefly still open door as the plane took off, flying low and fast over the war blighted night bound lands. Khari glanced up at MacCammon but made no sign of censure, just a saddened look of regret and understanding in her golden eyes. Jazriel sat back up against the plane's steel sides; Sivaya curled contentedly in his arms, like a pair of human lovers. Puzzled, Khari found she could not sense the pilot's mind. When she entered the cockpit, she found a familiar red headed Dark Kind at the controls. He turned to give her a foxy grin; his sharp features seemed so young, no more than seventeen.

"Well, its hello again to Azrar's little pet. And before you get all human and sentimental, I have not joined this insane scheme despite Eshan's incessant pleas. I just wanted to make sure my own people got back from this madness in one piece."

Emboldened by the success of the mission, she gently kissed Garan's icy forehead and spoke in his language. "That's to say thank you —whether you like it or not— on behalf of the humans. We couldn't have made it home without you."

Back on a remote airfield in England, Joe Devane steadily broke the team's record for non-stop smoking as he awaited his people's safe return. Until that night, Jazriel held the record, undisputed chain-smoking king of the Spook Squad. Now Devane paced back and forth wearing the butt-littered sodden turf down to mud, scanning the clouded skies for the first drone of a plane's engines.

Reluctantly, he had accepted Eshan's late substitute pilot, realising it helped the mission's chances to have the ultra fast reflexes and incredible night vision of a Dark Kind flying them home. But he was uncomfortable with the malevolent, irreverent creature that appeared at Eshan's London home shortly before the mission. Eshan, with some tell tale uneasiness, explained Garan was a mischief-making maverick among his own kind and indiscriminately predatory by nature. He had no respect or interest in humans beyond their use as prey and amusement, but he could be trusted to get the Dark Kind operatives home.

"Just bring Khari and the others back safely, and I'll resist the urge to drive a sharpened stake through your black heart,"

Devane muttered to himself in the darkness, unprepared for just how deeply his feelings for Khari had become, to an extent they threatened to prejudice the success of the mission before it began. He knew she was vital for its success, but was reluctant to endanger her life. The youngest and most unworldly of his agents, she overcame this with an extraordinary raw courage that often took Devane's breath away. He felt a gentle, reassuring squeeze on his arm from Anna.

"Raker has just had a premonition. They are all okay. That young devil is coming through okay for us."

Devane nodded with a slight sigh, his emotions mixed. Perhaps it was an advantage to know the near future thanks to one of the team's clairvoyants. But they could also foretell bad times too and he knew without having any special abilities there would be plenty of those to come. Once his superiors found out about the success of the snatch and grab raid, deep in the heart of the enemy's homeland and his squad's existence justified, the stakes would be raised. He doubted many of his team would survive to see the war through.

    Naively, he once imagined the clairvoyants and Khari could be employed back in England, their powers utilised for interrogation and early warnings. Only the Dark Kind accompanied by skilled covert operatives would be risked on missions behind the German lines. Why else recruit vampires but to use them to kill? But this idealistic dream was already shot down. Their first mission was close to the highest risk imaginable beyond encountering Hitler himself in Berlin. And Khari was right in the thick of the peril.

Two hours later, Devane could hear the dragon drone of Garan's plane, the only indication of its arrival. Dropping from the night sky like a huge carrion crow, the black plane touched down without landing lights on the makeshift muddy grass runway. The team drove right up to its doors, not waiting for the engines to be cut and with the propellers still rotating, bundled their rescued defector away to the safety and security of the squad's house. As the mission operatives disembarked, Devane on a wave of relief driven euphoria swept Khari up into his arms and kissed her.

"It's right out in the open now, Joe. No more hiding our feelings for each other."

She managed to say with a joyful grin as an embarrassed Devane quickly put her down. Impulsive behaviour had never been one of his traits.

"I guess they all know already, this is the Spook Squad! Talking of which, where are my Dark Kind?"

The American stumbled over his words; deeply aware it was highly inappropriate for him to get emotionally involved with one of his operatives.

"They are still chatting to Garan but we had better hurry them up – it will be dawn soon. The Germans didn't manage to kill them; it would be too ironic to lose them now to sunlight."

Before Devane could reply, his second in command approached, his long features more dour than usual, "We have a big problem. The vamps made a kill. They had no choice, it was the only way to get us all out alive. But I am certain Colonel Banks of the regulars saw too much in the woods."

Devane groaned, his worst fears about working with anyone outside his squad confirmed. He asked Khari to scan Banks's mind while he organised getting the Dark Kind back to the Manor safely. But before he reached the plane, a belligerent Banks intercepted him.

"May you rot slowly and painfully in Hell for the evil you created, Devane. We are supposed to be morally better than the Nazis."

Devane's reply was firm and unapologetic, "They are just another form of weapon, I'll use anything to bring down that evil regime, anything to protect the innocent."

"You sanctimonious bastard, how dare you talk of the Nazis' evil as if you are above them? How exactly did you conjure up those Hell-spawned demons. What sort of pact have you done with the Devil?"

"They are just mortal beings, Banks. Nothing to do with the supernatural or any religion. But you have seen for yourself their abilities, their strength, their night vision…how could I not use them as living weapons?"

"They kill people —the vilest of ways."

"They don't exactly have the monopoly on that. I can live with the deaths of a few Nazi troopers. It's bombing defenceless German families from the air, I find harder to live with."

"War will always be a filthy business. You have taken it onto a whole new level of evil with these monsters."

"They are monsters, but at least they are our monsters."

Banks went silent as he watched his team prepare to leave. He acknowledged their calls to get a move on with a dismissive wave.

"What are you going to do?"

"I want to go back into that plane with a sharp stake, a machine gun—anything to wipe them off the planet."

Khari interrupted the British agent, his anger fuelled by a very understandable terror; his entire belief system had been shattered by the reality of the vampires. Her gentle voice had a new edge that Devane had never heard before, "You would not last five seconds before they tore your throat out. They are on our side, just leave it at that. Try and forget what you think you saw. Not much point blowing our cover. Who would believe you?"

Devane took Khari's arm and started to walk away. "Put it all down to a bad dream, Banks. "

The agent stared in silent, impotent fury as they joined the rest of their squad preparing to leave the airfield. Once out of the agent's earshot, Khari squeezed Devane's hand as their van drove away, slipping and bumping over the mud and ruts.

"We both know Banks won't let it be. We have made another enemy – one closer to home."

Chapter Eighteen

Arpalathian Mountains, Isolann, 1940

"Steady old man, it is nothing but thunder, just lights and noise…steady now, or you will harm yourself…"

Azrar held his terrified horse's head in a tight grip, as he fought to stop it from plunging around in dangerous panic. He spoke to it in a special tone using firm but soothing words in his own language. Wild eyed, soaked with the white foam of equine terror, the horse finally stood still, its slender legs shaking, its nostrils flared; but it had stopped its dangerous plunging in the narrow confines of a cave full of people.

Azrar was far from his keep, seeking shelter with his human fighters—deep within a cave network beneath the towering Arpalathians. Outside, Hell rained down, turning the deep, narrow valleys into infernos; deep wells of fire designed to wipe out the Isolanni and their flocks.

With the stallion quietened, Azrar was able to glance at his fighters, heartened by the lack of fear and cold resolve their eyes. Nazi flames would burn out to windblown ash; it could not destroy their spirit. The Jendar's people were safe within their cave hideaways; land born enemy troops had little chance of reaching them. He did not care how much Hitler bombed the landscape; it just drained the madman's resources and overstretched the Luftwaffe. The land would recover.

An earlier German expedition force from the south had floundered disastrously in the bog lands long before reaching Lake Beral's shores at the border between Isolann and Svolenia. Airborne attacks by Nazi parachute regiments had been cut to pieces by Azrar's fast moving native fighters. Azrar himself had drunk his first 'pure' Aryan blood and found without surprise that the master race tasted no different from any other human.

Now, in an act of desperation, fiery death dropped from the skies over Isolann in an intense campaign over many days and nights as the full thwarted fury of the Third Reich struck at Isolann's heart.

The unbreakable resilience of its tiny population led by their Prince– the mysterious Black Wolf of Isolann, infuriated the Nazi regime looking for another front to attack Eastern Europe. The Svolenians had given them clear passage through their country to smash Isolann but it proved a solid barrier of resistance.

The robust strains of an old folk song recalling some ancient victory over the Ottomans rang around the cave. To Azrar, that victorious battle was but yesterday, the blood-soaked memories remained fresh in his mind. One of his men dug out a pheeral –a flute-like instrument, and joined in the refrain. Azrar watched as they made a campfire and began to eat from their provisions.

With his men settled, the horses calmer, Azrar reached into his saddlebag for an intelligence message dropped earlier by the Allies. He needed no light to read the encrypted document which spoke of the allies great admiration and support for his peoples' unrelenting courage but gave no hope for sending re-enforcement's or more arms.

Azrar was unconcerned; he did not expect anything. His people's struggle for survival was mirrored all over Europe. Azrar believed despite Isolann's lack of modern weapons and equipment it could cope with the onslaught better than most. It did not just have a brutal landscape and a harsh climate; Isolann was the only one to have a genetically engineered vampire warlord with countless successful millennia of combat experience – a creature once recognised by human and Dark Kind alike as a ferocious genius of military strategy.

The message went on to ask for Azrar's help if any allied airmen were shot down, or escaped prisoners of war sought sanctuary in Isolann. He wondered of his true nature was known by the allied leaders by the last paragraph of the message, "*Please treat these soldiers as if they wore the black wolf amulet.*"

Azrar gave a shrug of dark amusement; these modern humans had much to re-learn about the unswerving nature Dark Kind honour. He would never treat allied soldiers as prey.

Chapter Nineteen

Chess Manor, The Chilterns, England. 1941

To Joe's relief, Khari's duties kept her busy in London for the next six months after their first mission. His shadowy superiors in command of the squad commandeered her to assist in the interrogation of captured enemy spies and would-be defectors. Although he missed seeing her at the Manor, Devane was content to let her remain in this vital role for the rest of the war.

Anna was another squad member he wanted to keep safe on home soil, he was very aware she was a young widow and mother to three small children. Her courage and determination to fight the Nazis made her reluctant to take a background role, but her protective instinct as a mother overruled her desire to fight. Devane found her formidable powers as an empath made her a natural trainer and she excelled in making the others more confident with their abilities, gently pushing them to new levels of achievement.

In buoyant spirits after their initial success, the rest of the team were eager for more action. Devane was now confident of their abilities and able to loan his human spooks to other covert groups. The Dark Kind he kept back unless accompanied by himself or MacCammon.

With Ffitchie away on a mission, the crunch of wheels on the gravel drive was the first indication of a car arriving late one night to the Manor. The Dark Kind slipped into the shadows, fangs drawn ready to attack. The humans grabbed handguns and waited, fully alert to the danger of a counter assault from German agents. The vehicle did not stop long; it paused with engine running to drop off one passenger then disappeared back into the night.

To Devane's relief, it was Khari, home one night on a short leave. Throwing aside her valise, she ran into the oak-panelled hall, arms out stretched in delight to see her friends again. Devane stayed in the background as she hugged and kissed the human team members with great delight. The two female Dark Kind stood back, aloof and haughty in their cold, hard beauty. Delighted at seeing his friend again, Jazriel was more forthcoming, sweeping Khari up into his arms and whirling her around, his handsome face lit by a dazzling smile of genuine warmth.

"Put me down, you crazy vampire. Put me down now or I won't give you the brand new music recordings I bought for you in London."

Jazriel carried her over to Devane and handed her over with the pretence of a solemn bow. "I believe this important delivery from London is all yours, boss."

Khari, embarrassed, tidied up her crumpled suit and wayward hair to avoid Devane's eyes. She knew the American still wanted her but was hesitant to openly show his feelings. First there was the question of protocol; he was her commander. Secondly, their lives were too dangerous to risk the hurt of a romance. "I'm sorry about that, Dark Kind are not subtle creatures by nature."

Devane smiled for the first time since her return.

"It's a beautiful night; let's go for a walk after dinner—completely alone."

Khari's face lit up with a joyous smile, delighted his feelings towards her had not changed while she was away. "That's the best idea I have heard for months. I need to breathe in good fresh country air again; my lungs feel solid with coal dust and car fumes. And I need to walk on something soft and green after all that concrete."

Far more than that, she needed to feel Devane's arms tightly around her, to kiss him again. But she would let him find that out for himself. "I'll change for dinner."

"Wear the jade and silver gown you brought from Isolann – I love seeing you in that."

Khari laughed as she ran up the stairs to her room. She paused briefly to call down to him. "I'm back less than five minutes and you are ordering me about already."

"Well, as the Jazzman said – I am the boss."

Breathless from rushing, Khari ran down the stairs to a very American wolf whistle of approval from Devane. "When I see you covered in filth and mud, wearing baggy combats tackling the assault course, you look like a beautiful young woman. Now, with your hair loose, wearing that lovely floating silk gown, you look, well, magical! From another world!"

Khari laughed and made Devane give her arm a gentle squeeze…

"See, I am just flesh and blood, just a very ordinary person."

"That will always be an impossibility!" Devane replied, shaking his head with a rueful grin as he walked with Khari through a field close to the Manor. The long hot summer had baked the footpath as smooth and hard as a road. A full moon, looming huge in the sky lit their way as surely as daylight, its softly silver light emphasised Khari's fey features.

"I cannot begin to imagine what life was like for you, cooped up in that cold, draughty gloom-shadowed castle."

"It was never cold, never gloomy. Azrar's human household filled the keep with life and warmth. Ileni and Sandor made sure I was always surrounded by their love and every simple joy of human life."

"But Azrar must have needed to keep it dark; that must have been very frightening for a child."

"Nothing in the Prince's keep frightened me. I loved the dark —it was like being wrapped in a black fur cloak — soft, luxurious and protecting."

Devane took her hand to help her over a stile, beyond it a little brook of clear water chuckled over polished pebbles. Above it, tiny bats swooped and flittered in their hunting dance after flies. Their tiny cries made Khari smile, as she remembered the larger bats hunting above the towering battlements at home.

"But surely Azrar himself must have frightened you. Eshan said the Jendar is a ferocious creature; far more imposing, much more menacing than the Dark Kind on our squad."

"Azrar is all of these things and more but he never frightened me. He is my guardian, as a Dark Kind warlord he is honour and duty bound to protect me."

Even in the darkness, Devane could hear the open adoration in her voice and see the brightness of love shine in her golden eyes. His heart felt crushed with disappointment. "You love him very much."

Khari turned to the American and held both his hands. "Yes, I love him. But not in the same way as I love you. Azrar is the forbidden, pointless and unrequited love of my soul. You are reality; you are a wonderful human man, the love of my heart, my mind, my body – my whole being."

"I guess I can live with that."

Devane replied as he brought her close to kiss her. But somewhere deep within, he felt cheated of something he could not define. He felt destined to love this woman forever, yet he had to reconcile himself to sharing her with the black murderous heart of a vampire. The moon had lost none of its brightness; not one cloud hid the glory of the stars. The night air was still and warm. But Devane was suddenly cold, shuddering as the night wings of an icy dark shadow passed over his soul. He didn't know or care whether Khari read his mind or not; he had no secrets from her. Apart from one. She looked into his eyes, her face solemn, her voice firm and strong.

"I am all yours, Joe. Never doubt that. Not now or for the rest of our lives."

Chapter Twenty

Special Forces Detention Centre, London, 1941

Jay Parrish flinched at the nerve-grating sound of metal against metal as the locks on his door begin to open. It was a long-winded procedure, giving him enough time to get off the low iron bed with its too few thread-bare, grey blankets and sit upright on his only other piece of furniture, a rickety wooden chair. Dignity was all he had left. If that golden eyed bitch was coming back to torment him, he'd lose even that scrap of self respect. On her last visit, she'd broken into the precious sanctity of his mind and ransacked it for secrets. How could he hide anything from this intrusive desecration of his privacy? Especially his mind's awareness of the treacherous betrayal of his body – the base unwanted physical desire for her that refused to go away.

He was able to forget these anxieties when a stranger entered, briskly dismissing the guards with an authority beyond his years. Introducing himself simply as Banks, the stocky young man in civilian clothing had the disturbing gleam of the zealot in his eyes. Parrish coughed before addressing the visitor with a world-weary drawl," If you are here to save my soul, forget it. All I want to know is when I can go back to sanity, back to the USA?" The man ignored him. He walked over to lean against the dank wall of the cell, crossing his arms, as he fixed Parrish with his unsettling stare, "So you know about vampires?"

Surprise and relief dawned on Parrish's pallid face. A faint light of hope glistened in the gaunt man's water-pale eyes. Was this visitor a possible ally? Then, remembering the devious bastard Devane, a self-protecting edgy wariness kicked in. He took a proffered cigarette and took his time before answering, taking many long drags from the precious offering from the stranger.

"The last person I confided in stole all my notes, my vital and important evidence then betrayed me. Sent me back to these murdering limeys. Why should I speak to you?"

Banks smiled a cold and unpleasantly shark-like grimace. "Because we have something in common; we both hate vampires and Devane in equal measures. We should work together to bring them to justice."

"I just want them all dead," Parrish replied bitterly, his dreams of acquiring the world's greatest treasure house of ancient knowledge long ago receded. His day to day survival, wrongly convicted and condemned as a spy for the Nazis consumed his every thought, well, nearly every thought. He still found space to fantasise on what brutal revenge, what agonising pain he would inflict on all of them; on Devane and his little bitch, Khari and that blood-drinking monster still thriving in his Balkan lair.

"Then we are of one mind, Professor Parrish. Shall we get going?" Banks walked away from the wall and with another shark-like smile, offered his hand to the American.

"What do you mean? Go where?" Parrish stuttered, unsure what was happening. Was this another devious, intelligence-gathering trick of the damned Spook Squad? Banks put his arms around the prisoner's thin, bony shoulders. "To war my friend, a crusade of righteousness against those Hell-spawned demons and their vile human allies."

He had been right, Parrish's initial opinion that the man was some sort of religious zealot returned. He did not care. He was a free man again.

Part Three

The Winter Thunder

Chapter One

Arpalathian Mountains, Isolann, 1942

Bruised and frozen, huddled beneath a stinking sheepskin blanket, the exhausted man did not understand a word from the bustling people around him, but he sensed their intentions were honourable.

Just hours before, Steve Railton was a member of a British bomber crew, on a high-risk spy mission over the Upper Balkans. They had embarked on such a perilous mission fully aware of its importance, finding out just how far the Nazi push through Europe's backdoor was progressing was vital. No allied force could spare any desperately over-stretched resources to fight on this remote front.

Railton's surveillance mission ended brutally in a terrifying explosion as the Lancaster took a direct hit from a German fighter squad. The pilots struggled to keep the wounded war bird aloft long enough to clear Svolenian air space. Coming down in mountainous Isolann was risky but at least the crew would be among allies. In the end there was just enough time for them to bail out before the Lancaster exploded somewhere above the border.

Railton had no idea what happened to the others, only that his parachute had drifted through the night air on high mountain winds to land in a deeply gouged narrow valley. He remembered seeing the distinctive black rock of the Arpalathians with a sigh of relief before losing consciousness from a punishing bad landing. He awoke in a dimly lit narrow cave. Wincing at the pain from many lacerations and bruises, he found himself lying on a bed of pungent sheepskins; his wounds tended and his uniform replaced by hand-woven woollen native clothing.

On hearing his gasp of pain on awaking, Railton was attended to immediately by a sloe-eyed young woman, her shy smile gentle and concerned. Her features were typical of the ancient Steppe nomads of Isolann; her gold skin, black almond eyes and long plait of thick dark hair made him sigh with gratitude. He had landed on the 'safe' side of the border; at least this country was not under Nazi occupation.

With the woman's help, Railton gingerly sat up, his back propped by a thickly padded sheepskin bolster. He sipped some aromatic hot liquid from a wooden beaker. Thankfully it contained a simple chicken broth; he smiled with gratitude, it was delicious. He could feel his strength and hope return with each sip of the soup; his last memories after bailing out of the stricken plane were drifting in the darkness to an uncertain fate in the limbo between friend and foe.

Railton gave a prayer of thanks to the courageous pilots whose actions saved his life. He believed he was in one of the well-hidden caves that thwarted the ambitions of the Nazis to conquer this harsh, backward region. The sparse population of this mountainous realm had taken to an ancient system of caves deep within the Arpalathians in a well-organised and meticulously prepared exodus to carry out their war from the safety of their rocky protectors.

A mixture of modern arms and ancient savvy made these deceptively simple people the scourge of the Nazi war machine. Peasants from scattered villages and different tribes were forged together as a formidable fighting force by the inspiration and resolute leadership of their prince, known now throughout Europe as the Black Wolf of Isolann. No one outside Isolann had ever met their enigmatic Prince; Railton wondered if he would have the privilege of seeing such a courageous and inspirational leader in person.

Railton soon found out why these people adopted a near nocturnal lifestyle. As the faint light from another dawn filtered through the outer caverns, he could sense a growing tension ripple through the Isolanni. Children were gently but firmly ushered further back into the cave system, as men and women alike gathered up machine guns and heavy mortars to guard the cavern entrance.

As the day lengthened the first ominous drone of aircraft could be heard, approaching from the south. Railton got to his feet and gestured for a weapon. An Isolanni tribal leader –a wizened, wiry little man, almond eyes like shards of carved jet, scrutinised Railton's craggy Yorkshire-bred features. He realised they had no reason to trust this tall foreigner who'd fallen from the skies; one who could easily turn the gun on them. But the tough little man grunted assent and picked up a high powered rifle. Railton took it, offering his gratitude in English, hoping they understood the difference in languages.

That day, luck was on their side. The frequent patrols of German fighter planes, which swooped down to strafe the valleys and bomb indiscriminately, chose to strike a more distant region of Isolann. As the sound of the attacking planes faded, the men-folk of the tribe cautiously left the cave's shelter to forage for firewood and fresh water. Railton accompanied them, but found it hard to keep up with their agility and stamina. Like mountain goats, they easily scaled the harsh, sheer landscape, confidently jumping from one narrow rock face to another and over deeply gouged crevices.

Railton was too stubborn and proud to admit his exhaustion but was grateful for every brief rest where his generous and good-humoured rescuers shared their meagre provisions of hard salty black bread and spiced water. As he ruefully rubbed his aching calf muscles, he caught sight of a large mountain goat grazing in a nearby by steep clearing of lichen covered loose scree. Offering to bring it down, he raised his gun in question to his hosts. They nodded assent hastily and Railton –a sporting crack shot in peacetime— raised the rifle and killed the goat with one clean head shot. Two of the strongest men rushed off to retrieve the prize and carried it back in high spirits.

As night fell, the caverns soon filled with the mouth-watering aroma of roasting meat. Railton's goat was received like a great treasure by these brave, besieged people. Railton was deeply grateful for the chance to repay their hospitality – repaying their gift of his life would take far more than a goat.

Railton awoke early, shivering as an early snowstorm blew freezing, sharp pellets of ice into the cave mouth. It was now three weeks into the British airman's stay with the Isolanni tribe and though comfortable with their ways, he was eager to find a way home. He knew the only way to repay his debt to these people was to return to the war and help defeat their common enemy. It was also so hard knowing how much anguish his family must be suffering now they had the dreaded news he was missing in action.

He strode over to the cave mouth and helped pull some dark brown cowhides over the entrance to keep out the bitter storm. Finding a way to communicate was still a problem. Railton struggled to learn their language but he had never been much of a scholar. His skills lay in his sharp, observant brain that could cope with complex, fine details, which led to his role in the RAF as an ace map-reader and navigator.

Railton came from an old Yorkshire family who had kept vast flocks of sheep on the moors since at least the Doomsday Book and probably long before. Not quite gentry – but more than ordinary farmers, the Railtons were a strong close-knit family as rough hewn as the moors landscape they all loved so much. This background gave him a natural resilience to the harshness of the Isolann's exiled life and the practical skills needed to help them tend their small flocks.

Later that morning, in warm sunlight, the pre-dawn snowstorm now just a memory, he helped with the daily, furtive fuel gathering under the shadow of constant threat from the skies. The soft clatter of unshod hooves brought great excitement as a group of horsemen rode into the valley. After tethering their animals well beneath the shelter of an old wind twisted pine tree; they approached on foot, making the steep craggy climb look easy. Railton's nomads greeted them with a great deal of good-humoured banter and the whole group sought shelter under another pine to share their rations.

One solemnly handed Railton a small parchment scroll sealed with black wax embossed with a silver wolf design. He gently unravelled the scroll and found a message in English, hand-written in an old fashioned elaborate style, clearly by an impatient though firm hand. Railton was surprised to read it came from the Prince himself, and wondered how the leader of this besieged land could find time to concern himself with one downed airman. "My apologies for your continued enforced stay in my realm. Everything in my power is being done to see you safely back home but by now you will be aware of the grave difficulties we face in Isolann. I have been able to contact your government and your family knows you are safe. Jendar Azrar, High Prince of Isolann."

Railton gave a deep sigh of relief. The most distressing part of his exile in this remote land was the lack of contact with his commanders and home. Sadly, he noted there was no mention of any other crew members in the Prince's message. With his own people reassured of his survival, Railton had a new resolve. He was trapped in Isolann for an indefinite time, but he wanted to do more than gather wood and take wild pot shots at passing Stukkas. He wanted to join the Prince's main army and fight. That night, as the nomads entertained the Prince's messengers while their horses rested, Railton packed up his only possessions –his uniform. With a tortuous mixture of sign language and the odd bit of their language, he was able to let them know his intentions.

    The next morning, as the riders prepared to leave; his nomads brought him a thin but sturdy chestnut mare. Railton had hunted across the moors since a small child. He laughed with the Isolannis at the mare's bad tempered attempts to bite his behind as he prepared to mount. As if the generous gift of a horse was not enough from a people with so little, a nomad woman stepped forward to hang an intricately carved stone amulet around his neck. She gestured anxiously, urging him he never to remove it; the others shared her nervous manner and reinforced he absolutely must not remove it. Railton signalled he understood and nudged the ratty little mare into a trot to join the others on their journey to rejoin the Prince. He turned back to wave farewell to the generous, hospitable folk who cared for him so well without wanting anything in return. Respecting and keeping one of their old superstitions was the very least he could do in return.

Chapter Two

Somewhere Beneath London, England, 1942

Tightly clenched fists held beneath the desk, unseen – Joe Devane's only outward sign of his inner turmoil. The American listened, his chest tightening alarmingly, as his superior officer, the urbane English gentleman with no name or rank spoke the words Devane dreaded most. Khari was to be sent deep undercover to Berlin, right into the slavering maw of the Nazi monstrous war machine.

"This is hard for you, Joe. She is an extraordinary asset to the war effort here in England. We know she is an asset we would be quite mad to risk, but risk we must. We need her close to the top decision makers."

Devane glanced up at the patrician features of the other man; no emotion showed on his pale, even features or in the flinty grey eyes. His commander, he mused, probably came from old noble Anglo-Saxon blood; it showed in his accent and mannerisms, his relaxed military bearing. He inherited the same cool, calculating eyes from ancestors that had commanded armies, men who had faced down marauding Vikings and taken on Napoleon's crack troops. "This plan is reckless and ill-conceived. It is far too dangerous. Even with my best agents to support her."

Joe Devane noted the commander's lack of reaction and waited to be over-ruled. He knew this day was coming. His success with the Spook Squad and their many missions behind enemy lines was a double-edged sword. A Damoclesian sword. Once he felt great relief to be vindicated was over his outrageous plan to form the team. It was on the wildest edge of credibility but he had done it and the squad worked brilliantly. Now of course, he realised it functioned too well. As he expected, these orders for another deep cover mission were on a whole new level of danger, they were horrendously high risk, shattering his hopes to keep Khari in England for the duration of the hostilities.

He had kept her as safe as anyone could be in a country at war, helping interrogate people such as Hitler's astronomer in a secure location in London. Now it seemed, high command wanted her deep undercover in Germany, as close as possible to the Fuhrer's closest aides and officers. Devane knew he could not hold her back, his personal feelings were an irrelevance in this time of world-wide pain and self sacrifice. Her abilities to read minds would give extraordinary highest level information, even possibly from the twisted mind of Hitler himself, information that could shorten the war and save millions of innocent lives. Devane sighed, knowing any arguments would fall on deaf, uncaring ears and listened instead to the commander.

"Khari is the greatest gift your squad had to offer their war effort, Joe. Her blonde beauty is acceptably Aryan. In common with all the team, she now speaks German with a native born fluency and her Svolenian ancestry is not problematical now it is one of Germany's closest and most loyal allies. Think of the advantages. Living the most innocent of roles would yield a virtually untraceable source of undiluted information."

There was no disputing this fact. Getting the information out of Germany undetected was more peril-laden and worried Devane more than anything else. A weakness at that point could lead back to Khari with disastrous and inevitably tragic consequences.

"Think who you want to send in with her, Joe. I am prepared to sanction assigning all the Spooks, if it will make this mission work."

Saddened, but resolved, Devane thought long and hard over this on his way back from London through the

Bucks countryside to the Manor. Though Sivaya was another blonde, a fierce, tough killer, she was still too unpredictable for Devane to send her to Germany with Khari with confidence. Eshan was a possible weak link with her refusal to kill humans. It had to be Jazriel. He was steady and courageous and he loved Khari as a friend but his dark beauty was problematical in a country ridden with murderous racial paranoia.

Devane's plan began to take shape. They would enter Berlin as cousins, royalist Svolenian nationals from a family long exiled from the now overthrown communists. Devane hoped the Nazis knew that dark hair and lightly golden hued skin did occasionally occur among the Svolenian population, a relic from long distant and unwanted steppe nomad genes.

To his relief, there was no one in the main hall as he entered the manor to the aromatic wafts of dinner and the sound of human laughter. He needed more time to collect his thoughts. The thought of losing Khari in Berlin made his chest tighten in fear with the foretaste of grief to come. He walked to his office and sat for an hour in the darkness, nursing a large tumbler of neat whiskey.

In a rare coincidence every agent was back at their headquarters. He had sent them on dangerous missions many times, but this was on such a whole new level of peril. The door opened without knocking, and he heard the slight swish of soft fabrics against the wooden parquet floor. He did not need to turn his head; he knew who was behind the silent footsteps and exotic floral fragrance, "Good evening Lady Eshan."

"I take it you have bad news, Devane."

He spoke to the vampire noblewoman until a lightening sky threatened her with dawn's first rays of rosy sunlight. Exhausted, he felt his eyelids grow leaden. He gratefully gave in to sleep, his head resting on his arms and slumped on a worn leather covered mahogany desk. Sleep was good; it meant he did not have to face his beloved Khari for a few more hours. The one person he could never deceive.

It was mid morning by the time Devane roused himself from his uncomfortable sleeping position on the desk. He stood up slowly, stiff and aching but not regretting the extra hours of much needed solitude. A gentle tap on the door brought reality crashing back. There could be no more hiding and prevaricating. Khari walked in bearing two mugs of steaming near-coffee. She put them on the desk before raising her face to Devane, a haunted, sad smile on her ethereal face. As he kissed her, Devane struggled with controlling his emotion, fighting back the tears welling uncontrollably. As a distraction he tackled the coffee, wincing as he sipped the brown liquid and the acrid taste assaulted his tongue. Rations – another reason to stop this damn war.

"It's going to be okay, Joe. We knew this day might come; I am only surprised it took them so long. The entire squad are ready; we need to get on with finishing this vile war." Khari stood up on her toes and kissed him lightly on the forehead. "We will speak again later, tonight, when we can be alone."

Devane watched her leave, even in shapeless khaki combats she looked every inch a fairy princess, beautiful and fragile as a moonbeam. Wild thoughts of running away from the war, abandoning his duties, taking Khari to some distant neutral country and living out their lives far from danger came into his mind. Wild fantasies that was all. Honour and duty meant too much, he was no coward. He pushed away the wild thoughts. Khari would despise anyone turning their backs on this fight for freedom.

Devane, forcing himself back on track to organise the new mission, sought out the views of his Jewish agent Lenny Dawn. He found the showman working hard on his telekinetic skills, as yet to be tested on a mission. Devane held his breath as the man, his lean face pale and contorted with effort, concentrated on moving a pen across the polished oak surface of a table. At first nothing happened; then the still air became charged with a curious vibrancy. Devane felt the hairs at the nape of his neck rise, goose bumps appeared all over his body. There was a slight, almost imperceptible movement in the lacquered fountain pen, so small it could be mistaken for a trick of the light, of the eye. Then it gathered a jerky momentum, faster and faster until it spun crazily around the table before flying across the room, landing on the wooden floorboards with loud clatter.

"Wow," was all Devane could manage, truly astonished by what he had just witnessed. Lennie shook his head as if disappointed; his skills were too erratic, too uncontrolled.

"I think it will be some time before I will be used to diffuse bombs from a safe distance!" he muttered ruefully. Devane patted him on the back. He knew how desperately Lennie wanted to contribute to the squad's war effort and resented every minute spent holed up in some luxury mansion in the English countryside while London burned and his own people in Europe disappeared from the face of the earth, their fate still unknown.

"Lennie, I need your advice, it's a bit of a sensitive issue."

"Fire away, commander. "

"I want to send Jazriel into Berlin undercover. Will he be mistaken for a Jew? I was told it happened to him in Vienna back in 1938."

Lennie laughed without a trace of humour at more evidence of the murderous malice of their mutual enemy. Nice Jewish boys did not have razor sharp fangs. A pity, though. They would be something useful to fight back with. Lennie pushed away the frivolous daydreaming and assured

Devane there was no trace of any Semitic features in Jazriel's sharply chiselled features.

"Surely, even the most rabid Nazi won't mistake him for one of us. Personally, I think it is hilarious – those jack-booted morons think we Jews are monsters – just wait till they see the Jazzman's fangs in action."

"Hopefully they won't. This is a deep undercover, low key mission. If it is successful, they will notice Khari and Jazriel because they are good to look at. No more than that."

Devane went on to explain his plan was for Khari and Jazriel to be hidden in relatively plain sight, to live openly and quietly in Berlin. There was no need for excessive risk taking and subterfuge when Khari could glean all the information she needed straight from their minds. She never had to ask any awkward questions or visit any sensitive areas.

Very dark glasses and the cover story he was blind solved the problem of Jazriel's beautiful but obviously alien eyes. He even had a trick up his sleeve to re-enforce this story. All Dark Kind eyes darkened when angry. But in a reverse action, Jazriel could blanche all the colour from his until they looked like the milky opaque eyes of a blind human. Demonstrating this trick one night made the team, human and Dark Kind alike, recoil with groans of disgust to the amusement of an unrepentant Jazriel.

Party trick aside, it had been another vital survival tool over the centuries. Passing as a human was hard enough; his looks and charm were never enough to escape the Inquisition's fires or the pointed stakes and nooses of the lynch mobs. Finding a way for Khari to meet high-ranking Nazis in a neutral setting was a difficult obstacle. Lenny came up with the solution. "What things have Jazriel and Khari got in common? We know they both speak many languages fluently including Svolenian, German and the vamp— sorry, the Dark Kind language. But they also are gifted musicians. If they got jobs as entertainers in some classy night club, they would be working with access to a wide range of German officials."

Devane smiled broadly in gratitude to the wiry magician, now even more sorry he could not go with them. His sharp intelligence and intimate knowledge of Berlin's night life would have been incredibly useful. But it was impossible. Lenny, as a Jew, was lucky to be alive, escaping Germany at the earliest days of his people's cruel and brutal persecution.

"Mr Dawn, as ever you are a genius. It is the perfect cover for Jazriel, playing the club by night – people would expect him to sleep by day. And Khari can access information without even having to speak to the bastards."

Devane broke the news of the mission that night to the whole team. The mood among them became deeply sombre and silent. After the team's briefing session, Anna urged them all to head for the music room. She felt they needed some momentary distraction from the rising anxiety they all felt. This was one Hell of a dangerous mission. "Thrown into a pit of angry vipers," — the apt expression used by Ffitchie.

Lenny walked over to the piano and brought back a battered leather case, once black now a scarred and faded grey. He removed the glistening old saxophone within and gave it an affectionate stroke before handing it to Jazriel. "Here, take my Ruthie, Jazzman. She's yours now. Look after her well; she's escaped from Hell once already."

Jazriel accepted the golden instrument, deeply aware of what it meant to Lenny. Ruth was the name of his Polish wife, now lost to the work camps, her fate still unknown. "Hey, man- it's just a short term loan. We are all coming back soon, including this beautiful old girl."

Devane did not share the vampire's confidence. He couldn't imagine his team going undercover so close to the heart of evil and all returning to Britain. Accepting losses were part of the gamble was fine when on paper at the start of this project; now the team were flesh and blood beings, it was not just Khari; he knew he couldn't bear losing any of them.

MacCammon was also going to Berlin but keeping a low profile in a safe house, keeping watch over the others; ready to pull the plug on the mission. Devane glanced over at Eshan, they had worked together for long enough to anticipate each other's thoughts.

"I know what you are going to say, Joe. We need Garan to fly them in safely. I will see what I can do, but I cannot say it often enough. We cannot trust him—ever."

"What about all this talk of Dark Kind honour," Ffitch-Brown ventured cautiously, still uneasy in the company of vampires.

"I think even we are allowed the one exception–just one maverick amongst all the survivors of our species. He is dangerous and unpredictable, with no respect for anything. We use him at out peril."

Chapter Three

Arpalathian Mountains, Isolann, 1942

Steve Railton had nothing but respect for the foul-tempered scrawny little mare he rode across Isolann's sharp, arid rock scape. But respect for her sure-footed courage through deep ravines and up frighteningly narrow passes did not help his aching backside.

Hours spent following hounds on a sleek armchair ride hunter was no preparation for the tortuous punishment of riding a thin, bony animal on an ancient saddle made of bone hard leather. He ended up making a pad out of his uniform and putting it on top of the saddle – to the uproar of hilarity from his native guides. And of course, the mare used this opportunity to try to tear chunks out of his arm and legs with her long yellow teeth.

"Pack it in, you miserable old bag – you are making me look stupid."

Railton pushed her lean bony head away with one elbow, but the mare answered with a well aimed cow kick that luckily did not reach her target, somewhere in Railton's mid region, due to his experience with horses. He got back on, gingerly lowering himself onto the makeshift padded saddle before joining his companions to negotiate a narrow pass, the jagged rock face just inches from their heads. One fighter leant back and pointed to the chestnut mare

"Se'renshee---aga nan Se'renshee."

Railton found out later it meant the mare's name was 'Sweetness' - no doubt an example of nomad humour.

Their journey was long and arduous, worsened by a deliberately indirect route that was not just due to the landscape. Every day, the German fighters returned, flashing through the valleys hunting any Isolanni to strafe with machine gun fire or bomb. Railton could imagine the frustration of the Nazi war machine trying to conquer this peculiar little country. They were up against a fearless nomadic population that could not just hide from attack but thrive in their mountain havens.

There was no capital city to defend their leader; the Prince lived among his people, sharing their hardship and fighting beside them. Azrar never remained in one place, but kept his small guerrilla army constantly on the move. It must be like fighting shadows – but deadly ones with teeth.

Isolann was far too mountainous for a mechanised assault from the ground; there was not one made up road in the entire country. But any illusion the Isolanni were trapped totally in the Dark Ages was belied by their formidable weapons...all were the most recent models available and all British made. Only a full scale assault by a huge army of infantry could be possible here and Railton doubted the Germans would be able to spare such a major resource in manpower just to subdue one tiny Balkan state.

The daily bombing was their only response, designed to terrorise and wear down the moral of the people. It was not working. The only historical fact Railton knew about this country was the proud boast it had never been conquered in its entire history. Living in Isolann and seeing for himself the unswerving courage and toughness of its people, he could now see why.

They journeyed by dawn and twilight, full daylight brought too much danger from aerial attack. By the sixth day's travelling, Railton noticed a rise in tension among his escort, which grew throughout the short riding time before they needed to seek shelter. A rider held up his hand and Railton followed his companions' example as they anxiously checked the tightness of their horses' girth straps. It was clear signs of some dangerous riding ahead.

Railton's heart sank into his boot when he discovered the cause of their anxiety. The narrow path they were on had been cut through ahead of them by a landslide. The gap looked enormous –far below in the sheer side chasm were jagged rocks like witches' talons reaching up from Hell. The path was too narrow to turn the horses around, but Railton sensed this was never an option with the Isolanni. The lead rider gathered up his reins held tightly onto his horse's head while spurring it on at the same time. This caused the horse to collect itself up, weight well back on its haunches. The rider gave a loud shout and spurring on hard, releasing the horse's head which leapt forward in a sudden burst of speed and power.

For a sickening moment, it seemed to drop its head and hesitate, hooves slipping and scraping on the very edge of the chasm. Then with a cat-like jump, it launched it self into space, landing on the other side with only inches to spare. Every one broke into spontaneous cheering and the next rider began his preparation to make the dangerous jump. His horse jumped more freely but was slightly short of the other side. For a horrific moment, rider and horse hung unbalanced, closer to plunging to their deaths then safety. Then with supreme effort, the animal scrabbled frantically with its front legs, hauling itself up with a deep grunt of exertion. The next two riders leapt across without incident, leaving Railton the last to go.

His little mare watched the others jump with growing impatience and agitation, her teeth snapping the air like insane castanets, ears flat back, her tail lashing and swishing furiously. She did not wait for any signal from Railton but pricked her ears forward and bolted towards the chasm and sitting right down on her spring-like hocks, leapt like a gazelle. For one sublime moment, Railton thought she had sprung wings like Pegasus as she took to the air, suspended above death with scornful ease. Then she landed with feet to spare, tossing her head and squealing in celebration of her own cleverness.

Railton bent down and hugged the ratty little mare's scrawny chestnut neck, gasping with astonishment and relief.

"You were named well after all. Sweetness, you are a wonderful mare."

She rewarded his compliments and praise by dropping her neck and one shoulder down to deposit Railton painfully on the ground. Ignoring the hearty laughter around him, he ruefully looked up at the mare, snapping her teeth and stamping her rock-hard unshod hooves. Then he gazed down at the sheer, death-dealing drop they had just leapt.

"I meant it, you old rat bag; you are a wonderful mare!"

By mid morning, the search for shelter became before desperate. With air attack from the south imminent, they were far too exposed on the mountain narrow passes but there was one factor they had no choice over. There was no turning back.

"We are caught between the proverbial rock and a hard place, Sweetie."

Railton muttered grimly to his mare and got her full ear flattened evil-minded snapping in return. The screech of carrion buzzards and the raucous arguing of ravens brought the riders to an abrupt halt –sensing something bad, the horses began to turn dangerously agitated. Everyone tightened their reins and drove their legs firmly against the horses' sides, trying to hold them. There was no room for any animal to turn around on itself along the narrow ledge. Any horse panicking now could doom them all to a horrible death at the bottom of the ravine.

Ahead there was a slight indentation in the rock face, enough to let one horse pass another. The lead rider signalled for Railton to come to the front. Had he not experienced the mare's courageous leap over the chasm, he would have been suspicious, wondering if there was a sinister reason for leading the way. Now Railton knew they all needed her indomitable pig headed courage to survive the mountain.

Once in front, the mare's character changed immediately, her ears pricked forward with enthusiasm and her step became jaunty and eager as if her thin legs had acquired springs. She led them around the serpentine winding of the ledge and down into a narrow valley where the stench of death hit like an assault. The valley, once a peaceful oasis of green with a noisy river of melted snow cutting though the centre, was now a charred nightmare.

What must have been a nomad tribe, risking the air raids to water their goats, lay in misshapen and unrecognisable fly-blown lumps of burnt flesh, which the carrion birds now fought over. The grass around them was reduced to ash and scorched earth, the valley's sparse tree cover now black, jagged stumps pointing upwards like charred accusing fingers.

One of the nomads somehow dismounted his frightened horse to be violently sick. Railton's own roiling stomach was only too ready to join the nomad in an outward show of horror and revulsion. His war had been so clinical up until this point, travelling in bombers unleashing death from high in the night skies. Sometimes crews did not return, sometimes planes returned badly damaged, their crews burned and maimed. The sight of what once had recently been families and their livestock reduced to rotting crow meat brought a harsh new reality.

Railton followed the others example and tied a scarf over his nose and mouth. Risking a similar fate to the nomads, they spent the rest of the morning gathering the pieces of body and burying them as decently and respectfully as they could. Cremation was out of the question, attracting the interest of the German fighters whose planes could be heard patrolling distant valleys. Railton rode on in deep thought. If he returned to Britain, his skills were too valuable to waste and he would be put straight back in the air, doing the same to German civilians. The only way he could get through this war with his sanity intact was to fight the Nazis with a gun in his hand, meeting the enemy eye to eye.

Chapter Four

London England 1942

"You will kill them all." Garan's eyes blackened and turned to narrow slits of fury as he confronted Eshan. They met in a central London Park, making no sound as they walked slowly across piles of drifting brown, dry leaves, long fallen from last autumn. It was nearly winter now, with long dark nights falling on a city that embraced self-imposed darkness in its long fight for survival. The lengthening evenings and the ongoing blackout was perfect for a predator like Garan but London held little pleasure for him. Eshan's arrival only added to his rancour.

"You flew for us before," Eshan pointed out, her tone even and unthreatening. This was not a time to pull rank; she needed Garan's help too much. Garan spun around to face her, fangs now drawn with the intensity of his hostility. Eshan gave a low growl of despair and quickly looked around; there could be no witnesses, and any hapless passer-by seeing the Dark Kind youth like this was as good as dead already. For once her luck held, they were still alone on the small path as it went up over a little iron-railed bridge over an ornamental duck pond.

But they would not be alone for long. Even at nightfall in early winter, St James's Park was a popular spot, an attractive short-cut for office workers from around Birdcage Walk heading for Green Park station and for visitors strolling through to see the Mall and Buckingham Palace. Workers would soon spill out of the handsome old buildings in the area at the end of their day. Garan could cause bloody mayhem in this mood. Eshan took his arm to try to propel him along the path but he shook her off with a low angry snarl.

"Zaard Agranat, Ha'ali! I flew them out of danger but I'm damn well not flying them to their deaths in Berlin."

There was no sign of Garan retracting his fangs. , Eshan began to get increasingly anxious – a human was bound to walk along this route soon. More innocent blood pointlessly spilt to assuage Garan's capricious and vicious moods.

"Are you totally insane now, Eshan? " He took his platinum-topped cane and slashed angrily at the bridge's metal railings, sending up sparks as metal struck metal. Eshan took hold of his wrist in a tight grip as Garan prepared to attack the rails again, the elegantly wrought iron bars miraculously not yet given up to the war effort. He shook off her hand, eyes now darkened to totally jet-black with his fury. "Would you sacrifice Jazz and Sivaya to your bizarre and craven campaign to become a docile pet to the humans?"

His remarks pierced through Eshan with a barbed accuracy but it was not enough for the enraged vampire. "And what of your beloved Azrar's ward? It's eating you up inside with jealousy isn't it? You cannot bear the fact she is more useful to him then you will ever be. Is that why you will risk her life too?"

He was unjust and cruel, jealousy was a human trait and Eshan felt nothing but goodwill towards Khari. Garan had always enjoyed provoking Eshan but this night was different, his taunts were not motivated by malice alone, his anger was heartfelt and deep.

"Your brooding Balkan recluse wants the girl back in Isolann, to be at his side. He wants the same thing as King Dezarn had with his own little witch, the first Khari. Forget Dark Kind honour, your life is over if anything happens to her."

Eshan took a deep breath to gather her thoughts, most of what Garan said was barbed, malicious rubbish but it still hurt. "I cannot stop Khari; she is determined to do this to help stop this war. Jazriel and Sivaya are free to make their own choices. No one is making them go to Germany. Can't you see? It would greatly increase their chances is you take them in."

Garan swore again in the vampire tongue. "I will have no part in this madness. No Dark Kind blood will stain my hands."

And with that he gave the railings one last clattering swipe with his cane and sped away to be swiftly lost in the night. Eshan's heart was heavy with disappointment. Garan's help would have made such a difference. He could fly very low and fast over mainland Europe in total darkness, the only clue to the aircraft's passage through the night sky was the low drone of its engines. Now the squad must rely on brave Resistance fighters in France and Germany to get them to Berlin, with all the perilous uncertainty that entailed.

Inevitably, she heard a man's scream of pain and terror echo across from the far side of the park. Garan's fangs had found another victim. It was wartime; death for humans came in many horrible forms. But meeting a violent and bloody death on a night's stroll across a park, to satisfy the bloodlust of an angry vampire who did not need to feed that night, seemed a death too much for Eshan. The screams had already brought people running across the park; it would be too late, Garan's victim would be dead already. This was not a safe place for a Dark Kind. Eshan pulled down the veil from her hat and walked slowly but purposefully out of the park. Damn Garan. Damn it, he was right. The Dark Kind should not risk their precious lives in a human conflict. But what other way forward was there? Co-operation or annihilation – that was what the few scattered survivors of her once great race now must face. The sound of growing alarm, angry shouts and police whistles behind her at the discovery of a still warm body with its throat torn out and drained of blood hastened her steps. She had no choice but to head back to Chess Manor, to the human and Dark Kind covert team she helped create. But her lone quest to find peace with humans never seemed further away.

Chess Manor, 1942

Precious darkness fell at last allowing the Dark Kind agents to stir from Rest. Jazriel left his room to take delivery of some eagerly anticipated parcels; they had arrived with Eshan and Devane back from London from a visit to headquarters in London. The parcels contained a new consignment from Jazriel's Saville Row tailor and as he picked them up from the hallway with a sigh of pleasure, Khari stepped out of the kitchens and gave him a hug, laughing gently, "You have to be the vainest creature on this earth, Jaz. The annoying thing is you'd still look gorgeous in a filthy, ragged old sack!"

Jazriel's impossibly handsome face broke out into a broad smile of agreement, "I can't help it; I was made this way!"

"The age-old Dark Kind excuse, it's nonsense, Jazriel, I managed to change."

Joe Devane and Eshan's arrival into the hallway put a stop over their light-hearted banter. Jazriel's turquoise eyes darkened briefly to a stormy navy as he answered Eshan in the low growl of their own language, "I know I am vain, a common-bred drifter with no high purpose, just my pursuit of pleasure. But at least I am full Dark Kind. I know what I am and I love my life. What exactly are you Ha'ali, other than pathetic and weak?"

Khari understanding every word, sought to defuse the tension by asking their commander about some official looking documents he had in his hands. Any good humour in her face blanched away, as the full impact of the papers hit her as she murmured in a quiet voice, "Joe's brought back our new German identity papers from head office."

Jazriel lightly kissed Khari's forehead as he took his papers off her and after giving a low formal bow to Eshan, returned to his room. The innocuous-looking papers were solid proof that the mission was going ahead and that they were off to Germany very soon, maybe even that night. This was a time for the two sets of lovers in the squad to be alone with each other, maybe for the last time. Once in his room, he studied the identity papers. The documents gave him a new name – Count Mikhail Cheryniaz, aged twenty-four and a legitimate nationality – a Svolenian who had taken German citizenship. He was greatly amused by what Eshan put down as his occupation: 'gentleman'. It confirmed her long held views he was just a hedonistic wastrel.

As a distraction, Jazriel tried on his new clothes and looked at his reflection in a dusty, full length gilded mirror checking the crisp lines of the tailored suit. It was made in a fine, deep charcoal silk and wool mix and flattered his elegant height and broad shouldered, slim-hipped figure. The suit's simplicity of design pleased him; he had no time for the ostentatious frivolity of some human fashion over the centuries. His great wealth–even the small amount he had access to during the war, at least bought immunity from the rations and restrictions the humans imposed on themselves in wartime.

He caught a glance of Sivaya behind him in the mirror, still in deep Rest on bed sheets wildly rumpled after their daylight hours spent in lovemaking; her long mane of blonde hair spilling over the pillows likes rivers of molten gold. Her body was porcelain pale, cold to the touch like exquisitely carved marble but with a raging heat within that never ceased to enflame his desire. She was so beautiful.

But difficult to be with, loving him with such fierce intensity that bordered on obsessive. Their relationship was severely strained since arriving in this country, would she ever forgive him for insisting on going to Germany?

Before this adventure joining the Spook Squad, Jazriel had preferred an easy going lifestyle. He needed the freedom to follow his own adventurous whims and enjoy his passion for human art and music – though admiration for the creativity of humans did not curb his appetite for hunting them for their blood.

It was all his idea to join Eshan on the Spook Squad rather than sitting out the war in some tedious neutral bolthole or living in an atmosphere of permanent dread and deprivation in Nazi-occupied Europe.

With Sivaya still in Rest, Jazriel lit a cigarette before slotting his wafer thin platinum cigarette case into the inside pocket of the new suit. He needed to check if they ruined the near perfect fit with any unsightly lumps. War or not, that would be just too unthinkable.

Eshan strode out into the darkness, needing to put plenty of space between herself and the rest of the squad. Her disastrous meeting with that malevolent creature Garan had left her disorientated and uncertain. Was this uneasy and dangerous collaboration she had worked so hard to forge with humans really just an elaborate form of death wish? Something she had often believed motivated Garan. Why else would he take such risks? Why did he openly kill so many humans – far more than he needed to survive, and make no attempt to hide signs of his predation. Unless on some subconscious level, he wanted to be caught. There was no doubt hiding true Dark Kind nature for so many centuries had a corrosive effect on the survivors. Something only Jendar Azrar still ruling his little mountain realm had avoided so far. Staying with the Spook Squad, for all its inherent dangers, at least allowed the Dark Kind to be true to their nature, to be valued for their abilities.

Another thing troubling Eshan was the signs of strange behaviour among the Dark Kind. Garan had warned in the past that too much close proximity with humans might affect Dark Kind nature. Could this be why Sivaya was showing signs of possessiveness and jealousy –none of these were Dark Kind traits? And now she too was displaying strange alien emotions. Why had she rounded on such a straightforward and simple being as Jazriel? Deep down, in a bad dark place that should not exist for her species, was she too jealous and angry with the handsome, louche commoner? He once had all she had ever craved for and he could so easily have it back again. Was that the source of her unreasonable anger with him?

Or was all this turmoil the effect of her self-imposed weakness. Regressing to hunting and killing humans for blood would give her full, ferocious strength back. But would it return her to confident self-belief again? It would be so easy. The hunger never left her, gnawing at her whole being, a pain so raw it almost had a malevolent life of its own. It certainly had its own voice—urging her to kill every night as she rose from Rest.

The voice never left off its strident call, especially when walking London's war-darkened streets—perfect hunting grounds for a desperately hungry Dark Kind. She wondered what would happen if she made just one kill, enough to silence the voice and ease the pain. But she knew it would never be enough, the hunger would always return; she had been cruel and hypocritical to Jazriel. The Dark Kind could not change, the hunger, the need to kill had never left her. She blunted it with carrion – bottles of donated dead blood from her laboratories. The vile-tasting cold liquid kept her alive in a weakened state but abstinence couldn't make her any less a killer. Maybe she could no longer hide from that horrible word of the humans – maybe she could not hide from being a vampire.

Eshan decided to test herself. She took a car from the converted stable block and drove to the nearest large town to the Manor. High Wycombe's narrow streets were dark from the blackout but people still wandered from their homes to the many pubs – a human monster like Hitler was not going to wreck their hard-earned social life. Behind closed doors, the sound of jolly piano music and human laughter brightened the rain drenched darkness of the town. It brimmed with life; the blood scent filled her senses and her body became alert and tense with predatory awareness.

Eshan waited in a pitch-black alleyway and watched in an uncomfortable silence as a courting couple took advantage of the darkness. Dark Kind had no voyeuristic interests in human mating rituals. To her relief they left quickly, disturbed by the clumsy approach of an inebriated young man who staggered into the alley, looking for a place to relieve himself before finding the next hostelry.

Eshan's whole being rebelled in self disgust. Is this what she was reduced to – skulking in the shadows like some common human murderer? This was no way for a noble-born Dark Kind lady to behave. She began to walk briskly out of the alley but the man tried to block her way with a stocky well-muscled arm. She could easily have snapped it like a twig with just one hand and the hunger grew more strident with the blood scent so close, so hot, so sweet.

"What's the rush, beautiful? The night is still young."

Eshan looked at the young man, desperately fighting back the urge to draw down her fangs and rip open his throat. She wanted to kill him, needed to kill him –her hungry body screamed for her to attack, but her mind fought for her to stop. A kill so close to the Manor could jeopardise all that she and Joe had built together—all the trust and open co-operation between human and Dark Kind destroyed by one moment of weakness.

"You are lucky – the night is not as young as you think."

Eshan pushed past the man, her greater strength sending him flying to the floor. By the time he found his feet, she was lost to the night. Eshan returned to the Manor, greatly relieved she had tested herself to the limit and triumphed over her true nature. But on seeing Jazriel at his language studies with the others, she was compelled to approach him and kissed him in the Dark Kind way on the lips.

"I'm so sorry, Jazriel. I was very wrong."

Unconcerned, Jazriel shrugged and smiled, too easy going too be concerned over a mere spat.

"This human slave driver is making me do these German verbs all over again; make him stop."

Eshan shook her head and glanced up at Lenny with a conspiratorial smile. "Under no circumstances. He's all yours, Lenny, do your best. You must be fluent by the time you get to Germany."

Chapter Five

Chess Manor, The Chilterns, 1942

A brisk night breeze caressed Jazriel's face, flicking through his blue-black hair like a playful lover. He took in a deep draw from a cigarette and paused to watch thin, elongated tendrils of cloud race across the night sky like malign high-flying spirits seeking victims. It was the last night in England before starting the mission and he needed some time to steel himself, to find a way to say goodbye to the beautiful, demanding but never boring female he shared his life with. Lost in his own thoughts as he walked through a woodland glade close to the manor, he did not notice Sivaya's stealthy, silent approach behind him until she addressed him.

"Why are you doing this?" she demanded, anxiety making her voice harsher and strident. "Why are you throwing your precious life away to help these humans fight yet another of their endless violent, petty squabbles?"

Jazriel gave a deep, heart-felt sigh, it seemed yet again they had to have this pointless argument over his loyalty to the squad, he had thought the matter finally resolved. He took another long drag from his cigarette without turning to face her, though he felt the blaze of her dark green eyes burn through him. He stood silently, as if still contemplating the strange shape and speed of the clouds. What answer could he give? He did not really know why this collaboration with humans had appealed so much; it was more than mere boredom, more than pique at the Nazis who had threatened the lives of his Austrian tailor and his family. Alhough, getting a beautifully cut and finished suit would be an utter bore now.

The answer lay buried deep in his past, but he did fully understand it himself, he had a subconscious need for self-validation, to have a reason to exist beyond the eternal pursuit of indulgence. Although he still enjoyed pursuing life's many pleasures with an enthusiasm that showed no sign of diminishing. He could not articulate any of this inner turmoil, especially to Sivaya. To admit his need for more meaning to his life was to accept there was something missing in their relationship. And this would break her heart, a pointless cruelty to one who had only ever loved and supported him.

"Don't do this. Walk away from here tonight with me."

Sivaya stood in front him, desperation clouding her eyes to a smoky dark grey. "You know I would do anything for you," she took his face in her hand and turned it towards hers. Her heart raced at the thrill of touching him, even after so many centuries he never ceased to make her weak with desire. Would her overpowering love and need for him ever fade? Deep down, she knew he did not share such an obsessive devotion towards her; that his heart was and always would be elsewhere. She always hid this awareness but now it rose again in a tidal wave of old, repressed pain. She held out her wrist and drew down her fangs,

"This is how much you mean to me. I would rip open this vein right now with my own fangs, if you wanted me to."

Jazriel gasped in horror as the sharp tip of one fang grazed the skin, drawing a thin trail of purple blood as she went on, "I would die for you. Right now, in this glade if you asked me to. I would kill every human infesting this planet if it pleased you."

Jazriel groaned and shook his head; taking her wrist, he kissed the wound tenderly, her sweet, perfumed blood on his lips. Sivaya pulled her hand away, unwilling to be distracted from her purpose as she continued, "Don't you understand? I love you so much I would do anything you asked. I want just one thing in return. Walk away from this suicidal lunacy, to prove your love for me."

Jazriel pulled her towards him, taking her face in his hands and kissed her passionately, long enough to take her breath away before addressing her in a quietly insistent voice, "I don't ask for dramatic gestures to show how much we love each other. Just let me go to Berlin, with no explanations, no more recriminations. This is something I need to do."

Sivaya's eyes were now all black, anger rising at his determination to risk his life for humans. "Then hunt with me tonight, we have all tomorrow's sunlight in Rest to make love before you go. Let's hunt and pull down strong, feisty prey together as we always have. Let's go wild, get drunk on blood like we did after the masked ball in Venice at the start of this new century."

Jazriel sighed, reaching into his coat pocket for his platinum cigarette holder and lighting up again. He waited until he had taken three long drags on the cigarette, buying time before speaking, "You know I cannot do that. We are under an oath of honour not to kill any humans here."

"I cannot believe my ears, my fierce and deadly Jazriel, as weak and pathetic as that sorry excuse for Dark Kind. Ha'ali Eshan's folly has infected you like a disease. If you go to Berlin you will die. For the love we have shared for so long, I am imploring you, Jazriel, leave with me now."

It was Jazriel's turn to feel anger, his iridescent turquoise eyes turned to darkest navy as he grabbed Sivaya's shoulders. "Why did you say I will die? What do you know about the mission, have you been talking to the squad's clairvoyants?"

Sivaya shrugged him off and stepped back into the clearing, "I have no time for human superstition and nonsense. The future has not happened yet, how can it be foretold! You will be in terrible danger in Berlin because you will be alone, working with humans and vulnerable to their inevitable lies and treachery."

Jazriel did not want to hear any more. He swept her up into his arms and firmly lowered her onto the soft, mossy floor of the glade, using his greater weight and strength to stop her running off into the night in search of human prey to assuage her anger.

"There is only one way to prove my love for you tonight, not by ruining my honour by killing protected humans and not by running away from this challenge in Berlin, just by making love…."

Sivaya fought back, snarling and raking the air with her fangs but as in any past duel between fury and desire, her passion for Jazriel always won. Her ferocity became refocused into making love but though her body was soon lost in the thralls of intense pleasure, her mind never lost the unbearable truth. That Jazriel could be lost to her in Germany and the memory alone of these powerful sensations from this wild ride may have to last her an eternity. This she could not bear, she had to have Jazriel totally to herself. To be at his side every night as she followed his endless quest for new sensations, new pleasures, or together hunting prey through the hours of darkness. And most importantly, she needed him inside her as they shared the hours of Rest when the accursed sun rose in the sky.

As an uneasy, fragile calm returned to the glade, Jazriel lay by her side and caressed her, her shimmering gold hair spilled through his fingers like liquid metal. "Beloved, we have shared our lives long enough for me to know what you are thinking. Do not wreck this opportunity for me. You must do nothing to stop me going on this mission. It is such a short separation, what is a few months, a few years, a few decades, to beings such as us?

Sivaya struggled to get away, the fear of losing him and anger at his obstinate instance returning in a flood of emotion. Something had to pay for her hurt – something human. Jazriel held her arms and with an intensity so at odds with his characteristic indolent manner, addressed her, "I love you, Sivaya. I *will* come back; *nothing* the humans can do to me will prevent my return."

Chapter Six

London, England, 1942

There was no turning back. The squad prepared to be airlifted into the outskirts of a German country town, then escorted by allied undercover agents into Berlin. With just days to go, Devane took Khari into London, to make a last contact with Jendar Azrar and her human family in Isolann before her undercover mission began.

It was then that Khari made a new discovery about the Dark Kind—how claustrophobic they were. Joe Devane was assigned London headquarters for his covert group, deep down beneath the capital in a secretive offshoot of the underground railway system. His Dark Kind operatives point blank refused to go anywhere near it. It was impossible to force them to do anything so the human operatives alone took advantage of the extreme privacy and security offered by the subterranean chambers.

She too felt a rising panic as she descended into the dark labyrinth. Like distant monsters, the underground trains rumbled on and on; the thought of the sheer weight of earth above her head made her heart race. She held onto Joe Devane's hand tightly and fought to control her breathing, realising the danger of hyperventilating in panic.

Once calmed down by Devane's strong, reassuring and unflappable presence, she recalled Jendar Azrar's place of Rest in Isolann. His lightless and vast stone vault lay deep beneath his keep and she remembered just how large and airy it was. She recalled the high ceiling and its amazing and realistic illusion of night sky complete with slowly moving stars and fleeting clouds. It made sense now: all the illusions of open space were designed to fend off the innate claustrophobia of his species.

Khari could well understand their discomfort as she settled on a tatty old overstuffed sofa to wait for the radio transmitter to warm up. Around her thin rivulets of water dripped alarmingly down the cave-like yellow walls. Devane said it was just normal condensation but this gave Khari no comfort; she knew the River Thames flowed right above them and a discreet mind probe told her Joe was equally uneasy and wary of it too.

She grimly endured the dank, musty rooms, with their cold, dim light – in order to be there when the radio sparked into life and she could hear Azrar's voice magically appear. The harsh steel melded with the honey of his voice would transport her to the high, wild, barren mountains of home. In her mind, it was always night – Azrar's own kingdom of darkness and strange secretive beauty. She could see the moon silvering the tops of the pine trees, the dazzle of millions of snow diamonds, the silent swoop of a hunting nighthawk. She could hear the sadness in the keening wind through the valleys, and the answering howl from the wolves.

Somehow the unending grimness of this terrible war drove out all joyous memories of Isolann. Summers spent in the mountains, travelling with the nomadic tribes and joining in nights of ancient folk songs around the campfires. Winter nights sharing laughter and sweet hot bread and spiced wine with Ileni and Sandor. Galloping through the trees, racing with Azrar astride his black war horse, and her brindled old Wolf loping loyally by her side.

Joe Devane busied himself by preparing some truly appalling coffee. As a Yank he deemed the weak brown sludge a grievous insult to true coffee. He always dreaded these rare, brief contacts with Isolann, despite their importance for intelligence gathering to the allied effort in the Balkans.

Having Khari at his side meant the whole world to him, he could pretend the war would end tomorrow and their lives would go on together, like any normal couple. He daydreamed about contented family life in a little New England town of neat, flower decked, shutter-boarded colonial homes with hordes of small children and friendly dogs running about in the summer sunshine.

But when she spoke in that outlandish harsh language to the prince, it brought him back to brutal reality. Khari was not like other women; she could read human minds and strangest of all, she had been raised from an infant by a vampire, a deadly being she loved with all her being. He could see it in the electric shiver of excitement that went through her – the brighter, lustrous glow in her golden eyes when Azrar's voice came clear on the radio. How could he, a mere human male, compete with the dark, charismatic power of Prince Azrar? He had never seen the Jendar but knew that like all Dark Kind he would be young and handsome with the hard-edged beauty they all shared. His looks would never fade with time and when Devane was a decrepit old man, Azrar would remain youthful and strong. He would go on living, unchanging and ageless when Devane was forgotten dust. This was hard to bear.

Devane did his best to hide his jealous pain and watched his beloved Khari as she waited for the signal to come through. Tactfully, she tried to hide her impatience and excitement but failed, as the radio warmed up filling the cave-like room with crackling static and eerie whines. Devane fiddled around with the confusing array of lights, knobs and valves until his patience was rewarded with a deep male and inhuman voice coming through. He handed the mike to Khari and readied himself to take any intelligence notes she dictated.

It was clear from the start there was seriously bad news, Khari's already porcelain pale face drained of colour and her eyes filled with tears. Shaking uncontrollably, her hands gripped the mike tightly as if her life depended on not letting it go. She carried on the conversation as best as she could as Azrar relayed the latest German movements in the region. Business as usual, though Devane could see her heart was breaking. When the Prince signed off, she collapsed into Devane's arms and broke down in heart-rending tears. Nearly ten minutes passed before he found out what happened as she struggled to explain through her grief-stricken sobs. Ileni's eldest son Dobruz and all his family were dead, their lives lost in a German bombing attack as they fetched water from a stream close to their hideout.

Helpless in the face of her grief, Devane held her tightly, unable to find the right words of comfort. The woman he loved beyond all reason had just lost much-loved family, what was the point of any words now.

Khari fell headfirst into a black well of grief, her mind haunted by memories. Some were bittersweet —of lost happiness, the many years growing up along side Ileni's growing family, sharing good natured banter with Dobruz. Then like a jagged knife twisting in her heart, she remembered the little ones, five cherished children and another not yet born, snuffed out in an act of unthinkable brutality. Ileni needed her; Khari could not imagine what her mother was going through now.

Her first reaction was to try to flee back to Isolann. Like a moth trapped beneath a glass, she explored every possible exit from England. Eventually, with a sense of crushing defeat, she realised how impossible this would be; Europe was on fire; there was no way through the inferno – and for what? Ileni and her other sons and families would take their grief with them into the mountains, and she would be alone with Azrar and his icy indifference to her loss.

The Prince had broken the news to her so dispassionately with as little concern as telling her about a favourite mare lost in foaling. She knew she could expect no more from the Dark Kind warlord, but it still hurt. Dobruz had served him with unswerving loyalty for many years. Joe's arms held her tight as she cried through the night and as the blur of shock subsided, an iron resolve took over. Any doubts she had over the mission were gone. Khari would do anything to defeat the enemy, the brutal regime who dropped death from the skies on unarmed peasants –anything.

Now she just wanted the waiting to be over and to be in Germany, in her own small way helping to bring down Hitler and his monstrous Third Reich. But she was not oblivious to Joe's pain. Even without her gift of *Knowing*, it was clear the thought of losing her to the undercover mission was torturing him. The addition of his continued jealousy over Azrar did not help his mental state. She kissed him, at first lightly then with all the passion she could bring, "What do I have to do, Joe? What will make you realise that I belong to you and only you? Forever."

"Marry me."

Devane could not think of a less romantic place to propose than a filthy, dank vault, or a more ill-timed proposal just minutes after his beloved Khari heard of the loss of her family– and on the virtual eve of a terrifying mission. Khari gave a sad smile, and kissed him again. With love shining from her lustrous golden eyes she addressed him, her voice trembling with emotion. "Perfect timing Devane. Lets get this nasty business in Berlin over first; then we will talk."

Khari felt wretched for side-tracking him, hated herself for causing the hurt clouding his eyes; but she was convinced it was the wrong time for further complications.

Their love affair was already creating so much heartbreak; the separation to come was unbearable, already too much to take. They both knew there was every chance she would not return. The only way for Khari to get through was to focus on her wartime duty with a single-minded fervour beyond anything she had ever experienced in the past. Over the next months, perhaps even years, she was prepared to lie, to betray and to kill. Not seemly thoughts for a bride-to-be.

Chapter Seven

Arpalathian Mountains, Isolann, 1943

Thin wafts of yet another goat stew made Railton's stomach cramp with hunger; exhaustion had blunted his senses but the wild herb enhanced aroma brought it back with a vengeance.

He strolled across to the mouth of the day's cave shelter, firmly pushing away the short tempered but loyal, lean brindled dogs that guarded the rock hideaway. Always on the move with the small band of nomad fighters – Railton had not slept in the same rock shelter twice. He helped Tigh, his closest friend among the Isolanni, dish out the stew into light wooden bowls carved from mountain pine and sat in companionable silence as they enjoyed the frugal but sustaining meal.

Tigh, a sturdy squat young man with the most infectious smile in the Upper Balkans was first to hear the ominous droning whine –the first warning of another German air attack. The fighters sprang into instant action, dropping their precious meal and grabbing their weapons. None were much use against fighter planes. The British had supplied them with excellent personal defence weapons, aware that only guns that could be easily carried by men climbing across rugged terrain would be any use in Isolann. But this fiercely proud, independent people refused to watch each attack passively from their mountain refuge. The German fliers were able to inflict their damage, yet always kept just out of gun range.

Railton walked to the cave mouth, focused and calm waiting for the attack, his machine gun ready to aim at the oncoming fighter planes. When the Stukkas dived down into the valley, the locals shot away wildly but he stayed calm, his knowledge of aircraft's most vulnerable sites giving him a slight edge. The Isolanni dived for shelter amongst the rocks as the fighter planes began their strafing run. Railton saw one get too close; whether through arrogance or misjudgement, it was the perfect chance to down a Stukka. He aimed for the fuel tank and fired with deadly precision.

The pilot, aware he was badly hit, took the plane into a steep climb, hoping to extinguish the flames or to gain air space when he baled out. Railton saw the German leap, his parachute safely unfold as the plane crashed into a mountainside in a thunderous explosion. Spurred on to increased fury by the loss of a colleague, the German planes wheeled around to attack again, targeting the area where Railton's team launched their attack – but they were already gone, like long morning shadows melting into the mountains as the sun rose.

From their shelter in the rocks, the Isolanni watched the Germans attack time and time again until they were forced to leave as their fuel ran low. Amid the noisy celebrations that followed, all centred on the hero of the hour –the Englishman and his sharp shooting, Railton overheard a whispered conversation. It appeared to be something about hoping the downed pilot was still alive, that the Prince would need him soon. When the valleys finally fell silent, a small group of nomads slipped away. Railton guessed they went to search for the German pilot.

He decided he had had more than enough of mysteries and secrets from these people; he put his life on the line for them every day, honesty was surely a small price for his efforts and sacrifice. As he walked beside Tigh, he was determined that only forthright answers to his questions would do.

"Why does the Prince need that pilot alive?"

Tigh averted his eyes and Railton could see the instant cloak of secrecy descend, it always did whenever he asked awkward questions of the Isolanni.

"It is not our business to question our Prince, nor should it be yours, Englishman."

"I fight with the Isolanni and I may well die protecting your country and its Prince. I think I deserve to know what is going on."

"Our neighbours, the Svolenians call Isolann 'the Land of Secrets and Shadows'. There must always be secrets from outsiders here."

"Is that what I am to you, Tigh? An outsider?"

Tigh sighed and gave Railton's arm a strong squeeze.

"You are our treasured friend and always will be so. But even if you dwell with us for a lifetime, the secrets must remain."

Railton was having none of it.

"I'm a Yorkshireman, born and bred. This means nothing to you now Tigh, but you will see how blunt and determined I am. I do not intend to live in a shadowy manner, full of whispers and rumours but only by plain speaking and straightforward dealings."

Railton pulled on his dark grey dyed sheepskin coat; aware he probably stank like a rancid old ram by now. The luxury of bathing was also one of many things he missed from home. Slinging his machine gun and several belts of ammunition over his shoulders, he saddled the ever furiously snapping Sweetness and rode out, heading in the direction of the downed pilot. Nobody tried to stop him. The independent nature of the Isolanni, combined with their respect for the British airman who shot Stukkas out of the sky like game birds, gave him the freedom of movement he needed to seek out Azrar, and he had had enough of mysteries for one war. The thud of hooves behind him was no surprise. He paused to let Tigh's horse fall into step beside his.

"Someone has to watch your back, Steve. These are not your Yorkshire moors."

Despite Tigh's obvious reluctance, he helped Railton follow the other nomads searching for the downed German pilot. The nomad's tracking skills were evident as they soon found a ragged scrap of torn parachute silk in a cruel black barbed thorn bush which led them to an accurate trail.

"What will you do if we meet with the Jendar?" Tigh asked tentatively, a tell tale tremor of growing anxiety in his voice.

"I will ask damn awkward questions!" Railton replied. "I've seen your Prince up close, remember. I don't know what he is, but the word human doesn't exactly spring to mind."

"I wish I could tell you Steve, just to stop you enraging the Jendar. Even a bearer of the wolf talisman is not totally safe from danger. But there are things I cannot ever tell an outsider."

"Then I go on, till I get the truth from the black wolf's mouth, if I have to."

Tigh shook his head. This foreigner was either dangerously pigheaded or brave beyond words. He suspected Railton was both things but in the end it made no difference. If Prince Azrar felt threatened by his demands, his fate would be the same. As an ally and wearer of the talisman, Railton's throat would be safe from Azrar's fangs. But in Isolann, there were so many other ways to die.

A week's hard journey brought them finally to Azrar's latest camp on the Prince's continuous roving patrol of his principality. They arrived in late afternoon as the last drone of enemy planes faded in the yellowed sky. The two men collapsed on the cave floor, rubbing aching calf muscles from a steep climb, having left their tired horses in a deep cave lower down the mountainside. Someone brought refreshments and to Railton's relief, there was no sense of any hostility and no one challenged the reason for their arrival; it was not the Isolanni way.

Railton glanced about the cave for any sign of the German pilot but there was no evidence he had ever reached this camp. Somehow he didn't expect to find the man alive, this was not a land where the conventions of war were recognised and respected.

Shortly after dusk, Railton was aware of a ripple of nervous anticipation through the inhabitants of the caves. He too felt an uneasy tightening of the chest; his resolve to shamelessly challenge the Prince began to falter. The caves were well lit by crude pitch torches and warm with cave-mouth fires over which the inevitable goat or mutton stews boiled away. He made a mental note to hunt the next day for some game to relieve the monotony of his diet.

Nothing had changed, the torches and the fires were still merrily blazing, but an eerie shadow seemed to fall, and an icy sensation chilled Railton's blood. The cave fell silent, the tribesman got to their feet and moved swiftly to the sides. Azrar strode in, sending shock waves of his curious ice power around him—a swirling black cloak billowing around him like a wall of smoke. All Railton could focus on was the imperious blaze of his alien eyes, chilling in their lack of humanity, their raw predatory menace.

At first, Azrar ignored Railton, taking and studying the latest reports from his commanders scattered across the mountains. Then, with a sinking heart, his resolve completely destroyed, Railton saw the Prince summon him over. On legs now treacherously weak, Railton instantly obeyed. This was not a being to keep waiting.

"You are most welcome, Mr Railton. I have heard great things of efforts on our behalf. My people are deeply in your debt. Are you ready to return home now? I will make the arrangements immediately."

Somehow Railton found a voice, one that sounded distant, small and as if not his own.

"I would like to stay and fight on – with your permission of course, my Lord."

"Permission is granted with my deepest gratitude, we need all the help we can get, especially from a man who can drop Stukkas from the sky with just a machine gun."

Railton could see the Prince was already impatient to move on; his brief audience was now over. Making small talk was clearly not the Jendar's forte. Some small courageous or foolish demon from deep inside Railton suddenly blurted out unchecked.

"Prince Azrar, will I ever be allowed to know about you? I suspect your people would rather die before telling me anything."

The Jendar's eyes became momentarily darker, a black cloud crossing the brilliant emerald and the tension in the cave became almost unbearable. Azrar's sharp-planed, marble-pale face began to relax, the relentlessly cold eyes returned to their former glittering verdant glory.

"What do you need to know?"

The Prince's strangely compelling voice sent a sliver of sharp ice down Railton's spine; at first it sounded deep, melodious, yet beneath it was a harsh timbre, like lush velvet, lightly covering jagged shards of glass.

Somehow Railton found his own voice, embarrassed by how thin and reedy it sounded before a creature that seemed as lethally beautiful as a black winged fallen angel.

"I need to know about you, Jendar Azrar."

The brilliant emeralds did not darken, instead the Prince seemed amused and curious. "And what if there is a price to pay for such knowledge? The highest price of all – your life?"

Railton took a deep breath, fighting to keep his composure calm and assured. He was all too aware of how perilous his situation had become – a danger entirely of his own making. He believed this warrior Prince – whatever dark place he came from, would respect courage. It was all he had to gamble with.

"I risk my life day and night in Isolann. If the Germans don't get me, then a landslide or a fall down a precipice from my rat bag horse may do the trick, or failing all that, food poisoning from rancid goat stew."

The Prince raised one elegant eyebrow in amusement as Railton continued, emboldened by the slight relaxation in his austere demeanour.

"I have given up worrying all the time about my life, but I have to ask. Is my immortal soul in danger from you?"

Again, the creature looked amused rather than angered.

"I have no idea what a human soul is and therefore it is in no danger from me. I am Dark Kind – from a species that has dwelled on Earth since the birth of modern humans. I am not a supernatural being or a demon. I will give leave for young Tigh over there to tell you whatever you want to know – providing you swear on something you hold dearest to your heart – that you will not take this information beyond Isolann."

Railton gave a solemn nod of assent and brought out a tattered pocket-sized and very dog-eared bible from the folds of his clothing. His precious good luck charm from his flying days; pressed into his hand by his mother on the day he left Yorkshire for the war.

"On this most holy book, I solemnly swear all the secrets of Isolann will never leave my lips but stay locked in my heart forever."

Azrar began to walk away on silent, powerful strides but turned to address Railton once more. "Not that anyone would ever believe you."

Railton was aware this dark creature had a fleeting, slight smile as he said it. The Jendar had a dry sense of humour – hopefully this was a good sign. Azrar became serious again; a harsher edge came into the honeyed voice.

"Do not rush into asking questions, Englishman, not knowing everything will not affect your stay with us. There are many doors in this land best left locked. You will have a less troubled life if you leave them firmly bolted."

The Prince and his small band of fighters left the cave shortly after. He rode out in silence on his black war horse and soon became part of the night; the darkest shadow and greatest secret in what was truly a land full of secrets and shadows. Railton took his advice and thought for many days before tackling young Tigh. Knowledge once gained could not be erased from the mind and Railton believed that the truth about Azrar would be very dark – even downright evil. There could be a corrupting effect from this knowledge, possibly permanently staining his soul. And if souls did not exist, knowing the truth about Azrar and the Pact would change him as a person. He would not allow something this momentous to happen on a mere curious whim. One day, fate willing, he would return to his native Yorkshire.

Just how serious his responsibility was to the future of these enigmatic folk began to dawn on him. As one they had treated him like a cherished brother without pre-judgement or for their own motives and gain. Their vulnerability began to hit home. It could well be threatened by a few misjudged words back in England. Railton made a Pact of his own that night, never to betray his Isolanni friends or their uncanny ruler.

Chapter Eight

Berlin, Germany. 1943

Blue-grey trails of cigarette smoke wafted lazily around the ceiling of a night club built in the basement of a once fine private home in Berlin. Always a smart venue, this night it was filled with the usual crowd of socialites. Couturier clad, pencil thin women, glittering with jewels accompanied wealthy businessmen in black formal suits. Their veneer of urbane glamour gave the illusion of a relaxed, privileged society at leisure – with no sign of any inconvenient war disturbing their social whirl. This illusion vanished at the sight of many uniformed guests, some in the pristine black of the sinister, ever present Gestapo.

There was an extra frisson of excitement buzzing through the club that night. Interest in its new singer, a little Slav songbird, had spread through Berlin society. It attracted the curiosity of Major Heinrich Dassler who sat surrounded by fellow regular army officers and their wives close to the front of the stage. He was a much admired and highly decorated war hero and his presence added to the excitement among the tightly packed guests. The club had never been so full.

A career soldier from an ancient Prussian noble family, Dassler tried to avoid eye contact and therefore ignore the raised salutes of greeting from the black clad officers. A tough military veteran of the Great War, he had no time for the hyena-like tactics of the Gestapo but was wise enough not to antagonise them.

He also studiously ignored the avaricious eyes of many of the society women in the club. Dassler was still handsome for his age despite an old duelling scar that bisected the right side of his face from forehead to chin. He was still blessed with heroic craggily hewn features, close cut, dark blonde hair now heavily flecked with silver grey and a tall, well honed body. His family's wealth was intact and he was divorcing his Hungarian born wife who had fled to America in disgust on the rise of the Nazi party. He knew these bejewelled hard-eyed women saw him as quite a catch but Dassler had no interest in their wiles. He had but one aim – to win the war with the least amount of spilt German blood.

The club was an unlikely venue for Dassler but he desperately needed some mental release from the war, a few hours of entertainment before returning to duty. He heard talk of this beautiful young woman who sang like a nightingale. Dassler fully expected to be disappointed; no doubt all he would see was a peasant girl with a thin veneer of tawdry glamour, he thought as the lights dimmed and a shiver of expectation shimmered through the crowd.

Dassler expected a peasant but found instead a fairy-tale princess walking with an elegant grace across the stage. She gently guided a handsome young man wearing very dark glasses and carrying an old saxophone and helped him to his seat behind her. Then with her blind cousin settled, she turned to face the audience with a sweet smile of welcome. She wore a simple, alluring but modest pale green bias cut silk gown. Her silver blonde hair was worn up in a simple unadorned chignon and she wore no make up – her astonishing gold eyes needed no enhancement.

Dassler was enchanted. Here was a Rhine maiden; an elfin princess come to life from the pages of the storybooks. His delight grew as she began to sing, with only the plaintive tone of the saxophone weaving a complementary pattern around her sweet pure voice that caressed his soul like a spiritual balm. All the ugliness of war seemed to vanish in the gentle lilt of her voice, all the carnage of battle and never-ending pain and humiliation from his loss of his much loved wife temporarily forgotten.

On stage, Khari began her carefully chosen repertoire. In this lion's den, surrounded by so many hardened Nazi party members, she never used material written by Jewish composers or any black blues or jazz. She started with a modernised version of an ancient Isolanni lament, so hauntingly beautiful it brought tears to all but the most hardened eyes, despite no one understanding the lyrics. As she paused for the rapturous applause to settle down, she gave the room a quick scan, desperately trying not to physically recoil in disgust at the foul contents of so many minds. Deep within, as ever she felt soiled, corrupted by the foul poison from so many evil human monsters. She wondered if she would ever clear her mind of the terrible images; would having them become part of her own memories end in madness? It seemed sadly inevitable.

One mind interested her; it belonged to a high ranking officer yet a man of honour and integrity. This could be the ideal subject for her to cultivate. A man high enough in the German chain of command to have access to useful information but one not too steeped in barbarity for Khari to visit his mind. She glanced across to Dassler and saw his interest in her without needing to read his thoughts. She lowered her eyes shyly and looked away, knowing already the high value he put on modesty and virtue. It was enough – the fish was hooked on the bait.

Behind his impenetrable dark glasses, Jazriel watched the crowds with the cold steady gaze of a seasoned predator. There was almost a danger of sensory overload for a creature with such sharp-honed awareness – the women drenched in Guerlain and Worth, the smoke from countless cigars and cigarettes and the clashing aroma of many cocktails. And beneath this superficial onslaught was the drum beat of a hundred hearts all pumping red life blood – the hot sweet elixir that gave him life and strength. His attention was caught by a tall white blond officer rudely inviting himself onto Dassler's table, his pristine black uniform so well cut and crisp it looked unreal. The man settled down to fix him with an intense glare. Jazriel was accostomed attracting the admiring attention of both male and female humans, something he often used to his own advantage. But he had never seen such an explosive combination of raw lust and intense hatred.

Khari had also seen this man fixing his attention on Jazriel and immediately probed his mind. What she found made her recoil in horror and disgust, completely losing her ability to continue singing. Swiftly, Jazriel disguised her confusion with a wonderful solo, a virtuoso performance that brought the audience to its feet in a standing ovation. The man had triggered Jazriel's own hunger, his blood lust – the instinctive need to kill to live. Soon, perhaps that night, in some dark alley he would hunt down and drain the Gestapo officer. One monster ridding the world of another.

As Jazriel finished his solo, Khari recovered her composure, deeply grateful for the vampire's quick mind and Lenny's genius in teaching him to play so well. She had thought she'd already plumbed the depths of depravity in so many Nazi minds but what this officer had planned for Jazriel went beyond all boundaries of evil. Her only consolation was that he could never be a defenceless human victim but a ruthless predator far more ferocious than any Gestapo monster.

She recovered to sing a medley of popular German folk songs and had every man in the room in love with her by the end of the performance. As she expected, they both received an invitation to join Dassler's table, which she accepted with a shy smile of appreciation. Dassler stood and raised a glass of champagne to toast her arrival at his table.

"You are most welcome, Fraulein Cheryniaz. Sadly, all I know of Svolenia is a remote ice-bound country full of superstitious peasants and ravening wolves. If I had known it contained such beauty, I would have visited it many years ago."

"Your first conclusion was correct, you were right to stay away. That is why I was so happy to become a German citizen, this is my beloved home."

Khari replied with a demure, shy smile.

"I thought Svolenia was a Slavic nation; your musician looks pure gypsy to me."

The Gestapo officer sneered with a dangerous contempt. His surly interruption shattered the atmosphere of growing rapport between Khari and Dassler who was livid at such bad manners at his table. One of the women guests lay a comforting hand on Jazriel's arm – gypsy or not, the blind musician was stunningly attractive.

"May I introduce you to my beloved cousin, Count Mikhail Cheryniaz – another Svolenian exile happy to live in Germany. There is no taint of despised gypsy blood in my family, we are all noble born."

Tactfully, one of the officers' wives swiftly switched the conversation to the latest Berlin gossip; everybody studiously omitting any mention of the war. This was a night of pretence, an illusion, to escape the growing horrors and fear. Khari tried to avoid the suspicious glare of the Gestapo officer, meeting his almost colourless blue eyes with innocent candour. But it was so hard to do, knowing what a hideous soul lay beyond those bland mirrors.

Khari picked up Dassler's intentions towards her; an honourable evening at a fashionable restaurant, this liaison would further their mission. She knew she had to go alone but was frightened for Jazriel. She spoke to him quietly in the vampire language.

"Jazz, my love, you must take great care. That Gestapo officer is an evil. filled with self loathing and perverse desires. He has murdered many young men already. He means to do terrible things to you."

A wickedly feral grin spread across Jazriel's handsome features. Khari caught a fleeting glimpse of his fangs as he reached across to kiss her hand.

"Do not concern yourself, little one. He is about to meet his fate, one beyond even his fevered imaginings."

"Don't take any crazy risks. Please be very careful."

"I'm a survivor, remember. Anyway, this is easy prey."

The evening progressed without much further incident, although their brief use of the vampire tongue triggered some unwelcome interest from one of Dassler's guests. The wife of one of Dassler's officer's leaned forward to speak to Khari.

"Erina, I apologise for being so forward, but I couldn't help noticing that fascinating language you use with each other. I am a professor of linguistics and anthropology and it has completely stumped me. It isn't a Slavic or Germanic tongue."

Her last words attracted the suspicious interest of the Gestapo officer. This situation was getting ever more dangerous. Khari scanned the woman's mind for any malice but only found genuine academic curiosity and was uncertain how to proceed; this woman's knowledge could lead them to danger. Thankfully, Jazriel was in great form and gave the professor the full power of his most disarming smile.

"It is an old family tradition. It's a child's game, a made-up language started by some of our distant ancestors as a childish prank to outwit their tutors. It's been added to and embellished by generations of Cheryniaz children, a process Erina and I continued as little ones."

"A charming tale," the woman replied, temporarily distracted by Jazriel's stunning looks. Dassler, tired of the company, decided to ask Khari out for a light supper at a discreet but high class restaurant.

"Count Cheryniaz, may I ask your permission to take Erina for a meal? It is a highly respectable establishment and I will bring her home promptly."

"*It's okay, Jazz. I know his intentions are completely honourable.*

"*How can I protect you if you disappear into the night with a Nazi major? Devane will personally throw me out into the sunlight if any harm comes to you.*"

"*And I will have to face Sivaya's fangs if you mess up hunting that Gestapo creep. I am going to be much safer than you.*"

Jazriel gave an elegant nod of assent to the Major.

"Look after my little cousin well, she is our family's most precious gem."

"Of course. Do you need help getting home?"

"It is but a short walk. If I take my time, my trusty cane will get me back in one piece."

Khari kissed the vampire lightly on his forehead and allowing Dassler to drape her white fox stole over her shoulders left the club, aware of the buzz of intrigued gossip her departure created in the crowds.

Jazriel left the night club with a few hours of darkness left, grateful to be away from the sensory clamour of too many humans crammed into too small a space. He strolled through the narrow network of back streets, the pavement slick with recent rain. There was little bomb damage, miraculously this area was not yet touched by the war from the skies. The late hour meant the streets were deserted but he still did not walk with his usual, confident prowl but with the halting measured step of a blind man in an unknown street, tapping ahead with his white cane which disguised the silence of his steps. He knew he was being followed and led his jack booted pursuer deeper and deeper into a network of back alleys.

Erich Gruber was delighted as the tall figure slowly made progress away from the main streets. It brought closer realisation of his fantasy – to inflict his pleasure on the handsome blind gypsy as he slowly killed him. Not as slowly and inventively as he would like but lust made him impatient. Gruber readied his handgun and continued to stalk his next victim through the slippery alleys. The man's blindness made his ambush easy as he reached out and grabbed him firmly by the shoulder.

"Wait, my handsome young friend, the evening is not over so soon."

The savagery in the human's voice amused Jazriel. It was like a fluffy kitten threatening a tiger. He turned to face Gruber, leaning against a wall with practised languid insouciance. Jazriel slowly put two cigarettes in his mouth and lit them. In a relaxed, elegant gesture handed one to Gruber, the erotic overture inflaming the German to recklessness. The clouds cleared and moonlight illuminated Gruber's round face and florid features, so bland they seemed unfinished. His plans were thrown by the foreigner's lack of fear, his apparent welcome to his advances. He found this both daunting and provocative; in the past he had only chosen to rape and kill the alluring but forbidden innocent, naïve young men with dark good looks of Jewish or gypsy background.

Then he realised that because this amazing looking man was blind, he could not see the reality of Gruber. He could not see the small, grossly overweight taunted child with the red hair and too many freckles, crammed tightly into his lederhosen like an over-filled bratwurst. He could not see him grow tall and lean, a proud member of the Nazi Youth until violated by an adult party leader beneath the piercing stare of the Fuhrer's portrait. He did not see him become the dead-eyed Gestapo officer who got his revenge on every school boy who taunted him, and the leader who betrayed his trust, contaminated his zeal for the Nazi party. He could not see the twisted young man who learnt to enjoy inflicting pain and death as he enjoyed the secret desires that would destroy him if ever discovered.

This beautiful blind man was the first not to flinch away with repulsion but regretfully he still had to die to preserve Gruber's secret. The foreigner tilted his head slightly letting the moonlight catch his perfect features. Gruber wanted him so badly; he fought for breath, his legs weak with desire. He reached out to touch the sharply chiselled features but Jazriel caught his wrist with a vice like grip that splintered bones. Gruber mewled with pain and shock as Jazriel snarled in disgust.

"No human vermin touches me."

Jazriel removed his glasses causing Gruber to collapse with shock at the blazing alien beauty of his eyes. His fangs engaged and Gruber began to thrash about in terror with a high pitched animal scream. As he voided himself copiously, a revolted Jazriel threw him down with a snarl of disgust, snapping the German's back and neck to silence the irritating wailing. No hunger was worth polluting himself with such a vile creature's blood.

The night was not a total waste as he heard the scrape of more jack-booted steps approach unsteadily towards him. Gruber's aide, too drunk to remember the command not to follow him from the club. More by bad luck than judgement, the fool blundered onto Gruber's route through the alleys. The aide was a big, hard-muscled man, proud of his athletic prowess and his many medals in the Berlin

Olympics. His size and strength made him more worthy prey and kicking Gruber's body into the shadows, Jazriel approached the second Gestapo officer with a purposeful loping gait.

Despite his inebriation, the officer put up a prolonged courageous fight for life, unwittingly hastening his fate by sweetening his blood with adrenaline. Jazriel revelled in his predatory skill, his agility and strength – playing with his victim until the hunger grew too great. He overpowered the man, who did not scream for mercy but raged and fought on with hate and anger right until the inevitable end. Jazriel forced the man to his knees and took the kill from behind, tearing into his neck with one powerful bite straight through to the jugular. He shivered and growled with intense pleasure as he drank deep of the man's gushing lifeblood, flooding his entire being with electric new life.

Fully sated, vibrant with renewed strength, he prowled away to return to his apartment anxious to reach it before dawn, his fedora pulled low over once more hidden eyes. He had left the two dead Nazi officers in such a compromising position, he doubted there would be further investigation of their deaths by a shocked and embarrassed Gestapo hierarchy.

Khari awoke to the smell of something close to coffee. She had fallen asleep in an old high backed armchair in her apartment waiting for Jazriel to return. She rubbed her eyes and glanced at an old mahogany clock on the mantle piece of their run-down apartment; there was just half an hour of darkness left before dawn. Jazriel handed her a steaming cup of the ersatz coffee before sitting opposite her. It was obvious to Khari he had killed and fed that night – his turquoise eyes glittered with greater brilliance.

"Devane is not paying me enough. I was sent here to protect your life, not look after your honour as well."

Khari smiled as she cradled the coffee.

"My honour is perfectly safe. Major Dassler is an old fashioned gentleman. The more chaste I remain, the more his interest will grow. He is high enough in Hitler's chain of command to be the perfect source of information. How was your night? Did you hunt down that Gestapo creep?"

Jazriel gave an exaggerated shudder of disgust.

"I'd rather sink my fangs into a dead slug. I still killed him – broke his neck like the filthy rat he was. Luckily he had a delicious big, strong aide close by to feed on."

Khari blew the vampire an affectionate kiss as he retired to his room for his Rest from daylight. She finished her unpleasant coffee and after a wash in cold water with the last of the soap ration, changed into day clothes. What kind of cold-hearted monster had she become, where she could calmly discuss the murder of two humans as no more than small talk with a friend?

The answer lay trapped in her mind, filling daily with yet more terrible images of the Nazis' growing list of crimes against humanity. Jazriel had no other choice; he was created a ruthless predator, a killer of humans to survive. Khari had become an accessory to murder by her life-long association with the Dark Kind. She knew her colleagues in the Spook Squad would defend her behaviour as necessary in the war against a greater evil. Even fuelled by her desire for revenge for her Isolanni family, she could not be so coldly dispassionate; her war grew harder by the day.

Joe Devane wandered by the brook that tumbled through the Manor's rambling overgrown grounds. Deep in his own troubled thoughts, he was oblivious to the beauty of the late winter morning. He did not notice tiny fish darting above the polished stones in the shallow, crystal clear water or the soft purple-tinged clouds driven by a stiff north easterly wind with their promise of snow flurries.

His mind was too full of thoughts of Khari and all that she faced in Berlin. She had been away for nearly nine months, but to Joe Devane it could have been nine centuries. Time had not made her absence any easier to bear; missing her became more painful every day, coupled with the constant soul draining dread, laced for good measure with so much guilt. He had sent his beloved golden girl straight into the heart of evil, into a viper's nest of menace. Devane's sanity was only saved by the steady stream of good intelligence coming from his agents in Berlin. The vampire language had been a godsend to their war effort. Any Nazi code-cracking unit would be gnashing their teeth with frustration if any of the Spook Squad's messages were intercepted. A language with no human speech pattern, with no common roots with any human tongue – an unknown language with no known records or written form, they would have to be beyond genius to decipher it.

The use of the Dark Kind language meant he knew that Khari and Jazz were still safe, settled in a shabbily genteel, discreet apartment close to the Grey Cat night club where they were both employed as entertainers. It had been an ideal cover. They were able to send back a steady stream of high quality intelligence without having to do anything risky; there was no need to break into offices or make dangerous contacts. They did not have to build up the trust of any high ranking officials. Jazz played the saxophone and Khari broke a dozen hearts every night with the beauty of her voice. On second thought, mused Devane, it was probably Jazriel breaking more hearts, he only had to smile.

Devane was certain that his two agents – both precious to him in their different ways – had been followed by the Gestapo many times, but they would have seen nothing suspicious. By daylight Khari and Jazriel rested in the apartment, perhaps Khari venturing out to a local shop to queue for hours for increasingly meagre rations, by night they spent every hour in the club. The only deviation was their rare night out with Dassler and his friends, all of them high ranking Germans including inner circle party officials, all beyond reproach, even for the most paranoid Gestapo agent.

Khari's chaste but high profile relationship with a German officer was more problematical to Devane. It was pure unadulterated jealousy of course. He trusted Khari implicitly and his head accepted Khari's tactics in cultivating Dassler were sound. The German officer was not a Party member but still close enough to the Fuhrer's elite inner circle to provide the highest grade information. It was Devane's heart that screamed at the injustice, why was this man, an enemy, enjoying Khari's company, while he languished alone in England?

Devane's reverie was disturbed by someone approaching; he looked up to see Anna Vandenberg walking towards him. Damn these empaths! He thought without rancour, they always knew when he was feeling unhappy and troubled! He tried small talk, knowing it would only delay the inevitable. "How are the new batch coming, anything we can use?"

"You know more than me, Joe, nobody studies his team's progress closer than you."

Devane bowed his head in defeat, nothing got past Anna who, with MacCammon in Berlin, had become his human second in command. Eshan still provided extraordinary support, with all the energy and drive of her Dark Kind strength and commitment. There were no half measures with the vamp member's of the squad.

"They still seem secure as anyone can be in that mad house of a country," Anna ventured, crouching down to let her hand dangle in the stream, the water was cold but it was still pleasurable to feel it trickling through her fingers. The sharp sensation felt like a form of spiritual cleansing after an arduous morning helping Ffitch-Brown interrogate a suspected double agent. Anna did not have Khari's extraordinary, intimate access to the dark heart of the human soul but she could pick up emotion, including those deeply repressed. The only problem was the effect it had on her. Other people's emotions seeped into her; she felt like an unwilling human sponge soaking up contaminating water. God knows how Khari coped with her more potent input.

"I want them out, now."

Anna nodded, agreeing personally with his determined statement, but she was a realist. "They are not in any greater danger now than a month ago, Joe. Our bosses won't want to pull the plug on this mission yet."

Devane sighed and crouched down beside her; pulling angrily at some water reeds, snapping the stalks with his fingers. Anna stayed his hand, "Hey, these poor things are not the enemy, unless the Nazi's have found a way to recruit plant life."

A sad smile flitted briefly across Devane's face and he left the plants be. He caught a glimpse of his face in the clear water and instinctively pulled back in revulsion. Anna's heart went out to him as she felt pent up waves of roiling self disgust pour out of Joe Devane and assault her unguarded soul.

"Joe, you are an amazing man, a brave and beautiful soul; that is the man Khari has fallen in love with."

Devane stood up and turned away abruptly from his reflection. "Khari was raised surrounded by the charismatic charms of Dark Kind allure…they are all so damn beautiful. I am certain Jendar Azrar is too. How can a monstrous thing like me compete? What if she discovers the truth? I cannot bear the thought of her turning away from me in revulsion."

Anna took Devane's arm and guided him away from the brook, "Joe, I told you before, Khari knows everything about you but she only sees a wonderful man, a man she loves with all her heart. The Dark Kind's outer veneer of beauty is illusion too; underneath they are monsters with hearts of stone. Khari does not want that – she wants you."

They walked back to the Manor in reflective silence. No member of the Spook Squad was an ordinary human being, all had an inborn gift – or curse, some strange ability; it was just that some chose not to reveal it.

Chapter Nine

Arpalathian Mountains, Isolann, 1943

In the months following his last unnerving encounter with Jendar Azrar, Railton and his Isolanni friends became all too aware of an intensifying of the German aerial assault. It felt like someone's bad strategy being pushed to the bitter limit in the vain hope that it might finally succeed.

Steve Railton arose early to help prepare breakfast for the other fighters in their cave hideout. "There's something different in the air today my friend," ventured Tigh hesitantly, handing the Englishman a piece of rock hard rye bread. Railton nodded, dipping the grey-brown bread into his herb tea to soften it enough to eat. Again last night there had been no ominous drone of oncoming death from the skies, the mountains free of made-made lightning and thunder. Five days and nights without a raid. Could it be the Germans had given up their brutal assault on this tiny realm? Railton did not believe it but one thing was without dispute. Isolann was still defiantly free.

The strange peace had given Railton time for reflection. For some time now, he was fully aware of the Prince's true nature and the ancient pact he had with his people. It had horrified him at first. The concept that vampires did exist and were not the stuff of over fervent peasant imagination took some coming to terms with. But in his heart, it did not surprise him. He had seen Azrar at close hand, experienced for himself the dark charisma and menacing power of this ancient warlord. As days turned into months, his initial horror turned to fascination. What wonders had this creature witnessed in his incredible lifetime? Had he seen sabretooth tigers and mammoths? Had he watched the building of the pyramids and known what happened to Atlantis? Did he know what Stonehenge was for?

That Azrar's life depended on human blood was the hardest to accept, possibly because he did not look like a ravening beast or spectral ghoul, but a handsome young man with strangely beautiful eyes.

Free from restrictions to talk to the foreigner Tigh had told him the Prince was able to feed on his people's many enemies over the centuries. It was scant assurance to the Englishmen, Azrar still took human life to exist. There was a cold black heart to Isolanni society, a tacit acceptance of murder to preserve their Prince. But balancing this was the vampire warlord's unbreakable bond with them, his unswerving duty to protect them against all danger.

It was so hard for Railton's Christian based morals to come to terms with. He knew he should condemn Azrar as utterly evil, an enemy of all mankind, a hellish thing to be destroyed. But he could not. If Azrar was a human, this would be the only outcome. But he was Dark Kind, an alien species as unaccountable for his predation as any wolf or bear.

He realised he would have no difficulty keeping his oath of silence once back home, as the Prince rightly said who would believe him? It would also condemn him in many of his countrymen's eyes as an accessory to murder, for once the war was over, the Prince's needs would remain. Nor did Railton want to endanger the Jendar's life and the security of his loyal people by betraying him. Railton could see the Isolanni clearly adored their prince; they respected his ferocious nature and obeyed him without question, but not out of any blind fear. It was a relationship of mutual trust and respect built over many centuries. Yet it was fragile pact as delicate as the finest cut glass vase, one that would take just one person's actions to shatter forever.

Railton's thoughts were interrupted by Tigh's hand on his arm. The nomad fighter pointed to some people moving through the narrow valley below, herding thin straggly goats, desperate for fresh pasture. Lured by the silence in the skies, it was clear some Isolanni began to move openly in the daylight. It felt too soon and Railton's anxiety grew as he watched the nomad families make their way through the gorge. It was only human nature, everyone wanted their normal life to return; it was no surprise to see the beleaguered families risking their lives to graze their livestock openly and attempt to replenish the seriously depleted feed stores in their mountain hideouts.

"This peace is false. The enemy will be back. We must stay vigilant," muttered Tigh. Railton nodded assent, eyes narrowing from the strong sunlight as he uneasily watched the families' slow meandering progress. If the Germans struck now they would not reach shelter in time. His eye was caught by a young nomad woman, she walked with the easy grace of her people, back straight, head held high, proud and unafraid. She managed to make flicking at the straying goats with a long willow switch seem as elegant a gesture as any queen commanding her subjects. As his eyes became accustomed to the strong light, he raised his binoculars for a better look and could see she was beautiful, with huge almond shaped black eyes and an impish smile that undermined her regal bearing.

"Mountain women, they are the most desirable of our people!" Tigh laughed as he spotted the focus of Railton's interest. The Englishman looked embarrassed but this did not phase the young fighter who called down to the valley in a burst of Isolanni too quick for Railton to follow. To his further discomfort, the nomad girl looked up and waved to him, her whole face alight as she responded to Tigh with good humoured banter.

"Her name in Lhalee and she wants to meet the famous Englishman who can down German planes with one shot."

Tigh teased, "And look, my friend, she is not wearing a red feather hair braid."

Tigh's disclosure that the young woman was unmarried did little to ease Railton's embarrassment, yet he did not object or resist when his friend urged him to walk down into the valley to meet her. In this unusually free society for women, wrongly perceived as primitive to the outside world, there was no need for a chaperone. In Isolann, no one would object to two young people meeting up and with the assurance from Tigh that no angry father or brother would chase him away, Railton climbed down to meet his future wife.

Months passed and a sort of uneasy stability fell on Railton's team of nomad fighters. Without the threat from air raids, they remained mainly in one cave network, allowing their hard driven horses to recuperate and gain much needed weight.

Railton's blossoming relationship with the spirited Isolanni beauty Lhalee was put on a very reluctant hold as she returned with her family to their tribal wanderlands to the northwest. Noticing the Englishman's gloomy mood at her departure from their valley, Tigh assured him they would find her again after winter when travel was safer— unless of course the Germans renewed their attack.

Winter, the oldest enemy yet also closest friend of the Isolanni people was stalking the Autumn like a black mountain wolf. Railton began to notice a new sharpness in the night air, often waking to find the ground beyond their caves frozen rock hard until the sun rose high. The severity of Isolann's winters were well known, even to a foreigner like himself and he resolved to learn every survival skill from his nomad friends before the first snows fell.

One morning, the sun seemed to have gone missing. Dawn arrived with a brief tinge of vivid pink before iron-grey clouds lumbered over the mountains, almost low enough to touch. As the day progressed, the cloud cover became increasingly dark and more ominous with distant rumbled of surly thunder. A wind, first skittish and playful as a yearling filly, grew in strength, building up to blustering storm force by dusk.

The nomads stayed close to the cave system and were well under shelter when a horrendous rainstorm descended, hurling sharp rods of ice mingled with the gale driven, near horizontal rain. Despite the wild banshee howling, their horse herd, already nervy from the roar of the storm began to stamp and whinny. The guard dogs went into a frenzy of howling as they warned of riders approaching in the night. The horsemen were Prince Azrar and his escort hurrying to find shelter from the storm.

Like a well-oiled machine, the newcomers' needs were met, horses taken away to be dried off and fed, the humans brought warm, dry clothes. Only Azrar stood apart and silent, a glowering presence deep in the shadows, just the emerald glow of his eyes showing in the darkness.

As the night drew on, once dry and refreshed the newcomers began to relax and join in the flow of campfire conversation; much concerned the urgent need to stockpile supplies before winter. The lull in the aerial bombardment had been timely but deeply mistrusted. Nobody believed their war was over – the Germans were planning something major. It was just a question of when.

Eventually, sleep took more and more of the Isolanni and the cave network soon became full of slumbering forms beneath their increasingly pungent sheepskin rugs that were also used as cloaks and saddle cloths. Railton pulled his cloak tightly around his shoulders as he felt the bone-deep chill of Azrar's presence increase. One of the Prince's fighters approached and escorted him to an audience with Azrar. It was a summons he did not welcome but could not refuse.

Azrar sat by a makeshift wooden table, studying a small pile of modern looking documents. He read one in obvious contempt, gripping it with his deceptively slender fingers. Railton remembered his friend's warning that the Jendar could break a man's spine with the same ease as a human squashed a troublesome insect–and with as much thought. Railton was found a chair and given a mug of a spicy warmed and robust red wine. It did nothing to ease the icy waves of power from the Prince, but he accepted the hospitality with gratitude; it was a welcome change from weak herb tea or goat's milk.

"The German Chancellor has issued me with an ultimatum. I must give his forces free and unimpeded access through Isolann or face complete destruction."

"Is it an option, my Lord? Can your people withstand the full fury of the German war machine if you refuse?"

Azrar held the document to a candle, unbothered by the flames as they licked at his fingers. He swept the ash to the floor. "Nothing has changed. The Germans still believe my people are racially inferior. It is just a rather pathetic ploy to make us relax our guard. I have dealt with the treacherous ways of humankind for too long to be fooled by such transparent trickery."

Railton nodded and took another long draught from the warming wine.

"Well, Englishman, you chose the more dangerous path. You now know all about me and my people's ancient pact. Are you planning to try the pointed stake option to rid the world of an ancient evil?"

Momentarily startled, Railton studied the vampire's austere pale face and saw one slightly raised eyebrow – an outward sign of Dark Kind humour – these creatures could not laugh or cry and most smiles were warning signs of growing danger. Railton answered, hoping his nervous wavery voice could convey the sincerity he truly felt, "My Lord, I will not break the oath I swore on my bible. I owe you and your people my life; I will never betray you. I would gladly forfeit my own life for Isolann."

"Fine words, Englishman. And what if the hunger dangerously weakened me – and thus imperilled my people – would you offer your neck to me?"

Railton again sought for clues in the carved marble of Azrar's fierce, handsome face and found nothing to help him. "You would never do that, Prince Azrar. You are a Jendar of the Dark Kind and bound by your honour to protect those loyal to the Pact and their allies."

Azrar seemed pleased with his answer and went back to studying his papers, clearly the short audience was at an end. Railton sat in uneasy silence, waiting to be dismissed from the vampire warlord's presence, eager to be far from the power waves threatening to turn his blood to ice. The Prince looked up briefly from his intelligence reports.

"You will need plenty of rest, Railton. Tomorrow night you will ride by my side, and for the rest of the war. Unfortunately I have always set a punishing pace for my human outriders, a leftover from the long gone days when I rode out with Dark Kind warriors. I am eager to learn all about your lands and the modern world. I also value fresh ideas and opinions, so feel free to express them. I am a dangerous creature to my enemies but I am no tyrant to my people – or my friends. "

Railton was astonished by this command, but excited too. There was so much he could learn from this fascinating creature. He bowed and began to walk away, but a sudden boldness made him pause and to speak to the Prince, "There's just one thing. My Lord, I speak with the deepest respect; your people seem immune to your power, but I find it physically very hard to be close to you. I am worried I cannot serve you well if I succumb to it."

Azrar nodded gravely not offended by his candour, "Generations of living by the Pact have indeed bred an immunity for the Isolanni. I will do my best to make you more comfortable."

Railton mumbled his gratitude and bowing low again, swiftly headed for the warmth and light of the nearest campfire and the comfort of human company. That night would add a whole new dimension to the deepening strangeness of his Isolanni odyssey; a wild adventure, he was glad no one would ever hear about if he ever made it home to England. He had learnt to respect, no, more than that, he actually liked and admired the vampire Prince; who would understand that back home? Railton just hoped he was mentally and physically strong enough to ride by the Prince's side in the darkness. What wonders would he learn about? Would he learn enough to satisfy his own great curiosity about the ancient world?

As a child, he read everything he could about the Ancient Romans, Greeks and Egyptians. Now he could actually speak to a being who breathed the same air as Cleopatra and Julius Caesar, who fought against Alexander the Great and won. And most important of all, who walked the earth at the same time as Jesus Christ.

Railton doubted he would be able to get much sleep that night with all the excitement and anxiety. But rest, he must, for he was still in a deeply imperilled country at war and Prince Azrar was at the forefront of its defence. The vampire warlord would not slacken his relentless pace for one unfit British airman.

Chapter Ten

London, England, 1944

Joe Devane watched the afternoon's sky turn dark blue than a ridiculously lurid salmon pink, scudded with fleet fluffy, baby-pink clouds. It looked unreal, a poorly painted daub hawked from a pavement. He wondered what sort of sunset Khari was watching over Berlin's sky. Even in her perilous situation, somehow he knew she would greet the garish sunset with delight, seeing only beauty. Khari had the gift to see the beauty in ugly things.

"That's quite a sight, Joe; God's gone a bit wild with the paintbox tonight."

Devane turned to see a distinguished looking older man approach down the path winding through St James' Park, in London. They paused on a small bridge of a little lake, leaning over the iron railing as if looking at the ornamental waterfowl beneath.

"I want my people home, now. This mission has gone on too long," Devane stated evenly but with conviction. The older man sighed, producing a crumpled paper bag from his coat pocket and throwing some stale bread crusts to the ducks and geese below. "You know that would be a mistake," he replied quietly, pausing until a gaggle of affronted housewives passed them, muttering pointedly at the waste of food in this lean, hard time of rationing.

"Joe, they are well settled in undercover now. The quality of information coming back is astounding. You have no idea how many lives they are saving, how much they are probably shortening this terrible war. I will not pull them out yet."

Devane did not answer. The man beside him was his superior, in charge of the Spook Squad. Yet he still did not know his name. Just that he was a well spoken limey in his early sixties. They never met in official offices or corresponded on paper, just these brief clandestine meetings in parks and woods in and around London. He had the growing and disturbing feeling of time and luck running out on his squad. Those not already deep undercover in Berlin had been used many times across Europe on missions of intelligence gathering or sabotage. He and Anna were currently the only ones left in England.

"It's tough on you, Joe. I appreciate that." The man continued, "It has been a longer haul for the three still in Berlin than we originally envisaged. But their roles seem to be accepted, they are okay."

Devane shook his head. The line between safety and detection from the Gestapo was so fine it was invisible. He had lived with this terror in his heart for nearly three years. If it had not been for Mac getting all too rare messages out of Germany written in the vampire language, he would have gone mad with worry. No message had been intercepted yet but Devane and the team was confident no German would ever decipher it, should this happen. Anxiety over her safety and missing Khari was eating into his soul. He knew his love for Khari would come with a high price; it was also an increasingly bitter one.

"Why this new urgency to pull back your team? Has Ffitchie had a vision about them?"

Devane shook his head. "No, nothing dramatic like that. Just my own gut instinct that we have pushed our luck too long. I want them out, now."

The man shrugged his shoulders, reluctant to lose this unique intelligence link so close to the monster, the bestial heart and mind of their Nazi enemy. He clapped Joe on the shoulder as he moved to stroll away. "I'll send a good man in. Not to make contact – that might compromise their cover. I'll get him to check out their situation, to put your mind at rest. If he recommends their removal, we'll do it, pronto."

Devane realised that this was all he could get from his boss – a typically British compromise. "Who will it be?"

"An excellent man in the field, virtually a native German speaker, nerves of cold steel."

"I need to know his name," Devane insisted. The safety of his people demanded he stand firm on this matter."

"Anthony Banks."

"Not Banks, absolutely not." Devane went on to explain the angry encounter he had with the agent after the Spook Squad's first overseas mission.

"Is that your only objection, Joe?" the man replied with a weary smile. Devane was a brilliant commander but like so many Americans, he was a bit too earnest, the perpetual boy scout seeing everything in black and white. In his world there were only infinite shades of grey. He started to walk away, his decision final. He paused and turned to say to Devane, "So, Banks hates vampires. Don't we all?"

By the time he returned to Chess Manor, Devane had made up his mind. The gaudy glory of the earlier sunset had long gone, in its place a peaceful star strewn night sky lay over the Manor like an artfully draped velvet cloak.

All the squad's humans were on assignments, leaving the two Dark Kind females behind, in a state of anxious impatience. As he expected, Sivaya was the first to meet him, running down the gravel driveway to intercept his car, unable to wait till he reached the entrance.

"Did you get the go-ahead, are they coming home?"

Devane switched of the car's engine and got out of the car. He took his time before answering her, choosing his words carefully; this deceptively petite, golden beauty could tear his head off with one hand.

"No, but we are getting them out anyway."

By now Eshan had joined them on the drive, and Devane leaned up against the car door to address them. "Ladies, as nonhumans, I have no jurisdiction over your movements. If one of you should contact Garan and slip away with him to Berlin, I do not have the power to stop you. I will also be powerless to prevent you bringing the team home."

Sivaya's face became radiant with joy, forest green eyes shimmering and sparkling. In a rare, impulsive gesture, she kissed Devane on his cheek and ran back to the manor. Devane ruefully rubbed the icy trace of her lips on his face.

"Are you sure about this, Joe?" the other Dark Kind female asked as they walked together in Sivaya's wake. Devane sighed, the thought of a wild card like Banks loose in Berlin frankly terrified him. It would take so little to tip the balance against his team, against Khari. "I just want them out, Lady Eshan. I have no spook abilities but something is screaming to my soul that there is evil stalking my people – and not just from the Germans."

Berlin, Germany, 1944

"That woman is just incorrigible. And she isn't the first persistent nuisance. This is getting dangerous." Khari addressed her fellow covert agent, Jazriel as he emerged at dusk from Rest.

She sighed, as usual the handsome devil looked unrepentant and she distracted herself from losing her temper by pouring herself a mug of another grisly substitute for coffee. Khari had queued all morning for the paltry rations, but it was an important gesture. Since her liaison with Dassler, hostile, suspicious eyes followed her every move. The Gestapo must be bored stiff by now of her uneventful life. Accepting any of the readily available black market goods offered to her at the club would also put her and Jazz at risk. So it was queue, queue, and endless queue for Khari and her fellow citizens of war-torn Berlin.

Jazriel, of course had his own, readily available source of nourishment, luckily he had not hunted for many months but she dreaded the night when inevitable hunger made him seek human prey in the darkness. Her current problem with her Dark Kind companion came from another source… his growing army of admirers. Khari's chaste liaison with her German officer kept unwanted attention at bay. Jazriel was another matter.

"Did you see the size of her? A coarse overstuffed bratwurst trying to wear a Worth original," he murmured, aware and amused by Khari's displeasure with him. "She thinks because I am blind she can fool me into falling for her and not just her Daddy's stolen millions."

Khari shuddered at the reminder of the lost innocent lives, whose looted wealth now lined the Braun bank vaults. "Fraulein Braun has dangerous connections –you must not be so reckless."

Jazriel shrugged with his languid elegant grace, and removing a cigarette from a slender platinum case, lit up the first of many that night. He also poured himself a generous glass of absinthe; he enthusiastically embraced as many human vices as possible, none would harm his Dark Kind metabolism.

"That is new, let me see it." Khari held out her hand and Jazriel handed the cigarette case over with a wicked and impudent smile. Khari tried to be angry but it was impossible, Jazz could charm the birds out of the sky.

The slim case was pre-war and very expensive, but it was the new inscription engraved inside that made Khari's concerns worsen.

'To my Blind Orpheus,
Your music holds my soul forever in thrall,'
To my dark Adonis,
My love is forever yours.
M'

"I take it the ghastly verse is from Fraulein Madchen Braun," Muttered Khari darkly.

Jazriel shook his head and took another swig from the dangerous spirit. "Actually, the M stands for Margot. It is from her mother."

Khari took out her anger over Jazriel's dangerous dalliances by some vigorous housework, beating the apartment's faded Persian silk rug. Once a vibrant kaleidoscope of warm russets, purples and gold, its worn glamour was in tune with their cover story; they were Svolenian aristocracy fallen on hard times after the countries communist revolution. And of course, Jazriel was playing his role of louche noble-born playboy as part of that cover. The trouble was he played it too well. His looks were magnetic attracting women, and under the Nazi regime, also some understandably fearful men. Many of the women were married and many were connected to dangerous men, like the predatory Margot Braun and her plump, dim daughter.

Though he was skilful at keeping his perfumed army of admirers at arms length, surely it was only a matter of time, before some besotted female made wild accusations or invented lurid lies about him. It was just too dangerous to continue. Jazriel needed an obvious and steady girlfriend

– or better still a respectable wife, to keep them away. But how could that happen? There were no more human Spook Squad females in Berlin, nor would she sanction risking another agent on this mission.

As Khari continued her assault on the Kelim rug, a man walked briskly past her and without pausing or looking in her direction made a strange low, growling noise without seeming to move his lips. No doubt one of the Spook Squad applying his gift for ventriloquism —the man had spoken a few rapid sentences in the vampire tongue. It was clear he had no idea what he said, by his incorrect inflection and mispronunciation of the difficult language, but it was understandable enough to Khari – it was a message from London. Not the one she yearned for. They were not coming home.

Distracted by the message, she re-entered the apartment, her assault on the rug forgotten, as was her bad mood with Jazriel. To make amends, he had run her a shallow but hot bath, throwing in some precious drops of rose oil to scent the grey water. "There you are, Princess, I thought you might need to soak away that dust."

Khari's face did not soften at his gesture, and he dropped his head in mock penitence, "I really am in big trouble this time."

She glanced up, finally able to get her mind around the message from London. Something told her, the new orders were not from Joe.

"It's me that is in big trouble, Jazz. Our bosses want me to get close to Hitler himself. I don't think I can do it."

The vampire's vivid turquoise eyes darkened to the colour of a sullen, storm-lashed sea, his voice turned to an angry wolf growl and for the first time, Khari could see a flash of gleaming white fangs. "You will ignore that idiotic order. You are in enough danger already. "

"Do I have a choice?" Khari replied bitterly. The tenuous security the pair of Allied agents had created was built around their narrow little world, centring on the Grey Cat club. They did nothing out of the ordinary, never went anywhere risky or spoke to anyone controversial. Khari had hoped the Gestapo would soon lose interest in them, though she knew they were still being watched in a half-hearted fashion. Forcing a meeting with the German leader was fraught with danger and would re-awaken their closer interest. Khari took advantage of the bath; she needed time to think before her nightly visit to the club.

Jazriel waited until she was in the bathroom, before picking up his white cane and quietly leaving the apartment. He knew the British agent would head for MacCammon's hovel-like basement near the club, tracking the man was easy, he left the scent of fear floating on the night air. When no one was watching, the vampire moved swiftly through the shadows, easily catching up and overtaking the agent. With the swift, silent swoop of a consummate predator, Jazriel pulled the human into a dark rubble strewn alley. Proximity to the vampire made the man shiver with abject terror; when the creature's fangs dropped, he nearly passed out with fright. "Don't make a sound," he purred, but the velvety tone was pure menace. "Neither of us want to attract those Gestapo bastards trying to follow me."

"What do you want? You are honour bound not to hurt me," the man managed to whimper, though his throat was being restricted by the vampire. His pre-war training as an entertainer did not prepare him for confrontations with blood draining monsters—especially in the heart of Nazi Germany!

"Not your blood, little man. Or your life. I just want you to get a message back to Mac. Tell him Khari will not be meeting up with that madman, not while she is under my protection."

Jazriel let go his vice-like grip on the man's throat. "Get out of here. I spotted three Nazi agents following me, I will deal with them."

The man ran out of the alley then walked swiftly away, not looking back. He did not see Jazriel wait in the shadows, poised like a spring to ambush the Nazis. He was spared the sight of the vampire skilfully toying with his enemies, making light of their brawn and gun power before making three swift kills. And most mercifully, he did not witness Jazriel drinking his fill of Aryan blood.

Back at apartment, Khari was beside herself with worry. Where the Hell was Jazriel? She had finished her bath, ruefully recalling the luxurious days when she travelled Europe with Ha'ali Eshan. Then she could soak for hours in hot deep baths filled with expensive perfumed bath oils if she wanted, as they stayed in the most prestigious, most expensive hotels, Europe's capitals had to offer. She dried herself quickly and dressed ready to go out searching for Jazriel, it would soon be time to begin their first set at the club.

Just as she grabbed her coat, Jazriel strolled in. Khari noticed with alarm he had just fed and fed well. His eyes glittered with new power; his whole body seemed to spark with electricity.

"I hope that was discreet, we are in deep enough trouble with your women and now this order."

Jazriel did an extravagant bow, took her hand and kissed it.

"Never doubt my abilities my little human Princess. No one will trace those that gave me life tonight, nor will their last moments before going to Hell lead a trail back to us."

Khari shivered, proximity to Jazriel's renewed energy was uncomfortable as was the stark reminder that her charming and attractive companion was in reality a ruthless nonhuman predator.

"I have news. Our orders have changed. You will not have to come face to face with that odious little runt, Hitler."

Khari snatched back her hand, shocked. What had he done? Had he attacked the British agent and drank his blood? She cursed her inability to reach Dark Kind minds. Jazriel smiled, his most disarming, dazzling smile, the one that always worked.

"Sweet thing, I have not harmed a single hair of any of our people's heads. The agent is safe with Mac the janitor now, and will be back to England and his family soon, I am sure. But I gave him a clear message. I was given the solemn and precious duty to protect you by Joe Devane, speaking not as your boss but the man who loves you. I would fail my duty if I allowed you to be at any further risk. I am Dark Kind, we vamps cannot fail a duty of honour."

Khari ignored the power waves and reached up to kiss Jazriel's cold face. "What would I do without you, Jazz? You are a devil."

"You missed out the handsome bit."

Chapter Eleven

Chess Manor, The Chilterns, England, 1944

Joe Devane had taken the news of his vampire agent's flagrant insubordination with a secret smile of delight; it validated his leadership skills, he'd chosen Khari's protector well. The order from London for Khari to get close to Hitler had been reckless and ill-advised. Devane had argued in vain against it, sending his anxiety levels over Khari's safety to dangerous levels. Well, good for the Jazzman on standing firm against it, though of course, his own head was at risk from this barmy order.

The vampire's refusal to co-operate had enraged his secretive bosses in London, but what could they do about it? The Dark Kind agents were laws unto themselves; that they worked so well along side the human squad members was miraculous enough. Though Devane would stay worried sick until Khari came home, at least she was in the relative security of her cover story, with a ferocious vampire and a besotted German officer to keep her safe. It was an ironic and bizarre situation, but one that typified Devane's war. He ran a squad full of strangely talented beings, mind readers and vampires, telekinetics and clairvoyants. All doing their best with their unique talents to win the war. He wondered if the Spook Squad's story would ever be told. What would the world think!

Berlin, Germany 1944

War-weary, Heinrich Dassler returned to Khari's apartment, ordered back to Berlin from the French battlefront. He did not know the reason for the summons but he desperately wanted to see Erina first. Dassler was dispirited and increasingly frightened for their safety; the unexpected call at the height of pitched battle only added to his dread. Hitler's murderous rages were worsening and increasingly paranoid and dangerous as the tide turned against the Reich. It was as if the enemy could always second-guess the Fuhrer's plans, every manoeuvre anticipated and prepared for – even ones he still had in his mind.

The security leak must come from the highest level but even the closest scrutiny by top Gestapo investigators came up with no answers. Hitler was increasingly convinced supernatural forces were being used against him but this proved impossible to prove. It was proof to many that their once all-conquering leader had lost his mind. Dassler was at too low a level to be under the strictest surveillance and Erina had been investigated many times, she gave no concerns to the Gestapo. Her life was simple. By day she kept to her apartment, looking after her blind cousin Count Mikhail, by night she sang at the Grey Cat Club accompanied by Miki on the saxophone. That was all. She never spoke to anyone but Dassler's friends and never of the war. Her life was an open book, with mainly blank pages.

The most dangerous thing in their lives was Dassler's own doubts about the Fuhrer, and these he never voiced, not even to Erina.

Khari watched as her protector slumped down on the old overstuffed brocade settee. On each increasingly rare visit, Dassler looked older, more diminished as the stalwart Teutonic warrior was brought down by defeat, the horror of his losses of men and equipment. He was worn down by the cruel incompetence of his superiors and Hitler's insanity.

Too much a patriot to ever consider joining a plot against his leader's life, Khari knew from her mind probing he just wanted an end to the madness that was rending Germany apart—the Fatherland now a fatally wounded beast at bay. Khari knew it was time to leave Berlin, she and Jazriel had done all they could here without endangering their lives anymore. But for now, she wanted to give Dassler the peace and solace he craved. She held him in her arms until he fell asleep, slumped on the sofa and then crept out of the apartment to seek out any meagre rations.

Outside, she hurried head down, picking her way carefully through the rubble-strewn debris of the bomb blasted city. She pulled her battered felt hat down hard, hiding her face in its shadow, wanting to be as anonymous possible as she queued for five hours for food. The city was slowly starving; anything at the end of the long wait would be welcomed. She found herself dreaming a lot of the heady, sensual pleasures of Ileni's full tables. Khari queued in silence, her face down. She had become a minor celebrity, a brief glimpse of glamour in the desolation of a war-torn land but wanted no attention now.

As she waited, drenched from a horizontal, cold relentless rain, a riot broke out in the queue ahead of her; perhaps someone tried to push in. A group of nearby troops rushed across to brutally quell the disturbance with fists and rifle butts. She became aware that during the pandemonium, a note had been dropped in her pocket—probably by MacCammon's clever sleight of hand—Lenny Dawn's lessons had obviously paid off. Sivaya wrote the note in the vampire language—untranslatable if it fell into the wrong hands, but familiar to Jazz and herself. It was good news – it was time to go home.

Dassler was awake on her return and the change in his appearance shocked her. His sturdy, muscular frame always younger than his years, was now wasted and thin. His handsome face – once Hitler's ideal of Germanic perfection, was pallid and gaunt, his blue eyes dull and deep shadowed. He had obviously been distraught with anxiety but made a show of bravado as she re-entered the apartment with some stale, rat bitten bread.

Khari scanned his mind and was genuinely saddened. Dassler was the enemy but he had been good to her and Jazriel. He had treated her with love and honour, respecting her desire to remain a virgin until they were married, providing a comfortable home for her and her cousin. She knew she had the downfall of an honourable man on her conscience but it was a bitter price she had to pay without question. Honest though Dassler was, he was still part of the Nazi monster devouring the world. She had no doubt about exploiting his man's love for her if it could save just one Jewish family or one battalion of allied troops.

Dassler's mental anguish was painful to experience – a wild roller-coaster ride of nightmares and confusion blended with the wildest fantasies. Since her assignment, Khari had relived his brutal loveless childhood. Raised by a series of anonymous and ever changing nannies and tutors in an austere Schloss in Prussia; he'd been sent to cadet school at a young age and all his early memories were of there. He did not remember much of the beautiful but remote figure that was his mother, or the stern authoritarian tyrant of a father.

He entered the Great War as an eager, raw young officer – from an already archaic world of bravado – duels, impressive uniforms, his head full of thoughts of dashing cavalry charges. Months later, he lay badly wounded, trapped in a fox hole with the putrefying remains of his colleagues, helpless as the ruin of their faces were gnawed at by huge fearless rats. Above him roared the endless brain shattering bombardment. He cried out for help but no one could hear. Then the rain came, filling the foxhole with stinking mud and he was in danger of drowning in the liquefying remains of his own men. He was within an hour of this horrifying death when rescue came during a brief lull in the bombardment. His injuries kept him away from the trenches for the rest of the war, but couldn't save him from the haunted memories.

Throughout this he had never cried; any show of feelings beaten out of him since a tiny child. Khari knew his every moment of horror and hidden fear, every suppressed emotional need. She cradled his head in her lap and cried for him.

She remained statue-still, silently holding him close as he sank into a mercifully dreamless sleep. She watched the progress of a half-hearted sun drop gratefully below the horizon. Jazriel would soon stir from Rest and she urgently needed to discuss plans to get out of Germany with him. They were able to talk openly in front of Dassler by using brief bursts of the Dark Kind language, which he assumed, to be their invented language. They spoke it very rarely; conversing in their own language in front of their benefactor was a sign of ill-bred bad manners, which no true aristocrat would dream of.

Dassler awoke a broken man, his face taut with an expression of hopelessness and desolation. He held her tightly in his arms and began to ramble incoherently about how much he loved her. Then his self control returned and his mind began to find some focus again. "Erina, my dearest little one, you must get out of Berlin tonight. Get as far away from here as possible."

Hating herself for her falsehood, Khari made a show of protest, crying bitterly, clinging to his arm. "I will not leave Germany without you, Heinrich."

"You have your whole beautiful life ahead of you and you have a big responsibility looking after poor Miki. I will put you on the train for Svolenia tonight. I will join you later.... I can transfer to a Balkan command post."

She knew in reality he was due to face the Fuhrer's wrath on the failure of his exhausted and ill-equipped battalions to hold back the allied advance. A failure he would pay for with his life. A loyal honourable and courageous soldier deserved so much better. Khari sighed, genuinely sad as she heard his lies. His only appointment now was with the barrel of his own gun. She prayed she and Jaz would be safely en route home before he pulled the trigger. So acute was his desolation, this final desperate act could happen any time. She would not try to save him. This would be a merciful end; a far kinder fate than what awaited him at the hands of the allies or his own crazed leaders.

"Promise me now you will not do anything rash. I will not leave until you assure me you won't take any risks."

Dassler held her close, unable to speak. It was if she could read his mind…

"Filthy vermin!"

Major Rolf Werner slammed his considerable fist down over an archaic map of the so-called Three Kingdoms, tearing the fragile, yellowed document into tattered fragments. His square carved-in-wood face contorted with disgust at the disintegration of the only map of the area his aide could provide, and he swept it off the table in frustration. Despite being centuries old, the precious ancient parchment lay discarded on the polished oak floor – just more old world rubbish.

"We must wipe these slant-eyed rats from the face of the earth, but we cannot find them; they hide like cowards deep in the mountains of that infernal primitive backwater."

Dassler struggled to control his shaking hands as he helped himself to a large measure of schnapps. Just minutes before the same hands held a pistol to his mouth, ready to end his life. Tears had rolled down his cheeks as he kissed a portrait of Erina, his final farewell to his only true love. He looked at the painting again, seeking solace in her gentle smile. The image gave a fair account of her ethereal beauty, capturing it forever as she sat dressed in a shimmering, pale lilac silk gown and adorning her slender neck, a subtle string of ivory pearls, their gentle lustre beautifully caught by the artist.

As Dassler prepared for the mercy of oblivion, the concierge let his old friend, Major Werner into Erin's apartment block. By a bizarre quirk of fate, he had knocked lightly on her door just as Dassler was ready to die. Dassler steeled himself, expecting the door to be knocked down by a gang of Hitler's enforcers. The unexpected sight of an old friend stayed his hand. He hastily threw his pistol into a drawer, struggling to control his emotions, forcing himself to speak to Werner in a relaxed, normal manner.

"Don't you think we have wasted enough resources on these people? Let us win the war, then we can go back and destroy them at our leisure."

Werner began to calm down; it was good to be able to express his rage and frustration with Dassler, an honourable career soldier whose wisdom he respected and whose discretion was absolute.

"It would make sense but our Fuhrer wants the Isolanni crushed now and their leader taken alive. Your fiancée and her cousin are from Northern Svolenia. What does she know of Isolann?"

Dassler curbed the urge to cry at the mention of his beloved; he was reminded again of her beauty and fragrance by a crystal bowl of white roses placed above the ornate fireplace.

"She told me they are a backward, hostile people – an ancient, ferocious warrior race. It is a source of great pride for them to never have been conquered since they gave up life on the open steppes to settle in Isolann."

"And what of their leader, the so-called Black Wolf?"

"She has never mentioned him," Dassler replied curtly. He did not want his precious fairy princess dragged into his terrifying world of death and treachery.

Werner nodded grim-lipped, unsure whether to further confide in the courageous old war-horse. If Dassler had any dangerous doubts about their leader, this was not a time to add to his misgivings. He had too much respect for Dassler to endanger him.

"You are a lucky man, Heinrich. She is a lovely young woman and obviously utterly devoted to you. I believe she is of old aristocratic stock too."

Dassler finally let a sad smile break free, making him look ten years younger, catching an echo of the handsome man he'd been in his youth, "Her family lost everything when the communists seized power in 1922. Her parents sought sanctuary in Germany with her blind cousin, who is now the Count. But they have fallen on hard times and make their living with their music."

"I know. I have heard her sing – magical, like an enchanted Rhine maiden," Werner agreed, with a smile and a mock sigh, mimicking some love-struck school boy.

"Listen to us, two grizzled old soldiers who are really just romantics at heart," Dassler smiled sadly. He had only known the dangers and rigours of a soldier's life. Once the thought of spending his last years at peace, enjoying the company of his lovely young wife was foremost in his thoughts, but with Hitler refusing to admit he no longer had the resources to smash all opposition and expand the boundaries of the Third Reich, peace was a distant memory.

Dassler ventured to question the bull-framed Werner, "Why is the Fuhrer so determined to capture Prince Azrar alive? It will surely crush his people's morale more to kill him."

Werner was unsure whether to answer. Hitler's interest in the occult was well known in their leader's inner circle of command. But Dassler was not in this elite circle. He represented the old guard, the solid backbone of loyal, steadfast professional German soldiers. He was too valuable to risk with the bizarre knowledge that Hitler believed Jendar Azrar of Isolann was not human but a non-ageing vampire warlord. Werner knew that Hitler had received garbled intelligence reports from his troopers operating near the Isolann border under heavy assault at night from local fighters. The reports included hysterical accounts of the Prince himself entering the battle, tearing open the throats of his enemies with long sharp fangs and drinking their blood.

Also, some years before Hitler had expected an American professor to bring him solid, first hand proof of Azrar's bizarre descent. Unfortunately the man had been intercepted and captured by the British authorities, which meant the allies had this arcane knowledge.

It was all nonsense. Werner did not believe in astrology or vampires – all were dangerous distractions to their leader's' focus on winning the war. But he would never voice these views, nor should a loyal servant of the Reich like Heinrich Dassler be subject to such mental pollution.

"Heinrich, you are one of the Reich's most experienced officers – wasted in a messy European war. We need your focus and valour in the Balkans. I want you to spearhead a small but elite force. Infiltrate Isolann and go hunting. Bring our Fuhrer the black wolf alive and you will be the highest decorated officer in the army."

Dassler sank onto the sofa. Just a few swift minutes changed his destiny from the grave to new hope, another chance of life. Werner was throwing him a lifeline – getting him out of Berlin and far from Hitler's wrath. It meant he could take Erina back to her homeland. Perhaps an assignment fighting the Black Wolf was a poisoned chalice. But it was more honourable to chase shadows in the mountains, than answer for his failings at the end of an executioner's rope or firing squad in Berlin.

Chapter Twelve

Berlin, Germany, 1944

Anthony Banks stifled an urge to laugh out loud. All that he needed to destroy one of the vampires and torture Joe Devane was here in one convenient package in Berlin. And he could do it with a clear conscience, and without being labelled a traitor.

Joe Devane, or more likely his clandestine superiors, obviously believed in the saying, "It is better to keep your enemies close." Banks had been surprised when he was assigned to go undercover in Berlin to survey the situation for the Spook Squad. Now it was so easy to rip into the heart of this unnatural collaboration with the Devil. Just one short phone call, just one tip off to the Gestapo and the spooks would be decimated. Joe Devane would live with guilt at his girlfriend's death for the rest of his life and the whole world would be alerted to the reality of vampires living among them.

Banks recalled the last meeting with Devane before he left for Germany - the American madman had pinned him up against the wall and threatened him,

"Never forget these are our people, even the Dark Kind. Betray any of them and it will not be bloody vampires who rip out your throat – it will be me."

But who could prove it was he who led the Germans to the spooks? Especially if he did all he could to save them –save some of them. Banks watched in his guise as a Russian front officer on leave, as Devane's lover stepped onto the stage. His own German was perfect, learnt from birth from his beloved Bavarian mother and honed by long, happy stays in Germany as a child. Banks was never afraid working deep undercover so close to the heart of evil. Devane, in his last confrontation, believed Banks's lack of fear made him dangerous but Banks was scornfully dismissive of this view, he was convinced it just made him a better agent. Banks's eyes narrowed with hatred at the sight of the dark haired vampire beside her, it was an intolerable situation – but not for much longer.

A weasel-featured Gestapo officer strolled over to join his table and a relaxed, confident Banks calmly gave a realistic, word perfect account of his recent campaign in response to questioning by the black clad agent. Such was his arrogance he believed he could pass for Hitler's brother if he wanted to. On stage, 'Erina' bowed her head with a slight smile, graciously accepting the rapturous applause before starting another German folk ballad, a guaranteed crowd pleaser.

"She is lovely – such a bright joy in these dark days."

Banks raised his glass in agreement. "It is nothing, merely a temporary darkness; the dazzling brightness of the thousand year Reich will dawn tomorrow."

The Gestapo officer gave a slight thin lipped humourless smile of approval. "Few are returning from any front with such optimism."

"Then they are dangerous fools that must be weeded out and destroyed. They are a foul cancer sapping our soldiers' strength and our vital resolve to win."

The conversation was cut short by the loudness of even more rapturous applause as Khari finished her song. How easy it would be to destroy her now. All it would take was a few words of doubt in front of this Gestapo minion to sew the seeds of her destruction.

Khari paused as she collected herself before her next song. Her success was not just down to her beauty and lovely voice but the overpowering emotion she put into every word. When combat hardened officers fresh from battle in the audience cried, she knew her cover as a singer was still holding. A 'wrongness' in the atmosphere of the club made her sharply alert, swiftly scanning the minds of the audience. She spotted the British agent Banks talking to a Gestapo officer and she recieved his imminent betrayal. She whispered to Jazriel in the vampire language.

"Change of plan – play the opening to 'Treacherous Heart'."

Jazriel launched into a smoky, soulful song – a pre-arranged code to alert MacCammon. Uncomfortable with the choice of song, Banks sensed it was her unspoken threat to betray him first. He rose abruptly to leave the club, saluting the Gestapo officer.

"This music is not to my taste – too decadent, too American. Tell me friend, has the opera house survived the despicable destruction by the enemy?"

Khari watched Banks leave and her anxiety grew to outright terror. She scanned the Gestapo's officer's mind; there was no memory of any betrayal by the British agent, only his lurid sexual fantasies about her. She stayed in the Nazi's mind; naivety made her curious at first, then she pulled away in disgust as the fantasies turned increasingly violent and murderous. His mind was full of vile thoughts, but he did not suspect either of them.

The evening, already nightmarish, became far worse when a smiling Heinrich Dassler entered the club. He held out his arms towards her, beaming broadly. Khari dipped into his mind and learnt about Major Werner's offer. It was an outlandish quirk of fate, instead of lying with his brains decorating the apartment, he prepared to head a mission to trap Azrar in Isolann and planned to take her home.

The set ended in a thunder of enthusiastic applause, foot stamping and hearty cheering. The beauty of her singing had the power to raise the spirits of a besieged people surrounded by ugliness and brutality. Khari had no choice but to join Dassler at his table. She turned to speak to Jazriel but he had already left the stage. Khari walked calmly through the crowd, smiling her acceptance of their praise. Outwardly she was bright and vivacious, without a care in the world. Inside she fought against the incessant clarion call of rising terror, every instinct told her to flee the club, now – and run for her life. Instead she smiled and signed autographs and made merry small talk with the eager club goers.

Where was Jazriel? Not for the first time, she cursed her lack of ability to reach out into Dark Kind minds. Normally after a set, she would despair as she pushed her way through the gaggle of adoring females waiting off stage to besiege the Jazzman. Tonight was different, this time Khari prayed the vampire was with one of them now, flashing his dazzling smile, charming his fan until her knees went week with desire but still skilfully keeping his distance, as only he could.

Getting the blood-draining bastard out of the club was almost too easy; Jazriel was obviously primed to expect an escape plan. Banks quelled the handsome monster's reluctance to leave Khari, promising MacCammon was getting her out through the main entrance in a luxury saloon. After all, he reasoned the crowds expected her to have star treatment.

The clouds parted and a full moon gave the rubble filled streets brightness and borrowed beauty they did not deserve. It was a bombers moon; soon the sky would thunder with flaming death.

"We must hurry; MacCammon is getting Khari to a safe house. We will meet them there."

Jazriel halted with a low growl, suspicion making him fully alert. Banks in turn now felt real fear for the first time since a small child. He had happily exchanged banter with a Gestapo officer relaxed and without a qualm, where just one slip would have doomed him to torture and death. This was a whole new world of nightmare; he was strolling alone in a dark alley with an inhuman creature of the night – a vampire. Reality of just how vulnerable he was hit him hard, he had seen for himself how strong, fast and lethal this creature was.

Sirens screeched their warning as the first sound of allied bombers droned towards the cowering ruined city. The night sky became strafed with deafening defensive fire and raking searchlights. A group of terrified citizens ran past, nearly knocking into them as they sought any shelter from the bombardment. A bomb fell, perilously close, sending Banks flying from the shock wave. A scarred apartment building in front of them took the full brunt, exploding in a fireball. In a scene straight from Hell, burning debris fell in a deadly rain, burning people ran from their ruined homes, their screams were silent, unheard above the roar of the inferno and yet more explosions as more bombs fell.

The attack deadened the sounds of the trapped and dying still under the blazing rubble but Jazriel's sharper senses made out the desperate cries of children. He ran to the blazing ruin of a small shop and began tearing at the rubble with his bare hands.

"Come over here, I need your help."

Grateful the vampire called out in German, Banks tried to pull him away.

"We don't have time for this; we have to get to the rendezvous now."

Jazriel shrugged, coldly indifferent to Banks's demands. He continued to pull away at the flaming debris, hauling huge sections of brick and wooden beams with ease. Banks reluctantly joined in, unwilling to let his hands become burned by the flames. They reached the first trapped victim, and the gentleness and compassion the vampire showed towards the badly injured and shocked child astonished Banks. A bedraggled young soldier joined them; a private in a torn and burnt uniform covered with debris dust. The young man was too anxious to reach the trapped family to notice the uncanny strength of one of the other rescuers who tore away large sections of heavy masonry.

They found the bodies of two adults, most likely the parents. Jazriel callously threw their bodies out of the way as just more rubble in his determination to reach the rest of the children. He found them cowering beneath a wooden table that had saved their lives, coaxed them out with gentle words. Once all the little ones were safe, rushed off by other rescuers to the nearest medics, Jazriel paused to light a cigarette. It was at this moment of calm and relief, the German private seemed to notice their tall seemingly blind rescuer for the first time.

"I have never seen anything like that. How could you lift such huge weight or touch red hot metal without burning your hands?"

Jazriel gave a slight smile and shrug, making Banks groan in despair at the inevitability of this young man's fate. He was an enemy solder but at this moment was an exhausted, frightened youth condemned to die for choosing the wrong family to rescue. Banks should have turned his back and walked away, but a horrified curiosity made him stay.

Jazriel was silhouetted against the raging inferno, a vision of demonic power and horror. He removed his glasses and his turquoise eyes blazed with cold fire, at once both beautiful and terrible. He held the soldier around the neck in the grip of one hand, his long fangs dropped and the soldier's silent futile struggles ended with one fast tearing lunge. Jazriel drank fast and deep, throwing the body into the depth of the blaze. Banks, in near panic, stumbled away over the smoking debris, pausing to be violently sick. Jazriel, his whole being vibrant with renewed energy from his barely adequate kill approached, his voice still the wolf growl of a hunter.

"It was your choice to witness that kill. It had to be done, he saw too much."

"He was so young, no more than a frightened boy in an oversized uniform," Banks muttered, embarrassed, trying to regain some dignity as he wiped the vomit from his mouth. The appalling sight of those curving fangs tearing open the youth's neck would haunt him for a lifetime – even beyond.

"He was an enemy soldier, one who would have us both exposed and shot. You are a covert agent; you must have killed the enemy."

"Yes, many times. But I do not drink their blood."

"Then be thankful you were born a human and not created Dark Kind. You can keep to consuming dead vegetation and charred animal flesh to survive."

Banks remained unmoved; this thing was responsible for the horrible death of a lad who seemed too young to be defending his homeland–murdered for rescuing children. He felt his soul was now stained for his part of this killing that had no place in warfare. Restitution must be made— starting with the destruction of the monster at his side.

Grey Cat Club, Berlin, 1944

Khari graciously accepted a glass of ersatz champagne from a fan, and let Dassler, with a brave smile kiss her hand. Around her the crowd applauded this open display of affection. The chaste and honourable love between the grizzled hero of the Third Reich and their favourite songbird was a welcome romantic distraction from the worsening horrors of the war. Dassler was highly agitated, excitedly brim-full of plans for their future but Khari heard nothing. Like a trapped animal, she searched for a way of breaking away from the German officer, while still keeping her poise and a bravado outward show of calm.

"I must find Miki; I am really worried about him."

"Relax my darling. You know what a terrible flirt he is. Let him enjoy his time delighting the ladies. Besides, he needs to find a rich wife so he can truly live as Count Cheryniaz again."

Khari nodded but her rising panic would not go away. She looked out for a waiter to send word backstage for Count Mikail to join them at Dassler's table but was thwarted by the first banshee wail of an air raid siren. Dassler gently held her arm and steered her towards the shelter beneath the club.

"I must find Miki; he may have difficulty getting down the stairs to the cellar with all these people rushing past him."

Khari's heart was gripped with rising fear – there was no sign of Jazriel backstage or in the shelter.

"He's probably left with one of his conquests." Dassler tried to soothe Khari, who wrung her hands with genuine panic.

"If you are looking for Mikhail, he was seen leaving the club with a uniformed officer," a fellow musician ventured nervously in a low whisper to Khari, as if this implied an undercurrent of a highly dangerous sexual liaison. Everyone knew the death camps awaited males of that persuasion. Khari sensed it must be Banks, and prayed his treacherous thoughts would be held in check until after the mission. She accepted his hatred of vampires as perfectly normal and understandable, but Jazriel was an allied agent and therefore surely Banks must honour this and protect him?

Chapter Thirteen

Berlin, Germany, 1944

"Don't you just love it when the apes have their little squabbles," muttered Garan unconvincingly. He pulled out the slender blade of his sword-stick embedded in the chest of a middle-aged German and threw the body face down into a filthy water-filled bomb crater. With Sivaya keeping watch, he leaned against the remains of a chimney stack and tumbled the bricks down to cover the body.

The man, a civilian, had been well dressed and well spoken, he would be missed soon. His only mistake was to stumble upon the two Dark Kind as they moved swiftly through Berlin's streets in the dark, and question who they were. Now he was yet another unseen body under the rubble. That was the price paid by anyone hampering their progress. And there had been many.

As Garan and Sivaya continued their slow progress, they stayed in the shadows of yet another reeking charred rubble-strewn street. Travelling through the bombed-out heart of a besieged Nazi Germany had an extra sense of very real peril. For the first time in many centuries, humans were hunting them down, humans who knew exactly what they were looking for.

Hitler had found out about the Dark Kind and knew the allies were using some as covert agents. The Fuhrer wanted his own vampires and sent intelligence teams throughout occupied Europe and Russia to track some down. No doubt the German leader reasoned that evil creatures of the night had no interest in human politics or possessed any moral imperatives and could be recruited by anyone for the right price. He was wrong. The Dark Kind would never physically harm what they considered taboo, vulnerable humans. Their awareness that the Nazis had massacred defenceless women, children, the elderly, sick and disadvantaged, appalled even hardened cynics like Garan.

Progress in tracking the Spook Squad was slow and frustrating, despite the vampires cutting a ruthless path through the city streets. Simply hiding from any encounter was not enough to protect their survival, and they left a trail of bodies, like the last victim, dumped under the rubble in their wake. It was a high risk strategy. They tried to lessen the obvious signs of vampire predation by not tearing out any throats or breaking necks, only killing with blades, cowardly human weapons but a necessary compromise. They didn't want to make it easy for Hitler's goons to track them down.

Sivaya held out her hand to signal a problem ahead. They ducked into the remains of a doorway to observe with low growls of dismay as their route ahead was blocked by a large troop of soldiers disembarking from three lorries. Their commander barked out some orders and what was clearly a well-organised, systematic search began through the rubble.

"Zaard!" Garan swore bitterly in the vampire language. The stench of betrayal had hung in the air since the start of this suicidal mission.

"We must get out – now!" he snarled at Sivaya. "We will be lucky to get out of this putrid cess pit with our lives."

Sivaya stood her ground, eyes darkening, her fangs bared. "I'm not leaving Berlin without Jazriel."

Garan shrugged as he scanned the darkness for an escape route. "Something in my blood tells me it's too late. I'm getting out of here, you do what you want."

Two more military vehicles pulled up, a black clad Gestapo officer stepped out and began directing the operation from one, the other disgorged tracker dogs and their handlers. The German troops were too far away to make out any conversation but were steadily getting closer.

"Damn," muttered Sivaya in mounting despair. "Once those dogs have got our scent, we are finished."

Garan's mind raced, dogs normally had a healthy respect for Dark Kind, regarding them as superior predators and giving them a wide berth. These were trained trackers, giving chase to a Dark Kind scent did not compromise this primeval deference.

"Help me get that lump of carrion from under the rubble," Garan snapped. He knew Sivaya would try to fight her way out; he had no intention of dying as she proved her courage. They dragged their last victim's body up from the crater and over to the mound of charred debris that was once a large, fine house. Garan pulled furiously away at the rubble until he found a caved-in cellar. There was a small gap in the debris, just big enough for two slender, lithe Dark Kind to slip down into the cellar below.

"Get down there. I'll pull our friend back over the entrance."

Once through, the gap, there was a twelve foot drop straight down into deep, freezing, stinking water filling the cellar. Sivaya and Garan waited in the darkness, up to their chests in the foul water. Within minutes, the dogs had tracked their scent and were howling their triumph to their handlers.

"What is it?" barked the Gestapo officer. "Have they tracked down a vampyr?"

"No, sir, just some poor sod, another bomb victim."

Garan and Sivaya waited with the complete silence and stillness of their kind until all signs of their pursuers had gone. Garan looked around the vault-like wine cellar; the walls were rounded, slick and sheer, the gap too central to climb up to. Garan searched for anything in the cellar but there was nothing left to utilise to help them climb, the vault's contents long ago looted. Escaping was a major problem.

"Any more bright ideas?" Sivaya snarled, loathing being stuck in the reeking water. If the Germans had the knowledge that Dark Kind existed and that they were openly hunting a vampire, then Jazriel's life was in the gravest danger. Being stuck down a water-filled cellar was more than uncomfortable and ignominious, it was catastrophic.

"Actually, I have," Garan replied. He reached into his pocket and took out a slender rod of grey crystal. A piece of the alien technology of unknown origin, used only by the Dark Kind. As he held it in his hand, the crystal began to glow with a faint blue light, gradually building to a pulsating blue-white radiance.

"It's a beacon. Eshan gave it to me before coming to Berlin. She will be able to direct the local Resistance to us, contacting them from London."

"You are going to trust humans after what has just happened. Have you gone completely insane?"

"No," sighed Garan, "Just very wet."

"This is madness, we cannot reach the rendezvous tonight. We need to find shelter, a cellar – anything."

Jazriel reluctantly agreed with the human agent as the bombing grew in ferocity. He was assigned to protect Khari; this separation was wrong. But Banks's fear was well founded; they were now alone in the streets, totally encircled by high walls of raging flame. Blazing debris crashed down around them in a deadly thunderous bombardment as they ran through the empty burning streets like the last creatures alive on the planet.

The vampire's well-honed instinct for finding shelter from daylight in emergencies paid off. After frantically pulling aside some blazing debris, he found a deep, abandoned wine cellar beneath a ruined restaurant.

"It will be daylight soon. I'll leave then to make contact with the others, then get you out at sunset. "

"Forget it, Banks. I won't be pinned down in this filthy, stinking rat hole. I can get back to base by myself. Unless my cover has been blown of course."

"No, it should still hold. This blitz is a blessing. Erina's disappearance will not be noticed for weeks, presumed killed by the bombing. It will buy us time to get you out safely."

They waited in an uneasy silence till the bombing ended with dawn's approach; Jazriel watched the agent scramble free of the cellar and disappear. It was time for Rest but he could not let his guard down to succumb to sleep. He sought the deepest, darkest part of the cellar and sharply alert, his fangs drawn and waited for darkness to fall again.

A few hours into his vigil, Jazriel growled with fury as he heard the tramp of many boots and the shouting of urgent commands above him. He had been betrayed, caught in Banks's trap with nowhere to go. Above him daylight's lethal furnace blazed – it would leave him powerless and permanently blind if forced to run from this lightless sanctuary.

After much crashing about and shouting, the human troopers found the entrance to the cellar and he heard the click of their weapons reading to fire. His Dark Kind sense of immortality shattered like glass, a lifetime measured in millennia now was down to the last few heartbeats. He pushed out distracting thoughts of regret and grief, channelling his whole being ready to attack; his only weapon surprise and speed. He had to destroy as many of the enemy as possible in the first few minutes – or be mowed down by the sheer weight of numbers and firepower.

The darkness tore apart with the retina-scorching beams of torchlight as the first troopers ran down. Jazriel leapt forward, bullet-fast, crushing the skulls together of the first men down the steps, wrenching their machine guns from their dying hands. But as their bodies dropped, gunfire strafed the cellar from above and the rest of the troop rushed in. Jazriel's body shuddered, thrown back with the impact of many bullets. Snarling with fang-bared fury, he realised he'd been shot many times. He struggled to his feet, fierce eyes black and glittering as he fought on, ignoring the pain and blood loss in a desperate fight for life.

In the darkness and confusion, he killed many times, with the machine gun and by breaking necks, and slashing at throats till a deathly silence fell.

A broad shaft of pain-filled sunlight now breached the darkness of the cellar. Mortally wounded, Jazriel, the old saxophone still in his hand, somehow hauled himself across the gore-spattered floor to avoid this ancient enemy. Most of the troopers were dead, but a couple were still alive though badly wounded; their groans broke the silence of the cellar, now stinking of blood and cordite.

A black clad Gestapo officer pulled himself up to aim a handgun at Jazriel. The vampire was too weak from blood loss to avoid the shot. It hit him in the chest in an explosion of black bone and thin purple blood. He sank to his knees but managed to reach for a gun to finish the Nazi off.

"Bastard. Why won't you die?"

A young trooper whimpered from a corner. He was the last of the squad, barely alive and terrified. Jazriel sighed at the realisation his injuries were fatal and he had so little time left. He tried to reach for a last cigarette, but was too weak. If no more humans came down, perhaps he could regenerate enough to escape at nightfall but he knew in his heart, such optimism was pointless, pure survival instinct not backed by any fact. Unable to walk, Jazriel crawled across the floor, slippery with gore-slicked debris and bodies. By the time he reached the trooper, his life was ebbing away with each second. He had no strength left to attack but found a hidden inner reserve of raw tenacity at the thought of being parted forever from the one true love of his long life.

The human was unable to fight back. Jazriel slowly tore away at the man's scrawny neck, too weak to make a good fast kill, too weak to hold his victim and drink. The vampire sank to the floor beneath him, letting the precious life giving blood trickle down his throat from a small wound in the victim's neck. Jazriel lost consciousness many times as the pain wracked his broken body, but the human blood kept him alive.

It wasn't enough. Ashen faced, now little more than a living corpse, Jazriel waited in the shrinking shadows for the precious gift of darkness. He knew he faced death and prepared to meet it with all the courage and dignity he could muster. He was nothing more then a commoner, created without the inbred unwavering courage of the warriors. He had lived for many thousands of years but now was desperate for a few more hours of life, so he could feel the cool caress of night once more. A last glimpse of the stars – that was all he could hope for now.

A different unfamiliar darkness clouded his vision; he knew he would not make nightfall. He took in one last breath, enough to call out his lover's name before falling into the black pit of forever-silence.

Khari reached out for Dassler's hand and crawled up from the wreckage of the night club. Over half lay in smoking ruins, the remaining precarious barely upright walls were buckled, burnt and hazardous. Lazily swirling grey dust clouds hid the early morning sunlight, drifting sharp grit into her eyes. There was little left of the street, sleepwalking with exhaustion, a small group of rescuers picked through the rubble in a desultory way. The silence beneath the smouldering rubble told them everything they needed to know. Dassler tried to comfort his love, her blind cousin's vulnerability was a burden she bore so well, until now.

"I know you must be frantic with worry about Miki, but I am sure he is either asleep back at the apartment or safe between the legs of some wealthy socialite."

Khari sank down head in hands, onto a pile of debris, unconcerned that her treasured jade silk ball gown was filthy and torn. Dassler grew agitated; every minute spent in Berlin was perilous. Werner's orders could easily be overturned on the Fuhrer's whim, Dassler wanted to put as many miles as possible between them and their leader. To Dassler, the much-hated Upper Balkan front was a precious refuge, a chance for survival.

"Erina, we must hurry. I must get you on a train to Svolenia this morning. I have been ordered to leave for the Upper Balkan front today."

Khari could not allow herself to be hustled onto a train. Her mind raced with stalling tactics. Gently, she took Dassler in her arms; anxiety had aged him overnight, and the stalwart Third Reich warrior turned to a frightened old man.

"I cannot go to Svolenia alone. It was never my home; it is a country of hostile strangers, the same people who killed my father and uncle. I was born in Germany, it is my homeland now and I feel German. But I understand it is Miki's birthright to return as Count Cheryniaz; it is my duty to help him return. I need to find him. Leave me in Berlin, and we will meet in Svolenia."

Dassler could not argue with her, there was no time. As they hurried through the ruined streets, he prayed her blind playboy cousin – the charming, handsome wastrel who meant so much to his beloved was back at the apartment —instead of a deadly deputation from the Fuhrer.

Getting away from Dassler was now imperative; Khari could not go to Svolenia. Her cover story held fine in Germany, as there had indeed been a noble Cheryniaz family in the remote northern region close to the Isolann border. But in reality none had escaped a shameful massacre in 1933, the facts long hidden from the Svolenian people. A mission to find out what happened to the doomed Deret expedition had the misfortune to be lead by a vicious, lazy and cowardly commander. Unwilling to risk entering Isolann itself, he took out his frustration on the Cheryniaz villages in Svolenia, wiping out everyone—peasant and noble born alike. But there was always the risk of unknown survivors; it would only take one to destroy Khari's cover.

They returned to Khari's apartment, it had survived the night's bombing raid and mercifully there was no sign of unwelcome visitors. But also there was no Jazriel. Khari threw some clothes for both of them in a bag but refused to leave the apartment.

"Heinrich, I am in no danger from the authorities in Berlin. But you will be if you are not on your way to your new command. I must find my cousin. Only then will I go to Svolenia."

Dassler sighed in quiet desperation. Of course she was right. Yet he sensed when he walked away, he would never see her again. Khari picked these thoughts up and kissed him with all the passion she could feign, it was the only way to save them both.

"My darling Heinrich… I promise I will join you in Svolenia, even if something terrible has happened to Miki.

Our family home is so close to the Isolann border, it will be easy to meet up."

Dassler, eyes welling with tears, nodded. He believed her. He turned and left the apartment without another word or backward glance. It was time to be strong again.

Khari waited until he was out of sight, praying her contacts were watching the apartment, ready to get her out of Germany. A strange coldness around her neck made her reach for her silver wolf amulet. As she held it tightly in her hand, it became uncomfortably icy. In her mind, she heard a terrible howl of Dark Kind grief, a raging unearthly cry that echoed around the distant mountains of Isolann and pierced her heart. She knew now with all certainty, her vampire friend Jazriel was dead.

Chapter Fourteen

A field somewhere in England, 1944

Joe Devane absentmindedly accepted a steaming mug of watery tea from one of his team. He rubbed the back of his neck, painful and aching from watching the skies for hours. The night was nearly over, already the tumultuous outpouring of bird song began in the thick hedgerows and there were signs of grey light behind the clouds. He had no idea who was coming home from Germany that night, he could only wait and pray the whole team made it back safely.

With an hour left before dawn, Ffitchie announced the plane was approaching. Now the anxious, useless hours standing around waiting could be turned into effective action. The whole team ran across a frost rutted abandoned cornfield to light temporary beacons, just enough to get the plane down. With the minimum navigational lights on, the blacked out light plane touched down, bouncing and swerving across the uneven ground.

Devane's heart pounded with anxiety as the tattered remnants of his squad disembarked to pick their way over the deeply rutted earth. He was a realist, he expected losses– it was an inevitable part of the dangerous game they played with the enemy. But seeing Khari step down first made him determined never to risk her life again on such a dangerous mission. Anna ran forward and threw a blanket over the girl's slender shoulders. Khari rested her head against the Dutch woman's broad shoulders; she was physically and emotionally exhausted.

Devane gave MacCammon a hearty welcoming bear hug in sheer relief at the sight of his agents safely home. "Thanks, old man. You did it."

MacCammon shook his brindled head in cold fury. He glared murderously at the other human agent strolling from the plane, whistling quietly to himself.

"There's unfinished business. There are no Dark Kind agents in the plane. Jazriel is dead, Sivaya has disappeared. Khari told me on the flight home that Banks betrayed us. Why was that bastard ever sent on our mission?"

Devane's mind reeled with the grievous loss of Jazriel and also by default, Sivaya. MacCammon continued, as they watched Banks pause to share a cigarette and relaxed banter with the pilots. "I was ready to throw the filthy bastard out of the plane over Germany. But there were witnesses, the pilots are from the regular SOS. Then, I thought, damn it! You had the most right to deal with him. He's destroyed all your hard work gaining the vampires' trust. And we've lost all chance of getting that vicious but useful little shit Garan on board now."

Incandescent with rage, Devane moved to gently push past a quietly sobbing Anna but she held his arm, needing to speak to their leader. "I know the Jazzman was not human, just a vampire –something I should hate and fear, but I still couldn't help liking him. Am I such an evil person?"

"Not at all, we all liked him; he was very special."

Devane gave her shoulder a comforting squeeze. Then he strode away from his squad and threw a hearty punch at Banks sending him flying across the beet field in a crumpled, indignant heap.

"What the Hell are you playing at, Devane? Have you gone mad?"

Banks struggled to his feet with difficulty, blood pouring from an already swelling broken nose. The pilots moved to intervene but MacCammon held them back, expression grim, nonchalantly cradling his handgun for emphasis.

"Steady laddies, this is strictly personal business."

"You are crazy, all you spooks are crazy – stay away from me."

Devane, white with fury grabbed Banks by the lapels, roughly hauling him out of earshot of the pilots.

"What exactly happened to Jazriel? I'd like to hear your version of his death."

"I have no reason to think he is dead. We got separated from MacCammon and Khari in the air raid. We found a cellar and when I returned after nightfall after contacting Mac there was no sign of your vampire."

"He couldn't leave that shelter 'til nightfall; no Dark Kind would meekly allow himself to be captured. Was there no sign of a struggle?"

"Clean as a whistle."

Devane's fury was further frustrated by his inability to tell Banks about Khari's powers. Only she could know what really happened.

"I cannot tell you why or how, but I know for certain Jazriel is dead and you are responsible for betraying a British agent. There's nothing I can do now, but I advise you to sleep with the light on and a gun in your hand— for the rest of your worthless and now considerably shorter life."

"My conscience is clear, Devane. Even if you or one of your blood-drinking demons manages to murder me I will always have that. Nothing will ever wipe away this evil from your black soul. You are damned Devane, damned for eternity."

Eshan ran back to the specially adapted van that kept the vampires safe when travelling by daylight. She wanted to put some distance between herself and the humans. Instinct urged her to howl to the dwindling darkness, to pour out her rage and grief to the uncaring stars. Ancient Dark Kind custom brought all the sad words of final farewell back to her heart for the first time in centuries. Wisdom urged restraint; there was nowhere remote enough in this overcrowded land to voice her sorrow without attracting unwelcome attention.

Khari, grey faced with exhaustion found her. The girl's red rimmed eyes mute evidence of her own grieving.

"It's okay, Eshan. You are too harsh with yourself sometimes. You must allow yourself to be Dark Kind, especially after this tragedy."

Eshan nodded in agreement, aware and grateful for Khari's unique understanding of Dark Kind ways.

"I must cry my farewell to Jazriel in my heart. I cannot risk myself or the rest of the squad."

Again Eshan's thoughts were of Jendar Azrar, fighting for his life in his distant mountain realm. She could only guess at the torment he was enduring now.

The squad returned to Chess Manor, lost in their thoughts and in solemn silence. Banks had disappeared with his pilots but not before Khari had relived Jazriel's last hours through the traitor's memory. She witnessed the Jazzman's compassion and gentleness as he rescued the buried children, his brutal slaying of a young German soldier. It was the first time she had seen a Dark Kind kill and the savagery made her recoil in revulsion. Finally she managed to catch a fleeting memory of Banks and Jaz entering the cellar. She hated that her last memory of her friend was seeing him trapped like a hunted animal in a filthy tomb-like vault. It was no place for a being who revelled in the finer things life could offer; Jazriel dwelled in a world of exquisite art, music and perfectly tailored clothes. A vain, hedonistic and savage monster, yet one of the bravest, most loyal beings – human or Dark Kind, Khari had ever known. She would miss him so much.

When they reached the Manor, Eshan hurried to the dark sanctuary of Rest, eager to be alone with her sorrow. Khari went into the lounge. Lenny had lit a merrily crackling fire in the spacious hearth and brought in a tray laden with pots of fresh tea and a huge pile of hot buttered toast. The cosy ordinariness of their British base now seemed increasingly surreal. It was a world of comfort and certainty she no longer belonged to, and perhaps ever could again.

Khari stared in the fire, as if the flames could burn away the terrible images polluting her mind – nightmarish memories of death camps and massacres she'd gleaned from the Nazi's she lived among only hours before. She was unaware of the warmth of the manor; the ice cold of pure terror still ran in her veins. The months spent waiting for the crash of jackboots through the door, the shrill cry of denouncement from some acquaintance or club customer. That these had never come was no comfort. Only luck and her gift kept her alive and these were not enough to save Jazriel.

Devane walked in, his fury unabated.

"What a bloody nightmare, what a bloody waste. I nearly had you all home. That bastard will pay – in blood and pain."

Khari wanted to reach out to Devane, to find mutual comfort in each other's arms, but his anger was too hot. She waited in silence until he got his thoughts under more restraint. She realised just how much self-control and discipline it took for him not to have shot Banks on the makeshift airfield. She waited until he calmed down enough to take in her small scrap of news; news she hoped would soften the full impact of Jazriel's loss to the squad.

"I scanned Banks many times in the plane. He recalled in his thoughts, returning to the cellar at nightfall. The

Gestapo were finishing cleaning up the sight of a massacre – some unknown German troops. They were clearly furious, there was no sign of a vampire body."

"Thank God that is the only good news to come of this mess. "

Inwardly, Devane sighed with heartfelt relief. He was fearful the Germans would gain possession of concrete evidence of the existence of the Dark Kind. Since the dawn of their existence on Earth, the vampires never allowed their dead to fall into human hands. He hoped Sivaya and Garan had removed the body and completely burnt it.

Devane looked at Khari, still tightly wrapped in the thick blanket despite the fire's heat. Her porcelain-pale face was now drained grey with exhaustion, her golden eyes huge and tear-filled. This was not a time for any more words. He pulled her close and held her tightly for the first time since the long mission began, Khari began to cry. Devane scooped her up, amazed at how light she was, her frame as elfin as her ethereal looks. He took Khari to her room, settling her under the blankets.

"You need sleep, Khari. You are utterly exhausted."

Khari took his face in her hands and kissed him on the mouth.

"No, Joe. Right now, I need you."

She pulled him down towards her with a low moan of desire; her whole being felt a surge of renewed love. She had yearned for this moment every minute of every day in Germany, forcing herself to hide how much she missed him, how much she wanted him.

They made love for the first time, tenderly at first as if frightened to break something fleeting, something fragile. Then as their pleasure and confidence in each other grew, their lovemaking grew wilder in passion and intensity. They did not need to be Dark Kind; two human souls in love could touch too.

In the darkness, Joe reached out and stroked her face tenderly; her cheek was wet with tears falling unchecked. "Anna told me, you know, you have seen that my appearance is an illusion. How can you bear my touch, knowing the truth?"

Khari took his face in her hands and gently kissed every inch without flinching at the touch of the maimed flesh. "There is no illusion to me; there is only one true face of the man I love. The perfect one you show to the outside world and the sad, scarred one you keep hidden; they are one and the same to me."

Dawn was still an hour away but Devane could not sleep. A white-hot anger had returned, taking over from the sheer relief at Khari's safe return and the joy of their lovemaking. He rose and dressed, leaving Khari in the deep slumber of complete exhaustion. He walked swiftly across the frost-hardened ground and into the forest beyond with no aim in mind. His anger was an uncontrolled, unfocused energy force, needing violence to quench its fire. Devane's fingers curled into fists so tight the knuckles turned white. He had spent a tortured year waiting for the inevitable bad news from Germany; such was the extreme danger of the mission.

Now he knew all his agents could have come home, they had been a few paltry hours from safety. To lose Jazriel to a British operative was beyond bearing. The vampire was his best Dark Kind agent, a charming yet ruthless killing machine, tractable and loyal to the squad. No vamp would ever trust humans again and their unique abilities were lost to the allies forever. With Sivaya gone too, he doubted he keep hold of Ha'ali Eshan. What a pointless damn waste!

Devane took his anger out on a log in the manor's winter woodpile, imagining each axe blow was connecting to Anthony Bank's neck. But when he threw the axe down, exhausted, his hands blistered and red raw, the anger was still there.

He returned to the Manor and found Khari awake in his room. She sat on the wide window seat, wrapped in a patchwork counterpane looking out over the Manor's grounds, but he guessed she was not taking in the fragile beauty of a fine English morning. She was so pale, as if drained of blood, her eyes were shadowed and tears had worn deep red lines down her cheeks. She turned her face away from him, needing to be alone in her sorrow, but Devane sat beside her and took her in his arms.

"It is right to mourn, he may have been a vamp but the Jazzman was your close friend and a brave protector in Germany."

Khari nodded but her grief ran far deeper than her own personal loss. Her mind was overburdened, so full of terrible memories, of whole families, slain and tortured by the Nazis. Innocent lives, young and old sacrificed by a complicit nation to feed one man's insane grandiose dreams of power. She always called her gift of *Knowing* a curse. Azrar had once told her that the word for *Knowing* in the original Khari's language was 'trguur' which had both meanings. For Khari, it was all a curse now.

She took no comfort in knowing that she, along with Mac and the Jazzman had saved many lives. It was an abstract concept, formless, nameless. It was all the lives she couldn't save that would haunt her forever – they had names and their faces, their terror, their pain was etched into her soul as if with searing acid. Devane realised no words could comfort her now but sat holding her tightly, wishing he could trade the power to hide his ruined features for those that could chase away the horrors in her mind.

Chapter Fifteen

Berlin, Germany, 1944

A slight, dark clad figure walked with brisk yet silent steps through a vision of Hell. The only sound came from the click of a metal-tipped cane as he passed through the once elegant city devastated from years of bombing raids.

Garan was oblivious to the charred and occasionally still smouldering shells of once grand fin de siècle buildings as he passed by their rat-infested ruins. Nor was he concerned at the very real threat of yet more fiery death raining down that night. He carried a rough hewn, heavily laden sack over his back. His heart was heavy too with sorrow, but his mind full of determination and resignation as he faced up to the grim but necessary duty he had to fulfil in some smoking ruins along the road ahead.

Focusing only on the horror the night would hold for him, Garan's fangs were already partly bared. He was ready to kill any human without hesitation who impaired his progress.heedless of his own safety. Thankfully the rubble strewn ruined streets were empty, with only the banshee wail of sirens, and the ominous drone of approaching bombers to accompany him on his journey.

He found the ruins and discovered Sivaya was down some steep stone steps at the entrance of what was an old ice storage cellar. Despite the bombed out building above, the cellar, now empty of ice blocks, had lost none of its coldness, every stone and brick was deeply permeated ancient perma-frost.

Garan's night eyes could see how her terrible grief had wrecked her beauty. Her once golden hair was lank, and she had torn out much of it in great ragged handfuls. Her hollowed eyes had an awful glaze he had seen too many times before – the outward sign of madness that sometimes accompanied vampire grief. The Dark Kind did not have the widely varied range of emotions enjoyed by humans but those they did possess were powerful and intense. Garan had vowed never to let such overwhelming forces have a hold on him and the sight of the once proud, beautiful and poised Sivaya reduced to this pitiful state confirmed the wisdom of his decision.

"I am so glad to see you," Sivaya sighed, kissing Garan on the lips in the Dark Kind greeting.

As she walked further into the light-less cellar, Garan decided to slip the bag discreetly behind his back; there was no need to re-enforce the grisly reason for his arrival, it was distressing enough for her. But despite his efforts to spare her feelings, Garan sensed she may have glimpsed the bag, for there was a brief moment of sudden clarity in her eyes. The look of realisation and horror was so heart rending, Garan was almost relieved when the glaze of madness dimmed their brightness again.

He followed her across the frozen stone floor. His carefully built wall, the protection of a deliberate lack of emotion, tumbled down instantly. He gave a low animal moan of distress. It had been so long since they had lost any of their kind but none of the sharpness of the pain and feeling of desolation had gone. It was obvious Jazriel had been dead for some time. All the honey gold of his skin had turned to a chalky bloodless white, though miraculously his still wondrously beautiful face framed by his blue-black hair had been untouched by the gunfire.

What lay further down was another story. Garan pulled away Jazriel's cashmere coat, carefully laid by Sivaya to hide his injuries, and gasped in shock. The whole torso had been shot to pieces with the devastated region now a mess of ragged black bone fragments and ruined organs. There was no sign of any blood left in his body at all. It was clear that Jazriel was beyond regeneration. With a soul deep sigh of intense sorrow, he gently kissed the pale forehead, closed each eye and finally the stone cold lips of the beautiful being who had long been a friend. He would give the whole world – and all the blood of every treacherous human in it –to see that famous dazzling imitation of a human smile for one more time. But it was not to be. He murmured a formal farewell in their language.

The sound of the words of farewell in the aeons old Dark Kind tongue alarmed Sivaya. She grabbed his arm, seemingly oblivious to her nails sinking deep into his flesh, her eyes wide and wild like a cornered animal.

"He will be fine, Garan. There is no need for goodbyes. I know it looks bad. But Jazriel is very strong with so much determination to live. All he needs is peace and time here in the darkness and lots of fresh blood. I can bring it to him. I can help him come back to us."

This was going to be harder and more harrowing than Garan had expected.

"Sivaya, nobody could doubt your love for Jazriel but it is over. Say your goodbyes and get yourself to safety. I will do what is needed here."

"He will come back. Damn you, leave him alone!"

Her voice had become a low ferocious animal snarl of fury and fear. Her fangs were completely bared as she prepared to do the unthinkable and attack another of the Dark Kind, desperate in her fight to protect Jazriel's body from Garan and his weapons of complete destruction.

"There is no easy way to say this. Jazriel is dead. His spirit needs to be released into the adventure beyond and his body made safe from desecration by humans. Every second you delay me could endanger us all, and risk his body being stolen and violated by the humans in their search for knowledge of our kind. Let me get on with this."

"No, if anyone has the right to do it, it must be me. I was the last of our kind to hold him in their arms, I must be the one to send him onward, if that is what needs to be done."

Garan held his anger in check with difficulty. It was a time for resolute and swift action not this pointless and time consuming argument.

"It is not right or seemly for you as his last lover to do this. The memory of how wonderful it felt to have him must be enough. Keep that memory beautiful and untainted by this horror and leave here now."

"I will not, Garan."

Her voice had deepened to a low even more dangerous snarl. She looked beyond reason. With a heavy heart he decided it was time for shock tactics.

"Can you honestly swear to me that you will be able to dispassionately pour this foul, stinking petroleum over the once beautiful body of the being you love so much and calmly set it alight? Can you stand there and watch as the fire mutilates and wrecks it 'til it is reduced to just a pile of smouldering ash and bone? Could you take this sledgehammer and pound and pound at the ash and bone till it is nothing but black dust? I am repulsed at the thought of what I have to do to Jazriel's body, but I will do it as my last duty to a friend."

"Leave me the bag and go, Garan. I do not need a lecture on my duty. I am Dark Kind and I love Jazriel with my whole being. How could I risk letting the humans get their filthy hands on him? I swear on Dezarn's noble memory no human will ever desecrate him."

Garan was caught in a trap. He could not push past her and set the pyre alight without enraging her and possibly starting a fight. The Dark Kind did not harm each other. He had no choice but to give in. But the consequences were horrific if she did not go ahead with the burning. Firstly Jazriel's spirit would be trapped, unable to find final rest or journeying to whatever mystery lay ahead for them after death. There was no knowing what an unending nightmare that would be for a lost vampire soul. Secondly modern humans would be in possession of irrefutable proof of Dark Kind existence. His remains would be dissected and probed then preserved forever for yet more study. The knowledge gained could threaten all the survivors still living in the shadows.

Garan had no choice, he had to trust her but it hung heavy on his heart. He also feared the terrible, dangerous rage of Jendar Azrar that would inevitably descend on them both should Sivaya not fulfil her last duty to Jazriel.

"If you fail him now, you will be despised for all eternity by all Dark Kind. If you truly loved him, you will do it now without a second's hesitation"

"Go, Garan, I will do what is right for my Jazriel."

Unconvinced, Garan handed her the sack noting with foreboding her shudder of revulsion and horror as she took it from him. Soon there would be grave danger for them both. The air raid was nearly over and the Nazi patrols would be back on the streets. It was imperative to find a safe shelter from both humans and daylight.

"Just do it now, Sivaya, there is no more time left."

He returned to the street and kept a watch on the ruins for as long as he dared. Bombs were falling close by and an explosion of intense white fire lit up the sky from the general area of the ice cellar. He gambled dangerously, relying on her Dark Kind courage, on her honour. Had he made the right decision? Though the thought filled him with revulsion, he prayed the searing light had been Jazriel's body being completely consumed in the inferno. "Fly free, my old friend. I hope there is fine champagne and a good supply of cigarettes in the adventure beyond."

PART FOUR

The Storm's Last Thunder

Chapter One

Arpalathian Mountains, Isolann, 1944

Jendar Azrar responded to reliable reports of a Svolenian assault force heading up the narrow gap beyond Lake Beral towards the forest clad foothills. Aware it might be a joint diversionary tactic with the Germans, the Prince did not commit a large force to engage the threat. He rode on hard through the darkness with a small but tough band of his finest fighters, with the British airman Railton doing his best to keep up with the furious pace across the Arpalathians. An even speedier surveillance team went on ahead, unhampered by the Prince's need to find shelter from the sun.

Since joining the Prince's entourage, Railton became adept at catching moments of sleep in the saddle, trusting Sweetness to follow Azrar's black stallion in her own grudging but sure-footed and courageous way. Sometimes, he needed a discreet nudge back into the saddle from his fellow outriders as he slipped perilously to one side. But no one, including the Prince, seemed to mind these slips of weakness; Railton did not delay the relentless pace of Azrar's continuous progress around his lands. The Prince had not exaggerated the difficulty and hardships they endured every night. Even with the vampire's perfect nocturnal vision, the route was always dangerous and exhausting. One slip of a horse's hoof on loose scree could lead to a rider plummeting to his death down a ravine; heavy rain brought the danger of rockslides and flash floods. Yet Railton never heard one word of complaint from his new companions, instead the danger brought out a dark humour among the Isolanni fighters.

The greatest revelation had been his growing friendship with Azrar, something he could never have envisaged in his wildest imaginings. He never forgot Azrar's status as a Prince even in the most relaxed moments of conversation and always spoke to him with respect and a certain formality of speech. Nor could he ever forget Azrar was a vampire; the edge of permanent very real danger coloured their every interaction.

Yet Railton's respect for the Prince was more than a natural necessity to avoid his fangs – the airman had yet to see them in action and hoped he never would. He observed Azrar at close range, saw for himself the total dedication to his people. He also saw their open and unforced adoration for their Prince, not based on fear and subjugation but an ancient mutual respect built up over centuries.

Azrar was undoubtedly a charismatic figure – the Isolanni people's protective dark angel, sternly handsome and fearless. The thought of a German bullet or bomb bringing down the ancient yet always youthful warlord made Railton shudder with distaste. Yes, the world would lose a fearsome predator but would also lose a precious living link to humanity's past and the Isolanni would lose their dark heart and soul.

Could they learn to live without Azrar? Of course they could, if they miraculously survived the Nazis' plans for their genocide. Railton believed if this happened they would no longer be a unique, proud and independent nation but become another lost and dwindling band of refugees buffeted by the cruel tides of world history.

Such musings were a luxury now, as Railton steeled himself to face his first engagement with the enemy. Until now his war had been detached, observing the theatre of war from high above in his bomber or from the uneasy safety of an Arpalathian cave. There was every chance he would soon see the enemy, not as some abstract idea, but as ordinary men before him, trying their best to kill him. And he must look an enemy soldier in the eye and do the same. It was something his valiant British countrymen in the infantry faced every day – he hoped he could be as brave as them.

A bitter wind howled like a banshee through the valleys almost masking the telltale crackle of a rusty old radio coming to life. Railton rushed to its operator side – praying he had a message from home. It was physically impossible to bring any documentation into Isolann and it was too remote and dangerous for any Red Cross package drops. Railton relied instead on the country's only form of communication with the outside world – the unreliable old portable radio. This temperamental but vital relic was strapped to a spare horse and taken on all the Prince's travels. Whenever it crackled into life, Railton would always try to be close, desperate for news from home. Knowing German ears would be listening, all communication was conducted by the Prince in his own language, to what Railton presumed was another Dark Kind, a female, based in London.

Railton found it bizarre hearing messages from home relayed in the harsh, wolf growl vampire language no German expert could ever decipher. It had a surviving written form, but no comparison or shared basis in any human tongue; its strange cadences and structure a mystery to every human alive. Hearing homely tales from his family such as little London evacuees living at Wildways, his home in Thwaite, was bizarre coming from a vampire warlord. But this important contact made sure his family knew he was safe and this kept his moral high. The airman wrote down every word of his personal messages on any scrap of paper he could scrounge and kept them safe, folded in his lucky bible.

Railton waited tense with anticipation as the female Dark Kind's voice came through, as ever faint and wavering. Whatever she said triggered an immediate violent reaction from the Prince. Azrar ordered everyone out of his section of the cave with a fang-bared ferocious snarl and stormy black eyes. No one argued, not least Railton who had caught his first glimpse of the vampire's fangs and was shocked at their unexpected length and silvery scimitar shape.

A terrible, heart-stopping howl instantly froze every man in the outer caves. Despite coming from an inhuman creature, there was no mistaking the great soul-deep outpouring of overwhelming grief and a fearsome murderous rage all combined in the nerve-shredding sound, followed by complete silence, perhaps more awful than the great resonating howl.

Then Azrar stormed out, his face white and gaunt, composed entirely of sharp deep shadowed planes. He barked some terse orders to his headman in Isolanni too rapid for Railton to follow, then disappeared into the night alone. He did not return that night.

As dawn broke, everything – each blade of grass, each leaf was heavily glazed with a hard frost from last night's storm. Unusually, the headman ordered they broke camp by daylight and once the treacherous coating of ice melted in the still warm autumn sun, travelled on without Azrar. No one would discuss what happened the night before with Railton, who once again felt isolated – an outsider in a land of secrets. Yet, he instinctively knew that once Azrar returned, he would not ask questions of the Prince about what happened that night. There were times when curiosity and folly could dangerously override courage; knowing when not to cross the line was the secret to surviving with the vampire Prince.

Azrar drove his heels hard into his stallion's sides. Startled, the black horse threw up its head in protest at the harsh signal then surged forward in a powerful plunge, its hooves throwing up sparks against the black granite scree. The Prince rode on hard, lying low against the animal's hard muscled neck, driving it on to gallop flat out through jagged ravines and rock strewn valleys at dangerous speed through the wind lashed night.

Normally the most considerate of riders, Azrar knowingly risked wrecking his horse's legs galloping across the bone breaking terrain, desperate to put great distance from his humans. They were in mortal danger from him; no Pact or carved amulet could protect them from his murderous rage, from his raw pain. His whole being screamed out to spill human blood, to kill and kill again. Azrar craved the sensation of human terror at his terrifying presence, their hard flesh rent apart by his scything fangs. But he was still three days hard ride from the advancing Svolenians – with no enemy to attack, his own people's lives were at terrible risk.

He rode to a hilltop and dismounting, climbed to the highest point, broadsword in hand. He threw back his head and howled again and again into the night, the tortured sound caught up by the icy winds and carried by them throughout his mountain realm. His fangs raked at the darkness, he gripped his sword hilt so tightly a thin trickle of purple blood seeped through his fingers. He would kill any human he found that night, in too much pain to see reason, unable to control his volatile, ferocious emotions. By daybreak, in the solitude of Rest, he would remember that an ocean of red human blood would not wash away his pain. Now he was all predator, all fury, all sorrow.

Railton and the Prince's team of fighters were finally reunited with their leader after a weeks hard travelling. The arduous terrain and the hard pace exhausted the British airman as they raced for the lower foothills. The worsening weather added to their difficulties, the late autumn season was a time of upheaval and transition for the Arpalathian region. Some days they travelled in baking sun unrelentingly harsh and energy draining. Other times, the sheer brutal force of the winds made travelling impossible, attacked by shards of ice carried in the storms like raking talons. Tigh commentated that Isolann was preparing to protect itself again from invaders and Railton believed him. It did seem this strange country was a living force of nature, as cruel to its own people as it was to outsiders.

Azrar arrived one night unannounced and silent. His face was gaunt and haunted; only his green eyes seemed alive, coldly glittering with their unearthly great power. The humans had travelled all day when Isolann's hostile weather took turns to assault them; they experienced both brief but hard-driving hailstorms and searing heat on the same day. But without a questioning word, they re-saddled their tired horses and rode out into the night to follow Azrar towards the battle with the Svolenians.

They neared the enemy camp two days later. By then Railton wondered if Jendar Azrar would ever speak again. The Prince rode ahead of his men, his head low, shoulders hunched beneath his wolf skin cloak. Railton could even feel the vampire's pain in the energy waves that surrounded the Prince but sensed there was nothing he could do to comfort the warlord.

As they rode slowly through the tangled forests that cloaked the Arpalathian foothills, they came across a large pile of wolf-strewn human bones and bloodied scraps of khaki uniforms. Railton counted nearly a dozen human skulls in what appeared to be a recent kill; the ripple of tension among the Isolanni convinced him the Svolenian patrol was not slaughtered by wolves. He looked towards the Prince, but he rode on ahead, his face as impassive as a white marble statue.

The enemy force had overcome the natural barrier of Lake Beral by using tough new amphibious vehicles but their timing showed the age old lack of respect for Isolanni winters that had routed so many other would-be invaders.

"We could just leave them alone; winter and the wolves would quickly finish them off,"
the headman muttered quietly to Railton as they surveyed the enemy camp from the tangled forest's dense screen. Railton saw the tension building in the Prince, a coiled spring of murderous intent and knew this would never be an option. He reasoned whatever triggered this grim mood in the Prince would only be assuaged in blood. For all the Svolenians' superior firepower, the Isolanni held all the advantages by night, and by the look of Azrar's murderous rage, it would be a massacre.

The Svolenian captain lit a pungent Turkish cigarette and ruefully surveyed the black wall of trees that blocked his progress through the empty wasteland. He fervently hated his assignment to this empty country, little more than a remote haven for wildlife. It was a complete waste of his military skills but this small invading force was a political sop to Svolenia's new best friend Germany and therefore had some prestige back home.

Captain Grban Jerskiu would willingly forgo the potential prestige just to be back in the capital, sipping coffee with his pretty new wife at a tavern in St Alaric's Square. With a cloudless darkness falling fast, he ordered his men to make camp. He prayed the night stayed calm, hating the grim prospect of weathering another vicious ice storm. He posted guards around the perimeter of the camp, aware of the contempt in their eyes.

From the moment the Svolenian force crossed through the barbaric ancient poles that marked the border into Isolann they had encountered no opposition. In fact they encountered no locals at all, not a village or any sign of nomadic life. It was as if Isolann was empty of all human life. Jerskiu did not believe this for one minute. He had carefully hand picked his team, weeding out any harbouring old superstitions about the so-called Land of Secrets and Shadows. He was immune to wild peasant tales of vampire Princes and wolves as clever as men.

He duly ignored the frisson of nervous tension and the unexpected chill to his blood as they drove over the border with its screaming blood stained human skulls on their high poles. He was more concerned by the growing complacency among the men; with no contact with any hostile locals, they saw night patrols as an irksome waste of time. Jerskiu believed them more important now than at any time on their journey through Isolann. He sensed malevolent unseen eyes watching their every move, but he did not anticipate an attack – yet. The Isolanni were a mountain people, they would wait until their enemy was on their home ground where they held all the advantages.

But Jerskiu's assignment was not to engage the Isolanni. He was sent by Hitler himself to search for the ancient Keep, the stronghold at the heart of this backward country. German intelligence said it was hidden somewhere between the forests and the surrounding girdle of mountains. Jerskiu had no idea why it had such considerable importance to the German leader who he believed was a dangerous madman. He just followed orders.

With a few hours before the welcome first light of dawn, Jerskiu's unease increased, though still without cause. He could not sleep and left the spurious shelter of his command tent to check the perimeter guards. The icy night air was still and clear under a dazzling panorama of stars, their remote, scintillating beauty not eclipsed by any overpowering moonlight. He paused to light up a cigarette and study a wondrous show as a shower of shooting stars streaked across the heavens.

Unable even to gasp, Jerskiu's throat was clamped in a powerful painful grip, his feet flailed and fought for the ground as he was raised by the neck high above the ground. He tried to reach down for his pistol but screamed in silent agony as his wrist was crushed to a bloody pulp. Unable to see or fight back against his inhumanly strong assailant, the captain watched in silent horror as a swift, shadowy team swept through his camp, slaughtering his sleeping men before the alarm could be raised. A few awoke in time to fight back but were hampered by the darkness and the speed and ferocity of their surprise attackers.

The first light came from violent earth shaking explosions, the Isolanni were destroying all their vehicles. No one was going home alive. Jerskiu felt his body turn slowly in the air, he closed his eyes unwilling to face his attacker. But a dark, harsh voice speaking his language compelled him to open them. Still unable to make a sound through his crushed throat, inwardly Jerskiu screamed in horror as he faced a monstrously handsome young man. No, not a man – not with those curving fangs, those terrifying green eyes. It was his last coherent thought as he succumbed to agony and blood loss, his throat ripped open in one slash.

Azrar swiftly drained the Svolenian, then sought more prey – his broadsword ready to take on his enemies. Even with his people's efficiency in night attacks, there were plenty of survivors for him to hunt down and kill. By the time he sought shelter from the coming dawn his blood lust was fully sated but the raw emotional pain remained. It was if his heart was kept permanently torn open by a sharp jagged knife and nothing, not even the passing of time could remove it.

After dawn, Railton helped his comrades clean up the battleground, burning the Svolenian bodies in one huge pyre. It was a horrific, grisly task, made more so by so many bodies with torn out throats or rent apart by sword slashes – the unmistakable signs of Azrar's attacks. The complete destruction of the Svolenian force was a true baptism of blood; Railton knew he had to accept such horrific slaughter was a factor of war. There were no rules of fair play, no awareness of conventions and treaties in this remote, primitive region. The Isolanni had to do what ever they could against better armed and more powerful foes.

Railton's only relief in the midst of so much horror was he had not seen the Prince make his kills or drain his victims of their life blood. That may come another night and he would face the consequences then. Now he was unsure whether he could still ride at Azrar's side after witnessing his true vampire nature.

Chapter Two

London, England, 1944

Professor Jay Parrish pulled his coat collar higher against the rain. It appeared to have a malicious, personal vendetta against him as thin tendrils of cold water determinedly worked their way down his neck. Another year stuck in Britain loomed, another year of war and deprivation, and every night, the fearful anticipation of fiery death from the skies.

He wanted to go home to Boston but America was in the war now; he knew the damning stigma of his attempted collaboration with the Nazis would precede him across the Atlantic, endangering his freedom, even his life. There was no point taking a risk of slipping into the USA unnoticed, he had no visa nor could he obtain one through official means. He remained in London under the stifling but necessary protection of Banks and his intelligence network, free to move about the city but still feeling very much a prisoner.

It was so monstrously unjust; his life had become an increasingly bizarre nightmare. Damn it, he was only an academic, an ordinary man of learning with lofty ideals far beyond the petty transient squabbles of modern nations. For this he had been branded a traitor. When would the nightmare end?

It seemed the heartless harridan of fate wanted his torment to continue. A woman fell into step beside him, linking her arm with his. "Listen to what I have to say rather than brush me away with angry words. You know they are watching."

Parrish glared at the woman. A streetwalker, by her clothing and garish heavy makeup, with greying mousy-brown roots appearing in her peroxide blonde hair. She was probably once attractive, but middle age and the harshness of her profession had thickened her waist and hardened her face.

"I don't have time for questions." Her voice was a low urgent whisper, though she smiled lasciviously for any onlookers, " If you want to be free to take the library away from that monster, go to Spice Island wharf at ten tonight. Alone. If you agree to this, give my arm a squeeze then push me away."

Parrish had no doubt this woman was a Nazi agent. His mind flinched away from further contact with such dangerous forces but his heart screamed dissent. Forever branded a traitor, the allies would never let him go to Isolann. This could be a trap but equally it could be his only chance to return to the land of Secrets and Shadows, to fulfil his destiny as the world's guardian of ancient wisdom. He had nearly lost his life before following his quest, what was one more risk? He gave the woman's arm a firm squeeze of assent then pushed her away.

"Betray us and you will die," she whispered. Parrish gave her arm another squeeze, acknowledging her threat; then he shouted loudly, "Not at any price! Get away from me or I will call the police."

"It's your loss, duckie!" the woman laughed and disappeared back into the rain-washed streets. Parrish stared around him, looking for any signs of Banks's agents but could see only fast moving passers-by, factory workers, pre-occupied in getting home before dark and the nightly air raids. To be finally free of Anthony Banks and his increasingly sanctimonious preaching against the occult and the forces of evil – that alone would be worth keeping his Thames side rendezvous!

He pulled his collar up again in his futile battle against the persistent rain. Leaving the foul British weather behind for the clear, cold air of the Arpalathians, surely that was another valid reason to keep his appointment.

Berlin, Germany, 1944

With an explosive snort of disgust, Major Werner studied what passed for maps of the region – the lack of information was infuriating. He angrily tossed aside the old documents and their vague and inaccurate depiction of the remote and little known Upper Balkan region, now considered to be strategically important as Europe's secret backdoor. The most up-to-date and accurate records came from aerial photographs taken by the Luftwaffe during its long campaign bombing and strafing Isolann. An embarrassing failure as far as Werner was concerned, the flyboys only succeeded in blowing up a few goats.

Though Werner believed the Fuhrer's determination to crush the Isolanni Resistance had already cost too many German lives and wasted precious resources, he would never voice this. A loyal party member, he had even turned a blind eye to the cruel deception that cost his old friend Heinrich Dassler, his life.

An honourable fool, Dassler's failures on the battlefields of Northern Europe had enraged the Fuhrer and thus doomed him. Lured by the false promise of an Upper Balkan posting, Dassler had been seized by the Gestapo while waiting for his Svolenian mistress at the rail station. His noble life of loyal service and courage ended with a shot to the back of his head on a filthy bombsite. This tawdry death, to be disposed off like the corpse of a rabid dog would not happen to him. Werner was at home with the dangerous intrigues and political manoeuvring of their leader's inner circle, like a barracuda swimming through its home waters. The Gestapo was merely an irritant, minnows compared to his own covert skills.

Now Werner was ordered to make what he hoped would be a last ditch attempt to subdue Isolann by capturing or killing its ruler. Werner agreed with his leader that the heart of Isolann's courage was its Prince – take him out and the tiny principality that stubbornly blocked Nazi advance through the Upper Balkans would crumble and fall.

Regular troop movement was impossible in such a steeply mountainous country without any roads. The aerial assault had clearly failed with their spectacular lack of success. Werner finally had his way and was given free rein. Now he could execute what should have been done from the start – send in a crack team of elite mountain warfare specialists, hardened killers with the agility and toughness of mountain lions. Men with the same ability as the Isolann nomads to blend into the landscape, living off the land and disappearing at will like ghosts. Named the Lynx Squad, Werner was proud of his team, it had taken him a year to assemble these gimlet-eyed fighters.

He had wondered about telling them the reason for Hitler's order to capture the Prince alive, then chose not to. He himself was uncertain whether to believe Jendar Azrar was some kind of inhuman monster, a terrifying ancient Vampire Warlord of Upper Balkan legend. He saw the highly top secret evidence of the British using vampire agents in Germany and found it too nebulous to draw a definite conclusion. But Hitler had been adamant.

"If these fearsome creatures exist and serve the British, I demand to have vampire agents of my own."

The Fuhrer's scientists were also eager to have a specimen – alive or dead. What secrets to benefit the Reich could these monsters hold, locked in their un-ageing bodies? What if Aryan man could also live without ageing for thousands of years? Every inferior race on the planet would be swept away by the might of the new species – Homo Superior.

Werner pushed thoughts of his discussions with the Fuhrer and his team of advisors. He had a job to do, one that had to start and end before the brutal Arpalathians winter smashed down like a gigantic ice fist. He called in his aide, a man so discreet, so subservient, he silently appeared and disappeared – as if melting into the fading yellowed chintz wallpaper of the Svolenian country house Werner had appropriated for his mission.

"Fetch in the American. He must have rested enough from his long journey."

A few moments later and his aide ushered the strange character Professor Jay Parrish, into his war room. Werner studied the stooped, balding figure with the nervous, shuffling gait, marvelling at how old the professor looked, yet knowing he was a young man in his thirties. The American's internment and close brush with ignominious death under the British authorities had nearly destroyed his health and sanity. The man's pallid grey tinged skin looked completely bloodless, a barely animated near-corpse – his life force drained away by stress and fear. The only animation remained in the manic glitter of his colourless eyes.

At first Werner said nothing, but fixed on the man, like a laboratory specimen awaiting dissection; holding him with the force with his authoritative and chilling stare. It was a well practised technique that often reduced his troops to nervous agitation. When he finally spoke, the release of tension was tangible. Parrish gave a little sigh and a flicker of relief flitted across the American's eyes.

"Considerable precious resources have been used to get you away from the allies. I hope you are worth the risk of so many brave and loyal German patriots."

"That is not for me to say, Major," Parrish replied tersely, showing a surprising strength and defiance in his voice that belied his weak and nervous appearance. Again Werner used his intimidating stare; he wanted this eccentric academic malleable. He intended to drain him of all useful information then swiftly dispose of him. Unlike the weak and vacuous British authorities, the professor's powerful American connections held no power in the Third Reich. Parrish was getting angry.

"I am no traitor. My vision spans more than this temporary state of war between nations. What that monster holds prisoner in his keep is a treasure beyond all imagining, beyond all the world's wealth. It is truly priceless. Azrar's library belongs to humanity."

Werner snorted with derision, "A few musty tomes – is that what all this is about?"

Parrish curbed his fury at this crass but highly dangerous Philistine. Werner was his only chance to reach the Isolanni keep. The British and Americans did not want to add the Upper Balkans to their theatre of war. But the Russians were not ruling this region out. His gorge rose at the thought of the Red Army vandals rampaging through Azrar's keep

"I tried before to come to Germany because you are a nation that treasures culture and learning. You are not destructive barbarians or dangerously ignorant. When your army comes across art treasures and ancient artefacts you do not destroy them but protect and preserve them."

Parrish's much diminished and tarnished conscience pushed aside the reality, the true horrific images of mass murder, genocide and shameless looting in the name of the Reich; he needed Werner as an ally and protector. "What Azrar possesses in his stronghold is truly mind blowing – a vast treasure house of ancient scrolls and priceless books – knowledge of our past, lost for thousands of years."

"Some say the past is irrelevant. That human history began when our beloved Fuhrer came to power."

"Your esteemed leader has a great thirst for knowledge – he knows it means power. He wants this collection for the good of the Reich."

Werner could not argue with this, the stick thin, maggot coloured American was perfectly correct. The order to bring Parrish to Germany came directly from Hitler himself. "And what of this so-called stronghold, this mountainous keep? The Luftwaffe have extensively flown over Isolann and seen nothing, not even a village or town exists in this vermin infested wasteland."

Parrish gave a humourless thin high-pitched laugh and shook his head. "You can fly directly above it and not see it. That's the cleverness, the genius of its bizarre design. Even on foot, you cannot distinguish it from the Arpalathians until you are right up close to the outer compound."

Werner paced the intricately inlaid wooden floor. "I fully respect our leader's wisdom and desire to gain possession of this library. I also see the strategic importance of clearing a route from our loyal Svolenian allies through to the rest of Europe. But I cannot accept I have to capture Prince Azrar alive because he is not human but some sort of monster–a blood drinking vampire for God's sake. This is totally preposterous."

Parrish's face developed a sly, rictus grin, "You don't have to believe it just because your leader does implicitly. Deliver the prince as a trophy to your leader and make yourself his most well favoured officer in the German army. But I warn you now, it won't be easy, Azrar's cunning and survival skills have kept him alive for a very long time."

Werner returned to the maps, still strewn across the worn oak table and on the floor. "Show me on these maps where Azrar's hidden keep is situated."

Parrish was no fool. He had played this game twice before and nearly lost his life both times – first to Azrar's fangs and then to a British noose. He knew the Germans would only keep him alive while he had some use to them.

"It is impossible to find it on an outdated conventional map or an aerial photograph. But I can take you right up to the main doors of Azrar's keep. I am the only one alive who can. The only man to stare straight into that devil's emerald fire eyes and survived his fangs with my throat intact."

Chapter Three

Isolann, Upper Balkans, 1944

Jendar Azrar reined in his horse. There was that same exhausted look on the pale faces of the nomads who rushed out to greet him as he rode through the narrow passes crossing the Arpalathian range. His people were too thin from a life on the move, surviving on poor rations, their lives constantly disrupted by the besieging enemy. There had been too much sorrow, too much fear in his land.

Azrar sent outriders onwards, as he called for a meeting of his headmen. For three long, hard years there had been no bonding or new life naming ceremonies among his people. Such occasions were too dangerous, for the Isolanni nomads held all their special events under open skies. A family event was a happy excuse for parties lasting many days and nights, everyone whatever their tribe was welcome and many travelled for days to take part.

There was one place in Isolann potentially safe enough to hold such celebrations – the outer compound of Azrar's keep. The Prince decided to risk a gathering of all who had babies to name, or couples wanting to bond. The morale of his people was at an all time low, it was time for them to celebrate their hard fought for status as a free people.

Steve Railton also made an important decision. When he heard of the planned ceremonies, he sought out the Prince to seek permission to take a short leave from his duties. He found Azrar alone in a small glade of mountain ash, the trees bent and stunted from the harsh winds that scoured each black granite gorge and valley. The Prince had cast aside his wolf pelt cloak and had unsheathed his broadsword.

Railton watched in fascination as the Prince went through a swordplay routine, marvelling at the balletic yet deadly movements, each parry and scything slash represented an enemy brutally slain. The heavy weapon flew through the air in a moon-silvered arc faster and faster until it became a blur yet Azrar seemed tireless, silently moving with speed and a muscular warrior's grace. The Prince was equally adept at wielding the blade with either hand, throwing and catching the sword as if it was as light as air yet Railton knew no human was strong enough to even lift it from the ground.

"You wish to speak to me, Englishman." Azrar addressed him without pausing his routine. Railton explained that he wanted leave to seek out Lhalee to ask her to bond with him as his wife. The Prince stopped the swordplay to fix Railton with the full powerful scrutiny of his emerald eyes. "This is good, Steve. A human life is too short to lose the chance of love and companionship. Go. Find your woman in the northern hills."

Azrar's Keep, 1944

Fresh meadow flowers wafted soft scents across the courtyard, to compete with the stronger aromatic smells of baking bread and roasting meats. To Steve Railton his first visit to Azrar's stronghold was an assault on all his senses.

The most under stress was his sense of wonder; the towering keep was mind blowing in its huge scale and complexity of its structure. Who were these builders who could seamlessly construct an edifice out of the living mountain? There was nothing like it anywhere in the world. Railton tried to keep his attention away from the brooding battlements, so high above that they were cloaked by cloud and circled by high flying ravens. He knew that many of the craggy battlements housed powerful new anti-aircraft guns; the Prince was taking no chances, knowing his people could still be attacked in what should be a happy time.

The same care was taken in the foothills surrounding the keep and outer compound where nomad tribes turned the rolling grassland into a colourful camp site. This too was ringed with heavy armament and manned by eagle eyed and vigilant soldiers. The mixture of fete and war sat uneasily with Railton, the merriment in the people's eyes was also under-shadowed by their own anxiety. It was clear to Railton that the Isolanni actively embraced this chance to celebrate their culture and freedom but was realistic enough to know it could come at a heavy price if their enemies chose to attack now.

Railton smiled nervously to himself, it was nearly time for his own bonding vows. He forced aside his unease of the foreboding alien splendour of the keep and looked up at the stronghold, knowing Lhalee was being bathed and dressed by the womenfolk of her tribe. He wore his own RAF uniform, as clean and pressed as he could manage and was accompanied by his ever loyal friend, Tigh. As it was mid day, there was no way that the Prince could make an appearance; in fact Tigh told him, Azrar never attended any human ceremonies. Railton felt a strange mixture of disappointment and relief over this. But perhaps it was best the Dark Kind warlord stepped aside from his subjects' special times – to let them forget the Pact for just a brief moment in their lives.

The eerie, visceral sound of a ram's horn announced Lhalee was ready and to his surprise Railton found his hands shaking. Tigh clapped a hefty arm around his shoulders. "It is good for a man to marry, but quite normal for him to fear it too! Come my friend, your beautiful woman awaits."

Unable to contain their wide smiles of joy, Railton and Lhalee stood surrounded by a circle of her tribe beneath a fragrant arbour of wild meadow blooms. More of the white, pale blue and soft yellow flowers were braided in her jet hair. She wore a new tunic of soft pale green lambs wool, embroidered with gold and purple patterns, ancient designs passed down through the generations from a time when her people roamed free across the steppes of Eurasia

The tribal shaman, an elderly woman as old and craggy and seemingly indestructible as the Arpalathians themselves, loosely bound their hands together with red woollen strands as she muttered an age old binding spell. Then Railton spoke his words of love and devotion to Lhalee in English and Isolanni. Lhalee began hers but the low deadly drone of an approaching warplane made her hesitate, eyes widening in fear.

"Finish, there is still time!" commanded the shaman and to Railton's relief, Lhalee carried on her vows to become his wife in time – just. Ripples of growing unease spread through the crowd as the Shaman cut the woollen bonds with a sacred knife. As the ominous drone of approaching enemy craft echoed down the valley, Railton grabbed Lhalee's hand firmly in his and rushed with the rest of the nomads for the shelter of the inner keep and the protection of Azrar's big guns. Anti-aircraft guns at the head of the valley swiftly foiled the attack, a foray by an opportunist Svolenian Marauder, but the people's rare and precious day of joy was ruined. The rest of the afternoon was spent feasting, the unease over the foiled attack never far away.

Everyone felt better when the musicians, emboldened by free-flowing wine, began to play. For a while the danger from the accursed Nazis and their pals the Svolenians were forgotten as the music swirled around the guests. At first the musicians played jaunty dance music that got everyone, young and old, to their feet, to dance off the plentiful food. Then as custom dictated, the women began their strange, primeval singing to bless the newly made union. Ancient steppe music with songs, passed down the generations, songs older then recorded history. The eerie yet beautiful sounds sent shivers down Railton's spine; how little he knew about his new wife's people and culture. Then there was silence and the excited hush of expectation. Lhalee stood up and was pushed forward by the female members of her family. There was a moment's awkward pause as she overcame a new shyness and then she sang a special bride's song to honour her husband. Railton thought his heart would burst with love; she and the song were so beautiful.

As the song finished, Railton reached out to embrace her but was jostled away by a boisterous but good natured gang of male relations. Tigh, laughing, explained to the bemused Englishman that it was his turn to sing to his bride. Slightly embarrassed – in the way of all Englishman abroad – Railton had no idea what to sing, though he had a reasonable voice. Doing his duty on Sunday's in the village church choir back home in Thwaite did not prepare him for this ordeal. There was only one song he could remember, a favourite of his mother. The cold granite walls of Azrar's compound resounded to Railton's enthusiastic but decidedly amateur tenor rendition of 'You are my heart's desire.' British honour was upheld and to Railton's relief, Lhalee was enchanted.

With twilight falling, torches were lit and the wedding party gradually and reluctantly dispersed; the celebrations of proper tribal weddings should last for many days. Another reason to curse the enemy! Railton and his new wife were escorted into the inner keep as honoured guests of the Prince, to give them a few precious hours alone. After a tribal wedding, the newly bonded couple would normally ride away together, to spend a week wandering the hills with the luxury of solitude, for there was little privacy in nomad life. The war made this custom too dangerous. Instead, the newlyweds were taken to luxurious private rooms festooned with fresh mountain flowers, courtesy of Azrar.

Lhalee ran around the rooms, eyes sparkling with wonder; she had never been inside a stone dwelling, let alone a vast royal palace. Her hands touched the soft silk tapestries with their richly glowing jewel colours adorning the black granite walls, marvelling at the scenes of wondrous unknown beasts and exotic plants. She bounced, laughing with delight, on the raised up bed, piled high with cloud-soft snow white lambs wool blankets, silken gold sheets and luxurious russet fox furs. Lhalee gasped with surprise as she found two gleaming matching gold and ruby rings left on the plump pillows as gifts for the newly weds from Jendar Azrar.

Railton smiled and carefully placed the ring on her finger, how had the Prince known of this western wedding custom? No matter, there were more urgent matters to attend to! He pulled Lhalee towards him. "Never mind all this fancy stuff; we have only a few hours alone…"

Some unknown hours later, Lhalee left her husband lightly sleeping off his happy fatigue and had risen from rumpled silk sheets. Despite the short-lived pain and discomfort in the first moments of their union, her whole body now glowed and tingled with pleasure. She was truly a woman now. She should be so happy. Lhalee pulled a fox fur blanket around her shoulders and walked across the bedroom to the balcony to sit on the wide sill. The sheer dizzying drop to the courtyard below meant little to a mountain bred Isolanni. She gazed up at the surrounding Arpalathians, their brooding peaks now shrouded with an evening mist and glowing with moonlight. The first night of what should have been a lifetime of joy and fulfilment with the man she loved. But it could all end tomorrow with the brutal rattle of machine gun fire or in the inferno from the skies. The continuing assault on her country had stolen lives and was close to stealing the Isolanni people's most precious weapon – hope.

She felt strong arms wrap around her.

"I want you to go back with your family tomorrow. I must ride with the Prince. It will be very dangerous and I cannot serve him if I am worried about you."

Lhalee started to protest but held back her tongue. She was a wife now; Railton's wishes must be respected. The only comfort was knowing how much he loved her. This war would end one day and they would spend a lifetime together. She refused to accept any other scenario in her mind.

The morning dawned, too sparkling bright and beautiful for farewells and heartbreak. It tore Railton apart to watch a distraught Lhalee ride away with her family. But yesterday afternoon's attack was a stark reminder of Isolann's continuing vulnerability. He had to ride and fight – for Lhalee and her people.

Chapter Four

**Northern reaches of Arpalathian Mountains, Isolann
1944**

Parrish awoke with a start at the hacking sound of a man's cough and gave a deep gasp of relief at living through to another grey dawn. He drew in a lungful of thin, cold air; he had survived another freezing night on the mountains. Forget getting his professorship at only twenty-two. Stuff getting the prettiest girl in Boston high society into bed. Staying alive for one more day – now that really was some achievement.

'You've really excelled yourself this time, Parrish,' he muttered to himself, trying to ease his cold, stiff muscles into action, seeking the warmth of a precious patch of sunlight. 'Could my life be any worse?' As if the brutal mountains weren't hostile enough, he had to add in the malevolent wildlife, enemy nomads armed with modern rifles, and a murderous bloody vampire ruling the whole shooting match. Sweet God in Heaven, his life just couldn't be more in danger. Oh, but yes, there was also the small matter of being forced to travel behind enemy lines with a load of grim-eyed fanatical Nazis who would shoot him without a moment's hesitation once his usefulness was over.

He adjusted a rough wool tunic that hung loosely over his pallid, skeletal frame and watched as his taciturn companions boiled water for their only breakfast – a rough, gritty watery oatmeal and salt gruel.

Three weeks of living off the land with an elite force of German commandos had nearly killed him with exhaustion and stress. Through his indomitable willpower he had endured; everyday he felt the physical hardship change him into a new man, fit and sinewy and alive. Parrish was driven by his single-minded determination to live long enough to take possession of Azrar's library. Long enough to see Azrar in chains dragged raging into the searing sunlight, broken, defeated and finally facing the long overdue death he deserved for centuries of cold-blooded murder.

The commandos took great care to keep Parrish alive. They had no idea just how sketchy and vague was his knowledge of Isolann's rugged terrain, but it was clearly enough to get the team deep into the heart of the mountain range unnoticed. They had forsworn the route Parrish was most familiar with, up the narrow swathe of gently undulating southern foothills, and then northwards beyond the Lake Beral floodplains through the deep swathe of tangled dense forests.

Parrish now knew this relatively easy route was an ancient trap to lure in the adventurous and the desperate from Svolenia as prey to feed the bloodlust of Isolann's demonic Prince. Instead, the commandos were dropped into a valley deep into the mountains while the Isolanni's attention was diverted with a south bound attack by Svolenian forces.

With Parrish's genuine knowledge of Isolanni garb, the German soldiers wore local style rough wool tunics and trousers in shades of dark grey, colours that blended well into the mountain background. He marvelled how well they could live off the land and move across it so stealthily but also with considerable speed.

Part of him, the small sane voice buried deep inside his mind, screamed that this too was an elaborate trap. There had been no engagements with any Isolanni – it was as if the entire population had disappeared from the face of the earth. Sometimes he even thought they were being watched by malevolent unseen eyes, but hastily put this down to natural fear, being so deep into enemy territory. Then another more arrogant part of his mind filled with scorn for the native population. Just what sort of enemy were they? – a bunch of goat herding nomads armed with sticks. Hardly a match for this highly skilled, ruthless and well armed troop of professional soldiers. And Azrar for all his fang-bared ferocity was still just one vampire. A mortal creature with vulnerabilities and blood that could be spilt.

Major Rolf Werner approached, his grim featured broad face more hostile than usual.

"We have been chasing mountain goats around these accursed mountains for weeks now without a single engagement with the enemy. When are you going to deliver the keep to us?"

"If it is Azrar you want, forget the keep for now. Even if we do find it, we can't get in without the key – a talisman the Prince wears around his neck."

"I refuse to go on chasing shadows. There must be a way of luring out this so called 'monstrous' Prince of yours."

"Find some locals to hold hostage – preferably some harmless little nomad family – then he'll be forced to come. The one thing this bastard holds dear is loyalty and duty to his people."

Werner nodded, having already planned such a move some time before. He knew now a people far better skilled at mountain guerrilla warfare watched their every move. A phoney show of carelessness and vulnerability may draw them out to attack. Once some Isolanni were held captive Azrar was as good as caught – dead or alive – the Fuhrer would have his black wolf trophy.

Azrar's Camp, Arpalathian Mountains, 1944

Railton stood watch at the cave mouth as the sun set with an extravagant glory. The sky was a riot of colour, fairy tale castle clouds of gold and purple against a deep salmon pink and glowing turquoise blue sky. "Show off!" he murmured saluting the Almighty with a smile of appreciation.

His attention was drawn away from the celestial showboating by some approaching Isolanni, a small group, they moved slowly, clearly exhausted and too tired to take cover. They climbed up towards the cave mouth, leading tired stumbling mountain ponies. Railton alerted his fellow fighters and ran to help the newcomers. As he neared them, his heart leapt with astonishment. Among the group was his new bride, Lhalee who had left straight after their wedding night to be with her family.

Her regal poise was undiminished but the impish humour was gone, burnt out by something terrible. Her dark eyes were wide, feverish and she flinched away in severe pain as Railton took her arm. All the group had torn clothes spattered with black dried blood, many with bad wounds. It was a tribute to the toughness and determination of these people they had made it this far.

Railton gently peeled back her cloak to discover a bullet had torn though her shoulder, mercifully it had gone right through. He noticed she wore a German pistol tucked into her belt. "My beloved Steve, you must tell our Jendar that we are here to fight," she managed to murmur before fainting, as a dangerous mixture of exhaustion of blood loss and shock took control.

Railton gently lifted her in his arms and carried her to the safety of the caves. She awoke as he cleaned and dressed her wound. Railton lifted a water bottle to her lips but after taking a long draught of sweet spring water, she forced herself up from the clean sheepskins.

"You must rest, my love, you've taken quite a hit."

"No time. The enemy have taken my family hostage..."

Railton already knew, the other nomads told them how the Nazis had slaughtered all the men folk of Lhalee's tribe and taken the women and children prisoner. A clumsily obvious ploy to lure Azrar out into the open; Railton realised with a sinking heart it was a plan that would succeed. He shivered as his back felt a wave of ice-charged air. The Yorkshireman stood to acknowledge the arrival of the Prince. He was ready to ride, already in his black wolf skin cloak, the wolf skull helm under his arm. "Stay with the wounded, we've lost two already to their injuries."

"My Lord Prince, it is a trap," Railton argued, desperately trying to keep his voice respectful, but anxiety clouding his judgement.

Azrar's elegant features broke into a humourless smile, exposing already primed fangs, "Of course it is my friend. But the price of my people's loyalty must be paid – even if it is in purple blood."

"Let me ride at your side, it will save another Isolanni life if one of them stays behind with the wounded."

Azrar looked down at the nomad girl as she tried to rise from her bed, grimacing against the pain in her shoulder. She was determined to ride with them, to fight for her family. The Prince addressed Railton in halting, heavily accented English.

"Love is too precious to be thrown away lightly, especially a fragile human love... stay with your woman, help her back to health."

"With respect, my Lord, what use is love if the Nazis are allowed to exterminate these people? It would be selfish and cowardly to stay here."

"Then saddle up that chestnut nightmare of yours and ride at my side."

As Railton dodged his mare's scything teeth and climbed up into the saddle, his heart sank as he spotted Lhalee fall into line, on a borrowed horse, her pale face betraying her pain. Steve rode over to her and halted up the animal by its reins. "There is no need for you to do any more, Lhalee," he pleaded, knowing how single-minded she could be. "You must give yourself enough time to rest and heal."

She leaned across to give Railton a kiss then pulled her horse away from his grasp, "Steve, you know how much I love you. How much I want a quiet life, wandering the mountain valleys or living in that stone farm house on the moors in your country, raising our many strong, beautiful children." Lhalee gave a sad smile and shrugged. "These evil men will not rest 'til every Isolanni is killed, in their eyes we are an inferior race, not part of their Master Plan. How can I walk away from this battle for life itself? I must ride with you, with our sovereign lord. I must fight on."

Railton bowed his head; he could not disagree with her reasoning. This was a tiny country, its people teetering on the edge of extinction. That was why he stayed to help them, and why he must let his beloved wife risk her life too, however much it terrified him. He glanced away from her, tears stinging his eyes, he must not show weakness now, not when she was so selfless, so brave. As they rode together into the unknown, he thought with sorrow that as a couple, they had never known anything but war. He said a prayer to his own Christian God – and for good measure, to all the world's deities and kindly spirits. "Please, end this war now. Let fate be kind and let them get through this Hell alive. Let them ride together in a time of peace."

Railton watched the shadowy form of his beloved Lhalee ride close by; he could tell it was her from the faint but unmistakable scent of wild mountain jasmine that he believed grew just to adorn her. How he loved her and how he hated the twisted little dictator who had brought such catastrophe to the world.

The Dark Lord led the mounted party out of their hiding place. As the Prince rode into the darkness, straight-backed in the saddle, head held high and proud, his long jet hair flying behind him in the gusty mountain wind, Railton could not shake the feeling this was the last night on earth for them all.

This was the role the Prince was created to fulfil, thought Railton as he watched Azrar spur on towards his fate, broadsword already in his hand. It could be no other way, but to the Englishman it was still not right. Unconquered and courageous, Jendar Azrar deserved a better end, a nobler destiny, than to die cut to pieces in a hail of German bullets in a cowardly ambush.

Azrar reined in his increasingly nervous horse to briefly pause; ever the predator, he inhaled the sharp night air. It smelt of death. Not the dreadful sweet-acrid cloying stench of human corpses, but the sharp, thin smell of nervous humans plotting ambush and hidden assault. The Prince had faced such moments many times before. His enemies had tried many ploys to bring him down over the centuries but he had always prevailed, using greater guile, experience, sheer ferocity and immeasurably greater skill at arms. This new enemy brought a new factor, the superior arms of this brash, fast-moving century. It could well be his own death he scented in the valley beyond.

Yet he could not turn back. The enemy commandos had captured three nomad families and by doing so challenged him to attempt a rescue. Ironically, he was all too aware that his greatest strength was also his greatest weakness. A human leader might consider sacrificing the families as tragic but inevitable casualties of war. As a Dark Kind warlord, Azrar could not. Somehow the Germans knew this and exploited it to capture or kill him.

He looked back at the small team of his best human fighters who had bravely ridden to this ambush at his side. Was it worth sacrificing them too in this impossible rescue attempt? Had they been an escort of ferocious Dark Kind warriors, there would be no question. But all his valiant, beautiful vampire warriors were long dust; these were just young humans with all their short lives ahead of them, most with families to support.

"Leave the horses with Railton and Lhalee. The next valley is swarming with Nazis. Try to drop down behind them as quickly as you can."

Railton pushed forward on his snappy little mare to protest as respectfully as he could. "My Lord, they will mow you down as soon as you enter the valley."

Azrar's eyes darkened fleetingly at the airman's impertinence – no human questioned his commands and lived, but the man's concern for his welfare was genuine and he knew his flare of anger was misplaced. It should be totally aimed at those who captured his people and held their children at gunpoint.

"It will take too long for my men to get behind the Nazis, if they can. The hostages are in too grave a danger. I must start the rescue process by taking them head on."

The ferocity of the vampire's tone forced Railton to obey but it felt like an act of craven cowardice, tempered only by knowing he could keep Lhalee safer here away from the ambush. The Prince sat back in the saddle, fingers tightening around the hilt of his broadsword slung across his back above the black wolf pelt cloak. Death held no fear for Azrar. Maybe it was time for him to move on. Now he would not be alone in the unknown beyond death. The one he most loved awaited him, they could journey together through eternity as they had in life – or both be lost to oblivion. Either way, he was ready to face death.

"Don't be too concerned, Railton. This is hardly a new situation for me. There is one lesson you humans never learn. I am very hard to kill."

In the end, Azrar did not ride on alone. Ten insistent volunteers among his troops were determined to ride at Azrar's side, knowing the terrible risks they faced. Some were relatives of the kidnapped families and wanted to take on the enemy head on. Azrar considered ordering them not to ride further with him, knowing they would obey without question. But he studied their anger hardened black eyes and knew they would go anyway – waiting till their Prince was out of sight before following. Strategically it made sense; it would give the others a better chance to surprise the enemy if their full focus was on the group riding into the valley. Railton's woman though exhausted and wounded rode forward. She did not bow her head low or avert her eyes, but met the Prince's imperious glare with a proud and bold expression. "I will not hang back with the horses, my Lord. As the last remaining elder of the Hansha tribe, it is my right to seek blood vengeance on my slain family. You cannot deny me."

Railton's mouth dropped in shock and he reached out towards his wife, "Please, Lhalee, no."

Azrar's eyes darkened at the woman's insolence. His voice was an angry, low snarl, "I am your Prince. You will do as I command."

Lhalee realising she had gone too far, dropped off her horse and onto her knees before the Dark Kind warlord.

"Remount your horse and ride with me," Azrar commanded curtly before turning to the distraught Englishman. "I am sorry Railton, but the woman has the ancient right to take her revenge."

The Prince turned his horse's head away, towards his appointment with fate in the darkness. "My command to you remains the same."

Chapter Five

The rhythmic scrape and clatter of many horses' hooves against the rough gravel strewn valley floor brought the Germans fully alert. Surrounded by sheer rock sides, the captives waited in the centre of the bowl-shaped valley, carved by a long lost glacial-melt eddy. A classic setting for an ambush.

At the sight of the Prince's glowing green eyes in the darkness, the captives began to wail, their pitiful distress enraging his human escort, pushing their horses into a canter to quickly get to their kinfolk. In a blinding flash, the night was lost to retina-searing white light as the valley became as day with bright flares. The humans struggled to control their panic struck horses but the Prince spurred on, broadsword in hand, his pained eyes scanning the dazzling wall of light for any sign of an enemy to attack. His men began to fire blindly up into the canyon but with no visible targets, it was like fighting ghosts.

In the rocky ledges above the valley, Parrish's heart beat wildly in excitement as he watched Azrar's foolhardy approach. Nothing had changed since their last encounter; the youthful vampire Prince had the same arrogant stance, the same warrior pride. He was just as handsome, just as deadly. For all his loathing of Azrar, Parrish could not help conceding there was something undeniably magnificent about this age-old creature at bay.

He watched dispassionately in the harsh artificial glare of battery spotlights, as the Germans aimed at the Prince and his men. Werner shouted an order and with casual ease, they picked off each Isolanni – tethered hostages and mounted warriors and even their horses – all were cut down in the hail of flaming death. The hellish attack went on and on, until they machine-gunned every living thing in the valley. The guns only fell silent when all that was left was the vampire Prince whirling around with fang bared defiance on his terrified war horse.

Azrar easily sat out the sweat bathed, bloodied animal's wild plunging, black broadsword held lightly in one hand, imperious alien eyes now all black but lit from within by fiery emerald sparks. Parrish heard Werner order one marksman to take out the sword – it flew from the Prince's hand with a spray of thin purple blood. The Prince howled not with pain but ferocious defiance, preparing to defend himself with the weapons he'd been created with – his vicious, long scimitar fangs.

"Take out the horse."

Werner's men emptied their machine gun fire into the black stallion's broad chest. It screamed, gave one last defiant rear before dropping dead, trapping the Prince's leg beneath the stricken beast. Azrar snarled in fury as he felt his leg bones crush to useless pulp. He realised the enemy strategy was to capture him alive – this would not happen. Ignoring the searing pain from what was left of his leg and shattered hand, he channelled all his indomitable life force, all his warrior strength to push the horse's carcass free of his trapped leg. He reached down to a nearby body grabbing a long wooden shepherd's pole from the hands of one of his slain people and used it to stand upright.

Werner watched from his vantage point – how easy it would be to bring this creature down now, a flurry of bullets and the legend of the Black Wolf would die. The thought of taking this monster back to Berlin appalled him; every inch of the journey would be a nightmare. Severely wounded and in chains, somehow Azrar would always remain a potent threat while he lived. Surely a corpse would serve science just as well?

"He's a beautiful monster – quite magnificent in defeat, isn't he?"

Parrish sidled up to Werner, whose whole belief system was shattered by the reality of the vampire warlord. They watched as Azrar readied himself to fight to the death, his long jet hair whirling in the sharp night air, his carved marble features still handsome despite the savage drawn fangs.

"I had to see this creature for myself; I would never have believed it could exist. You say it is thousands of years old?"

"Dark Kind have existed since the dawn of recorded human history – who knows how long before that – even they do not know. Jendar Azrar only looks about twenty-five doesn't he? In fact he is probably closer to twenty-five thousand years old."

Werner was increasingly disturbed at this discovery. This creature had lived through the rise and fall of many human empires, seen countless human races rise and decline. How could Hitler inspire his people to fight on with talk of their racial superiority and the power of the glorious thousand year Reich to come? What confidence would anyone have in this destiny when this nonhuman had first hand experience of human history? It had seen just how fragile human life was, could tell how human empires were doomed always to fall. There was only one answer. He removed his handgun from its leather holster.

"What are you doing?"

Parrish could see the Major's square jaw set in renewed determination.

"The first sane thing on this nightmare. The only sane thing. I am going to kill it."

"But what of the Fuhrer's orders? What of the consequences to your position?"

"This is the only practical solution. We will never capture this thing alive, never get it all the way out of Isolann, except in a body bag. It ends now."

"Let me come with you. I have dreamed of this moment for years. I must watch Azrar die."

Werner hesitated then nodded a curt assent. He knew Parrish's history with the vampire, how close the American had been to having his throat torn open by the monster's fangs. He ordered his men to hold their fire and they walked down to where Azrar stood – the vampire's courage alone keeping him upright and snarling in defiance and fury.

Azrar watched the German officer and another strangely familiar figure approach. He saw the pistol in the German's hand and knew how it would end for him. Yet he was not without hope, the rest of his men were still in action, clambering down the sheer sided valley with the agility of rock lizards. He just needed a little more time. He recognised the maggot-coloured bald man.

"I should have ripped out your throat from the start, my ward Khari said you were a treacherous, greedy little man."

"I have never betrayed humanity, Prince Azrar, only the misplaced trust of a monster, a blood drinking vampire. Soon all your vile kind will be wiped off the face of the earth. I am particularly going to enjoy watching you die, hopefully Major Werner here will make it very slow and agonising. Any pain you suffer will not make up for the centuries of suffering you have inflicted on your victims and their grieving families."

Azrar stood straight and defiant despite the agony from his shattered leg. "I have joyfully drunk the blood of many humans – all were my enemies. I do not have the innocent blood of women and children on my hands."

"You have still destroyed their lives," Parrish continued, "the tears of all those mothers, widows and fatherless children must run in rivers from your countless kills over the centuries. An ocean of your blood tears will not wipe away one salt tear of ours."

"You have misquoted that ancient poem, professor, but in essence it is true. I am Dark Kind, I do not apologise for my nature."

Werner was by now incensed by the exchange in Isolanni – a language he did not understand, his anger fuelled by his growing fear of the vampire. He had never believed such a dread creature could exist. And now the full snarling fire-eyed reality stood before him and all normal existence spun around him in a nightmarish blurring of reason. For once the weight of his handgun gave no reassurance. Even badly wounded and unarmed, the icy waves of raw menace from the demonic Prince terrified him. It would take just one raking slash from the creature's long, curved and wickedly sharp fangs to end his life. Somehow he found some strength to address the vampire directly in German, trusting the creature's long life would make it master of many languages.

"You are deeply honoured, my Lord Prince. You have an audience with our Fuhrer in Germany. There is no need for all this bloodshed. It is time our two proud nations became allies."

"But the reality is I will be an intriguing captive specimen for the curiosity of your scientists, while my people are exterminated and my lands plundered. It ends here for me. My people have great courage; they will fight on until every German is hounded out of Isolann forever."

"So be it, Prince Azrar. Your corpse will keep our scientists busy for many years. I doubt these goat herders will put up much resistance once you are dead."

"It will take more than one shot, Dark Kind can regenerate from even fatal looking injuries," Parrish urged, eager for the continuing danger from the vampire to be eliminated, eager to snatch the black crystal wolf-shaped key from around his neck – the key to the most wondrous treasure on earth; Azrar's fabulous library – worth far more than all the vampire's countless chests stuffed full of gems.

In Werner's mind, he calmly levelled the gun at Azrar's forehead and fired. In reality he paused, wondering if even wounded, the vampire could still leap, tearing at his throat before he fired the first shot.

"Just do it," hissed Parrish, alarmed by the delay in finally despatching the vampire.

"You have no idea how fast that bastard can move. Kill him now!"

As the night turned to brutal day, Railton recklessly ignored the Prince's order to stay with the badly startled and anxious horses. With Lhalee's help, he made them as calm and secure as possible, tethering them to a stand of twisted old mountain ash. The pain from her injuries had finally taken their toll and with great reluctance, she had agreed to stay behind with the animals.

"Just bring the Prince and my people back safely – all of them," she urged through clenched teeth. Railton too k her face in his hands and kissed her on the lips then followed the narrow trail through to the valley. He had barely reached the outskirts when the night exploded into violence. With a sudden blinding light, the harsh retort of machine gun fire and soul-tearing screaming – some clearly from small children. He rushed forward, following the terrible sounds and light but as he reached a rocky outcrop at the entrance to the valley, it was clear there was little he could do alone.

Railton grabbed onto the rock as his knees buckled with shock, his chest tightened painfully, his breathing becoming ragged. The carnage was sickening even by the Germans' brutal standards. The harsh spotlight illuminated slaughtered captives some still tied to trees, totally unarmed and helpless, they had been given no chance to run or hide. Around them lay the bodies of their rescuers, the dead and dying thrown like broken bloodied rag dolls over the awkward bulks of their slain horses – some still groaning and thrashing in their death throes. Then as each dying man and beast breathed their last there was silence.

Railton welcomed the unearthly hush; it meant at least the suffering of the grievously wounded was over. There was no time to grieve for the fallen. He saw the black coated body of the Prince's war horse and realised with a leaden heart the Nazis had brought down the extraordinary Prince of Isolann – it was a bad death for such a warrior. He turned to leave, self preservation making him cautious as the surrounding hills swarmed with German commandos.

Railton heard a familiar low growl; his heart gave a lurch of surprise and bewilderment as he saw the Prince haul himself to his feet, pulling away in great pain from his fallen horse. The Jendar stood miraculously still alive and proudly defiant, growling with fangs bared – challenging his enemies to fight on. Unable to reach the Prince in time with covering fire, a horrified Railton waited for the Germans to finish the slaughter but there was only silence. He guessed the Germans wanted the Prince captured alive – and why wouldn't they want the extraordinary prize of the last vampire warlord?

Jendar Azrar was a creature from the darkest nightmare, yet Railton desperately wanted this extraordinary eternally young being to live. For all his murderous nature, the vampire Prince had risked all for his people for centuries. He would never slaughter innocent children or harm the old and frail. Yet Railton could do little but watch in mounting alarm. The Prince was in a bad way. Jagged shards of black bone had torn through the black leather of his clothing, a steady stream of purple blood pooled around his feet. Azrar was dying yet he remained upright, propped up bizarrely with a wooden pole, still ready to tear at human throats with his savage fangs.

Railton saw a German commando approach with a pistol in his hands, accompanied by another man, smirking with open pleasure at the vampire's downfall and imminent demise. Perhaps they were not going to try to take him alive – a wise move on their part. The old cliché rang true, there was no creature more deadly than a wounded predator – and Azrar was the ultimate living killing machine. Railton was appalled to hear the weedy balding man address the Prince in English with a marked American accent. What the Hell was a Yank doing helping these murdering Nazi bastards?

It was time to even the odds – darkness was Azrar's greatest ally. Railton aimed his machine gun at the spotlights and with accuracy honed on the grouse moors back home, took them all out in a single sweep.

It acted as a signal for the rest of the Prince's men, the belated but still welcome re-enforcements to attack from behind, dropping down the sheer rock walls like spiders on threads. Railton took advantage of the chaos as the Isolanni fighters took on their enemy at close range, sprinting forward, he reached Azrar while the German officer in mindless panic, spun in confusion in the pitch darkness, firing his pistol around him blindly.

"Lean on my shoulder, my Lord...I'm getting you out of here."

Azrar's black eyes opened wide in surprise but the wolf growl defiance in his voice was low and dangerous. "I do not run from my enemies – I will have their throats for what they have done tonight."

Without thinking, Railton risked his own throat and hauled the weakened Azrar away from the Germans. He was surprised how light the Prince was for such a powerful predator. "With all due respect, with so much blood loss, you are probably dying, Prince Azrar. You are in no state to attack anything – even me, now let me get you away from this nightmare."

Railton was almost relieved when the Prince passed out from shock and blood loss. He threw the stricken vampire over his shoulder and ran through the darkness, grateful for the covering fire from the rest of the Isolanni fighters.

He found the horses and carefully put the Prince across Sweetness's scrawny back – he would trust no other horse with such an important burden. Railton was determined now that the last Dark Kind warlord was not going to perish by the hands of cowards. There was only one honourable death for a creature like Azrar and that was facing his foe with a sword in his hand. Lhalee threw him the reins of another horse, only too aware not all the warriors would survive the battle, and grabbing his own mare's reins galloped back down the ravine to safety.

A few minutes later, a low groan signalled the Prince had come to. Railton reined in the horses and helped him off the horse to sit upright with difficulty.

"What do you need to recover? I don't suppose there's any point fetching a doctor."

Azrar's still black eyes fought to stay focused and conscious, his voice was a rasping low growl as he fought each surge of searing pain.

"You know what I need, Englishman. I need a living human male – but not one of my people."

Railton made the gravely wounded vampire as comfortable as possible, binding the top of his shattered thigh in a futile attempt to stop more blood loss. Tying the recalcitrant mare to a bush, he retraced his route back, praying the enraged Isolanni had left some of the Germans alive. He met some fighters along the track.

"I have the Prince safe but his wounds look mortal. I don't think he can last much longer."

"We have overcome and scattered the enemy force, though far too many have escaped. Including the Yank. When we couldn't find the Prince's body, we prayed he was still alive. We kept some Germans prisoners, just in case."

Railton walked away to find Lhalee, this was Pact business, not a time for his presence, an outsider, a supposedly Christian Englishman. There were things he should not witness and keep his sanity. He found her in a very bad way, crouching down, rocking herself in a tight ball of pain as the awareness she had lost almost every person she had ever loved had struck like a thunderbolt of grief. Railton put his arms around her, to hold her tightly and comfort her but she had gone to a dark place beyond the mountain pass, beyond his reach.

He held her, not caring she did not know he was there, as more and more exhausted, wounded fighters arrived at this unlikely rallying point. It was like watching a parade of ghosts, even by the faint light of a half moon, he could see all hope all life was drained from their faces. The prince must not die. Without his unifying, undaunted and fearless leadership these people were lost. The horror of this night would be repeated across the land until the Isolanni were wiped from the face of the earth.

His guilt as an honourable, moral human being was now overpowered by the needs of a desperate people, the helpless children, the frail and elderly who would be mercilessly cut down by the Nazis. With a sad, reluctant sigh, Railton left the near catatonic woman as Isolanni fighters dragged a terrified yet still aggressive commando prisoner towards the Prince. By now, the vampire was too weak to support his head upright let alone make a kill. One fighter flourished a small curved but wickedly sharp knife and cut the prisoner's throat in one swift slice. Railton's gorge rose in revulsion but he stayed to witness the battle to save Azrar.

The Isolanni held the prisoner with difficulty as he thrashed and fought, jugular blood spraying wildly into the air but nothing was getting into the Prince. Railton quickly spotted the problem, no Isolanni dared actually to touch their ruler. Railton took a deep breath as he fought to stay calm and in control of himself as he stepped forward to cradle Azrar's body, holding the vampire's ice cold head still to allow the blood to pour down his throat. Railton surprised even himself with his grim determination to save the vampire Prince. It was no use. He growled a command to the others.

"Get another one. I can feel him sinking fast. We are losing him."

Another wretched German soldier was dragged forward, but Railton had by now mentally de-humanised these victims as mere vital blood donors, the impression of what they had done to the nomad families was seared forever into his soul. Again a clumsy attempt was made to get the blood to pour down Azrar's throat but he appeared beyond help. Railton grew angry and pulled open the Prince's leather and chain mail jerkin, tearing open a black silk shirt to reveal his chest. He searched everywhere for a heart beat, unsure where Dark Kind hearts were placed. His aggressive action alarmed the Isolanni who stepped forward to protect their Prince. Realising the danger, Railton spoke to Azrar in their language.

"You will not die, Prince Azrar. You are a Jendar and your people need you. Without you, the Nazis will wipe them from the face of the earth. Now open your damned mouth and drink."

With no response from the vampire, Railton forcible prised open his mouth, careful not to touch the razor sharp fangs and grabbing the German prisoner, positioned him above.

"Cut him again, this time go in much deeper."

Spurred on by the force of Railton's will, one of the Isolanni cut right into an artery and the thin red stream became a gushing flood. The tribesmen held the wildly thrashing prisoner over their fallen Prince, ignoring the German's cries as he vainly screamed for mercy. Then there was silence as every precious drop was drained. The silence remained as a baleful sense of death and defeat hung above them like a leaden coffin lid, ready to drop down, entombing them all.

With a deep sigh of anger at his own failure to keep Azrar alive, Railton lay the Prince gently down on the black granite scree. Frantically, he tore strips of fabric from his own woollen cloak and tightly bound the shattered leg – more as a matter of respect than practical use. It was just one more thing to do anything to postpone facing the world without Azrar.

How could something so powerful, so charismatic—an elemental whirlwind of a being that held such power across a continent for millennia be reduced to so little? With one ironclad fist grasping a broadsword, Azrar held his own destiny and the fate of his people against myriad foes. How many mighty armies had he faced down and defeated over the centuries? Now all that remained was a pathetic blood-spattered bundle of rags. Railton picked up the Prince's voluminous black wolf pelt cloak yet could not bring himself to cover him, to admit he was really gone.

More riders approached the rendezvous, Railton looked up to see Tigh run towards them, a brave young warrior reduced to a frightened child by the news. This was how it was going to be across the whole country soon. The Germans would have an easy task destroying Isolann.

"Is it true, is the Prince dead?" Tigh shouted through tears, "He cannot die, he is Dark Kind; he can live forever."

Railton could take little more, as he became overwhelmed by the horrors of the night, witnessing the pain of his distraught friend, the wordless keening of his traumatised wife and the sad remains of the slain warlord. He wanted to walk away, needing some time alone to collect his thoughts; his life was unreal, a nightmare. Without a moment's thought he had helped kill two unarmed men to save the life of a murderous vampire.

He looked back at the Isolanni soldiers as they stood around; their uncertain future had left them desolate and helpless. He couldn't even begin to imagine their state of shock. These simple people had a unique history, their ancestors shared thousands of years of security and certainty under one being's continuous protective rule. For the first time, they faced the future alone.

This was no time for weakness. Azrar had not picked a weakling to ride by his side in the darkness. They needed snapping into action with the very real threat from the remaining Germans still so urgent. He reverently laid the Prince's cloak over the body, leaving his face uncovered as if sleeping.

"The hills are crawling with Germans. I think the Prince should have his sword back."

The night sky had now totally cleared of flitting clouds and in the faint light of the moon, Railton could see a flicker of relief pass over their eyes at having something positive to do and the party of riders, including Tigh, melted back into the night. They returned with the intricately worked black sword placed over the backs of three horses. It took six men to lower it beside Azrar's body. Railton marvelled at how extraordinarily strong the Prince had been. How lightly he wielded the broadsword, swinging it above his head with one hand though it took many men to lift it, yet when he carried the wounded Prince away from the ambush, Railton found him lighter than a human.

Railton gazed down at the lifeless vampire Prince, pondering whether it was worth the risk of returning the body to the main camp for his people to pay their last respects. With so many German commandos at large, the risk of them capturing it was very high. Railton shuddered at the prospect of this great ruler reduced to dissected fragments as a laboratory specimen. But at the end of the day, it was not his decision. In death as in life, Azrar belonged to the Isolanni nation.

    He turned to go back to his horse and continue the fight when a slight scraping noise made him spin in surprise. He watched open mouthed in amazement as Azrar took in a great lungful of night air and reached out to firmly grasp the hilt of his broadsword. Still very weak, he tried to sit up with difficulty, using the sword to raise himself slowly, emerald eyes sparkling with a fierce light. A pain wracked but wry feral grin of triumph spread across his sharp-boned features. "Did I not tell you, Englishman? I am very hard to kill."

Chapter Six

Azrar's Stronghold

"Poor little mite," Ileni muttered, her heart heavy with sorrow and compassion. She watched as Sandor helped the Englishman carry the injured nomad girl down into the warm sanctuary of her kitchen domain in Azrar's keep. It seemed but days ago she had helped Lhalee prepare for her wedding to Railton in this same cosy haven. "Curse those Nazis!" she swore out loud, "German and Svolenian alike, for bringing so much death and misery."

Ileni fetched a warm wool blanket and wrapped it around her shoulders. Lhalee was so lost in her own darkness that she did not flinch as the older woman removed the rough field dressing over her wound, nor did she react as Ileni bathed it and reapplied healing balms. It was not a good sign; the wound though healing well was deep. Pain should have made her react but there was nothing, no reaction in her dark eyes.

Ileni turned to Railton, in stark contrast, there was plenty of pain in his eyes. This was a courageous man; he needed to be strong now for his wife.

"Railton, her mind is hiding in a very deep dark cave, far away from the pain of the real world." The woman sighed sadly, her sloe-dark eyes misting over. "A curse on this war and all who caused it. How I wish my Khari was here now, she could reach out to Lhalee and try to bring her back to you."

At the sound of his adopted sister's name, Sandor's eyes widened, he ran across the kitchen flag stones, sending a rush basket of apples spilling across the floor. Forgetting his shyness in front of the wiry, blond foreigner who dressed like an Isolanni fighter, he demanded, "Khari? Is our Khari coming home?" He glanced across to Ileni, the light of excitement and hope in his placid eyes.

Ileni gave the big man's hand a gentle squeeze. "Not long now, Sandor. The winds will soon turn against these invading vermin. With so many brave men and women like this Englishman risking their lives, it has to. The spirits of justice cannot sleep forever."

Railton stroked his wife's hair, it was like touching a lifeless thing, a life-sized doll with no means to animate it. Her lack of response to his caress was painful but his heart refused to seek out hope. "What am I to do, Ileni? I have tried everything to reach her."

Ileni looked deep into the Englishman's eyes, so much pain, so much anxiety. "She is beyond our medicine, beyond your gentle words and embrace. She needs time. Her spirit is in hiding and very frightened. Let her stay in the warmth and safety of Azrar's keep. When she feels safe, maybe she may return to the world."

Railton took Lhalee's hand, which lay lifeless in his palm like that of a marionette with broken strings. "I love you. I will wait for you, however long it takes for you to come back to our world."

Ileni looked away, tears stinging her eyes. Deep down she felt this was a journey the girl would never make.

Part Five

Echoes of the Departing Storm.

Chapter One

Chess Manor, the Chilterns, England, 1945

The war continued to devastate a broken but defiant Germany but the growing sense of hope among the allied forces made little impact on Joe Devane and his depleted Spook Squad. Devane was convinced the allied governments would end up like dogs fighting over Germany's carcass; he saw the signs of hostility and distrust and foresaw signs of a new dangerous instability in post war Europe. He was certain his team would still be needed, their strange work would go on but like Europe, his squad was a maimed and broken-spirited thing.

It was not just the grievous loss of the Dark Kind operatives, that was bad enough, with Jazriel dead, and Sivaya missing – by now most likely a dangerous enemy. Her grudging loyalty to the squad disappeared with her lover's death by Banks's lethal treachery. No human male throat among the squad was safe from her fangs.

Devane's team also lost their other priceless asset, Khari's *Knowing*. She had not recovered from her ordeal in Berlin, her mind remained haunted by other people's memories: the terrifying images from death camps and battlefields, from bombed-out cities and torture chambers. She had withdrawn into herself, exhausted from self-inflicted sleep loss–her nightmares were worse than the daytime torment. Anna did her best to exorcise Khari's demons but made little progress. Devane was terrified his beloved golden girl would lose her mind. While his superiors feted the squad as a great success despite the loss of the vamp agents, Devane counted the cost in ruined lives, human and Dark Kind.

He knew it had been worth it; they had helped shorten the war and saved many innocent lives. Helplessly watching Khari drift around the Manor and its grounds like a living ghost, did not make it any easier to bear.

One night, a large saloon with obscure diplomatic plates and blacked out windows arrived at the mansion. This in itself was strange and worrying, how had their security been so easily breached? It paused briefly to toss out something by the main entrance then left in a spray of gravel, speeding down the long drive from the mansion. Ffitch-Brown drew his pistol and aimed it at the back of the car but Eshan stayed his hand, "Leave it be, Ffitchie, it was flying a black wolf pennant."

Two small packages remained on the drive. Devane was first to reach them. He took them straight into his study, ignoring the groans of disappointment from his by now highly curious agents, and locked the door. Inside one parcel he found a battered leather case. Devane shuddered before opening it as he saw the dried purple blood stains on the scuffed leather surface. He touched it with considerable reverence, knowing it would contain a highly polished cherished old saxophone. Some one had helped the Jazzman keep his promise to Lennie Dawn. His Ruthie was back.

The other parcel contained a long roll of canvas, which Devane discovered with a gasp of astonishment was a painting of Khari. It was stunning, a masterpiece perfectly capturing her fey beauty. Devane rolled it back up, walked over to the fire and threw the painting into the flames. This belonged to her past. Devane felt no regret as he watched the beautiful artwork flare up then collapse into acrid ash. It needed to be destroyed; it was a reminder of a bad place, a bad time. Just more horrible memories that were slowly killing Khari.

He would commission his own portrait of the woman he loved. One painted in a time of hope and peace.

Paris, France 1945

Despite the loss of the other Dark Kind, much to everyone in the Spook Squad's surprise, Eshan had stuck with the team. Jazriel's death was a senseless tragedy but the Dark Kind's potential doom had not changed. She was convinced there was long term gain to her people from working with humanst – the right sort of humans like Joe Devane. The future of the dwindling band of Dark Kind survivors scattered across Europe, Russia and Asia, was still worth fighting for.

For the time being at least she was away from the squad, and humans she regarded as true friends as she took some time off to return to her Paris apartment for the first time since the liberation of France. To her astonishment, it survived mainly how she left it. Though the heavy boarding had been breached many times and all her antiques and furniture stolen, there was no bad structural damage or unwelcome squatters – with one notable exception. Garan used the apartment whenever he visited the occupied French capital on one of his many hunting trips. It was no surprise therefore to find him at her door that night, leaning against the doorframe with an insolent grin of over-familiarity.

"Hi, how's my favourite near-human? Just how are things in the exciting world of international espionage?"

Eshan growled with disapproval at his irreverent, sarcastic tone. He strolled in, his inevitable platinum handled ebony cane tapping on the oaken floor now stripped bare of its sumptuous Persian silk rugs. He had clearly made a recent kill; Garan's dark violet eyes glittered with new fire; he'd been dangerously careless as usual, with a fresh red bloodstain on his navy shirt.

"Get changed, then get out. I have no time for your nonsense tonight."

"That's no way to speak to a messenger from your beloved."

Garan threw a letter to her. Once fastened with the familiar seal of the black wolf, Eshan was livid that the seal had already been broken. Garan shrugged off her fury with a vulpine grin, "Mi casa es su casa – there are too few of us left to keep secrets."

Eshan curbed her fury at his outrageous breach of her privacy. With Germany's impending defeat, the route to the Upper Balkans was becoming gradually less perilous. Somehow a courageous human messenger from Isolann had got through to Paris. Eshan rapidly read the letter from the Prince –its contents were devastating. She sat down on the floor, head in hands, her mind reeling with the contents of the letter. In the missive, Azrar spoke to her of his nightmare existence since Jazriel's death. The Prince believed Jazriel's spirit was in terrible torment, haunting him by day and night, crying for Azrar's help to rescue him from a terrifying afterlife, some sort of hellish dimension.

Garan joined her down on the bare boards; the apartment's furniture was totally looted. For once he became serious, "We know Jazriel is dead but his spirit appears to be trapped in some awful place. We need to go back to Germany and find Sivaya. Somehow I know she is still there, that she has the answer."

Deeply shocked, Eshan thought awhile before answering. "We cannot risk entering such a heated war zone now, even with help from the others. Our intelligence reports a murderously vengeful Red Army getting ready to storm through Germany. It will be bad for anyone – human and Dark Kind alike, getting caught up in that firestorm of brutality."

"What others? "Garan sprung to his feet. "Those treacherous little apes you are still inexplicably a slave to?"

Eshan's voice was muted, weary of the constant arguing with Garan over her relationship with humans. "They will want to help; they all loved Jazriel."

"But not enough to keep him alive," Garan snarled, his eyes stormy with anger and contempt. "This is vampire business. Leave the humans out of it."

Eshan stifled her own anger at his constant and flagrant use of the old human insult to their kind; it was a losing battle. Jazriel had also found it amusing and used it many times in jest with the human squad members.

"In that case we must be patient. We have lost too much already to risk a trip into Germany now. It will fall soon and maybe movement will become safer once the Russians have slated their understandable thirst for vengeance. Jazriel has been dead for a year – we can wait a few more months."

Garan tapped his cane in a furious staccato rhythm on the parquet floor. He paced the floor, darkened eyes glittering in the unlit apartment. "Jazriel's spirit is suffering beyond the grave. I will not wait."

"Nothing ever changes with you, does it Garan? It is not just your careless, indiscriminate killing. This reckless impatience won't just condemn you – it risks all our survivors. I know there is no point commanding you as a Ha'ali to wait. Instead I will beg on my knees, do not go to Germany 'til it is safer."

Troubled by a curious new sensation – indecision, he walked over to a window, the glass still taped up against the threat of air raids. It was true Jazriel had never featured in his past, beyond Garan's fleeting physical desire on the rare occasions they did meet. He couldn't help it – Jazriel's looks had been outstandingly beautiful. Now all hope of any future liaison was gone. But Jazriel was still Dark Kind, in death as in life.

Garan had no interest in the concepts of Dark Kind honour and duty. Yet he still felt compelled to return to

Germany to pick up Sivaya's trail. Not to help the haunted Prince in his distant wolf-ridden land – just to do the right thing by Jazriel, a commoner like himself.

"If you will not wait, let me at least contact the rest of the squad. If this must be done now, it must be done properly. Much as you vex me, I do not want to lose another Dark Kind to the Germans. Their insane leader knows about us, he has a special squad searching for evidence of Dark Kind. Their greatest trophy will be any specimen – dead or alive." Reluctantly, Garan agreed. But he knew he had the option of breaking free at anytime and conducting his own search – in his own way.

Chapter Two

Islington, London, England, 1945

"Here's to one less blood draining bastard. Well, it's a start."

Professor Jay Parrish raised a glass of vinegary wine to toast his new partner as Banks recounted the bloody death of the Dark Kind agent. The two men met in a run down bomb-damaged town house in Islington. Banks used his connections to secretly fund the requisitioned house as the headquarters of his new covert organisation. Grandiosely called 'Nemesis,' it had merely three members but would soon have many more. It had one aim – the exposure and destruction of the entire vampire infestation.

Parrish had another more urgent personal agenda – to seize Jendar Azrar's extraordinary library, but the end of the war further thwarted his quest. He knew he was now completely obsessed with obtaining the outstanding collection, but he saw no wrong in stealing back the ancient lost knowledge that rightly belonged to humanity – not some demon-like vampire warlord. Parrish had mixed feelings over Azrar's great success in defeating every attempt to wipe him and his people off the planet. It meant the library had not fallen into enemy hands but post war the warlord was as secure as ever in his tiny mountain realm.

Killing off minor players like Jazriel brought him no closer to his prize but it gave great pleasure to Banks and he needed him. Odious as the shark-like Banks was, Parrish owed him his life and he had given his life purpose and hope.

"So who has the body?" Parrish queried. "This evidence is all we need to finally expose these creatures to the whole world."

Banks winced as he finished the foul wine, 'Roll on the end of rationing,' he thought ruefully. "That is the bad news. There was no trace found of a vampire corpse. The Germans searched extensively but came up blank."

Parrish pounded the side of his chair in frustration. "Then we have nothing! The creature may be still alive, out there somewhere in the darkness, preying on humans."

"No, it is very dead. Devane's mob must have found a way to dispose of the body. Devane thinks he is untouchable now, even after losing their pet vampire, the one with the matinee idol looks. It would be so much easier if the bastards looked like something from a Hollywood horror flick!"

"Indeed," agreed Parrish. "Some would say we are doing this out of jealousy. These things are unquestionably beautiful; they never age and can virtually live forever."

He remembered the hauntingly handsome face of Azrar. Injured, bleeding, so close to death. Parrish shuddered. No, he would not allow himself to recall that valley, that night of death and horror. His own death had come too close, far too close for such memories. His luck and the bravery of some resourceful German troopers who had led him to safety, that must be the only memory of that night.

Banks shook his head with vehemence, becoming uncomfortable at the direction the American was taking. "How could anyone be jealous of vampires? Immortality and beauty paid for in innocent blood? By cold-blooded murder. Only a damned human soul would envy the Dark Kind."

"Of course," Parrish answered hastily, misjudging the man's hard line loathing of the Dark Kind. "I only mention this because we must be vigilant in our choice of new recruits to our cause. There are so many foolish vampire myths made popular by the movies. Some deluded fool might think he could be turned into a vampire by being bitten in the neck. Getting a chance to be physically close to the Dark Kind might attract the wrong candidates."

This seemed to satisfy Banks and he relaxed into his diatribe again. "We want killers – as ruthless and dedicated as their prey." Banks's eyes gleamed with a missionary zeal. "But I want God-fearing Christian killers with intelligence, self restraint and integrity – it's going to be an uphill task to find the right men."

"Or women," Parrish interjected.

Banks nodded readily in agreement; he served with enough valiant female operatives to know only too well how tough the so-called fairer sex was in war. And his campaign against the Dark Kind was going to be a war, a Holy War. Parrish grew visibly agitated, draining a full glass of the foul tasting wine in one draught. He knew what he was about to say would aggravate Banks.

"There is just one important aspect we need to discuss," Parrish remarked slowly, as if waiting to gain courage to continue. "There is the considerable problem of our other opposition – the unknown but very powerful force that is working to stifle any information about the Dark Kind."

Banks snorted with ill-disguised derision and rose to leave the room. This matter was an obstacle to complete concord between the two men. "Not this paranoid nonsense again, Parrish. I have done extensive research into this. There are no covert forces at work."

Agitated, Banks began to pace the room before planting his hands on a table and fixing the American with an angry glare. "What evidence have you got? A sick old man's death by natural causes, and the coincidence of a fire at a library. You know books are highly inflammable objects."

Parrish was determined he was not going to be browbeaten over this. God damn it, he had survived Azrar's lair and the hangman's noose. He could take on one angry Brit. "And what of Colgramm's missing documents?"

Banks eyes narrowed as he answered, "He put them in the Library vault for safe keeping and they were all lost in the fire. Rather unfortunate but not particularly sinister."

The intelligence agent and his dismissive manner incensed the gaunt American. How dare he so breezily reject the facts? Parrish believed he had a right to be concerned; his very real fears had haunted him for years. Parrish's life had become a nightmare roller-coaster ride, with too many close escapes from death for one overwrought academic to take in.

"I don't care what you think, Banks. I know there is a conspiracy to hide the truth about vampires— one that has existed for centuries. Azrar's stronghold was not the only such structure. I believe the ancient world was once studded with the Dark Kind's mighty stone palaces, crammed full of their bizarre artefacts. Ornate swords too heavy for humans to lift, extraordinary gems and diadems, luxurious fabrics that never fade or decay. Where is all this valuable stuff now?" He paused, drew breath, plunged on.

"There is not one curious object of unknown origin likely to have belonged to the Dark Kind in any museum, nor are there any private collections of their artefacts. Doesn't that strike you as curious?"

Banks shrugged dismissively. He didn't give a damn about dusty museum collections. He had experienced the horrifying reality of vampires. That was enough evidence for him, enough to fuel his quest for their complete destruction.

Chapter Three

Chess Manor, the Chilterns, England, November, 1946

Joe Devane poked at the smouldering remains of a bonfire in a desultory manner, his mind full of his anxiety over Khari's future – and his place in it. The raging fires of war were dying out all over Europe, but they had left their own smouldering embers, still dangerous, still likely to flare up again into more conflict.

The ongoing turmoil meant the depleted ranks of the Spook Squad remained heavily engaged in intelligence gathering. The dangerous shifting sands of post war Europe and the cold hostility of the Soviet Block gave them much to do. One small consolation was traversing the ravaged continent had become a little easier. Devane was not interested in post-war politics that night.

He had distanced himself from his group to spend time alone in the Manor's gardens, clearing the dead foliage of summer past. Bonfires usually relaxed him, with their warmth, cheerful crackle and smoke, redolent of Fall campfires with his father and brothers on hunting trips in the woods back home. The therapy wasn't working.

Thankfully the war was over, yet his heart did not totally share the allied rejoicing. He dreaded the moment which surely must come soon, when Khari would say goodbye and return to her homeland. It might be the best thing.

His superiors still wanted her deeply involved in war criminal prosecutions, helping to determine the truth from prominent Nazis the allies had captured. Devane protested, Khari, though slowly recovering, was badly damaged, Devane wanted her to have no part of this. Khari had begun to smile again. Why should he subject her to more appalling mental pollution? What images festered in the minds of those monsters? He believed it could send her insane with horror. A view also shared by Anna Vandenberg, the team's top empath who best understood Khari's gift.

With deep sorrow, Devane accepted it was best if Khari turned her back on the modern world and returned to Isolann – back to the protection of Jendar Azrar, best for everyone – except for Joe Devane, the mere mortal who loved her so much.

He looked across at the Manor through the smoky twilight, framed by a cloudless pale sky swiftly darkening to purple then inky night-blue. Wraith-like, the wood smoke intertwined with low lying mist to insinuate around the winter-bare trees. Beauty was slowly returning to the world, but to Joe the end of the war signalled the loss of beauty from his life. Was it so bad to want her to stay with him? Or was keeping Khari by his side an act of appalling selfishness?

He heard footsteps crunch through the frost-crisped leaf mould, his second in command, MacCammon approached, two mugs of steaming liquid in each broad hand. He handed one to the American, "Here, laddie. You look like you need some warming up. It's supposed to be hot chocolate."

MacCammon answered the question in his commander's eyes. "Lennie liberated a tin of cocoa from some GI's on his last mission. I've given it a wee Celtic boost."

Devane took a tentative sip, wincing at the liberal lacing of bootleg moonshine, but grateful for the sudden flush of warmth as the poteen worked its way through his body. MacCammon picked up another stick and began to poke at the bonfire, sending a flurry of sparks dancing into the sky.

"Raker is bringing Eshan back tonight."

Devane nodded at the message, puzzled at the shortness of the Dark Kind lady's visit to her apartment in Paris, perhaps it had been destroyed during the German occupation. MacCammon coughed, uneasy to continue but feeling he needed to help Devane out of his increasing gloom. The war had forged a deep friendship between the two men, a bond of mutual trust and shared direction that formed the backbone of the squad.

"I don't need to be one of our psychics to know what's on your mind, Joe."

Devane did not answer but continued to stare into the glowing logs in the dying fire.

"She loves you very much. There is no way Khari will leave your side now. The war is over. Just marry the wee lass and be done with your dithering."

"It's not that easy, Mac. You don't know the powerful hold her homeland has over her."

"You mean Azrar"

Devane launched his stick onto the fire with a vehemence that surprise even him, in a release of pent up jealousy. MacCammon sighed, the underlying cause of the commander's gloomy mood was exactly what he thought.

"I cannot compete with him, Mac. I am just a guy, not some glamorous Dark Kind warrior Prince!"

MacCammon's tone was adamant, "Azrar can offer her nothing. He is a cold, heartless vampire, damn it, Joe. No love, no future, no wee bairns. Khari is an intelligent grown woman, not a dizzy adolescent girl. She knows you are the only one who can give her a happy life."

The flare of a car's headlights abruptly interrupted their talk as Raker drove the saloon up the drive towards the Manor. The two men kicked earth over the fire to put out the last of the embers and began to make their way back to the house. MacCammon suddenly stopped, determined to save his friend from losing the best thing in his life, "Don't be a fool, Joe, propose to her tonight."

They found Eshan in the drawing room and it was clear she had returned from Paris in some distress. She was talking with animation to Khari in the vampire languages—something she never usually did in front of humans.

"I'm sorry, commander," Eshan apologised to Devane for the breach in squad etiquette, "I will explain everything to you shortly, but I must speak to Khari first in private."

To Joe's dismay the two women walked out through the gardens of Chess Manor, soon lost to the smoky, ice crystal dusted beauty of the late autumn night. All thoughts of proposing disappeared; Devane was convinced there was only one subject that Eshan would need to speak to Khari alone about—returning to Isolann, to Azrar.

As Khari had risen to follow the vampire woman, she had seen the distress on Devane's face but accepted she had to talk to Eshan first. She had never seen the supremely confident Dark Kind woman so flustered. They walked down a forest path till certain they were alone.

"What I am about to tell you will seem bizarre and outlandish but it is all true," Eshan began. "I met that poisonous little monster Garan in France. He bought me the strangest news from Isolann. Khari, Jendar Azrar is in a bad way; he is being tormented by the lost spirit of Jazriel calling out for help."

Khari's eyes grew wide in wonder, unable to comprehend the full meaning of her story as Eshan continued, "When a Dark Kind dies, we do not know what happens, whether we go on to some afterlife or disappear into oblivion. We do not share your human comforts of faith. But we now know Jazriel's spirit survived his death and is somehow trapped, unable to move on. We need to help Azrar before he is driven insane by what I can only describe as a haunting."

Khari was puzzled, "But why Azrar? Surely if Jazriel needed help he would seek out Sivaya."

Eshan sighed; this was going to be difficult. "For many reasons. Mainly because Garan and I believe she has something to do with this horrible nightmare. Also, Azrar is a Jendar from a more powerful Dark Kind caste. And most important of all, Azrar and Jazriel were lovers in the distant past, and as I have explained before Dark Kind love remains forever."

Khari stifled a shocked gasp; she suddenly needed to be alone to absorb all these alarming revelations.

"I'm sorry Lady Eshan, I need to think about this – alone."

She ran away, seeking her favourite spot, a mossy bank by a little brook.

"There are doors that should remain forever locked."

Khari remembered Eshan's words. When Eshan knew she loved the vampire Prince, she tried a brutal 'cure', taking her into one of the few rooms Azrar had forbidden anyone to enter. Khari saw the portrait of the beautiful, doomed Zian and learnt of Azrar's obsessive adoration for her.

Now she discovered another chapter of Azrar's distant past but was unprepared for the devastating effect it had on her. As Eshan spoke of his past relationship with Jazriel, Khari felt cold and strangely detached. She heard her words but the shock waves they created numbed her to silence, as a lifetime's romantic, naïve dreams shattered in seconds. Her teenage years were spent secretly yearning hopelessly for Azrar, fantasising he would one day love her in return. The romantically tragic tale of his passion for Zian gave the perfect reason for Azrar's lack of interest in her. Of course, as a young adult, she knew that there could never be a relationship between them. It had always been an impossibility. Any fondness he might have for her was on the same level as the consideration he showed to his horses and wolves.

Now her mind had to come to terms with the revelation that another object of Azrar's desire was a Dark Kind male. This was too hard for her to understand. And it was not just any anonymous male from the forgotten past, but her own dear friend Jazriel. Not a day passed for Khari without tears shed for his loss. Now she discovered how important he had once been to Azrar and her feelings were confused, painful without truly knowing why. Her only experience of males loving their own sex was through human minds. She found her mind making mental pictures of Azrar and Jazriel together – images both beautiful and disturbing.

Eshan found her and asked if it was all right if she joined Khari on the bank. The human woman nodded assent, her mind still reeling with confusion. As if reading her thoughts, Eshan firmly took her hand. She had always known that Khari's feelings for the Prince ran deeper than the human girl would ever admit to. Now Khari was a grown woman with a loving, strong relationship with Joe Devane. It was finally time for her to let Azrar go completely from her heart.

"We are not like you. Dark Kind are very different – both emotionally and in our physical construction to humans. We have always had the ability to become emotionally involved and enjoy physical love with individuals of either gender. I myself have had female as well as male lovers. It is normal for the Dark Kind.

"What happened between Jazriel and Azrar finished a very long time ago. They parted amicably enough, when their affair had run its full course. This is perfectly usual for beings so long lived. What was not usual was the way Azrar treated Jazriel."

Eshan paused, hesitant, knowing what she was about to say would portray Azrar in a bad light. But she needed Khari and the human team members' help and believed only total honesty would suffice.

"To the rest of us Dark Kind, it seemed the Prince was unwilling to acknowledge Jazriel as his consort. He kept him hidden in the background, as if he was no more than an exceptionally good-looking but anonymous commoner, one he used purely for his physical pleasure. We will never really know. I suspect Jazriel's spirit sought out Azrar over all others because for all the inequality and indignities of their relationship, they really loved each other."

And then with an sudden bolt of clarity, Khari realised the root cause of her discomfort – her old demon – pure jealousy. Zian was not even a ghost. Just a long dead name from the past, a beautiful face in a portrait that stayed locked away. Azrar never visited the room and Khari could fantasise he never visited her memory in his heart. Jazriel, though dead was a vibrant presence in Azrar's life; his restless, tormented spirit still existed and now haunted him.

Khari's foolish reveries embarrassed her greatly and she was grateful no others shared her gifts to scan minds. The two women sat in silence for some time, Khari seemingly hypnotised by the sound of water tumbling over round river pebbles. Then she slowly rose to her feet, carefully smoothing out her skirt as if needing more time to gather up her thoughts.

"I loved Jazriel very much as a good friend. I cannot bear the thought of his poor, lost spirit being in such torment. I cannot imagine what Hell this must be putting Azrar through. Of course, I will help you find what has happened. Let's find Joe and tell him we are going back to Germany. He has always blamed himself for Jazz's death; I know he will want us to help."

Chapter Four

Berlin, Germany, 1946

Thin tendrils of mist trailed around the ruins like spectral fingers, reaching out to trap the unwary, a low sickly light from a sullen moon the only illumination. For the first time in her life, Khari was afraid of the Dark Kind.

Perhaps not of Eshan, who strode ahead, picking her way confidently across the charred rubble, the meagre light more than adequate for her night-born vision. Khari's new sense of fear was fuelled by the dread of meeting Sivaya in the darkness. In the past her lover Jazriel held the vampire woman's innate savagery in check. Now he was dead, Sivaya's fury and grief would make her a formidable and vengeful nightmare. Sensing her nervousness and hesitancy, Joe Devane reached out and held Khari's hand tightly, "Its not too late, we can still turn back from this."

"Jazz would never have turned away from us. I have got to see this through. Keep your revolver handy, if Sivaya is here, she will be looking for throats to tear out."

Devane nodded to reassure her, he already had his gun ready from the moment they started their journey through Berlin's ruins. Of all humans, he suspected he was second on Sivaya's hit list – after Anthony Banks, for his own part in sending her lover to his death in Germany.

Eshan raised a hand and the small party stopped in their tracks. Lit by the dull orange glow was a slight, pale faced youth. He leant against an exposed brick chimney stack, arms folded watching their approach with contempt.

He addressed them in a low, angry snarl," Well, what have we here? Lady Eshan, with a whole troop of performing monkeys."

"Cut the crap, Garan" muttered Devane with impatience. "Have you found Sivaya?" He was in no mood for this malevolent creature's insults, nor for the angry exchange that followed between them in the vampire language.

"This is Dark Kind business. These stinking apes defile Jazriel's memory by their presence."

"He was happy to call us particular humans his friends. If Sivaya has lost her mind, you will need all the help you can get, urged Khari in a conciliatory tone.

Garan ignored her words and snarled, fangs fully drawn, violet eyes darkened to a dangerous jet-black.

"Their deaths will be on your head, send them away now or I will stop them, permanently. Zaard, you disgust me Eshan, you have become a human with a pitifully weak mind and heart."

Eshan's own eyes changed from lavender to a smoky dark grey as she addressed the vampire youth. "These humans are under my protection. You threaten them at your own peril. If you think you can take me on, Garan, just think of Jendar Azrar's wrath if you harm his human ward."

Devane and MacCammon watched the furious, fang bared exchange between the two vampires with increasing anxiety. They did not need Khari to translate the fierce exchange in their harsh, growling language. They knew all too well their lives were being fought over. With the speed, power and ferocity of a vampire attack, they doubted if their handguns would give them any protection.

Garan continued to taunt the Ha'ali. "Oh, Azrar. Look how I am trembling with fear at his name. Has the great Jendar ever left his mildewed, crumbling keep? When was the last time he left the boundaries of that peasant-ridden medieval backwater he calls a realm? I am not afraid of Azrar."

Eshan growled with exasperation. "Then you are the one lost to the Dark Kind, not me. We can waste time fighting over these humans or we can find Sivaya, together as a team. That it is how it must be in the future. Any Dark Kind alone, skulking in the shadows will not last long in this century."

The two beautiful, deadly creatures faced each other, low growls still rumbling in their throats. Khari was now very afraid, their lives hung on a knife-edge. If Garan attacked, he could do great harm with those razor sharp, raking fangs and his ever present deadly sword stick. She doubted whether Eshan in her weakened state could restrain him. Nor was she sure what Eshan would do faced with a choice between harming a fellow Dark Kind over the lives of mere humans. And if Mac and Joe defended themselves with their guns, would Eshan be forced to defend her fellow Dark Kind?

Time lost all meaning, all reason, as the impasse between the warring vampires remained. The humans stood frozen and impotent in the face of two dangerous predators testing each others strength of resolve. Had Eshan backed off just a fraction, Devane knew the other vamp would have killed them all with ease. Suddenly the tension eased as Garan gave a shrug of feigned indifference. "Okay, let's get on with it. But that one stays behind."

Garan, still stormy eyed, his fangs still ominously drawn nodded towards Devane. Eshan agreed tersely, there was sense in this. Someone had to keep lookout for the American troops patrolling this area of a city turned to broken wasteland. Sivaya would be difficult enough to handle and would harbour a particular grudge against the squad's leader. Devane tried to argue against this decision but Eshan was adamant. She knew Sivaya had a reluctant respect for MacCammon and Khari had Azrar's inviolate protection.

"You will be a prime target for her fury. It is best for the mission if you guard our backs from unwanted attention."

Devane realised he had no choice; he could not force his authority on two vampires. As they left, Garan turned to grin with glittery-eyed malice, "You had better sleep with the lights on, Devane. We will meet again."

With Devane left seething alone in the darkness, Garan reluctantly led the others to a badly charred ruin. Both Dark Kind paused, scenting Sivaya's recent presence, sultry, like night blooming lilies. Eshan agreed to remain outside the cellar, her sharp senses vital to watch out for intruders.

With MacCammon's help, Garan broke down the heavy wooden door. It was a long and arduous job; the door was made of large planks of tough, solid oak, recently heavily reinforced with steel bars.

As the door finally yielded to their assault, the stomach turning stench of death assailed them, causing even the vampire to reel back in revulsion. Garan's long life dwelling among humans and the appalling aftermath of their endless wars had not robbed him of his loathing of the noxious miasma of human decay.

Below them lay a dank cellar in total blackness, Khari and MacCammon steeled themselves for horrors as he switched on a torch. To their relief there were no putrid bodies lying around, though the floor was revolting, sticky with fresh looking human blood and the black pools of long dried up gore. This was the most obvious source of the appalling stench. There was evidence of another room further down in the depths of the cellar but it was secure behind another door, this time of stone with no sign of a means to open it.

Garan hit the door hard with his fist accompanied by a fang bared growl of frustration, ignoring the gush of thin purple blood from his torn and bruised hand – such minor damage would soon heal.

"Steady, laddie," said the big Scot. "If there is a way in, I can find it."

MacCammon shone his torch around the cave-like cellar, and ran his long fingers around the stone door. "There's no a door an old pro like me canna tease open."

There were no passengers in the Spook Squad, everyone had a special gift. Now MacCammon's ability came into use. His strong, ultra sensitive fingers felt every inch of the cold, unyielding stone, sending back information straight into his mind, each minute change in the stone's atomic structure. With his gift, Mac was able to detect and trigger a secret catch, the door slowly and theatrically began to open. Again there was an assault of foul putrid stench. Garan's anger began to rise higher, how dare that crazy bitch condemn the once so fastidious and hedonistic Jazriel to lie alone in this filthy charnel house? This was no way to respect the body of the being she was supposed to love. His worst fears were confirmed as they entered the inner chamber. A stone sarcophagus lay in the centre surrounded by large unlit candles.

Garan threw back the stone lid with a furious snarl – what he saw made him step back in shock. Jazriel lay in the tomb, as beautiful as the day he died. There was no sign of any deterioration; in fact he looked merely asleep. He had been carefully dressed in a gem bedecked navy robe of bariola velvet; the ancient rich brocade of the Dark Kind.

The familiar sight of her friend's face, still handsome in death brought sobs of grief from Khari, who had until then kept a brisk and businesslike facade. MacCammon put his arms around her tightly; to his surprise he found his own eyes stinging with tears.

"I can't believe he is dead, Mac, he looks as if he is just lying there in a peaceful Dark Kind Rest."

Khari reached out instinctively to gently stroke Jazriel's face murmuring quietly in his own language. "My poor friend, you should not have ended up in this terrible place."

She pulled back in surprise at the feel of his skin. Expecting it to be stone cold and rigid with rigor, it was icy and pliant to the touch – just as living vampire skin would be. Garan growled and stepped forward to pull back the ornate robes, expecting to see the shattered ruined chest but, found everything miraculously intact. Yet despite the physical repair, Garan could find no sign of life; he was very much dead. It was unlike any normal regeneration, there was something unnatural and sinister about this strange restoration of Jazriel's body.

"Leave him alone. You meddling fools.."

The sound of a furious female vampire voice behind them startled the team into action; they had been expecting and dreading this confrontation. Garan curbed his rage with difficulty as he faced up to Sivaya. The years had not changed her appearance; she was still superficially a lithe-limbed golden beauty. But her blazing black eyes were madness incarnate and with fangs bared she prepared to fight to the death to protect Jazriel's body from these enemies, human and Dark Kind alike.

Garan tried reason at first, though his natural impulse was to turn on her with his own fangs, despite his species old taboo. "What have you done here, Sivaya? The body is intact and perfect again."

"I told you then he will come back. I was right. There were just enough cells alive to start rebuilding. It has taken a long time and a great deal of human blood but I did it"

"All you have done is preserve his body. He cannot come back. He is and always will be dead."

"Get out and leave us alone!" Sivaya snarled. "I know what you want to do, Garan. You and your apes want to destroy him, to burn him. You were always jealous of Jazriel; he is far more beautiful than you, he can have anyone he wants – human or Dark Kind." She stood between them and the sarcophagus, her features distorted with fury, "I won't let you touch him."

Garan sighed; the thought of flames consuming this perfect body, now it was golden and intact was too horrific to dwell on. But so was the thought of Jazriel's spirit being trapped in torment. He stepped forward, his own fangs bared. "What you are doing is sheer cruelty. His tortured soul is desperate for release. Anyway, we no longer have any choice. It is Azrar's command."

Sivaya paced the floor like a caged beast, her crazed mind racing. She was outnumbered here, and a suicidal attack would not save Jazriel from the flames.

"Azrar! How dare you say his name in my presence. He only used my beloved Jazriel. The mighty Jendar, too high born to treat him as anything but an object for his sexual pleasure."

Khari spoke, her voice compassionate despite the rising revulsion threatening to overwhelm her in this claustrophobic charnel house. " They were once very much in love. When Jazriel died, part of the Prince's soul died too. He is in contact with Jazriel's spirit and it is in terrible torment."

The human girl's knowledge that the Jendar and Jazriel once had an intense love affair infuriated Sivaya greatly. Yet, paradoxically, it also gave her a spark of wild hope. With an excited voice speaking the vampire language, she grabbed Garan and pulled him over to the stone tomb.

"There is still hope. Don't you see? If the Jendar is truly in contact with Jazriel's spirit, he could reunite it with this now intact and viable body? As mere commoners, you or I could not do it, but the Prince is very powerful, it might work."

Garan tried to push her away as if her madness was a contagion. "This is crazy talk, what you are saying is impossible."

Khari hastily translated the exchange between the vampires for the benefit of the other human. Though increasingly uncomfortable being between two warring vampires in such a confined space, MacCammon risked entering the debate. "This sounds like dangerous meddling in the supernatural. Do you know the consequences of what you are proposing, Sivaya?"

Unlike Devane, his boss, Archie MacCammon was never fazed by the strange world he inhabited, accepting each strange revelation at face value – they just confirmed his view that the world was a very mysterious place.

"It is irrelevant, this is all complete madness," Garan interrupted tersely. He hated the crazed female vampire for what she had done to the Jazzman. Now he hated her for planting seeds of doubt in his mind. How could he destroy Jazriel's body, knowing there may be a chance to restore him to life, however slim and bizarre sounding? Yet he believed MacCammon was wise to question the ethics of such unnatural meddling. What sort of life would it be? What horror to be returned as a re-animated corpse, trapped in the dead shell his spirit had sought to be free of?

Sivaya could sense his wavering and grabbed a candle. She lit it and as the light flared, illuminating the filthy bloodstained cellar with its inappropriate warmth and golden glow, she thrust the candle into Garan's hand.

"Go on then, use this to start your dirty work if you are so sure the Prince cannot help him."

Garan pushed aside the candle with a groan of confusion and despair. His entire life had been dedicated to self-indulgence, the pursuit of selfish fun and mischief – at the expense of human and Dark Kind alike. How had it all become so serious?

Khari ended the stalemate as the only one being in existence uniquely comfortable in both the human and vampire world.

"We have no choice but to take him to Isolann. One way or another the only way to end this tragedy is to leave it to Jendar Azrar to resolve. I trust him to do the right thing by Jazriel."

Everybody nodded at last all in agreement. But Garan still did not trust Sivaya, sensing that left alone, she might move the body to another hiding place. He stayed in the appalling vault guarding the tomb, refusing to sleep, while the humans left to prepare the paperwork necessary for a journey to Isolann.

They talked again with Devane in the privacy of their hotel. He listened to their story in wonder and mounting horror. How unimaginably strange his life had become – once an ordinary career soldier, he was now dwelling in an underworld populated by ghosts and vampires – what would he encounter next? As dawn spread a pale grey light over Berlin's ruined streets, he looked down at the tattered desperate lines of displaced humanity. Reality for them was the desperate search for the next meal, for any news of lost family. Reality for Devane was an ever-shifting sand of uncertainty. The world around him hid strange secrets, it was no longer rock solid, but a world made of moving shadows.

Over the next days, the squad's well-honed system to create forged documentation went into production. Khari made up some impressive looking papers, her silver wolf talisman easily recreated Isolann's royal seal and she could forge Azrar's signature with ease and style. Getting a false death certificate proved less easy, but Devane pulled every covert string he could. In the end, few officials in the chaos of post war Germany showed any interest in the repatriation of a body of a Resistance hero to a remote Upper Balkan principality.

Eshan contacted the Prince and told him of their intention to bring Jazriel back then joined them. They met at the bombed out ruin of a small town airport, where Garan had left his own plane. Due to the danger of being stopped and searched by customs, Devane insisted the body be transported in a traditional conventional wooden coffin. This caused great distress among the Dark Kind, who balked at such irreverence, but Devane was adamant.

The journey was virtually conducted in silence, any conversation desultory, and Khari stayed close to Devane. The thought of going home and seeing Azrar again would have under any other circumstances filled her with exhilaration. Now she wished with all her heart that this ordeal be over soon, and the healing process could begin at last. It had been a long cruel war.

Chapter Five

The Arpalathian foothills, Isolann, 1946

The big man thought he would die with joy at the sound of the flying machine circling above, searching for a safe landing on the uneven, hilly grasslands. He grabbed the thin, strong hand of the woman at his side, "She's coming home!" Ileni wiped tears from her eyes; there was no time for emotion now, and strangers meant more work for her household.

"Go down to the courtyard, Sandor and help the Prince with the horses, maybe he will let you ride out to greet your sister."

Sandor did not need any persuasion despite his continued nervousness near the Prince; Ileni smiled as he ran down the steps towards the courtyard. Sandor's nervousness close to the Prince was well founded. Ileni too had seen a gloom around the vampire far beyond his usual mysterious aura. With the return of the uneasy peace, Azrar had come back to his keep damaged: both physically and emotionally. He had not waited for his shattered leg to regenerate and heal properly in his desperation to get straight back to fighting the enemy invaders. His metal workers had fashioned a metal calliper forcing the ruined leg into shape, allowing him to ride, albeit in great pain. The limb was now healed but he walked with a limp, perhaps permanently. The wounds to his soul were harder to see. A light had gone from his emerald eyes but none of his human retinue knew why – not even the English soldier, Steve Railton who had fought at his side and saved his life.

Ileni liked the young man, and missed him after he had gone home, heartbroken at leaving his Isolanni love behind. He too had promised to return, but Ileni doubted the poor lass would have heard a word. She had tried so hard, to help Railton bring Lhalee back from the dark abyss of despair, but to no avail. The young woman dwelt in the keep, her body kept fed and safe, but her mind was gone.

Ileni touched her wolf amulet and with nothing but hatred in her heart, cursed the Nazis, as she had done every day since they brought their fiery death from the skies, stealing her eldest son and his family from her. But tonight a light had returned to give her comfort, the bright light that was her beloved Khari.

Garan's aircraft landed uneventfully on the grassy plains by the wild forest, as close to Azrar's fortress home as possible, with a few hours of darkness still in hand.

A visibly distressed Eshan pulled the coffin lid open, gasping in surprise as she saw for herself for the first time the unnatural perfection of Jazriel's remains. Shaking, she turned to the others to command, "Get the body out of this noxious wooden box. Azrar must not see him brought home in this human-made monstrosity."

They were met by a small group of stronghold guards, some driving carriages others held extra-saddled horses. Khari's heart leapt at the sight of the tall man patting the neck of an aged grey stallion. It was Sandor, her big brother. Unable to focus properly, blinded by tears of joy, she ran to throw her arms around him. Now she knew she was truly home.

"I love you, Khari," he stated simply through his own tears. She was only able to nod, so overcome with emotion. Recovering, she looked around for Azrar.

Staying apart from the human reunion, the Jendar sat motionless and grim-faced on a high spirited black stallion. As a small child, Khari would have run exuberantly into the Prince's arms – oblivious to protocol and deference to his status. This time she instinctively hung back, shocked by his appearance, as the clouds cleared and a huge full moon illuminated the plains in brilliant silver.

Always handsome in his austere way, his face appeared to be composed of sharp knife-like angles, the fierce emerald eyes deep shadowed and cold. He ignored his visitors and dismounted, leaving his horse unattended. Strangely it stood unheld in seeming respectful stillness, not even dropping its head to crop the grass or champ noisily on the metal bit. Khari bit her lip in shock as she saw Azrar's painful progress, and the clumsy metal frame holding his leg together. Instinctively everyone stood aside as Azrar entered the plane alone.

Outside became a vigil as everyone kept a respectful silence, even the seething and wretched Sivaya held her peace. Azrar reappeared holding Jazriel's body in his arms, the Prince's face visibly taut with the effort of containing his terrible grief. With his warrior's strength and a lover's gentleness, he remounted his stallion unaided, and cradling the body with his right arm, made strong with millennia of sword wielding, steering the horse with his left hand lightly on the reins. He rode ahead, the others following, keeping at a respectful distance. The vampires and Khari choosing to ride; the visiting humans grateful for the comfort of the carriages.

They soon reached a seemingly impenetrable tangle of dark woods, with a network of narrow paths winding in all directions to fool the unwelcome. The Prince's horses picked their way with sure-footed familiarity through the dense woodland, the path barely wide enough to take the narrow one-horse carriages. The sombre procession was silent, save for the dull rhythmic thud of shod hooves, the rattle of carriage wheels and the sharp snap of broken twigs. Occasional brief breaks in the overhead canopy of tangled branches lit the party with dazzling shafts of silver light.

Joe Devane could not take his eyes of his slender beloved, transformed into something fey and ethereal since their arrival at this strange land that seemed closer to fairy tale and legend than reality. She had removed her tailored jacket, to reveal a loose white satin blouse, and released her hair down so that it fell in a silver- blonde waterfall down her back.

She rode with a lithe elegance on her long maned stallion now pure white with age, confidently picking her way through the darkness. Every step of the journey was familiar; she knew the source of every strange sound in the forest, from the distant murmur of a fast tumbling brook fed by melted ice and snow from the mountains to the stealthy prowl of stalking wolves. Devane thought she looked like an elfin princess riding a unicorn. His heart was heavy with a strange melancholy – she was no longer the Khari he knew but a strange, beautiful creature of mystery and magic. She had come home and was as much a part of this enchanted landscape as the eldritch and sinister Prince of Darkness ahead.

McCammon could understand his friend's unease. He too had seen Khari transform into some unearthly beauty but he was confident it was only a superficial change – created by the magic of the moonlight and the strangeness of Isolann itself. He patted Devane on the shoulder and said in a quiet voice, "Don't worry, laddie. She is still your Khari; she is still the same sweet lass. After this sorry business is over, I know she will come back with us. She loves you very much."

"You don't understand Mac. I've always sensed I have had her on a temporary loan, that I have had to share her love with a more important memory from the past. The memory is made flesh. She is with him again and he is very real".

"He saved her life as a tiny child and raised her as his ward. It is only natural she loves him."

Devane shook his head with a slight sad smile of resignation. "She was raised by the castle retainers, a loving family of kind-hearted humans. Khari doesn't see him as a father figure. She loves the Prince with her whole heart and soul. She would do anything for him, even willingly die for him. I can't compete with that."

MacCammon disagreed, "You are so wrong, Joe; the next night or two will be traumatic for her, but she will come back with you. I bet my best twelve year old single malt on it."

Certain his whiskey was safe, MacCammon explained why. Devane dropped his head to stifle his laughter, so inappropriate in the sad circumstances of their journey, but there was no doubting MacCammon's sincerity with a bet of that importance to him. MacCammon felt secure he would win the bet, for it was obvious to him that Khari was both the wrong species – and the wrong sex – to interest the sinister Prince of Isolann.

They finally arrived at the sheer high wall of the outer keep, gloomily ominous in its alien gothic splendour and overpowering size. Inside the retainers silently took away the horses, allowing the rest of the party to cross the courtyard on foot towards the castle's huge main entrance. Suddenly, the dignified silence of the cortege was brutally shattered by Sivaya's shrieks of rage. In the centre of the courtyard was a carefully built pyre, stacked high with tightly packed aromatic branches already soaked with fragrant, inflammable oils. In the centre was a final resting-place, lavishly furnished with priceless and irreplaceable bejewelled Dark Kind brocades.

Garan solemnly nodded his approval to the Prince; this was a far more appropriate and dignified send-off for

Jazriel than the filthy charnel house vault. But the sight of the pyre enraged Sivaya beyond any scraps of reason she may have still possessed. She ran to bar the Jendar's progress with fangs bared and tried to pull Jazriel's body from his arms.

"You evil bastard, Azrar. I did not allow him to be brought back for this. I will not have him burned."

Shocked, Eshan and Garan leapt forward to restrain and silence her; terrified she would provoke the fearsome, dangerous rage of the warlord. To their surprise, Azrar pushed her back with a carefully controlled shock wave of his icy power and strode in silence into his fortress.

Inside, Khari, eager to find Ileni, was overwhelmed by the familiar sight of her old home; the differing emotions of her homecoming made her mind spin. But even before she could recover from the confusion, Garan's furious voice broke the silence.

"What if he fails, you crazy bitch? Do you think the Prince will allow Jazriel to dwell in torment for a second longer than is necessary? Only you are that cruel."

More compassionate than the contemptuous Garan; Khari stepped forward to comfort her. She was brushed away as the vampire female dared to confront them in front of Azrar.

"All of you killed Jazriel. The high and mighty Jendar began the process. Jazriel was nothing to you. A handsome commoner, to use as a sexual plaything till you got bored. He wasn't high born enough to be your consort so you dumped him for that crazy, scheming bitch of a Princess. You broke his heart but he never stopped loving you, poor loyal fool."

"Then you Eshan, with your obsession with co-operating with humans, betrayed his trust by dragging him into that suicidal covert squad. He was never the brightest star in our sky; he could not see the danger until it was too late. You humans used us to fight your dirty little war games, exploiting skills you could never possess as an ape-bred inferior race."

"But sweet little Khari who called him by an affectionate nickname and said you loved him as a friend; your betrayal was subtler. You could have stayed with him until the war was over. You could have protected him instead of abandoning him so you could run back to your German lover."

Sivaya spun on her heel to fix her black-eyed glare on the youngest-looking Dark Kind. "But I have saved the worst till last. Garan, you are his friend, you wanted to reduce him to dust, blown away by the wind to oblivion."

The injustice and inaccuracy of her accusations outraged them all, but they kept their emotions in check, out of respect for the grieving Prince.

"It's just the madness talking," muttered Khari, still unable to find it in her heart to condemn Sivaya. She doubted she would be any more rational if anything bad happened to Azrar or Joe.

"Dust is better than keeping this corpse preserved like some obscene waxwork. If the body was turned to dust, his spirit would be free from the horror you put it in."

Azrar snarled; a dangerous ice fire was alight in his green eyes. The vampires could see the warning signs and tried to gently pull Sivaya away from provoking him further. The Prince's violent rages were legendary among the Dark Kind. But Sivaya was beyond reason, she brushed off Eshan and Garan and strode over to confront the Prince.

"You lost the right to decide Jazriel's fate when you left him two thousand years ago. If you cannot restore him to life, I will take him away from Isolann to a place of safety. I will not have you burn him Azrar."

A powerful shock wave of telekinetic energy from Azrar's fury thundered around the vast hall; the vampires dropped down in a ground-hugging bow of obeisance, with the humans copying only seconds behind. His voice, usually like honey studded with sharp nails, was harsh and imperious.

"I will have respect in my domain. Sivaya, I have endured your ravings out of respect for the love I know Jazriel had for you. I will endure no more. I will attempt this restoration but if I fail, his body will be consumed by fire before daybreak. I alone have had to live with Jazriel's agonised spirit; I will not allow him to suffer any more. If need be, I will have you bound and taken beyond Isolann until this is over."

He turned and strode across the stone hallway and down into the dark vault where he took his Rest. Distraught at losing sight of Jazriel, Sivaya pushed against Garan's restraining arm and tried to follow. Unexpectedly, Azrar returned to the hall, having reverently lain the body on his brocade and fur strewn bed in his Vault of Rest.

"I do not know how this can be achieved, or even if it should be attempted. But I cannot do it alone. Khari, I need you to help me contact him."

"But my Lord Prince, I can read human thoughts, but not make contact with our own dead. I am not a medium. Nor can I link with Dark Kind minds let alone their spirits."

"But you are able to tune into something of the Dark Kind's emotions," Devane interrupted, turning her gently towards him. "Sweetheart, you can do this. Remember the night of Jazz's death? You became very distressed. You *knew* something bad had happened to him."

Azrar returned down into his resting place in the keep's underground vault and Khari followed without question, although she had no idea what she could do to help.

Away from the gaze of the others, the Prince relaxed some of his stern facade. He looked across at Khari, his face drawn and weary. "What are we doing? Have we all been lured into Sivaya's madness? I have no idea what to do, or whether we should be doing this at all. Of course I yearn to have the real Jazriel back, intact in body and spirit, but.."He faltered, for the first time in his long life, uncertain.

Azrar walked over to the raised bed and touched Jazriel's face. "He was my beloved, carefree, ever-loyal companion, who rode my horses too fast and filled my warrior's keep with human musicians and artists. I didn't care that he was too vain and pleasure-loving sometimes; everything he did was with such easy charm and good humour."

Khari joined the Prince at the bedside. "I want my dear friend back. I would even put up with that endless chain-smoking again. He only had to walk in a room to attract the attention of every human there. One smile and all the females, and some of the men, were under his spell. He was a shameless flirt. I loved him too."

The reminiscences made them both briefly smile, hardening their resolve only to try to bring him back to life if Jazriel himself desired it. The hideous and very real possibility of bringing back some soulless reanimated corpse was intolerable. With no real idea what to do, she suggested that they try to make a circle, imitating human mediums attempting to make contact with departed spirits.

Despite the icy touch, Khari thought it was wonderful to finally hold the Jendar's hand; how many years had she longed for any physical contact with him? But she had to suppress a shudder of horror at holding Jazriel's hand. It had the pliability and coolness of living Dark Kind flesh, but was utterly devoid of life, like a pathetic broken puppet with cut strings.

"Try to focus on a really strong positive image of Jazriel, perhaps the time when you were happiest with him. Then use that image to summon him here."

Khari found herself back in wartime Germany. The night they decided to forget about the war, and sought out a little club that promised good music and not too many military personnel. She remembered strolling through the blacked-out streets, arm in arm with her handsome companion, the inevitable plume of cigarette smoke rising in the star strewn warm night air. They spoke in the strange ancient vampire tongue, openly laughing and talking freely, confident no one overhearing could possibly understand them. It was just one night in the midst of so much fear and horror, but it was a good one.

Azrar's mind took him back to the lush foothills of the Himalayas, their distant snowy peaks silvered by the moon. Jazriel had gone ahead, as usual pushing his horse too fast, living just for the moment. They were hunting some bandit marauders who had raided a village under Prince Tevan's protection. Two of the bandits had got separated from their gang, and their fear-tainted scent was very strong, the closeness of the prey firing up the fearsome bloodlust of the vampires.

Azrar was a guest of the Prince, and had first seen Jazriel the night before at court. His incredible beauty had sent his senses reeling and this was the first time the Jendar had been alone with him. Azrar kicked his horse to catch up, but as he reached Jazriel's side the Prince impulsively reached down and grabbed the bridle of Jazriel's horse, abruptly halting the hard pressed animal.

Without a word, he pulled Jazriel towards him and kissed him, suddenly overcome with overpowering desire. To his relief, Jazriel's feelings towards him were equally as strong and he returned the fierce warrior's embrace with great passion, the forgotten bandits escaping into the night.

But happy memories and the use of a circle had no effect. An hour passed with no sense of any spirit presence. With a weary sigh so grief laden it tore into Khari's gentle heart like a jagged knife, Azrar stood up.

"It is over. We must finish this now. Please leave me alone with him for a few minutes then send Sivaya down here alone."

Khari did what he requested, but seconds after Sivaya entered into the vault, the silence of the vast keep was shattered by the vampire woman's terrible screams of denial. Khari could take no more. She ran out of the building and sought her special place of peace and serenity, her precious garden. To her amazement, despite the hardships of a long and cruel war, Sandor had lovingly maintained her little bower. The pure white roses she had planted still bloomed there, their gentle scent evoking so many memories of her contented childhood.

Her mind suddenly filled with a burst of love so intense it overwhelmed her senses, she spun around to see Ileni running towards her, arms outstretched.

"Mother!" she cried. It was the first time she called Ileni this; it felt so right, so deserved as she held the little nomad woman tightly in her arms, some bonds were stronger than mere blood.

In the inner keep, Sivaya had held tightly onto her optimism, like a drowning wretch grasping at any drifting object. Azrar's stern expression tore down all the walls of her desperate hope. He spoke with a quiet insistence, "Sivaya, let us forget for now that I am a High Prince. This is a time we must be of one accord. We both loved Jazriel. We both knew the pleasure of his body and the warmth of his love. We want him back and cannot bear the thought of destroying his beauty forever. I am sorry you did not share the merging of spirits when making love with him. But if you did, you would know how terrible it is to feel his pain now he is lost and alone in the darkness. You would not let him endure that pain a moment longer.

"Although it is breaking my heart to lose him, we must do it now. I have no idea what lies beyond the curtain of death for the Dark Kind. Maybe it is just oblivion; maybe he will join the others lost to us from this earth in a wonderful new adventure. Whatever it is, it will be better than this unending torment."

Azrar paused, then pleaded, "Do not fight me any more. Stand with me in dignity and pride and give our beloved Jazriel his deserved peace and release his soul from pain."

Emotionally exhausted, a defeated Sivaya had no choice but to drop her head in a signal of resignation.

So at last the final ordeal had to be faced. Jazriel had been placed on the byre by the Prince, with Sivaya in silent attendance. A tear-streaked Khari had placed one of her white roses on his chest. To spare them the horror of seeing the body burn, thick wrappings of brocade had been gently laid across it. The humans stood together, heads bowed in respect. With Ileni and Sandor at her side, Khari nestled into Devane's arms for support. Eshan stood by Sivaya, not just to comfort her but to prevent another unseemly outburst. Eshan doubted the Prince would tolerate any further disturbance to his farewell to his lover. She believed Sivaya's life would be forfeit to Azrar's fangs in this highly charged atmosphere of ultimate sorrow.

The Jendar, his face gaunt with grief, stood apart from the group, his head high, ever the stern warrior, in a brief moment of silent farewell. Close by, Garan waited for his signal, then handed him a flaming torch. The Prince strode over to the byre and lit it, hardly moving back as the wall of flame exploded twenty feet into the night sky, the aromatic oils feeding the violent power of the inferno.

A high scream from a human female voice rose above the fire's roar. Azrar leapt forward to see the human males trying to fight back the flames and reach the body, but were being defeated by the strength of the blaze.

Instinctively reacting, he leapt onto the byre, throwing the body off onto the ground clear of the fire. For one horrific moment, it looked like both Prince and corpse were engulfed in flames, but it was just his long black wolf fur cloak, and the heavy brocade shroud. As the flames were beaten off, a distraught Azrar looked to Khari for an explanation for the desecration.

"Azrar, I swear it's the truth. I heard Jazriel calling me, clearly and strongly. He wants to come back to us."

The pain on Azrar's gaunt face was terrifying. Stress had stripped all the honey from his voice, and in a harsh growl he demanded, "Are you absolutely sure? I will not endure another second of this nightmare."

Khari risked grabbing his arm, urging him to return to his vault in the keep, for dawn was not far away.

She said ,"There is another Dark Kind presence with me, he will tell us what to do. But time is short, this guiding spirit will not stay in the earthbound darkness for much longer."

" I have heard of the trickery of human evil spirits, what proof have I got I can trust this spirit?"

"He said he gave you his favourite sword with the golden dragon hilt for safekeeping, but he never returned to reclaim it."

Azrar uttered a low moan of recognition and the memory of the tragic loss of the great King Dezarn. He scooped up the body and hurried to the dark sanctuary of his resting place beneath the keep, Khari running by his side as behind them, the funerary pyre was allowed to blaze away unchecked. Once in the vault, Khari's head tilted slightly to one side as she listened to the otherworldly instructions in her head. She relayed them to the Prince.

"You must reach out with your spirit and catch hold of Jazriel's soul, somehow use your body to channel it back using your noble-born, warrior strength of will"

Breathless, she continued, "It will involve some physical closeness with the body, some form of intimate contact."

The Prince looked horrified, but Khari and her spirit guide were insistent, "Some form of close contact is vital.

You must hurry, My Lord Prince; this may be your only chance. Ah, we are alone again, the other spirit has gone."

Khari forgot all ancient protocol and gave Azrar a loving kiss on the cheek for encouragement, the trauma of the night emboldening her as she turned to make her way out of the vault.

"What must I do? Help me Khari, stay with me."

Khari had never heard the Prince uncertain and hesitant before, it seemed so strange, but this was a highly bizarre time. She found the courage to shake her head, it was the first time she had refused the Prince anything.

"I will be killed by your power if I stay. You must unleash the same energy you create when your kind make love, when your spirit leaves your body to touch your soulmate."

Alone, the Prince held the body and called out Jazriel's name over and over again, summoning him to return from the depths of torment. When nothing happened, despair and exhaustion unleashed his suppressed power and tightly reined emotion creating a vortex that span around the vault like a whirlwind of raw electric energy.

But still there was no sense of Jazriel's presence and now anger took over. "I command you to come back. You must obey me! I am Jendar Azrar. I will not let you leave me alone for eternity."

Azrar's despair-fuelled power shook the deep foundations of his keep, flattening the castle's inhabitants, both human and vampire to the ground as if being blown over by a mighty hurricane. Garan crawled to a corner, cowering, knees drawn up in a tight ball. Sivaya pulled sharply away from Eshan's supporting arms and fled from the great hall, across the keep courtyard and out into the valley. Overwhelmed by fear and grief, some buried sane part of Sivaya knew whether Azrar succeeded or failed, she had lost Jazriel and his love forever. She ran, blindly, not caring where as long as it was far from the keep. Not caring that the rising dawn threatened her sight, her life. She stumbled, falling over tree roots, oblivious to her torn clothing and scratched skin from vicious thorns untill halting at the edge of the forest howled and howled out in her anguish, her loss. Like grey ghosts, a pack of encroaching wolves took up her cry, echoing her sorrow around the mountains and beyond.

Chapter Six

His spirit reached out from his body and for a split second touched another. It was enough, Azrar's iron will forced the contact to hold fast, and bringing his spirit back into his body dragged the other with it. For a brief, wonderful second, he was filled with the vibrant spirit presence of Jazriel. There was no time to revel in the pleasure of such intimate contact, this sense of complete oneness with the being he loved beyond reason. He swiftly prised open the corpse's mouth and kissed it, the passionate evocative kiss of a lover, using his power to force the spirit out of him and into the lifeless form beneath him. He felt the spirit leave him, leaving a desolate emptiness at its departure. Exhausted, Azrar sank onto his bed with no idea if he had succeeded.

Then Jazriel's body began to convulse violently. It thrashed about wildly as each cell, each nerve ending, was charged with Azrar's energy. The Prince held on to it tightly, anxious there should be no physical damage from the uncontrolled convulsions. There was no sign of breathing —no heartbeat, no pulse, just a mindless random reaction to the intense stream of natural energy. Azrar remembered how new born things often needed stimulation to start breathing; he'd helped many a foal in difficulty enter the world. He grabbed the body by the shoulders and shook it violently.

"Breathe damn you, breathe for yourself."

From a timeless Hell of no sensation, the lost essence of Jazriel plunged into a new pit of pain. He'd become close to nothing, drifting alone in a silent darkness where only an increasingly vague awareness of self existed. Sometimes he'd try to scream for help, but nothing worked; he was adrift in a silent, wordless void, and his cries went unanswered.

A violent eruption of pain, as shafts of light pierced him like jagged knives, and huge cudgels of sound battered him. From weightless non-being, he suddenly felt crushed by a leaden weight. He began to panic, thrashing around like a trapped whirlwind, desperate to be free of the vice-like grip. Frightening new sensations flooded through him. With one mighty effort of will, he was free floating incarnate and pain-free again but this time not in any amorphous darkness.

As the panic gradually subsided, he rediscovered an awareness of place, time and form again, and memories reawakened.

He was in the dark vault beneath Azrar's castle, the familiar luxurious and comfortable Place of Rest. There was the Jendar. The spirit form of Jazriel surged with love for the warlord, but as his awareness strengthened, Jazriel could see the Prince was distraught, raging in the language of their kind. Beneath him was a dead Dark Kind body, marble white and still: a completely lifeless form. Jazriel reeled away in shock, as he recognised his own familiar features, statue-like in their stillness.

He found himself drawn closer to the scene, puzzled and disoriented, his memory disjointed and fragmented. As he approached, the power of Azrar's aura touched him and he became caught in a powerful vortex. His spirit filled with great joy as it touched that of Azrar's – for a fleeting second of wondrous reunion. Then he was back within the leaden tomb of flesh he now knew was his own lifeless body.

This time he did not panic but was unsure what to do. The sheer physical dead weight oppressed him, his natural inclination was to fly free of this dead shell, this long spent encumbrance. But the power of Azrar's will was unyielding, commanding him to remain and to find a way to reanimate himself.

The frustration was overwhelming. His body and spirit seemed incompatible now, separated for too long. All the living taken for granted, seemed impossible and alien to his trapped spirit. Even the act of breathing, taking in quantities of air to expand and deflate the lungs was an uphill struggle. How did he restart his heart to speed blood through veins and arteries? Where was the sparkle of electricity lighting the brain and nervous system?

Time passed and his blind panic began to wane as Jazriel found himself slowly re-merging with his body, before passing into a normal living sleep of sheer exhaustion.

On awakening as a living being for the first time in years, he discovered he was still unable to control any of his functions. He felt Azrar lift him gently, his revived senses reeling from overload – the dense velvet softness of the Prince's black bariola robes, the icy power of his touch ,the emotional charge as a strand of jet hair brushed his face. He tried to speak, but opening his eyes had taken every ounce of faltering will power. The Prince shook his head, his low silken voice cracking with emotion; a turbulent mix of love, anxiety and wonder.

"Calm yourself. You are safe, you are alive. One day soon we will ride together to hunt in the moonlight. But now, you must relearn how to live."

Jazriel struggled to speak, his throat desert-dry from so long without use. Azrar held a goblet of wine to his lips and waited patiently as his lover spoke his first words again as a living being.

"Zaard, I really need a cigarette."

Chapter Seven

Hours passed, warm golden daylight flooded the upper reaches of the stronghold's outer compound and the waiting Dark Kind sought shelter from its lethal rays in the lower reaches of the inner keep. Of Azrar and Jazriel they knew nothing. Something had happened, some shift in the balance of the world but what that change was, they did not know, nor had the ability to find out.

Khari and Devane lightly rested in each other's arms, wrapped up in voluminous wool cloaks. They had slipped in and out of sleep as they sat in the great main hall of the keep, cosy by the vast hearth well banked with a comforting fire.

McCammon could not rest as the strangeness of the past weeks caught up with him. Eager for a sign of normal human life, he explored the compound with its busy retinue of household staff and military personnel. A small group of Isolanni soldiers were cooking breakfast over an open fire. The smell of fresh coffee and sizzling bacon was incredibly intoxicating and he gladly accepted their invitation to join them. No shared language was needed, there was a mutual understanding between them—the easy companionship of fighting men, all survivors of a terrible war. There were signs of an underlying unease, the air, the entire environment was charged with static electricity. Yet every human was valiantly attempting to hide an inner nervousness.

There was no sign of Jendar Azrar until several hours after sunset, when all the human and vampires with the exception of the missing Sivaya joined the Prince's aides and military leaders in the main hall of the keep. He appeared from the depths of his vault, utterly exhausted, but his emerald eyes sparkled – clearly triumphant – as he announced, "Jazriel is back with us."

For a short heartbeat moment no one moved, no one said anything and then the tension, the fear and uncertainty fled as smiles and loud cheers erupted.

Azrar waited patiently until the celebration of astonishment and euphoria died down before continuing,

"He is very disoriented and confused. He is still unable to co-ordinate any of his movements; but he is back whole, sane and very much alive. Jazriel will stay here in Isolann while he recovers."

The Prince dropped his head as if to terminate the brief audience, but as he turned to leave he paused to address the humans in English.

"There are no adequate words to express the depths of my gratitude to the human and Dark Kind friends who brought him home to me. I thank you all from the depth of my being. The war and its aftermath have taken a heavy toll on our emotions. There must be a time of serenity and recovery. We will meet again in happier times."

He turned without another word to go back down to his vault. Khari felt her heart constrict with sadness, wishing for more time with Azrar. And of course to see the miracle of Jazriel brought back to life. But perhaps the Prince was right; a reunion in the future could be a happier event, a time for celebration of survival and the unique, strange friendship Devane's squad had forged between two species.

Chapter Eight

Khari stood on the battlements as the first tentative rays of a grey, sullen dawn cleared the mountain peaks. Below her, the nocturnal life of the foothills crept unseen to seek their refuge from the daylight as the sun-loving creatures took their place. In the keep, Joe and Mac had fallen asleep by the hearth and the Dark Kind had already disappeared to seek their Rest.

Though she was exhausted, Khari could not relax and she left her high vantage point to wander around the keep and its inner compound, rediscovering the familiar sights and sounds of her home. She marvelled again in delight at the many pure white roses still thriving in her garden, how did Sandor manage to tend them so well in a time of war? He was a wonder. She wiped away a tear at dear old Wolf's grave as her mind filled with fond memories of her loyal brindled friend. She met with Sandor in the stables, reaching up to kiss him on the cheek. "I have seen the garden, my lovely roses thank you for looking after them so well."

Sandor laughed, embarrassed, "Roses can't talk, silly."

They walked down the cobbled aisle, Sandor proudly showing her the horses born since her departure, including the Prince's new black war horse. Sandor's eyes filled with tears at the memories of what happened to its predecessor, but Khari knew his tears were not just for a horse, they masked the well of anguish he felt for all the innocent human lives in Isolann lost to the Nazis. Emotions too deep, too painful, for Sandor to express in words.

Khari, seeing the big man's fatigue, begged him return to his quarters. "There will be time for us to be together, my brother. Try to catch a few hours sleep."

When he reluctantly left her alone, Khari wandered through to the outer compound. Here the changes to Isolann were more apparent. She had left a country frozen in a bubble of time. The war had forced change and the twentieth century onto an unwilling people. Soldiers in Azrar's army now carried modern rifles, instead of bows and swords. The crackle of radios spoke of instant communication between the mountain tribes and the troops who defended them. She wondered how long before electricity and motorised transport would arrive, and perhaps with them the end of Isolann and its Prince. The Germans did not have to invade this land to destroy it.

But then again, maybe she underestimated the resolve of the Isolanni. It was also possible they would retreat into the way of life that served them so well, deliberately turning their back on this fast, brash century. Her thoughts were interrupted by a soft keening, wordless and sad beyond belief. She anxiously sought the cause of the sound and found a young nomad woman crouched in a corner of a courtyard, arms locked around her knees, rocking back and forth. She looked unkempt, like a captive wild thing, though both her body and clothes were immaculately clean. Khari reached down to comfort her, but she flinched away as if struck by a blow.

"Poor little thing. We do our best to care for her but nothing we do makes her any better."

Khari stood up to embrace Ileni who had brought down some food for the girl. As Khari helped her feed the girl, Ileni told her story. It was a grim account of Nazi atrocities and a young woman who faced the enemy with great courage. "It was all too much for Lheela, she saw too much horror, the mind is a fragile thing"

Ileni also told of the courageous English airman who chose to stay in Isolann to fight alongside the Prince.

"He was a good man who loved Lhalee dearly, but his love was not enough to bring her back to the light of reason. We owe him so much, Khari. He saved our Dark Lord's life and brought hope to our people. Of course he insisted on staying here by her side, but we thought it was too cruel to his own family in England. Why deny a mother a son when this poor creature cannot know whether it is night or day? He returned to his home, vowing to return for her. And one day he will."

Khari was fascinated what sort of man was this Railton? Probably an ordinary man in peace time; perhaps a teacher or a shopkeeper turned by adversity into someone heroic and good. The war had produced so many such men and women, restoring faith in humankind.

After snatching a few hours sleep, Devane and MacCammon sought the human heart of the keep. They followed the man Khari called her brother, Sandor, a gentle giant with mild eyes and an innocent, guile-free smile down from the main hall into the spacious kitchen area.

After the over-awing effects of the keep's alien-gothic, barbaric splendour, the kitchens were a welcome sanctuary of human warmth and ordinary life. As they entered , the two men felt their senses pleasurably assailed by the comforting aromas of fresh baked bread, dried fruits and pungent herbs.

Ileni, the undisputed queen of this haven beckoned them to sit by the hearth on two old, overstuffed armchairs. They smiled and nodded their gratitude as she handed them earthenware bowls with a cream- topped bread pudding, richly smelling of spices and honey. The tough years of strict rationing melted into bad memories as they sipped the delicious breakfast treat, for the first time since arriving in Isolann, they were able to relax.

"Shera vay," said MacCammon with a smile, eager to try out one of his three Isolanni phrases, as well as 'thank you', he also knew 'hello' and 'goodbye'. His attempt at their language prompted fits of good natured and flirtatious giggles from the kitchen girls. Ileni silenced them with one warning glare before breaking into a broad smile herself. MacCammon could see Ileni had a warm, generous heart combined with a core of inner steel. She had the courage to walk through a wolf and bear infested forest, holding a tiny abandoned child with the faint hope of finding sanctuary with a fearsome vampire Prince. She had endured the hardships of war and the loss of so many of her family, yet still she prevailed, undefeated and feisty. His reverie was interrupted by a familiar voice.

"So, you boys are getting the gar'ani treatment! Ileni must like you already. Only the most favoured visitors are offered her legendary sweet bread." Khari walked into the kitchen to sit on the broad arm of Devane's chair.

"It's such a relief to get away from all that overwrought Dark Kind passion," sighed Khari sadly. Devane put his arm around her and gave her waist a loving squeeze, this journey was a traumatic emotional roller coaster for Khari. He prayed it would be over soon – one way or another. He became aware of the nomad woman's close scrutiny as she crossed the room to hand Khari a bowl of gar'ani, he doubted much got past her sharply intelligent, black eyes. Ileni addressed him in the fluid, singsong Isolanni language and he looked to Khari to translate. To his surprise, she looked flushed with embarrassment and took some persuading to tell him what Ileni had said.

"Well, Joe," she finally managed to say, "my mother thinks you are very handsome and look strong enough to sire many fine, tall sons."

"Tell your mother, she is very wise and observant – and of course perfectly correct."

Khari gave his shoulder a playful mock punch, but translated Joe's words to her mother with a broad smile; the first for many months. Ileni spoke to Joe again, her face more serious. Again Khari paused before translating. "My mother says you are a good man and a brave warrior, but warns you that I must live somewhere far away from other people, that my gift of *Knowing* will always put my life in danger."

Devane nodded in agreement; he knew this already. Protecting Khari from the world had become harder and harder. Her work with the agency brought her to the attention of many undesirable elements, now the end of the war brought an end to the need for such a high level of secrecy. Khari would become a target for the rest of her life.

He had to leave her in Isolann, it was the only sensible solution. Devane got up abruptly and marched out of the kitchen, needing solitude and space to think. Khari sensed his emotions and rose to follow him but was restrained by the big Scot. "Leave him awhile, lassie. He needs time to find the courage to leave you here, safe again in your home."

Khari's golden eyes grew wide with dismay. "You don't understand, Mac, my home is with Joe. I love him."

MacCammon released his hold on her arm and gave a broad smile of approval, "Those are the only words he needs to hear; you'd better go and find him."

Chapter Nine

Somewhere over the Pyrenees, Andorra, 1946

Snug beneath a tartan wool rug, the sudden dip of the plane's turbulence woke Khari. Though still exhausted and ready to go back to her slumber, she glanced through the aircraft's small porthole. An amazing sight snapped her out of her sleepy state and made her catch her breath in amazement and awe. She realised they were flying somewhere over the snow-capped Pyrenees, poised in a brief, sublime moment between night and dawn.

In the same sky, Khari could see a deep blue star-studded night sky; the mountains below caressed by a full moon. She could also see a magnificent rising sun, resplendent in its rosy glory, filling the cloudless apricot and pink sky with golden rays. Khari's plane was flying towards the sun and its powerful warmth and light – it seemed to be more than just a symbolic direction.

She had known so much darkness; the festering evil in men's hearts and the agony this evil created in devastated innocent lives. Khari was raised in another kind of darkness, a human child dwelling in the night kingdom of a Dark Kind warlord. But no amount of blood shed by the vampire Prince compared to the obscene catalogue of horrors she'd experienced through human minds – abominations committed by humans on the most helpless and vulnerable. One of the war's victims was on the plane with them. She glanced across to a huddled form at the back of the plane. Protected by MacCammon's comforting large frame was the nomad woman, Lhalee. Everyone agreed she needed more help than Isolann could give her. If modern psychiatric medicine could not help her, maybe Anna Vandenberg could. Ever the optimist, Khari hoped she could be brought to full health and Steve Railton could one day be reunited with his loved one. A man like that deserved every happiness life could bring his way.

This journey marked the end of the Dark Kind's short experiment of co-operation with humans. Eshan remained in Isolann, caring for the deranged Sivaya. Garan could not wait to get out of what he described as "that primitive dump smelling of goat shit, where a vamp can't even enjoy sampling the locals." It took Eshan's threats and the uncomfortably close proximity of the formidable Jendar Azrar, but eventually with great reluctance he agreed to fly the humans to London. Khari wondered if the violet-eyed devil would try to throw them all out of the craft mid-flight, but so far there seemed no danger as he flew on in sullen silence.

Khari felt under the rug for the damson and gold bariola pouch Azrar had left for her on her departure from Isolann. It felt like a good time to open it. She broke the black wolf embossed red seal and slowly opened the pouch. Inside lay a glittering necklace of pigeon blood rubies: an opulent waterfall of stunning gems. Khari's pale, slender fingers felt the cold stones run through them like sparkling red chips of ice. It was beautiful; a cold hard beauty, like its giver. Khari recognised the jewellery, she'd last seen its image around Jendara Zian's neck in her portrait locked away deep in the keep. Carefully Khari returned the gems to their alien velvet pouch, and kissed the black wolf symbol. A kiss of farewell.

Her goodbyes to Ileni and Sandor had been scarcely less painful. Khari had promised to send for them once her life was again settled. " Surely, the Prince has enough staff to serve all his needs! I need you both in my life," she told them. To her relieved delight, they both joyfully agreed and on her journey away from Isolann, her mind was filled with plans for the future with her family.

An hour or so later, Khari looked down at the now dawn-lightened sea. The brownish-grey waves topped with storm driven foam marked the last stage of their journey, the short flight across the English Channel. It was the first stress free journey of her life and she smiled with pleasure as the rain-lashed white cliffs, topped by lush green pasture came into view.

An uneasy Joe Devane glanced across at Khari who seemed so transfixed by the view. Was she homesick so soon for Isolann and her adopted family? Her goodbyes to Sandor and Ileni had been heartbreaking to witness. Did she yearn to return to the inhuman creature that Devane knew she still adored? Khari turned to him, the love shining from her wondrous golden eyes and the warmth of her smile melted all his fears away.

"Let's go to your home Joe, let's go to America and get married. I have had enough darkness and sorrow, enough adventures. Let's just be boring, normal people. I want to have babies with you Joe – lots and lots of them."

Joe reached across and kissed her – tears of joy running unchecked down his cheeks. The war was finally over. He felt a slight but firm tug at his sleeve. He looked up to see MacCammon's dour long features breaking into a rare warm smile.

"That's a bottle of twelve year old malt you owe me."

"You can have a whole crate, Mac, and I'll help you drink it in celebration of peace, life and love."

"And hope, laddie, dinna ever forget that."

Chapter Ten

Wildways House, Yorkshire Moors, England, 1947

Steve Railton returned to Britain to a hero's welcome from his ecstatic family, but he was a deeply troubled man. The war had scarred every life it touched; no one could survive as the same person. Stranger demons than most tormented Railton.

He had learned that humans, himself included, behave like brutal monsters and had seen a real monster behave with great nobility. He no longer knew what was real anymore. If un-ageing vampires existed, what other wondrous or monstrous beings shared this troubled planet? What other horrors awaited man in the darkness? Could the worst nightmares of all be humans themselves?

There was a far more personal crushing guilt for him to bear. In an act that felt like cowardice, of treachery, he had left Lhalee behind, lost in her own dark place, hiding from the horrors she had witnessed. He had tried so hard to help her back but nothing could touch her. With not the smallest, slightest sign she even knew he existed, Railton had to think about the family he'd left in England. Could he abandon them? Heartbroken, he reluctantly left her safe in the sanctuary of Azrar's keep with its compassionate human household, to return home to his rejoicing family.

But the guilt grew worse, not better, by putting time and distance between himself and his Isolanni wife – abandoned to the private Hell in the prison of her own mind. Railton took to complete solitude, shunning his family and friends and though officially Britain's ambassador to Isolann, took no part in any diplomatic activity. His life became obsessed with long, exhausting walks across his beloved Yorkshire moors regardless of weather, without even a faithful dog as company. His hair grew long and unkempt, as was a straggly beard , often forgetting to wash or eat, collapsing to sleep on an old overstuffed chair in his kitchen.

Early one morning, a flurry of activity in his drive shook him from his withdrawn mental state. He watched as a horse-box rattled across the rain-drenched cobbles of the front yard. Incensed by the brash intrusion into his privacy, he stormed out to face the drivers. There had been no horses kept at his home since before the war. Perhaps they were delivering some hunters; they had certainly got the wrong address!

The driver jumped down from the cab, eyeing what he thought was a wild looking tramp with deep suspicion, before asking cautiously, "I have a delivery to the Hon. Stephen Railton, British Ambassador to the court of the Prince of Isolann. Is he here?"

Railton could not argue with that, they had the right address. Ignoring the confused delivery men, he walked to the back of the golden wood panelled lorry, a spark of curiosity lighting up his deadened soul.

"I am Stephen Railton, what have you brought me?"

Uncertain at first, the groom hesitated. He was expecting a distinguished diplomat not a smelly, unkempt hermit but he decided not to argue, eager to get rid of his charge. The groom lowered the ramp and in a flurry of angry hooves, down trotted a scrawny chestnut mare, her ears flat back, teeth snapping like castanets. He went to caress her familiar thin neck but she lunged away from her handler, biting Railton on the arm. Grateful for the thick tweed jacket that saved his flesh from her crushing teeth, he laughed – a warm, full laugh – the first it seemed for centuries.

"I can't imagine why a Prince would send you such a horrible old nag. Is this really the best his country can offer?" muttered the groom darkly, but glad to offload the troublesome mare, who had seemed determined to kick her way out of the box every mile of the journey from Dover. He was also eager to be free of its new owner, who appeared to be a filthy, wild haired madman.

"You don't understand: this is the sweetest, most wonderful mare in the entire world."

The groom and his driver shook their heads and returned to their lorry. As they drove away, the man's ecstatic greeting to the horse confirmed in their view that the dishevelled Railton was indeed a complete lunatic, most welcome to the vile-tempered scrawny mare.

Railton looked through the importation papers she arrived with; one was a letter from Azrar himself, in his now customary impatient but elaborate script, sealed with the black wolf symbol.

"Steve, my very dear friend. You may find this gift useful on those wild moors you told me about. You are actually getting two gifts in one; she is safely in foal to my new war horse, another black stallion of course! In the spirit of true friendship in war and in peace – Azrar, Jendar of Isolann, High Prince of the Three Kingdoms."

Railton took a tighter hold on the lead rope and risked a quick kiss on the mare's soft grey nose. She brought with her a gift of precious new life – such a potent symbol of future happiness. What Sweetness nurtured within her also brought Railton's troubled soul back to life, ready to experience hope again. He led her to his empty stable yard, one arm hugging her thin neck. "We are both home now, my darling old baggage. No more dodging bombs and bullets in mountain passes. Let's just take life easy and enjoy ourselves."

And a thought grew in his mind. If he could move on, maybe in time so could Lhalee, maybe one day they would be reunited and ride the wild Yorkshire moors together.

Chapter Eleven

The Monastery Gardens of St Valarin, Tobaar, Amantzk, 1946

Alejandro Reyes paused from his stroll to gently caress a yellow rose, the colour of early morning sunshine. He allowed his delight in the smooth satin petals and the rising delicate scent to distract him momentarily from his constant unending burden, and the weight of knowledge of what was to come. This was a truly wonderful world, an earthly paradise – even with all the sorrows and imperfections wrought by its human inhabitants and the dangerous wayward vagaries of nature.

Ah, humans, he sighed, there was nothing he would not do for them, he loved them so much. For despite their waywardness, their sins and shortcomings, they were all so precious, all worth saving. A beautiful, flawed species that trod a wavering tight-rope between extraordinary compassion and the vilest savagery. Human beings were truly a glory of creation. He had to protect them, even if it meant dealing with accursed, blood drinking devils in an ironic and increasingly desperate bid to save humanity from the future.

That was the hardest part, the true source of the leaden weight that bore down on his narrow shoulders and stole all peaceful sleep from his life. In truth, he never wanted to see another Dark Kind again in his remaining lifetime, never wanted to feel the ice cold aura of their being or sense the arrogant scorn from their pitiless fiery eyes. But it was his duty and he would not shirk from it. Could not shirk from it.

Reyes heard footsteps on the pale golden flagstones that meandered like a stone brook through the monastery garden: a tranquil, welcoming haven that managed to find room for flowers among the useful herbs, vegetables, fruit and medicinal plants. There was a balance here, the beautiful and purely ornate given pride of place with the more mundane but useful plants. He watched Father Gerard Mackie's approach; he was most definitely a useful plant! Gerry's florid, broad features with his trophy handle ears and flat, badly broken nose—courtesy of a hurley match 'accident'—would not fit into the decorative category. But as an aide and confidante and one day maybe a successor, Reyes could find no better man to work with.

"All the main players have survived the war, you must be so relieved," said the young Irish priest, shaking his bosses hand in a warm greeting. Reyes paused before answering. Strictly speaking he believed survival was a matter of opinion in one instance.

"Yes, my boy. I suppose we have something to be relieved about. If that is the right word. But our so-called success was all down to sheer luck. We did nothing to help them. "

"But that is good, is it not? queried Father Gerard. "It means we have not overstepped our assignment." The younger priest raised his hands in a gesture of bafflement. "But in truth, I do find the non-interference rule frustrating, hampering our objectives."

Reyes smiled with compassion and sadness, the younger man was eager to make a tangible difference to their assignment; watching and waiting was not enough for him to secure a good outcome. Reyes agreed, he shared this feeling of helplessness, but it was all they could do.

"And far too stressful, I know you agree with me, I can see the weariness and strain on your face," added Father Gerard, as ever worried about his mentor and superior.

Reyes continued his walk, beckoning the younger priest to join him, "Come, Gerry, let us take in this beautiful summer morning, this exceptionally wonderful garden. A tribute to the love and care of generations of pious monks in celebration of the Creator's genius. We could do with a break surrounded by beauty before we get mired down again, contaminating ourselves with protecting creatures that are not made by His hand. Beings that should not exist were never meant to be a part of His plan."

They walked together in silence, a comfortable quiet born from mutual trust and respect. Reyes halted, uneasy as he caught sight of a white rose bush, the blooms glacial and pure as new fallen snow, shuddering as he remembered the last time he saw such a rose growing. Would he ever enjoy the great beauty of nature again or was he forever condemned to view everything in the world touched by cold dark shadows and threatened by destruction and evil?

"The winter is coming, Gerry. Time is getting short."

Reyes hastened his pace, now the tranquillity of the monastery garden felt less like a safe haven than a beautiful distraction, diverting him from his mission. Beyond the garden lay the gentle rolling plains of Upper Amantzk, the well-tended fields still waving with unripe green barley and rye. To the north of this well-ordered, peace-loving land, lay Svolenia, a country as ever torn and suffering, at war with itself. And further still to the north, far to the north was accursed Isolann, the Land of Secrets and Shadows, its dark heart, and the unearthly blood drinker Prince. Despite the thousands of miles that separated the countries, it still felt too close.

Reyes shuddered, his whole being cold, despite the strengthening summer morning sunshine. "We face a winter with no end, my friend," he murmured, pulling the collar of his jacket up in a vain attempt to fend off the ice spreading like poison through his veins.

Chapter Twelve

Azrar's Keep, Isolann

There was no sense of time passing any more for Azrar; his whole life was centred on keeping Jazriel alive, and the exhaustion threatened to overwhelm him, but any sleep was impossible. He could scarcely believe what he had already achieved and as if doubting his own eyes, the Prince reached down and held his hand firmly over Jazriel's heart. To his relief, it was beating in a steady, normal rhythm. He had done this simple act of checking many times, such was the ongoing uncertainty of his success. Yet the miracle of Jazriel's revival made his mind reel with wonder. How could this have happened? As a direct result of some hidden power, Jazriel was alive. But his hold on life was still fragile, hanging on by a gossamer-thin thread.

Until now, Azrar had no concept of the full extent of his own power. No Dark Kind had achieved such an audacious feat, defying the ultimate and greatest enemy—Death itself. Could it be a simple solution? Was Dark Kind warlord arrogance and grief such a potent mixture it could bring a dead lover back to life?

He waited, quietly sitting by Jazriel's side, unwilling at first to risk leaving, as if this would trigger another catastrophic reversal. But Jazriel slept on in a normal peaceful manner, a slight smile on his perfect features. Weeks had passed since the last crisis, perhaps the reuniting of body and spirit would hold firm at last.

Unable to bear the tension of waiting until he awoke, Azrar risked leaving Jazriel's side for the first time and sought one of his favourite places in the keep. He strode through his shadowy corridors, the constant pain from his shattered leg a mere annoyance to be ignored. He now wore a carefully crafted fully articulated calliper, holding the fragmented bones carefully in place. Maybe they would heal straight and true – it mattered not to the Prince.

The new device was a vast improvement on the crude sword-iron frame hastily forged in a mountain cave. So eager to be back fighting the Germans, Azrar had ordered it fitted while the metal was still hot from the flames. Fangs bared in agony, he'd mounted Railton's brave, scrawny mare and ridden out to attack the invaders. The young Englishman had saved his life and by that act had saved the people of Isolann. He would never forget the foreigner's bravery and the debt of gratitude he owed him.

Azrar went to the stronghold's highest battlement and stood gazing over his lands with a fierce pride. A violent ice-barbed wind straight from the mountains lashed at him but he ignored the whip-stings to deeply breathe in the freezing air. It was intoxicating, tasting of freedom, of survival.

He was Jendar Azrar, the last Dark Kind warlord. The storm lashed his long jet hair and cloak to flow around him, his body surged with renewed vibrancy. Arcs of power flashed, sparked in an electric-blue aura. He threw back his head and howled above the storm's thunderous roar, a savage sound of triumph and exultant pride. He had prevailed into the twentieth century. He still ruled his lands – and he was no longer alone.

Epilogue

The white roses first caught his eye as he glanced around the bedroom; at least a dozen or more glacial buds arranged in a crystal cut glass vase. Perfect yet strangely cold – as if the blooms could only thrive in snow-melt water. Above them hung a portrait of a young woman, a silver silk shawl draped softly over her slender shoulders. The woman's Slavic features were delicate and portrayed with a gentle, slight smile, her face framed by silvery layers of fine, pale blonde hair.

Her eyes were an extraordinary colour – a lustrous gold – strange and ethereal, yet reflecting an inner warmth. She gazed confidently from the portrait, a woman who, with her unique insight into the darkness dwelling in human hearts knew too much of this world...

He saw beyond her fey beauty and the freshly offered tribute of the roses. As if mesmerised, he was drawn to her necklace, a generous waterfall of dark blood-red rubies and a dangerous rage welled within him. To anyone else, the lavish display of fabulous jewels would represent only opulent decoration. To the man, torn between hatred and fascination, they were the potent symbol of the woman's eternal damnation. For shamelessly, she wore a necklace of blood tears.

And for that she must die...

Author's Notes

A note to any would-be pedants and litigants!

Blood Tears is a work of pure fantasy; none of the characters are real and none are based on any actual person, living or dead. It isn't meant to be the real world so I have also taken outrageous liberties with history and geography – to create a world where the Dark Kind could exist.

It would be best to imagine the book set in a parallel universe. Then again, in an infinite universe with infinite possibilities, maybe out there somewhere Azrar and Jazriel and Co do exist!

I am indebted to Andy Hey for his tireless work on my behalf, Terry Hajowyj for the fabulous cover and eBiz Solutions for my equally wonderful website.

My thanks to Mal Phillips, treasured friend and computer genius, for his generous and unwavering help.

To anyone who enjoyed the Book...

Blood Tears is the first of a trilogy about the Dark Kind. *Blood Legacy* and *Blood Alliance* are well under way as is a prequel *Blood Legend* – but only if you want them!

The official website is www.bloodtears.co.uk

Raven Dane